"Why will you never marry?"

"What?"

She'd surprised him with that question. He leaned over, his face close enough to hers she felt the warmth of his breath. She could barely see his eyes in the dark. "As I said, you saw my scars this morning. What woman would ever want to marry me?" he asked very softly.

Ella closed her eyes, blocking out the brilliant blanket of stars in the sky and kissed him sweetly.

Time lost all meaning. For endless minutes Ella was wrapped in sensation. She could have halted time and lived forever in this one moment. It was exquisite.

JEWELS of the DESERT

Deserts, diamonds and destiny!

In the Kingdom of Quishari, two rulers with hearts as hard as the rugged landscape they reign over are in need of desert queens....

When they offer convenient proposals, will they discover doing your duty doesn't have to mean ignoring your heart?

Find out in Barbara McMahon's fabulous duet!

BARBARA MCMAHON

Marrying the Scarred Sheikh

JEWELS of the DESERT

HARLEQUIN®

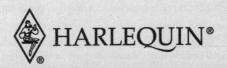

TORONTO • NEW YORK • LONDON
AMSTERDAM • PARIS • SYDNEY • HAMBURG
STOCKHOLM • ATHENS • TOKYO • MILAN • MADRID
PRAGUE • WARSAW • BUDAPEST • AUCKLAND

ISBN-13: 978-0-373-17651-9

MARRYING THE SCARRED SHEIKH

First North American Publication 2010

This edition published by arrangement with Harlequin Books S.A.

For questions and comments about the quality of this book please contact us at Customer_eCare@Harlequin.ca.

www.eHarlequin.com

Printed in U.S.A.

Barbara McMahon was born and raised in the southern United States, but settled in California after spending a year flying around the world for an international airline. After settling down to raise a family and work for a computer firm, she began writing when her children started school. Now, feeling fortunate in being able to realize the long-held dream of quitting her "day job" and writing full-time, she and her husband have moved to the Sierra Nevada mountains of California, where she finds her desire to write is stronger than ever. With the beauty of the mountains visible from her windows, and the pace of life slower than that of the hectic San Francisco Bay Area where they previously resided, she finds more time than ever to think up stories and characters and share them with others through writing. Barbara loves to hear from readers. You can reach her at P.O. Box 977, Pioneer, CA 95666-0977, U.S.A. Readers can also contact Barbara at her Web site, www.barbaramcmahon.com.

To Kelly-Anne, Jeff, Justin, Dylan and Bridgette:
Family is always best. Love from me.

Dear Reader,

Twins as adults are different from twins as kids. Switching places and fooling people are undoubtedly fun as children. However, as they mature, childish antics are put away. Still—from time to time they are undoubtedly misidentified.

In Khalid's story, he is unlikely to be mistaken for his brother, due to a scar obtained when fighting oil fires. His choice of career is unlike his brother's as well. He likes to be in the desert working in actual oil fields, vetting equipment and drilling procedures—or putting out dangerous conflagrations that most men never even consider facing.

It was one such fire that damaged his face and led him to believe no one would ever want to be close to him. So when he meets a stranger at the beach after midnight, he's struck with the novelty of being accepted solely for what he says, not for how he looks.

If you had loved and lost the one man you thought was for you, would you search for another? Or even be open to the possibility if one showed up unexpectedly? Ella considers any thought of marriage pointless. She'd already loved a wonderful man, and after his death planned her future alone. Running into a stranger on the beach was exciting—as long as they kept their meetings brief.

It's when they come face to face in the harsh light of day each realizes things are going to change in a big way. Two brothers—twins to boot—find love and happy futures in totally unexpected ways.

All the best,

Barbara

CHAPTER ONE

ELLA PONTI walked along the shore. The night was dark. The only illumination came from the stars overhead. No moon tonight. The wavelets gurgled as they spent themselves on the sand. Alexander had loved walking in the dark and she felt a closer tie than any other time.

He'd been dead for over a year. The crushing pain of his death had eased, as others had told her it would. Only a lingering ache where her heart was reminded her constantly that she would never see him again.

Sighing, she looked to the sky. The stars sparkled and shimmered through the heat of the night. Turning slowly, she looked at the black expanse that was the Persian Gulf. Nothing was visible. Some nights she saw ships sailing silently through the night, their lights gliding slowly across the horizon. Nothing there tonight. Turning toward home, she began walking, splashing lightly through the warm water at land's edge.

What a contrast this land was, she mused as she enjoyed the silence. Here at the seashore it was as beautiful as any Mediterranean resort; lush plants grew in abundance. She loved the leafy palms, the broad-leaf ferns and the flowers were nothing short of breathtaking. Each house around the estate she lived on seemed to flourish with a horticulturist's delight.

She enjoyed sitting out in the afternoons in the shady nooks of the garden, smelling the blend of fragrances that perfumed the air. While only a short distance from the capital city of Alkaahdar, it felt like worlds away from the soaring skyscrapers of the modern city.

She would go to bed when she reached her place. It was already after midnight. She liked to work late, as she had tonight, then wind down by a walk on the deserted beach—alone with only the sand, sky and sea.

With few homes along this stretch of beach, only those who knew the place well knew where to turn away from the water to follow winding paths through lush foliage that led home. Ella knew exactly where to turn even in the dark.

From a distance, as she walked along, she saw a silhouette of another person. A man, standing at the edge of the water. He was almost in front of where her path opened to the beach. In all the months she'd lived here, she'd never seen another soul after dark.

Slowing her pace, she tried to figure out who he might be. Another person who had trouble sleeping through the night? A stranger exploring the beach? Or someone intent on nefarious activities?

Ella almost laughed at her imagination. The homes along this stretch of beach belonged to the fabulously wealthy of Quishari. There were guards and patrols and all sorts of deterrents to crime. Which was why she always felt safe enough to walk alone after dark. Had that changed? She had only nodding acquaintances with her neighbors. Ella kept to herself. Still, one of the servants at the main house would have told her if there were danger.

She could cut diagonally from where she was to where the path left the beach, avoid the stranger entirely. But her curiosity rose. She continued along splashing in the water. The flowing skirt she wore that hit her midcalf was already wet along the hem. The light material moved with the slight breeze, shifting and swaying as she walked.

"Is it safe for a woman to walk alone at night?" the man asked when she was close enough to hear his voice.

"Unless you mean me harm, it is," she replied. Resolutely, she continued walking toward him.

"I mean no harm to you or anyone. Just curious. Live around here?" he asked.

As she walked closer, she estimated his height to be several inches over six feet. Taller than Alexander had been. The darkness made it impossible to see any features; even his eyes were hidden as he tilted his head down to look at her. No glimmer of light reflected from them. The traditional white robes he wore were highlighted by the starlight, but beyond that, he was a man of shadow.

"I live nearby," she replied. "But you do not. I don't know you."

"No. I'm here on a visit. I think." He looked back out to sea. "Quite a contrast from where I've been for the last few weeks."

She turned to look at the sea, keeping a safe twelve feet or so of space between them.

"Rough waters?"

"Desert. I wanted to see the sea as soon as I got here. I've been traveling for almost twenty-four hours straight, am dead tired, but wanted to feel the cool breeze. I considered going for a swim."

"Not the safest thing to do alone, especially after dark. If you got into trouble, who would see or hear?" Though Ella had gone swimming alone after dark. That had been back shortly after Alexander's death when she hadn't thought she cared if something happened or not. Now she knew life was so precious she would not wish harm on herself or anyone.

"You're here," he said whimsically.

"So I am. And if you run into trouble, do you think I could rescue you?"

"Or at least go for help." With that, he shed the robe, kicked off the shoes he wore.

Startled, Ella watched. Was he stripping down to nothing to go for a swim?

It was too dark to know, but in a moment, he plunged into the cool waters of the Gulf and began swimming. She had trouble following him with her eyes; only the sounds of his powerful arms cleaving the water could be heard.

"So I'm the designated life guard," she murmured, sitting down on the sand. It was still warm from the afternoon sun. Sugar-white and fine, at night it nurtured by its warmth, soft to touch. She picked up a fistful letting it run between her fingers. Idly she watched where she knew him to be. She hoped he would enjoy his swim and not need any help from anyone. She hadn't a clue who he was. For tonight, it was enough he had not had to swim alone. Tomorrow, maybe she'd meet him or maybe not.

Ella lost track of time, staring out to sea. So he came from the desert. She had ventured into the vast expanse that made up more of Quishari than any other topography. Its beauty was haunting. A harsh land, unforgiving in many instances, but also hiding delights, like small flowers that bloomed for such a short time after a rare rainstorm. Or the undulating ground a mixture of dirt and sand that reminded her of water. The colors were muted, until lit by the spectacular sunsets that favored the land. Once she'd seen an oasis, lost and lonely in the vast expanse of the desert. But her fervent imagination found it magical. Water in the midst of such arid harshness.

She wished she could capture that in her own work. Show the world there was more to the desert than endless acres of nothing. She began considering plans for such a collection. Maybe she'd try it after finishing her current project. Tomorrow was the day she tried the new technique. She had the shape in mind of the bowl she wanted to make. Now she had to see if she could pull it off. Colors would be tricky, but she wanted them to swirl in glass, ethereal, hinting and tantalizing.

She felt relaxed as the moment ticked by. It was pleasant in the warmth of the night, with the soft sound of the sea at her feet and the splashing in the distance. Would the man ever get tired?

Finally she heard him approach. Then he seemed to rise up out of the water when he stood in the gradual slope. She rose and stepped back as he went directly to where his robes lay and scooped them up.

"You still here?" he asked.

"As designated life guard. Enjoy your swim?"

"Yes, life giving after the heat of the desert." He dried himself with the robes, then shrugged into them.

She turned. "Good night."

"Thanks for keeping watch."

"I don't know that I would have been any help had you gotten into trouble," she said, turning and half walking backward to continue along the shore.

"Shall I walk you home? It would be easy enough for me to do." He stood where he was, not threatening.

"No." She did draw the line there. She knew nothing about the man. It was one thing to run into a stranger on the beach, something else again to let him know where she lived—alone.

"I might be here tomorrow," he said.

"I might be, as well," she replied, then quickly walked away. She went farther down the beach and then cut into a neighbor's yard. She didn't want to telegraph her location. Hopefully he couldn't see enough in the darkness to know which path she'd taken. She walked softly on the edge of the neighbor's estate and soon reached the edge of the property she rented. Seconds later she was home.

* * *

Khalid watched until he could no longer see her. He had no idea who the woman was or why she was out after midnight on a deserted beach. He was dripping. Taking a last look at the sea, or the dark void where it was, with only a glimmer of reflected starlight here and there, he turned and went back to the house his grandmother had left him last summer. Her death had hit him hard. She'd been such a source of strength. She'd listened to his problems, always supportive of his solutions. And she had chided him often enough to get out into society. He drew the line there. Still, he cherished her wisdom and her sense of fun. He would always miss her.

He thought about the woman on the beach. He could only guess she wasn't all that old from the sound of her voice. But aside from estimating her height to be about five feet two inches or so, he didn't know a thing about her. The darkness had hidden more than it revealed. Was she old or young? Slender, he thought, but the dress she wore moved in the breeze, not revealing many details.

Which was probably a good thing. He had no business being interested in anyone. He knew the scars that ran down his side were hideous. More than one person had displayed shock and repulsion when seeing them. Like his fiancée. Damara had not been able to cope at all and had fled the first day the bandages had been removed and she'd seen him in the hospital after the fire.

His brother, Rashid, had told him more than once he was better off without her if she couldn't stick after a tragedy. But it didn't help the hole he'd felt had been shot through his heart when the woman he'd planned to marry had taken off like he was a horrible monster.

He'd seen similar reactions ever since. He knew he was better off working with men in environments too harsh for women to venture into. Those same men accepted him on his merits, not his looks.

He had his life just as he wanted it now. Except—he had to decide what to do with the house his grandmother left him. It had been a year. He had put off any decisions until the fresh ache of her dying had subsided. But a house should not sit empty.

He walked swiftly across the sand to the start of the wide path that led straight to the house. It was a home suited for families. Close to the beach, it was large with beautiful landscaping, a guesthouse and plenty of privacy. The lawns should have children running around as he and his brother had done. As his father and uncles had done.

The flowers should be plucked and displayed in the home. And the house itself should ring with love and laughter as it had when he and Rashid had been boys visiting their father's parents.

But the house had been empty and silent for a year. And would remain that way unless he sold it. It would be hard to part with the house so cherished by him and his family. Especially with the memories of his beloved grandmother filling every room. But he had no need for it. His flat in Alkaahdar suited him. There when he needed it, waiting while he was away.

As he brushed against an overgrown shrub, his senses were assaulted by the scents of the garden. Star jasmine dominated the night. Other, more subtle fragrances sweetened the still air. So different from the dry, acrid air of the desert. Instantly he was transported back to when he and Rashid had run and played. His father had been alive then, and of course his grandmother. Who knew the odd quirks of fate, or that he'd end up forever on the outside looking in at happy couples and laughing families. That elusive happiness of families denied him.

Not that he had major regrets. He had done what he thought right. He had saved lives. A scar was a small price to pay.

He entered the house through the door he'd left open from the veranda. Bed sounded really good. He'd been traveling far too long. Once he awoke, he could see what needed to be done to get the house ready for sale.

* * *

Ella woke late the next morning. She'd had a hard time falling asleep after meeting the stranger on the beach. She lay in bed wondering who he was and why he'd been traveling so long. Most people stopped when they were tired. No matter, she would probably never see him again. Though, she thought as she rose, just maybe she'd take another walk after midnight tonight. He said he'd be there. Her interest was definitely sparked.

But that was later. Today, she wanted to try to make the new glass piece that had been taking shape in her mind for days.

After a quick breakfast at the nook in the kitchen, Ella went to her studio. As always when entering, she remembered the wonderful woman who had sponsored her chance at developing her skill as a glassblower and who had offered to help her sell her pieces when they were ready. She missed her. She pursued her passion two-fold now—for herself and for her benefactor.

In only moments, she was totally absorbed in the challenge of blending colors and shapes in the bowl she was creating.

It was only when her back screamed in pain that Ella arched it and glanced at the clock. It was late afternoon—she'd been working for seven hours straight. Examining the piece she'd produced, she nodded in satisfaction. It wasn't brilliant by any means, but it had captured the ethereal feel she wanted. For a first attempt at this technique, it passed. A couple more stages to complete before the glass bowl was ready for a gallery or for sale. A good day's work.

She rubbed her back and wished there was some way she could pace herself. But once caught up in the creative process, it was hard to stop. Especially with glass. Once it was at the molten stage, she had to work swiftly to form the pieces before it cooled. Now it needed to go into the annealer that would slowly cool it so no cracks formed. This was often the tricky part. Especially when she had used different glass and different color mediums that cooled at different rates.

It would end up as it ended up. She tried to keep to that philosophy so she didn't angst over every piece.

Once the bowl was in the oven, she went back to her kitchen, prepared a light meal and carried it to the small terrace on the shady side of the house. The air was cooling down, but it was still almost uncomfortably warm. She nibbled her fruit as she gazed at the flowers that grew so profusely. Where else in the world would she be so comfortable while working on her art? This house was truly a refuge for her. The one place she felt safe and comfortable and almost happy. She'd made it a home for one.

Thinking about the flat she'd given up after Alexander's death, she knew she had traded their happy home for her own. It had taken her a while to realize it, but now she felt a part of the estate. She knew every flower in the garden, every hidden nook that offered shade in the day. And she could walk the paths at night without a light. It was as if the cottage and estate had welcomed her with comforting arms and drawn her in.

So not like the home of her childhood, that was for sure. She shied away from thinking about the last months there. She would focus on the present—or even the future, but not the past.

Taking a deep breath, she held it for a moment, listening. Was that a car? She wasn't expecting any friends. No one else knew where she was. Who would be coming to the empty estate? The gardener's day was later in the week. For a moment she didn't move. The car sounded as if it were going away. Soon the sound faded completely. Only then did Ella relax.

After she ate, she rose and walked around the cottage. Nothing seemed disturbed. How odd that the car sounded so near. Had the sound been amplified from the road, or had it been in the drive for some reason?

The late-afternoon sun was hot. She debated taking a quick swim, but reconsidered. She wanted to walk along the beach tonight to see if the stranger returned. For the first time in over a year, she was curious about something—someone. Not many people shared her love of the night. Did he? Or had last night been only an aberration because of his long trip? Where in the desert had he been? She'd like to visit an oasis or drive a few hours into the desert, lose sight of any signs of man and just relish the solitude and stark beauty that would surround her.

She needed a car for that. Sighing softly, she considered renting a vehicle for such an expedition. Maybe one day in the fall.

Ella could scarcely wait until midnight. Very unusual, her impatience to see if the man was there again. For a year she'd felt like she was wrapped in plastic, seeing, but not really connected with the rest of the world. Yet a chance encounter in the dark had ignited her curiosity. She knew nothing about him, except he liked the sea and wasn't afraid to swim after dark. Was he old or young? Did he live nearby or was he sneaking through the estates to gain access to the private beach?

Would he be there tonight?

Promptly at the stroke of twelve, Ella left her home to walk quickly through the path to the beach. Quickly scanning from left to right, she felt a bump of disappointment. He was not there. Sighing softly for her foolishness, she walked to the water's edge and turned to retrace last night's steps.

"I wondered if you would appear," the familiar voice said behind her. She turned and saw him walking swiftly toward her. His longer legs cut the distance in a short time. No robes tonight, just dark trousers and a white shirt.

"I often walk at midnight," she said, not wishing him to suspect she'd come tonight especially to see if he were here.

"As do I, but mainly due to the heat of the day."

"And because you don't sleep?" she asked.

He fell into step with her.

"That can be a problem," he said. "For you, too?"

"Sometimes." Now that he was here, she felt awkward and

shy. Her heart beat a bit faster and she wondered at the exhilaration that swept through her. "Did you catch up on your sleep after your trip?"

"Got a few hours in."

"Holidays are meant for sleeping in late and lazing around," she said, trying to figure out exactly how to ask questions that wouldn't sound as if she were prying.

"If I were on holiday, which I'm not, I still require little sleep."

"Oh, from what you said…" She closed her mouth.

"I did come off a job at an oil field west of here. But I'm here on business. Personal business, I guess you'd say."

"Oh." What kind of business? How long would it take? Would she see him again after tonight? Not that she could see him exactly. But it was nice to share the walk with someone, if only for one night.

"I have some thinking to do and a decision to make," he added a moment later.

"Mmm." She splashed through the water. There was a slight breeze tonight from the sea which made the air seem cooler than normal. It felt refreshing after the heat of her workshop.

"You speak Arabic, but you're not from here, are you?" he asked.

She looked up and shook her head. Not that he could likely see the gesture. "I've studied for years, I can understand it well. Do I not speak it well?"

"Yes, but there is still a slight accent. Where are you from?"

"Italy. But not for a while. I live here now."

"With family?"

She hesitated. Once again safety concerns reared up. "Do you think I need a chaperone?" she asked, shying away from his question.

"I have no idea. How old are you?"

"Old enough." She stopped and turned, looking up at him,

wishing she could see him clearly. "I am a widow. I am long past the stage of needing someone to watch out for me."

"You don't sound old enough to be a widow."

"Sometimes I feel a hundred years old." No one should lose her husband when only twenty-eight. But, as she had been told before, life was not always fair.

"I'm sorry for your loss," he said softly.

She began walking again, not wanting to remember. She tried to concentrate on each foot stepping on the wet sand. Listen to the sea to her right which kissed the shore with wavelets. Feel the energy radiating from the man beside her. So now he'd think she was an older woman, widowed and alone. How old was he? She had no idea, but he sounded like a dynamic man in his prime.

"Thank you." She never knew how to respond to the comment. He hadn't known her husband. He hadn't loved him as she had. No one would ever feel the loss as she did. Still, it was nice he made the comment. Had he ever lost a loved one?

They walked in silence for a few moments. Then she asked, "So what did you do at the oil field?"

"I consult on the pumps and rigs. My company has a retainer with Bashiri Oil among others to assist when new fields are discovered. And to put out fires when they erupt."

"You put out oil fires?" She was astonished. She had seen the pictures of oil wells burning. Flames shot a hundred feet or more in the air. The intense heat melted and twisted metal even yards from the fire. She found it hard to work with the heat in her own studio with appropriate protective gear. How could anyone extinguish an oil well fire? "Is there any job more dangerous on earth?"

He laughed softly. "I imagine there are. It's tricky sometimes, but someone has to do it."

"And how did you get interested in putting out conflagrations? Wasn't being a regular fireman enough?"

"I'm fascinated by the entire process of oil extraction. From discovering reserves, to drilling and capping. And part of the entire scenario is the possibility of fire. Most are accidents. Some are deliberately set. But the important thing is to get them extinguished as quickly as possible. That's why we do consultation work with new sites and review existing sites for safety measures. Anything to keep a well from catching fire is a good thing. It's an interest I've always had. And since I could choose my profession, I chose this one."

"I just can't imagine. Isn't it hot? Actually it must be exceedingly hot. Is there a word beyond hot?"

He laughed again. She liked the sound of it. She smiled in reaction, not at all miffed that he was laughing at her questions.

"Oh, it's hot. Even with the special suits we wear."

He explained briefly how they dealt with fire.

Ella listened, fascinated in a horrified way. "You could get killed doing that," she exclaimed at one point.

"Haven't yet," he said.

She detected the subtle difference in his voice. He was no longer laughing. Had someone been injured or killed fighting one of those fires? Probably. The entire process sounded extremely dangerous.

"They don't erupt often," he said.

"I hope there is never another oil fire in the world," she said fervently. "No wonder you wanted to go swimming last night. I'd want to live *in* the sea if I ever survived one of those."

"That is an appeal. But I'd get restless staying here all the time. Something always draws me back to the oil fields. A need to keep the rigs safe. And a sense of need to return burning wells to productivity. Duty, passion. I'm not totally sure myself."

"So it's the kind of thing you'd do even if you didn't need to work?"

He laughed again. "Exactly."

She stopped. "This is as far as I usually go," she said.

"Ben al Saliqi lives here, or he used to," Khalid said, turning slowly to see the house from the beach. Only the peaks of the roof were visible above the trees that lined the estate, a soft glow from the lamps in the windows illuminating the garden.

"How do you know that?" she asked. There was hardly any identifying features in the dark.

He turned back to her. "I spent many summers here. At my grandmother's house," he said. "I know every family on the beach—except yours."

"Ohmygod, you're one of the al Harum men, aren't you? I'm your tenant, Ella Ponti."

CHAPTER TWO

"MY TENANT?" Khalid said.

"I rent the guesthouse on your grandmother's estate. She was my patron—or something. I miss her so much. I'm so sorry she died."

"She rented out the guesthouse? I had no idea."

"I have a lease. You can check it. She insisted on drawing one up. Said it would be better for us both to get the business part out of the way and enjoy each other's company. She was wonderful. I'm so sorry she died when she did. I miss her."

"I miss her, as well. I didn't know about this," Khalid said.

"Well, I don't know why you don't. Haven't you been running the estate? I mean, the gardener comes every week, the maids at the house keep it clean and ready."

"This is the first I've visited since her death. The servants know how to do their job. They don't need an overseer on site."

"It's the first visit in a long while. You didn't visit her the last few months she lived here. She talked about her grandsons. Which are you, Rashid or Khalid?"

"Khalid."

"Ah, the restless one."

"Restless?"

"She said you hadn't found your place yet. You were seeking, traveling to the interior, along the coast, everywhere, looking for your place."

"Indeed. And Rashid?"

"He's the consumed one—trying to improve the business beyond what his father and uncles did. She worried about you both. Afraid—" Ella stopped suddenly. She was not going to tell him all his grandmother had said. It was not her business if neither man ever married and had children. Or her place to tell him of the longing the older woman had had to hold a new generation. Which never happened and now never would.

"Afraid of what?" he asked.

"Nothing. I have to go back now." She began walking quickly toward home. How was she to know the mysterious stranger on the beach was her new landlord? She almost laughed. He might hold the lease, but he was nothing like a landlord. He hadn't even visited the estate in more than a year. She knew, because she'd never seen him there and she'd live here for over a year and had heard from his grandmother how much she wished to see him beyond fleeting visits in the capital city.

He easily caught up with her. Reaching out to take her arm, he stopped her and swung her around.

"Tell me."

"Good grief, it's not that big a deal. She was afraid neither of her grandsons would marry and have children. She was convinced both of you were too caught up in your own lives to look around for someone to marry. She wanted to hold a great-grandchild. Now she never can."

"She told you this? A stranger."

Ella nodded. "Yes. We became friends and had a lot of time to visit and talk. She came to the guest cottage often, interested in what I was doing." And had been a rock to lean against when Ella was grieving the most. Her gentle wisdom had helped so much in those first few months. Her love had helped in healing. And the rental cottage had been a welcomed refuge. One guarded by the old money and security of the al Harum family. Ella had found a true home in the cottage and was forever grateful to Alia al Harum for providing the perfect spot for her.

Sheikh Khalid al Harum came from that same old money. She hadn't known exactly what he did but it certainly wasn't for money. No wonder his grandmother had complained. It was a lucky thing he was still alive.

"And what were you doing?" he asked, still holding her arm.

"Working. You could call her a patron of the arts."

"You're a painter?"

"No, glassblower. Could you let me go?"

Ella felt his hold ease. His hand dropped to his side. She stepped back and then headed for home. So much for the excitement of meeting the stranger. She could have just waited until she heard him at the main house and gone over to introduce herself.

Now she wanted to get home and close the door. This was the grandson who was always roaming. Was he thinking of using the house when in the capital city?

"Oh." She stopped and turned. Khalid bumped into her. She hadn't known he was right behind her. His hands caught her so she didn't fall.

"Are you planning to sell the estate?" she asked.

"It's something I'm considering."

"Your grandmother wanted you to have it. She'd be so hurt if you just sold it away."

"I'm not selling it away. It's too big for one man. And I'm not in Alkaahdar often. When I am, I have a flat that suits me."

"Think of the future. You could marry and have a huge family someday. You'll need a big house like that one. And the location is perfect—right on the Gulf."

"I'm not planning to ever marry. Obviously my grandmother didn't tell you all about me or you'd know the thought of marriage is ludicrous. So why would I want a big house to rattle around in?"

Ella tried to remember all her sponsor had said about her grandsons. Not betraying any confidences, not going into detail about their lives, she still had given Ella a good feel for the men's personalities. And a strong sense that neither man was likely to make her a great-grandmother. The longing she'd experienced for the days passed when they'd been children and had loved to come to her home had touched Ella's heart. Alia had hoped to recapture those happy times with their children.

"Don't make hasty decisions," she said. Alia had died thinking this beloved grandson would live in her home. Ella hated the thought he could casually discard it when it had meant so much to the older woman.

"My grandmother died last July. It's now the end of May. I don't consider that a hasty move."

Ella didn't know what tack to use. If he wanted to sell, the house was his to do so with as he wanted. But she felt sad for the woman who had died thinking Khalid would find happiness in the house she'd loved.

"Come, I'll walk you back. You didn't use the path last night that leads to the house or guesthouse," he said.

"I didn't know who you were. I didn't want to indicate where I lived," she said, walking back. The night seemed darker and colder. She wanted to be home. So much for looking forward to the evening walk. Now she wished she'd stayed in the cottage and gone to bed.

"Wise. You don't know who might be out on the beach so late at night."

"I've been taking care of myself for a long time. I know this beach well." She was withdrawing. There was something liberating about walking with a stranger, talking, sharing. But something else again once actually knowing the person. She'd be dealing with him in the near future. She didn't know this man. And until she did, she was not giving out any personal information.

A blip of panic settled in. If he sold the estate, where would she go? She had made a home here. Thought she'd be living in the cottage for years to come. She had to review the lease. Did it address the possibility of the estate being sold? She knew Madame al Harum had never considered that likelihood.

As soon as she reached the path, she walked even faster. "Good night," she said. She wasn't even sure what to call him. Sheikh al Harum sounded right, or did she use his first name, as well, to differentiate him from his brother who also was a sheikh? She was not used to dealing with such lofty families.

When she reached her house, she flipped on the lights and headed for the desk. Her expenses were minimum: food, electricity and her nominal rent. It wasn't as if the al Harum family needed her money. But she had needed to pay her way. She was not a charity case. It wasn't a question of money; it was a question of belonging. Of carrying out her dreams. Madame al Harum had understood. Ella doubted the sheikh would.

She read the Arabic script, finding it harder to understand than newspapers. She could converse well, read newspapers comfortably. But this was proving more difficult than she expected. Why hadn't she asked for a copy translated into Italian?

Throwing it down in disgust, she paced the room for a long time. If she had to leave, where would she go? She studied the cream-colored walls, the soft draperies that made the room so welcoming. Just beyond the dark windows was a view of the gardens. She loved every inch of the cottage and grounds. Where else would she find a home?

The next morning Ella was finishing her breakfast when one of the maids from the main house knocked on the door. It was Jalilah, one who had also served Alia al Harum for so many years.

"His Excellency would like to see you," she said. "I'm to escort you to the main house."

So now he summoned her—probably to discuss her leaving. "Wait until I change." She'd donned worn jeans and an oversize shirt to work around the studio. Not the sort of apparel one wore to meet with a sheikh. Especially if doing battle to keep her home.

Quickly she donned a dress that flattered her dark looks. It was a bit big; she'd lost weight over the last few months. Still, the rose color brought a tinge of pink to her cheeks.

Her dark eyes looked sad—as they had ever since losing Alexander. She would never again be the laughing girl who had grown up thinking everything good about people. Now she knew heartache and betrayal. She was wiser, but at a price.

Running a brush through her hair, she turned to face the future. Was there a clause in the lease that would nullify her claim if the estate was sold? As they walked across the gardens, she tried to remember every detail about the terms Madame al Harum had discussed.

She entered the house and immediately remembered her one-time hostess. Nothing had changed since the last time she'd visited. It was cool and pleasant. The same pictures hung on the walls. Her first vase from her new studio still held a place of honor on the small table in the foyer, holding a cascading array of blossoms. She'd been so happy it had been loved.

The maid went straight to the study. Ella paused at the doorway for a moment, her eyes widening in shock as she got a good look at Sheikh Khalid al Harum. He looked up at her, catching the startled horror in her expression. His own features hardened slightly and she felt embarrassed she'd reacted as she had. No one had told her he'd been horribly burned. The distorted and puckered skin on his right cheek, down his neck and obviously beneath his shirt, disfigured what were otherwise the features of a gorgeous man. She'd been right about his age—he looked to be in his prime, maybe early thirties. And he was tall as she noted when he rose to face her.

"You wanted to see me?" she said, stepping inside. She held his gaze, determined not to comment on the burn, or show how sympathetic she felt at the pain he must have endured. She'd had enough burns herself in working with molten glass to know the pain. Never as big a patch as he had. What was a fabulously wealthy man like he had to be risking his life to fight oil fires?

Her heart beat faster. Despite the burn scar, he was the best-looking guy she'd ever seen. Even including Alexander. She frowned. She was not comparing the two. There was no need. The sheikh was merely her new landlord. The flurry of attraction was a fluke. He could mean nothing to her.

"Please." He gestured to a chair opposite the desk. "You're considerably younger than I thought. Are you really a widow?"

She nodded as she slipped onto the edge of the chair. "My husband died April a year ago. What did you wish to see me about?"

He sat and picked up a copy of the lease. "This. The lease for the guesthouse you signed with my grandmother."

She nodded. It was what she expected. He held her future in his hands. Why didn't she have a good feeling about this?

"How did you coerce her to making this?" he asked, frowning at the papers.

Ella blinked. "I did not coerce her into doing anything. How dare you suggest such a thing!" She leaned forward, debating whether to leave or not at his disparaging remark. "She offered me a place to live and work and then came up with the lease herself so I wouldn't have to worry about living arrangements until I got a following."

"A following?"

"I told you, I blow glass. I need to make enough pieces to sell to earn her livelihood. Until that time, she was—I guess you'd say like a patroness—a sponsor if you would. I rented the studio to make my glass pieces and she helped out by making the rent so low. Did you read the clause where she gets a percentage of my sales when I start making money?"

"And if you never sell anything? Seems you got a very cushy deal here. But my grandmother's gone now. This is my estate and if I chose to sell it, I'm within my rights. I don't know how you got her to sign such a lopsided lease but I'm not her. You need to leave. Vacate the guest quarters so I can renovate if necessary to sell."

Ella stared at him. "Where does it say I have to leave before the end of the five years?" she asked, stalling for time, trying to think about what she could do. Panic flared again. It has seemed too good to be true that she'd have a place to live and work while building an inventory. But as the months had gone on, she'd become complaisant with her home. She couldn't possibly find another place right away—and she didn't have the money to build another studio. And not enough glass pieces ready to sell to raise the money. She was an unknown. The plans she and his grandmother had discussed had been for the future—not the present.

"I do not want you as a tenant. What amount do you want to leave?"

She didn't get his meaning at first, then anger flared. "Nothing. I wish to stay." She felt the full force of his gaze when he stared at her. She would not be intimidated. This was her *home*. He might see it as merely property, but it was more to her. Raising her chin slightly, she continued. "You'll see on the last page once I begin to sell, she gets ten percent of all sales. Or she would have. I guess you do, now." She didn't like the idea of having a long-term connection with this man. He obviously couldn't care less about her or her future.

Madame al Harum had loved her work, had encouraged her so much. She appreciated what Ella did and would have reveled in her success—if it came.

Sheikh Khalid al Harum saw her as an impediment to selling the estate.

Tough.

"I can make it very worth your while," he said softly.

She kept her gaze locked with his. "No."

"You don't know how much," he said.

"Doesn't matter. I have the lease, I have the house for another four years. That will be enough time to make it or not. If not, I'll find something else to do." And she'd keep her precious home until the last moment.

"Or find a rich husband to support you. The estate is luxurious. You would hate to leave it. But if I give you enough money, you'll be able to support yourself in similar luxury for a time."

She rose and leaned on the desk, her eyes narrowed as she stared into his.

"I'm not leaving. The lease gives me a right to stay. Deal with it."

She turned and left, ignoring her shaky knees, her pounding heart. She didn't want his money. She wanted to stay exactly where she was. Remain until those looking for her gave up. Until she could build her own future the way she wanted. Until she could prove her art was worth something and that people would pay to own pieces.

Khalid listened to the sound of her hurried footsteps, then the closing of the front door. She refused to leave. He glanced at the lease again. As far as he could tell, it was iron tight. But he'd have the company attorneys review. There had to be a way. He did not want to sit on the house for another four years and he suspected no one would buy the place with a tenant in residence. What had his grandmother been thinking?

He leaned back in his chair and looked at the chair his unwanted tenant had used. Ella Ponti, widow. She looked like she was in her midtwenties. How had her husband died? She was far too young to be a widow, living alone. Yet the sadness that had shone in her eyes until the fire of anger replaced it, showed him she truly mourned her loss. And he felt a twinge of regret to be bringing a change to her life.

Yet he couldn't reconcile her being in the cottage. Had his grandmother been taken in? Was Ella nothing more than a gold digger looking for an easy way in life? Latch on to an old woman and talk her into practically giving her the cottage.

He was on the fence about selling. He remembered his grandmother in every room. All the visits they'd shared over the years. Glancing around the study, he hated to let it go. But he would never live in such a big house. Which left selling the estate as the best option.

He should have visited his grandmother more often. He missed her. They'd had dinners together in Alkaahdar when he was in town. Sometimes he escorted her to receptions or parties. But long weekends at the estate doing nothing were in the past. And in retrospect she'd asked after him and what was going on in his life more than he'd asked after hers. Regrets were hard to live with.

Though if she'd seen Ella's reactions, maybe she would have stopped chiding him that he made too much of the scar. Ella's initial reaction had been an echo of his one-time fiancée's own look of horror. He knew it disgusted women. That was one reason he spent most of his time on the oil fields or in the desert. He saw the scar himself every morning when he shaved. He knew what it looked like.

Shaking himself out of the momentary reverie, he picked up the phone to call the headquarters of Bashiri Oil. The sooner he found a way to get rid of his unwanted tenant, the better.

* * *

Ella stormed home. She did not want to be bought out. Why had Khalid al Harum come to the estate at this time? He'd never visited in all the months she'd live here, why now? She had her life just as she wanted it and he was going to mess it up.

And how dare he offer her money to move? She was not going anywhere. She needed this tranquil setting. She'd gradually gotten over the fierce intensity of her grief. She owed it to Alia al Harum. The older woman had such faith in her talent and her ability to be able to command top money for her creations. She had strongly encouraged Ella to prove it to herself. And she would for the memory of the woman who had helped her so much.

And no restless grandson was going to drive her away.

She shrugged off the dress and tossed it on the bed. So much for dressing up for him. He only wanted her gone. She pulled on her jeans and oversize shirt. Tying her hair back as she walked, she went to the studio. The glass bowl she'd created yesterday still had hours of graduated cooling to complete before she could take it from the oven. She was impatient to know if it would be as beautiful as she imagined. And flawless with no cracks from irregular cooling, or mixing different types and textures of glass that cooled at different rates. Fingers crossed. Patience was definitely needed for glasswork.

In the meantime, she picked up her sketchbook and went to sit by the window. She could do an entire series in the same technique if the bowl came out perfect. She stared at the blank page. She was not seeing other glass artwork, but the face of Khalid al Harum. What a contrast—gorgeous man, hideous scar. His grandmother had never mentioned that. She'd talked of her grandchildren's lives, her worry they'd never find happiness and other memories of their childhood.

When had the fire happened? He could have been killed. She didn't know him, nor did she care to now that he'd tried to bribe her to leave. But still, how tragic to have been burned so severely. She looked at the couple of small scars on her arms and fingers from long-ago childhood scrapes. Fire was dangerous and damaging to delicate human skin. Every burn, no matter how small, hurt like crazy. She shivered trying to imagine a huge expanse of her body burned.

Had it happened recently? It didn't have that red look that came with recent healing. But with all the money the al Harums had, surely he could have had plastic surgery to mitigate the worst of the damage.

Impatient with her thoughts, she rose and paced the studio. She needed to be focused on the next idea, the next piece of art. She had to build a collection that would be worthy of an exhibit and then of exorbitant prices. Had Madame al Harum spoken to the gallery owners as she had said she would do when the time was right? Probably not. Why speak of something that was years away from happening.

"Great. It's bad enough he'll try to get me off the property. I truly have no place to go and no chance of getting a showing if I don't have someone to vouch for me," she said aloud. She could scream.

But it would do no good.

"Deal with it," she said to herself. She'd take the advice she'd given him and make sure she made every moment count. He might try to evict her, but until she was carried kicking and screaming from the studio, she'd work on her collection.

The day proved interminable. Every time she'd start thinking about Khalid al Harum, she'd force her mind to focus on designing pieces using the swirling of blues and reds. It would work for a few moments, then gradually something would drift in that had her thinking about him again.

She didn't like it one bit.

After dinner, she debated taking a walk on the beach. That usually cleared her mind. But after the last two nights, the last thing she wanted was to run into *him* again.

She sat on her terrace for a while, trying to relax. The more she tried to ignore his image, the more it seemed to dance in front of her. She was not going to be intimidated by him. Jumping to her feet, she headed down the path to the beach. She'd been walking along the shore for months. Just because he showed up was no reason to change her routine.

When she stepped on the sand, she looked both ways. No sign of anyone. Slowly she walked to the water, then turned south. If he did come out, chances he would head north as she had the last two nights. She'd be safe from his company.

It didn't take long for the walk to begin to soothe. She let go of cares and worries and tried to make herself one with the night.

"I took a guess," a voice came from her right.

Khalid rose from the sand and walked the few yards to where she was. "I thought you might go a different way tonight and I was right." The smug satisfaction in his tone made her want to hit him.

"Then I'll turn and go north," she said, stopping and facing him. She'd tried an earlier time and a different direction. Had he come out to the beach a while ago to wait for her? She ignored the fluttery feeling in her stomach. So he came out. It probably was only to harangue her again about leaving.

"I am not stopping you from going in either direction," he said. He stood next to her, almost too close. She stepped back as a wavelet washed over her feet. The cool water broke the spell.

"You are of course welcomed to walk wherever you wish," she said. She began to walk again along the edge of the water.

Khalid walked beside her.

The silence stretched out moment by moment. Ella had lost all sense of serenity. Her nerves were on full alert. She was extremely conscious of the man beside her. Her skin almost tingled. She could see him from the corner of her eye—tall, silhouetted against the dark sky. She didn't need this sense of awareness. This feeling of wanting to know more. The desire to defend herself to him and make him change his mind and want her to stay in the guesthouse until the lease expired.

She kept silent with effort, wondering if she could outlast him. It grew harder and harder to keep silent as they went along.

"I called an attorney," he said at last.

She didn't reply, waiting for the bad news. Was there an escape clause?

"You'll be happy to know the lease is airtight. You have the right to stay as long as you wish. The interesting part is, you have the right to terminate before the end but my grandmother—and now me—didn't have the same right."

She'd forgotten. Madame al Harum had insisted Ella might wish to leave before five years and didn't want her to feel compelled to remain. At the time Ella had not been able to imagine ever leaving. She still didn't want to think about it. Would four more years be enough time?

"So if you wished to leave, I'd still make it lucrative for you."

"I don't live here for the money," she said.

"Why do you live here? You're not from here. No family. No husband. What holds you to the guesthouse, to Alkaahdar?"

"A safe place to live," she said. "A beautiful setting in a beautiful country. I also have friends here. Quishari is my home."

"Safe? Is there danger elsewhere?" he countered, focusing in on that comment.

She stopped to look at him. She wanted to get this through to him once and for all. "Look, I came here at a very hard time in my life—just after my husband died. Your grandmother did more for me than anyone, including making sure I had a place to live, to work, sheltered from problems and a chance to grieve. I will forever be in her debt. One I can now never repay. It hit me hard when she died. I grieve for her, as well. Now I'm coming to a place of peace and don't wish to have my life disrupted because you want to get rid of a home she loved and left to you in hopes you'd use it. Do not involve me in your life. I have no interest in taking a gazillion dollars to leave. I have no interest in disrupting my life to suit yours. I want to be left alone to continue as I have been doing these last months. Is that clear enough for you?"

"Life changes. Nothing is as it was last year. My grandmother is dead. Yes, she left me the estate in hopes I would settle there. You saw me this morning. You know why I'll never marry. Why should I hold on to a house for sentimental reasons, visiting it once or twice a year when some other family could enjoy living in it daily? Do you think it is easy for me to sell? I have so many memories of my family visiting. I know I'll face pressure from others in the family to hold on to it. But it's more of a crime to let it sit vacant year after year. What good does that do?"

"Why will you never marry? Did the fire damage other parts of you?" she asked, startled by his comment.

"What?"

She'd surprised him with that question.

Oh, this was just great. Why had she opened her mouth? Now she had to clarify herself. "I mean, can you not father children or something?"

He burst out laughing.

Ella frowned. It had not been a funny question.

"So you're all right in that department, I guess," she said, narrowing her eyes. "So what's the problem?"

He leaned over, his face close enough to hers she felt the warmth of his breath. She could barely see his eyes in the dark. "As I said, you saw me this morning. What woman would get close enough for me to use those other parts?" he asked very softly.

She stared into his eyes, as dark as her own, hard to see in the dim light of the stars. "Are you stupid or do you think I am? You're gorgeous except for a slight disfiguration on one side. You sound articulate. I expect you are well educated and have pots of money. Why wouldn't someone fall for you? Your grandmother thought you should be married. Surely she'd have known if there was a major impediment."

"I do not wish to be married for my money. I have a temper that could scare anyone and, I assure you, looks count a lot when people are looking for mates. And my grandmother saw only her own happy marriage that she wished replicated for her grandsons."

"So again I say what's the problem?"

"Maybe you are stupid. This scar," he said, reaching for her hand and trailing her fingers down his cheek, pressing against the puckered skin.

He let her hand go and she left it against the side of his face. The skin was warm, though distorted. Lightly, she brushed her thumb against it, drifted to his lips which had escaped the flame. Her heart pounded, but she was mesmerized. His warmth seemed to touch her heart. She felt heartbreak for his reasoning. He was consigning himself to a long, lonely life. She knew what that was like. Since Alexander's death, hadn't she resigned herself to the same?

But the circumstances were different. She had loved and lost. Khalid needed to feel someone's love, to know he was special. And to keep the dream his grandmother had so wanted for him.

Khalid was shocked. Her touch was soft, gentle, sweet. Her thumb traced a trail of fire and ice against his skin. No one had touched him since the doctors had removed the last of the bandages. When he released her, he expected her to snatch her hand away. It was still there. The touch was both unexpected and erotic. He could feel himself respond as he hadn't in years.

"Enough." He knocked her hand away and took a step back. "Tell me what it would take to get you to leave the guesthouse."

"Four years," she replied, and turned to resume her walk.

He watched as she walked away along the sea's edge. She was serious. At least at this moment. She didn't want money. She wanted time.

Why was she here? Was there anything in his grandmother's things that explained why she'd befriended Ella Ponti and made that one-sided deal with her? He hadn't gone through all her papers, but that would be his next step first thing in the morning.

He remained standing, watching. She didn't care if he walked beside her or not. If this was her regular routine, she'd been coming for nightly walks for a year. She didn't need his company.

Why had he come out tonight? He usually kept to himself. He couldn't remember the last time he'd sought out a woman's company. Probably because it would have been an exercise in futility. Ella had seen him in broad daylight. Tonight it had been like the last two: wrapped in darkness he could almost forget the burn scar. She had treated him the same all three nights.

Except for her touch tonight.

Shaking his head, he almost smiled. She shocked him in more ways than one. Was the reaction just that of a man too long without a woman? It had to be. She had done nothing to encourage him. In fact, he couldn't remember another woman standing up to him as she had, both tonight and earlier this morning. Deal with it, she'd said, dismissing his demand she leave as if it were of no account.

Which legally it proved to be. Maybe he'd stop pushing and learn a bit more about his unwanted tenant before pursuing other avenues. She intrigued him. Why was she really here? Maybe it was time to find out more about Ella Ponti, young widow living so far from her native land.

CHAPTER THREE

MAYBE she had finally gotten through to him, she thought as she walked alone. He had not followed her. Good. Well, maybe there was a touch of disappointment, but not enough to wish he was with her.

She clenched her hand into a fist. His skin had been warm, she'd felt the strong line of his jaw, the chiseled outline of his lips. Not that she wanted to think about his lips—that led to thoughts of kisses and she had no intention of ever kissing anyone else. It almost felt like a betrayal of her love for Alexander. It wasn't. Her mind knew that, it would take her heart a bit longer to figure that out. She still mourned her lost love.

"Alexander," she whispered. It took a second for her to recall his dear face. She panicked. She couldn't forget him. She loved him still. He'd been the heart beating in her. But his image wavered and faded to be replaced by the face of Khalid al Harum.

"No!" she said firmly. She would dismiss the man from her thoughts and concentrate on something else, anything else.

Wildly, she looked around. Out to sea she spotted a ship, gliding along soundlessly in the distance. Was it a cruise ship? Were couples and families enjoying the calm waters of the Gulf? Would they be stopping in one of the countries lining the coast? Maybe buy pearls from the shops or enjoy the traditional Arab cuisine. Maybe couples would be dancing. For a moment she regretted she'd never dance again. She was young to have loved and lost. But that was the way life was sometimes.

She had her art.

Stopping at last, she gazed at the ship for a long moment, then glanced back up the beach. Khalid al Harum stood where she'd left him. Was he brooding? Or just awaiting her return. She studied his silhouette and then began walking toward him. She had to return home. It was late and she'd had enough turmoil to last awhile.

When she drew even she stopped. "Now what?"

"Now we wait four years," he replied.

That surprised her. Was he really going to stop pressuring her? Somehow she had not thought he'd give up that easily. Yet, maybe he was pragmatic. The lease was valid. She had the law on her side—even against a sheikh. Dare she let her guard down and believe him?

"Since we'll be neighbors for the time, might as well make the best of things," he said.

That had her on instant alert. He didn't strike her as someone who settled for making the best of any situation unless it suited his needs and demands.

"And how do we do that?"

"Be neighborly, of course." He walked beside her. "Surely you visited with my grandmother from time to time."

"Almost every day," she said. "She was delightful. And very encouraging about my work. Did you know you have one of my early pieces in your house?"

"What and where?"

"The shallow vase in the foyer. It's a starburst bowl. Your grandmother liked it and I gave it to her. I was thrilled when she displayed it in such a prominent place."

"Maybe I'll come by one day and see your work."

Ella wasn't sure she wanted him in her studio or her house. But she probably had to concede that much. If he truly stopped pushing her to leave, she could accept a visit or two.

"Let me know when," she said.

Khalid caught up on some e-mail the next morning and then called his brother. Rashid was the head of Bashiri Oil. Khalid was technically equal owner in the company, along with an uncle and some cousins, but Rashid ran the business. Which suited Khalid perfectly. He much preferred the oil fields to the offices in the high-rise building downtown.

"What's up?" Rashid asked when he heard his brother's voice. "Are you still in Hari?"

"No, I'm at Grandmother's estate. Did you know she rented out the guesthouse last year?"

"No. Who to?"

"An artist. Now I'm wondering why the secrecy. I didn't know, either." Another reason to find out more about Ella Ponti.

"Good grief, did he convince her to sponsor him or something? What hard-luck story did he spin?"

"Not a he, a she. And I'm not sure about the story, which is the reason for the call. Can you have someone there run a background check? Apparently Ella has an airtight lease to the premises and has no intention of leaving before the lease expires—in four more years."

"A five-year lease? Have someone here look at it."

"Already done. It's solid. And she's one determined woman. I offered her as big a bribe as I could and she still says no."

"So, look for dirt to get her out that way." Rashid suggested.

"No, I think I'll go along with it for a while. I just want to know more about her. I respect Grandmother's judgment. She obviously liked the woman. But she also knew her and I don't."

There was a silent moment before his brother spoke again. "Is she pretty?"

"What does that have to do with a background check? She's a widow."

"Oh. Sure, I'll have one of the men call you later and you can give him what you have to start with. Bethanne and I are dining with Mother tonight…care to join us?"

"I'll take a rain check. I'm going through Grandmother's things. I still can't believe she's gone. It's as if she stepped out for a little while. Only, she's never coming back."

"Planning to move there?"

"I was thinking of selling the place, until I found I have an unbudgeable tenant."

"Then good for the widow. None of us wants you to sell."

"It's not your place. You got the villa south of the city."

"Where I think Bethanne and I will live. You love the sea. Why not keep it?"

"It's a big house. You don't need it—you have your own villa by the sea. Why let it sit idle for decades?"

"Get married and fill it up," his brother suggested.

"Give Mother my love and have someone call me soon," he said, sidestepping the suggestion. Rashid should know as well as he did that would never happen. But his brother had recently become engaged and now had changed his tune about staying single. He was not going to get a convert with Khalid.

Ella's words last night echoed. He shook his head. Easy to say the words in the dark. Harder to say when face-to-face with the scars.

He hung up the phone and looked again at the vase sitting on his desk. He'd taken it last night from the foyer to the study. It was lovely. Almost a perfect oval, it flared at the edges. From the center radiating outward was a yellow design that did look like a sunburst. Toward the edges the yellow thinned to gossamer threads. How had she done it? It was sturdy and solid yet looked fragile and enchanted. He knew his grandmother had loved it.

Seeing the vase gave validity to Ella's assertion she was an artist. Was she truly producing other works of art like this? Maybe his grandmother had seen the potential and arranged to keep her protégée close by while she created. She'd been friendly and helpful to others, but was an astute woman. She must have seen real talent to encourage Ella so much. So why not tell the rest of the family?

Khalid rose and headed next door. It was time he saw the artist in her studio, and assessed exactly what she was doing.

He walked to the guest cottage in only seconds. Though it was close, because of the lush garden between it and the main house there was a feeling of distance. He saw a new addition, obviously the studio. How much had his grandmother done for this tenant?

He stepped to the door, which stood wide-open. He could feel the heat roiling out from the space. He looked in. Ella was concentrating on her project and didn't notice him. For a long moment Khalid watched her. She wore a large leather apron and what looked like leather gloves that reached up to her elbows. She had dark glasses on and straddled a long wooden bench. At one end a metal sheet was affixed upon which she turned molten glass at the end of a long tube. As he watched, the glass began to take shape as she turned it against the metal. A few feet beyond was a furnace, the door open, pouring out heat.

Her dark hair was pulled back into a ponytail. He studied her. Even attired as she was, she looked feminine and pretty. How had she become interested in this almost lost art? It took a lot of stamina to work in such an adverse environment. It had to be close to thirty-seven degrees in the room. Yet she looked as cool as if she were sitting in the salon of his grandmother's house.

Slowly ,she rotated the tube. She blew again and the shape elongated. He was afraid to break her concentration lest it cause her to damage the glass globule.

She looked up and frowned, then turned back to her work. "What do you want?" she asked, before blowing gently into the tube again.

"To see where you worked." He stepped inside. "It's hot in here."

"Duh, I'm working with fire."

He looked at the glowing molten glass. She pushed it into the furnace. No wonder it was so hot; everything inside the furnace glowed orange.

She pulled out the molten glass and worked on it some more. Khalid began to see the shape, a tall vase perhaps. The color was hard to determine as it was translucent and still glowed with heat.

He walked closer, his scar tissue reacting to the heat. He crossed to the other side, so his undamaged cheek faced the heat. How did she stand it so close for hours on end?

"Do you mind if I watch?"

"Not much I can do about it, is there?" she asked with asperity.

Khalid hid a smile. She was not giving an inch. Novel in his experience. Before he'd been burned, women had fawned over him. He and Rashid. He'd bet Ella wouldn't have, no matter what.

"Did my grandmother build this for you?"

"Mmm," she mumbled, her lips still around the tube.

"State of the art?"

"Mmm."

He looked around. Other equipment lined one wall, one looked like an oven. There were jars of crushed glass in various colors. On one table were several finished pieces. He walked over and looked at them. Picking up a vase, he noted the curving shape, almost hourglasslike. The color was pastel—when held up so the white wall served as a background, it looked pale green. When on the table, it grew darker in color contrasting with the wood.

He wondered how much all this cost and would his grandmother ever have made any money as a return on her investment. She must have thought highly of Ella to have expended so much on an aspiring artist.

He looked at the other pieces. He wasn't a connoisseur of art, but they were quite beautiful. It was obvious his grandmother had recognized her talent and had encouraged it.

When he glanced back at Ella, she was using a metal spatula to shape the piece even further. He watched as she flattened the bottom and then began molding the top to break away from the tube. Setting the piece on the flat bottom, she ran the spatula over the top, gradually curving down the edge. He watched her study it from a couple of angles, then slide it onto a paddle and carefully carry it to the oven. She opened the top doors and slid it in, closing the doors quickly and setting a dial.

Turning, she looked at him, taking off her dark glasses.

"So?" she said. Her skin glowed with a sheen of perspiration.

"Interesting. These are lovely," he said, gesturing to the collection behind him. Trying to take his eyes off her. She looked even more beautiful with that color in her cheeks.

"I hope so. That's the intent. Build an inventory and hit the deck running. Do you know any art dealers?" she asked hopefully.

Khalid shook his head. His family donated to the arts, but at the corporate level. He had no personal acquaintance with art dealers.

She sighed and untied her apron, sliding it off and onto the bench. "Me, neither. That was another thing your grandmother was going to do—introduce me to several gallery owners in Europe. Guess I'll have to forge ahead on my own."

"Too bad you can't ride in on the al Harum name," he murmured.

Her eyes flared at that. Was he deliberately baiting her to

see her reaction? He liked the fire in her eyes. It beat the hint of sadness he saw otherwise.

"I was not planning to ride in on anyone's name. I expect my work to stand on its own merits. Your grandmother was merely going to introduce me."

"Still, an introduction from her would have assured owners took a long look before saying yea or nay, and think long and hard about turning down a protégée of Alia al Harum. She spent a lot of money in some galleries on her visits to France and Italy."

"I don't plan on showing in Italy," she said hastily.

Khalid's suspicions shot up. She was from Italy—why not show in her home country? He'd given what information he had to a person at the oil company to research her background. Now he wanted more than ever to know what brought her to Quishari, and how she'd met his grandmother.

"Do you think you can sell enough to earn a living?" he asked.

"Your grandmother thought so. I believe her, so yes, I do. I don't expect to become hugely wealthy, but I have simple needs, and love doing this creative work, so should be content if I ever start selling."

"Have you sent items out for consideration?"

"No. I wanted to wait until I had inventory. If the pieces sell quickly, I want more in the pipeline and can only produce a few each month. I have a five-year plan."

He met her eyes. Sincerity shone in them. It seemed odd to have this pretty woman talk about five-year plans. But the longer he gazed at her, the more he wanted to help. Which was totally out of character for him. He broke the contact and gave a final glance around the studio. Heading for the door, he paused before leaving. "I say give it a test run, send out some of your best pieces and see if they'll sell. No sense wasting five years if nothing is worth anything."

* * *

Ella stared out into the garden long after Khalid had left. He made it sound so simple. But it wasn't. What if she didn't sell? What if her pieces were mundane and mediocre? She could live on hope for the next few years—or have reality slap her in the face and crush her. She was still too vulnerable to venture forth to see if her work had merit. Madame al Harum had been so supportive. Now she ran into a critic. She had to toughen up if she wanted to compete in the competitive art world. Could she do it?

She cleaned up, resisting the temptation to peer into the lower part of the annealer to check the progress of the piece she'd done yesterday. She hoped it would be spectacular. Maybe Khalid al Harum was right. She should not waste time creating glass pieces if they would never sell. The slight income from Alexander's insurance would not carry her forever. If she couldn't make a living with glass, she should find another means to earn her livelihood.

Only, she didn't want another means. She loved making glass.

Once she finished cleaning the studio, she grabbed her notebook and went to sit on the terrace. The arbor overhead sheltered it from the hot sun. She enjoyed sitting outside when planning. It was so much more pleasant than the hot studio. She opened the pages and began to study the pictures she'd taken of the different pieces she had already made. She had more than one hundred. Some were quite good, others were attempts at a new technique that hadn't panned out. Dare she select a few pieces to offer for sale?

What if no one bought them?

What if they skyrocketed her to fame?

She did not want to rock the boat. She liked life the way it was. Or the way it had been before Khalid al Harum had arrived.

Idly she wondered what it would take to get rid of him. The only thing she could think of was moving out so he could sell the estate. She wasn't going to do that, so it looked as if she were stuck with him.

He was so different from his grandmother. Distracting, for one thing. She'd known instantly when he appeared in the doorway, but had ignored him as long as she could. Of course he had the right to visit his property, but his grandmother had always arranged times to come see what she was working on. There was something almost primordial about the man. He obviously was healthy and virile. She was so not interested in another relationship, yet her body seemed totally aware of his whenever he was near. It was disconcerting to say the least.

And distracting.

Ella stayed away from the beach that night. She listened to music while cataloging the pieces she thought might do for a first showing. She only had a couple of photos of the first batch of vases and bowls she'd made when she moved here. She needed to take more pictures, maybe showcase them in one of the salons in the main house. It was an idea she and Madame al Harum had discussed.

Good grief, she'd have to ask Khalid and she could imagine exactly what he'd say to her proposal. Or maybe she could sneak in when he wasn't there. Surely there was an oil field somewhere in the world that needed consulting. If he'd take off for a few days, she was sure Jalilah would let her in to photograph the pieces sitting in prominent display in the main salon. It would add a certain cachet to her catalog and maybe garner more interest when she was ready to go.

She went to bed that night full of ideas of how to best display the pieces she would put in her first catalog. The only question was if she dare ask Khalid for permission to use his salon for the photographs.

By the time morning arrived, Ella regretted her decision to forego her walk. She had slept badly, tossing and turning and picturing various scenarios when asking Khalid for his help.

Maybe she should have been a bit more conciliatory when discussing her lease. She planned to stand fast on staying, but she could have handled it better.

Only she disliked subterfuge and manipulation; she refused to practice it in her own life.

After a hasty breakfast, she again dressed up a bit and headed for the villa. Walking through the gardens, she tried to quell her nerves. The worst he could do was refuse. The guesthouse had a small sitting area, not as lavish as the main dwelling. She could use that, but she longed for the more elegant salon as backdrop for her art.

Jalilah opened the door when she knocked.

"I'd like to see Sheikh al Harum," Ella said, hoping she looked far more composed than she felt.

"He has someone visiting. Wait here."

Ella stood in the foyer. Her vase was gone. She peered into the salon; it wasn't there, either. Had something happened to it? Or had Khalid removed it once he'd learned she made it? That made her feel bad.

"Come." The maid beckoned from the door to the study.

When Ella entered, she stopped in surprise. Two men looked at her. Except for their clothing, and the scar on Khalid's cheek, they were identical.

"Twins?" she said.

Khalid frowned. "Did you want something?"

"Introduce us," the other man said, crossing the room and offering his hand.

"My brother," Khalid said.

"Well, that's obvious." Ella extended her hand and smiled. "I'm Ella Ponti."

"I am Rashid al Harum. You're the tenant, I take it."

She nodded. "Unwanted to boot."

"Only because I want to sell," Khalid grumbled. "Rashid is trying to talk me out of it, too."

"Good for you. I told him your grandmother wanted him to have the house. She could have left it to a charity or something if she hadn't hoped he'd live here," she said.

"It's a too big for one man," Khalid said.

"So—"

He raised his hand. "We've been over that. What do you want?"

Rashid glanced at his twin. "Am I in the way?"

Ella shook her head, bemused to see her vase in the center of Khalid's desk.

"Not at all. I came to ask permission to photograph some of my work in the salon. Give it a proper showing—elegant and refined. The guest cottage just doesn't have the same ambiance."

"You want to take pictures of my house?" Khalid asked. "Out of the question."

"Not the house, just some of my special pieces sitting on a table or something which would display them and give an idea of how they would look in another home. The background would be slightly blurred, the focus would be on my work."

"Use the table in your workroom."

"That's elegant."

He frowned. "I don't see—"

"—any problem with it," Rashid finished before his twin could finish. "I was admiring your vase when you arrived. Khalid explained how you made it. I'd like to see more of your work. I bet Bethanne would, as well."

"She'd do anything you say," Khalid grumbled.

"Bethanne?" Ella asked.

"My fiancée. She's making some changes to my villa in preparation of our marriage and moving in there."

"So the consumed one is getting married—wouldn't my grandmother love to know that?" Khalid asked.

"What are you talking about?" Rashid asked, glancing at his twin.

"Nothing, only something your grandmother said to me once. I'm happy for you and your fiancée. You might tell your brother how happy you are so he could go find someone to make a life with and leave me alone," Ella said hastily.

Rashid looked at her and then Khalid.

"Forget it. We've been over this before. I'm not marrying," Khalid growled.

Rashid looked thoughtful as he again looked back and forth between the two others in the room.

"I, uh, have to be leaving. I'll bring Bethanne by tomorrow if that suits you, Ella. She'd love to see the glass objects. Khalid, you have what you asked for. Let me know if you need more." He nodded to both and left, a small smile tugging at his lips.

Ella hated to see him go. He was much easier to be around than his brother.

"So I can use the salon?" she asked. Rashid had indicated yes, but it was still Khalid's place and his decision she needed.

"What if I say no?" he asked, leaning casually against the side of the desk.

"Then I'll pester you until you say yes," she replied daringly. "Maybe it'll help sell some of my work earlier than originally planned and I could move away sooner."

"How much sooner?"

"I don't know, five days?"

A gleam of amusement lit his eyes. "For such an early move, how can I refuse?"

"Thank you. I'll give credit in my brochure so everyone will know you helped."

"No. No credit, no publicity."

She started to protest but wisely agreed. "Okay. I'm cooling a couple of pieces now and once they are ready, I will begin taking pictures. I appreciate this."

"You weren't on the beach last night," he said.

He had been, obviously.

"I, uh, needed to get to sleep early. Big day today."

"Doing what?"

"Coming to ask you about the salon" sounded dumb. What else could she come up with?

He watched her. Ella fidgeted and looked around the room. "Just a big day. Why is my vase in here?"

"I was looking at it. I thought it was mine."

"I guess. I should have said why is the vase I made in here instead of the foyer."

"I wanted to look at it. I like it."

She blinked in surprise. "You do?"

Amusement lurked in his eyes again. "You sound surprised. Isn't it good?"

She nodded. "I just can't imagine you—"

"Having an eye for beauty?"

"I wasn't exactly going to say that."

"You haven't held back on anything else."

"You are very exasperating, do you know that?" she asked.

"Makes a change from other names I've been called."

If he drove the other people he knew as crazy as he did her, she wasn't surprised.

Khalid stood and moved around to sit at the desk.

"So, you'll be on the beach tonight?" he asked casually.

Ella shrugged. "Thanks for letting me use the salon for the photographs."

"One caveat," he said, glancing up.

She sighed. It had been too good to be true. "What?"

"I get to give final approval. I don't want certain prize possessions to be part of your sales catalog. No need to give anyone the idea that more than your glass is available."

"Done." She nodded and turned. At the door she stopped

and looked at him over her shoulder. "I do expect to take a walk tonight as it happens."

She wasn't sure, but she suspected the expression on his face was as close to a smile as she'd seen.

CHAPTER FOUR

ELLA and Khalid fell into a tentative friendship. Each night she went for a walk along the beach. Most evenings Khalid was already on the sand, as if waiting for her. They fell into an easy conversation walking in the dark at the water's edge. Sometimes they spoke of what they'd done that day. Other times the walks were primarily silent. Ella noted he was quieter than other men she'd known. Was that his personality or a result of the accident? She gathered the courage to ask about it on the third evening after he said she could use the salon.

"How did you get burned?" she asked as they were turning to head for home. She hadn't wanted to cut the walk short if he got snippy about her question.

"We were capping a fire in Egypt. Just as the dynamite went off, another part of the well exploded. The shrapnel shredded part of my suit, instant burn. Hurt like hell."

"I can imagine. I've had enough burns to imagine how such a big area would be almost unbearable. Were you long in hospital?"

"A few months."

And in pain for much of that time, she was sure. "Did you get full mobility back?"

"Yes. And other parts were unaffected."

She smiled at his reminder of her attempt at being tactful

when he said he wouldn't marry. A burned patch of skin wouldn't be enough to keep her from falling for a man. She suspected Khalid was too sensitive to the scar. There were many woman who would enjoy being with him.

"Good. What I don't get is why you do it?"

"Do what?"

"Put your life at risk. You don't even need to work, do you? Don't you have enough money to live without risking life and limb?"

He was quiet a moment, then said, "I don't have to work for money. I do want to do what I can to make oil production safe. Over the last fifty years or so many men have died because of faulty equipment or fires. Our company has reaped the benefit. But in doing that we have an obligation to make sure the men who have helped in our endeavors have as much safety guarding them as we can provide. If I can provide that, then it's for the good."

"An office job would be safer," she murmured.

"Rashid has that covered. I like being in the field. I like the desert, the challenge of capturing the liquid crude beneath the land, or the sea. I like knowing I'm pitting my skills and experience against the capricious nature of drilling—and coming out on top more than not."

"Still seems ridiculously dangerous. Get someone else to do it."

"It's my calling, you might say."

Ella was silent at that. It still seemed too dangerous for him—witness the burn that had changed his life. But she was not someone to argue against a calling. She felt that with her art.

She turned and he caught her hand, pulling her to a stop. She looked up at him. The moon was a sliver on the horizon, the light still dim, but she could see him silhouetted against the stars.

"What?"

"My mother is hosting a reception on Saturday. I need to make an appearance. I want you to go with me."

Ella shook her head. "I don't do receptions," she said. "Actually I don't go away from the estate much."

"Why?"

"Just don't," she murmured, turning to walk toward home.

He still held her hand and fell into step with her.

"Consider it payment for using the salon," he said.

"You already agreed to my using the salon. You can't add conditions now."

"Sure I can—it's my salon. You want to use it, consider this part of the payment. It's just a reception. Some people from the oil company, some from the government, some personal friends. We circulate, make my mother happy by being seen by everyone, then leave. No big deal."

"Get someone else."

He was silent for several steps.

"There is no one else," he said slowly.

"Why not?"

"I've been down that road, all right? I'm not going to set myself up again. Either it's you, or I don't go. My grandmother helped you out—your turn to pay back."

"Jeeze, talk about coercion. You're sure it'll only be people who live here in Quishari?"

"Yes. What would it matter if foreigners came? You're one yourself."

"I am trying to keep a low profile, that's why," she said, hating to reveal anything, but not wanting to find out her hiding place had been found.

"Why?"

"I have reasons."

"Are you hiding?" he asked incredulously.

"Not exactly."

"Exactly what, then?" He pulled her to a stop again. "I want to hear this."

"I'm in seclusion because of the death of my husband."

"That was over a year ago."

"There's a time limit on grieving? I hadn't heard that."

"There's no time limit, but by now the worst should be behind you and you should be going out and seeing friends. Maybe finding a new man in your life."

"I see my friends," she protested. "And I'm not going down that road again. You're a funny one to even suggest it."

"When do you see friends?"

"When they come to visit. I'm working now and it's not convenient to have people over. But when I'm not in the midst of something, they come for swimming in the sea and alfresco meals on my terrace. Did you think I was a hermit?"

"I hadn't thought about it. I never see these friends."

"You've lived here for what, almost a week? No one has come in that time. Stick around if you're so concerned about my social life."

"Mostly I'm concerned about your going with me to the reception this weekend."

"No."

"Yes. Or no salon photos."

Ella glared at him. It missed the mark. He couldn't see her that well. And she suspected her puny attempts at putting him in the wrong wouldn't work. He did own the estate. And she did need permission to use the salon. Rats, he was going to win on this one. She did not want to go. She was content in her cottage, with her work and with the solitude.

Only sometimes did it feel lonely.

Not once since Khalid had arrived.

Dangerous thoughts, those. She was fine.

"All right, we'll go, greet everyone and then leave."

"Thank you."

They resumed the walk, but Ella pulled her hand from his. They were friends, not lovers. No need to hold hands.

But her hand had felt right in his larger one. She missed the physical contact of others. She hadn't been kissed in ages, held with passion in as long. Why did her husband have to die?

"I'll pick you up at seven on Saturday," he said.

"Fine. And first thing tomorrow, I'm coming to take photographs. I don't want to miss my chance in case you come up with other conditions that I can't meet."

He laughed.

Ella looked at him. She'd never even seen him smile and now he was laughing in the darkness! Was that the only time he laughed?

"I expect I need to wear something very elegant," she mumbled, mentally reviewing the gowns she'd worn at university events. There were a couple that might do. She hadn't thought about dressing up in a long time. A glimmer of excitement took hold. She had enjoyed meeting other people at the university, speaking about topics far removed from glass making. Would the reception be as much fun? She felt a frisson of anticipation to be going with Khalid. She always seemed more alive when around him.

"You'll look fine in anything you wear," he said easily.

Just like a man, she thought, still reviewing the gowns she owned.

The next morning Ella carefully took two of her pieces, wrapped securely in a travel case, and went to the main house. Ringing the doorbell, she was greeted by Jalilah.

"I've come to take pictures," she said.

"In the salon, His Excellency has told me. Come." The maid led the way and then bowed slightly before leaving.

Ella put the starburst bowl on one of the polished mahogany tables.

Khalid appeared in the doorway. He leaned against the jamb and watched.

"What do you want?" she asked, feeling her heartbeat increase. Fussing, she tried pictures from different angles. She could hardly focus the lens with him watching her.

"Just wanted to see how the photo shoot went."

"Don't you have work to do?"

"No."

She tried to ignore him, but it was impossible. She lifted the camera and framed the bowl. She snapped the picture just as the doorbell sounded. She looked at Khalid. "Company?" she asked. Maybe someone who would take him away from the salon.

He looked into the foyer and nodded. "Rashid and Bethanne. Good timing. They can help."

"Help what?"

"You get the best pictures. You want to appeal to the largest number of buyers, right?"

"Of course." The sooner she started earning money, the sooner she might move.

"Hello," Rashid said, coming into the room with a tall blond woman. "Ella, this is my fiancée, Bethanne Sanders. Bethanne, this is Ella Ponti. Now, can you two talk?" he asked in Arabic.

"I also speak Italian and French and English," Ella said, crossing the room to greet the pair.

Switching to English, Rashid said, "Good, Ella speaks English."

"I'm so delighted to meet you," Bethanne said, offering her hand.

Ella shook it and smiled. "I'm happy to meet you. My English is not so good, so excuse me if I get things mixed."

"At least we can communicate. And you speak Arabic. I'm learning from a professor at the university. That's not easy."

"And the maid," Rashid said softly.

Bethanne laughed. "Her, too."

"Would that be Professor Hampstead?" Ella asked.

"Yes, do you know him?" Bethanne asked with a pleased smile.

"My husband worked at the university in language studies. I know the professor and his wife quite well. He's an excellent teacher."

"We came to see your work," Rashid said. "I see you've started on the pictures."

"Photographing some pieces for a preliminary catalog. I'd like to see if I can move up my timetable for a showing. Once I have enough pictures, I can make a small catalog and circulate it."

"Why are you taking pictures here?" Bethanne asked, walking over to look at the bowl. "Oh, this is exquisite. You made this? How amazing!" She leaned over and touched the edge lightly but made no move to pick it up.

"I think the ambiance of the other furnishings here will show it off better. I want the background to be blurry, with only the glass piece in clear focus, but to give the feel that it would fit in any elegant salon."

"And Khalid was all for the project, obviously," Rashid said with a glance at his twin.

"Obviously—she's here, isn't she?" Khalid said. "You two can help with the project. Give us an unbiased perspective and select the best pictures."

"I'd like to see the other pieces you've made," Bethanne said.

"I'm happy to show you. Shall we go now?"

"Finish the pictures of these, then when you go to your studio, you can bring some more over," Khalid suggested.

The next couple of hours were spent with everyone giving opinions about the best angle for pictures and which of the different art pieces Ella had created should be included. Rashid said he'd see if his mother had some recommendations on art galleries who would help.

Ella felt as if things were spinning out of control. She and Alia al Harum had discussed the plans, but they'd been for years down the road. Now so much was happening at once.

Khalid looked over at her at one point and said, "Enough. We will return to the main house and have lunch on the terrace. Bethanne, you haven't told Ella what you do. I think she'll be interested."

Ella threw him a grateful smile. "I'll just tidy up a bit and join you."

Rashid and Bethanne headed out, but Khalid remained behind for a moment.

"They only wanted to help," he said.

"I'm glad they did."

"But you're feeling overwhelmed. You set the pace. This is your work, your future. Don't let anyone roll over you."

"Good advice. Remember that next time you want your way," she said, sitting down on her bench, touched he'd picked up on her mild panic and dealt with it. She hadn't expected such sensitivity from the man.

"You are coming for lunch?"

"Yes. I just need a few minutes to myself."

"I'll come back for you if you don't show up in twenty minutes."

"Did anyone tell you you're a bit bossy?" she asked.

"Twenty minutes," he said, and left.

Ella took less than the twenty minutes. After a quick splash of cool water against her face, she brushed her hair and lay down for ten minutes. Then hurried to the main house. Khalid and the others were on the terrace and she walked straight there without going through the house.

Lunch was delicious and fun. It was a bit of a struggle to remember to speak English during the meal, but she was confident she held her own in the conversation that ranged from

Bethanne's career as a pilot to Rashid's recent trip to Texas to the reception on Saturday night.

"Are you coming?" Rashid asked his brother at one point.

"Yes," Khalid said.

Rashid and Bethanne exchanged surprised looks.

"Great."

"I'm bringing Ella," Khalid continued.

Both guests turned to stare at her. She smiled brightly. Was this such an amazing thing? Surely Khalid had brought other women to receptions before.

"Condition of using the salon for the pictures," she murmured.

"Of course," Rashid said with another quick glance at his fiancée.

"Great. Maybe you could go shopping with me before then," Bethanne said. "I'm not sure I have anything suitable to wear."

Ella hesitated. She hadn't been shopping except for groceries since her husband's funeral. Dare she go? Surely it would be okay for one afternoon. It wasn't as if anyone was hanging around the main streets of the city looking for her.

"I don't know if I would be much help." She felt Khalid's gaze on her and glanced his way.

"Help or not, don't women love to buy beautiful dresses?"

"I don't need one. I have several," Ella said.

"Come help me find several," Bethanne urged.

Rashid watched the interaction and then looked at his brother. He narrowed his eyes when Khalid never looked away from Ella.

"Okay, I'll go tomorrow afternoon," Ella said fast, as if afraid she'd change her mind.

When lunch finished, Ella thanked her host and fled for her cottage. She'd had more activity today than any time since Alexander had died. And she'd agreed to go shopping—out along the main district of Alkaahdar. Surely after all this time it would be safe. She had a right to her own life. And to live it on her terms.

That night she debated going for a walk. She was getting too used to them. Enjoying them too much. What happened when Khalid moved on? When he went to another oil field to consult on well equipment, or had to go fight a fire. That thought scared her. He was trained; obviously an expert in the field. He knew what to do. It was dangerous, but as he'd explained, except for that one accident, he'd come through unscathed many times.

But that one could have killed him. Didn't he realize that? Or another one similar that might rip the helmet and protection totally off. She shivered thinking about it.

She went for her walk, hoping he'd be there. It was better than imaging awful things that could happen.

He sat on the sand near the garden.

"It's warm," he said when she appeared, letting some sand drift from his hand.

"Sometimes I sit on the beach in the night, relishing the heat held from the day."

"Sand makes glass," he commented.

"Yes. I've heard that lightning strikes on beaches produces glass—irregular in shape and not usually functional. I'd like to see some." She sat beside him. "I like the fact I'll know your brother and Bethanne at the reception."

"And me."

"Yes, and you. We aren't staying long, right."

"I said not long. Why are you nervous? You've been to university receptions—this would be sort of the same, just a different group of people. You'll be bored out of your mind with all the talk about oil."

She smiled at his grumbling. "Is that the normal topic?"

"With a heavy presence of Bashiri executives it usually is. The minister of finance is not in charity with us right now. Rashid closed a deal he didn't like. But I'm sure a few million for pet projects will sweeten his disposition."

Ella didn't want to talk about money or family. She jumped up. "I'm going to walk."

He rose effortlessly beside her and kept pace.

"Tell me more about the oil fields you've been to," she said, looking for a way to keep her thoughts at bay. She liked listening to Khalid talk. Might as well give him something to talk about.

The next afternoon Ella had a good time shopping. Once inside boutiques, she didn't glance outside. While in the car she had seen no one that appeared to be paying the two of them any attention. Bethanne was fun to shop with. She looked beautiful in the elegant cool colors that went so well with her blond hair. Twice, salesclerks offered jewel-tone dresses and Bethanne had suggested Ella try them on. Of course the sizes were wrong. Ella was slight, almost petite, not nearly as tall as the American. She was tempted, but conscious of her limited funds, cheerfully refused. She had dresses that would suit. She wasn't going to spend a week's worth of groceries on a dress she'd wear for about an hour.

Bethanne decided on a lovely blue that mimicked the color of her eyes.

"Done. Let's get some coffee. And candied walnuts. They're my favorites," she said when she received the dress in a box.

Having the chauffeur stow the dress in the limo's trunk, Bethanne asked him to take them to an outside café. When they found a coffee house with outside seating on a side street, she had him wait while she and Ella went for coffee.

"This was fun," Bethanne said. "I hope we can become friends. I will be marrying Rashid in a few months and don't know but a handful of people in Quishari. And most of them don't speak English. So until I master this language, I'm left out of conversations."

"I would like another friend. Tell me about Texas. I've never been to the United States."

"Where have you been that you learned so many different languages? And that's not even your career, like the professor's is."

"I went to school in Switzerland for a few years and in England."

"And the Arabic?"

"That I learned because Alexander was learning it and planned to come to an Arabian country to work."

"Alexander was your husband?" Bethanne asked gently.

Ella nodded. "We knew each other from when we were small. I loved him it seems all my life."

"I'm sorry for your loss," Bethanne said.

"Me, too." Ella didn't want to think about it. Every time she grew sad and angry. It had happened. Nothing could change the past. She had to go on. Today she was with a new friend. And beginning to look forward to the reception on Saturday.

Ella worked through the next two days culling her collection, deciding which pieces to display and which to hold in reserve.

She tried on the dresses she'd worn to university events, dismayed to find she had lost more weight than she'd thought. They all were loose. Finally she decided on a dark blue long gown that shimmered in the light and almost looked black. If she wore her hair loose, and the pearls she received when she was eighteen, she'd do. It wasn't as if it were a real date or anything. But she wanted to look nice for Khalid's sake. If he broke his normal habit of nonattendance, it behooved her to look her best.

* * *

Saturday evening, Ella prepared for the reception with care. She had some trepidation about venturing forth into such a large gathering, but felt safe enough since the guests would most likely all be from Quishari. Her hair was longer than she usually wore. The waves gleamed in the light. She hoped she would pass muster as a guest of a sheikh. Her heart tripped faster when she thought of spending the evening with his family and friends. And some of the leaders of the country. She planned to stay right by Khalid's side and remind him how soon they would leave.

Promptly at seven he knocked on the door of the cottage. She picked up a small purse with her keys and went to greet him.

"You look lovely," he said when she opened the door.

She thought he looked fantastic. A man should always wear a tux, she decided.

"I could say the same. Wow, you clean up good."

"Ready?"

"Yes." She pulled the door shut behind her. To her surprise, Khalid had a small sports car waiting. She had expected a limousine as Rashid used. She liked the smaller car; less intimidating. More intimate.

"If we were going for a spin in the afternoon, I'd put the top down. But not tonight."

"Thank you. I spent hours on my hair."

"Literally?"

She laughed, feeling almost carefree for the first time in months. "No, I just washed and brushed it."

He reached over and took some strands in his fingers. "It feels soft and silky. I wondered if it would."

She caught her breath. His touch was scarcely felt, yet her insides were roiling. She looked out the windshield, trying to calm her nerves. It was Khalid, cranky neighbor, reluctant landlord. She tried to quell the racing of her heart.

When they arrived at the reception, Ella was surprised to

find it held in a large hotel. "I thought your mother would have it at her home," she commented when he helped her from the car. A valet drove the sports car away.

"Too many people, too much fuss. She prefers to have it taken care of here."

"Mmm." Ella looked around. She hadn't been to such an elegant event in years. Suddenly she felt like a teen again, proud to be going to the grown-up's affair. Excited. She could do this, had done so many times before. But she preferred smaller gatherings, friends to share good times. Like she and—

No, she was not going there. Tonight was about Khalid. She owed him for his reluctant help. So she'd do her best to be the perfect date for a man of his influence and power.

"Khalid, I'm so glad you came. Rashid said you would—but your track record isn't the best." A beautiful woman came up and embraced him. She smiled at him, patted his good cheek then turned to look at Ella.

"Salimeia, may I present Ella Ponti. Salimeia is my cousin," Khalid said, looking somewhat self-conscious.

Ella couldn't imagine he felt that way. She was aware of his self-confidence—almost arrogance when around her. She watched as he gave a quick glance around the gathering.

An older woman, dressed in a very fashionable gown came over, her eyes fixed on Khalid.

"I am so glad you came," she said, reaching out to grab his hands in hers.

"Mother, may I present Ella Ponti. Ella, my mother, Sabria al Harum."

"Madame, my pleasure," Ella said with formal deference.

"How do you do?" Khalid's mother looked at him in question, practically ignoring Ella.

"I'm glad he came, too. Mo is here. I'll find him and tell him you're here," his cousin said. She smiled and walked away.

"Ella is my tenant," he clarified.

She looked horrified. "Tenant? You are renting her the house your grandmother left you?"

"No, she has the cottage on the estate and has lived there for a year. Didn't you know about her, either?"

Ella expected the woman to shoo her out the door. She was not the warm, friendly woman her mother-in-law had been.

Sabria al Harum thought for a moment. "The artist Alia was helping?" she guessed.

Ella nodded once. She felt like some charity case the way the woman said it.

"I did not know she had her living on the premises." She said it as if Ella was a kind of infestation.

"I do live there and have an airtight lease that gives me the right to stay for another four years," Ella said with an imp of mischief. She did not like haughty people.

"Nonsense. Khalid, have our attorneys check it out." His mother sounded as if any inconvenience could be handled by someone else.

Ella hid a smile as she looked at Khalid.

"Already done, Mother. Ella's right, she has the right to live there for another four years."

Other guests were arriving. Khalid took Ella's arm and gently moved her around his mother. "We'll talk later," he said. "You have other guests to greet."

"Gee, is she always so welcoming?" Ella said softly, only for his ears.

"No. She is very conscious of the position our family holds in the country. Perhaps because she came to the family as an adult, not raised as we were. Come, I see someone I think you'll enjoy meeting."

She went willingly, growing more conscious of the wave of comments that were softly exchanged as they passed. She caught one woman staring at Khalid, then looking at Ella. Giving in to impulse, she reached out to take his arm. It automatically bent, so she could have her hand in the crook of the elbow. He pressed her against his side. She moved closer, head raised.

Khalid introduced her to a friend and his wife. They chatted for a few moments, Khalid mentioning Ella's art. Both were interested.

"My uncle has a gallery in the city. Do send me your catalog so I can send it to him," the wife said.

"I would love to. Thank you." Ella replied.

They mingled through the crowd. Once the complete circuit of the ballroom had almost been made, she tugged on Khalid. He leaned closer to hear her over the noise. "Once we've made the circle, we leave, right?"

"If you're ready."

"Ah, Khalid, I heard you came tonight." A florid faced, overweight man stepped in front of them. "Tell your brother to stop sending our business outside of the country. There are others who could have handled the deal he just consummated with the Moroccans." He looked at Ella. "Hello, I don't believe we've met."

"Ella, the finance minister, Ibrahim bin Saali. This is Ella Ponti."

The minister took her hand and held it longer than needed. "A new lovely face to grace our gatherings. Tell me, Miss Ponti, are you from Quishari?"

She tugged her hand free and stepped closer to Khalid. "I've lived here for years. I love this city."

"As do I. Perhaps we can see some of the beauty of the city together sometime," he said suavely.

Ella smiled politely. "Perhaps."

"Excuse us," Khalid said, placing his hand at the small of her back and gently nudging her.

They walked away.

"That was rude," she said quietly in English.

"He was hitting on you."

"He's too old. He was merely being polite."

"He does not think he's too old and polite is not something we think of when we think of Ibrahim."

She laughed. "I don't plan to take him up on his offer, so you're safe."

Khalid looked at her. "Safe?"

She looked back, and their eyes locked for a moment. She looked away first. "Never mind. It was just a comment."

Khalid nodded, scanning the room. "I think we've done our duty tonight. Shall we leave?"

"Yes."

He escorted her out and signaled the valet for his car. When it arrived, he waited until Ella was in before going to the driver's side. "Home?"

"Where else?" she asked.

"I know a small, out-of-the-way tavern that has good music."

"I love good music," she said.

He drove swiftly through the night. What had possessed him to invite her to stay out longer? She had attended the reception, he got some points with his mother, though she hadn't seemed that excited to meet Ella. They could be home in ten minutes.

Instead he was prolonging the evening. He'd never known anyone as interesting to be around as his passenger. She intrigued him. Not afraid to stand up to his bossiness, she nevertheless defended Ibrahim's boorish behavior. He smiled. Never could stand the man. He had been afraid for a moment Ella might be tempted by Ibrahim's power and position. Not his Ella.

He had to give her credit. No one there had guessed she'd come as part of a bargain. No one made comments about how such a pretty woman was wasting her time with him.

The tavern was crowded, as it always was on Saturday nights. It was one place few people recognized him. He could be more like anyone else here, unlike the more formal events his mother hosted. There were several men he knew and waved to when they called to him. Shepherding Ella to the back, they found an empty table and sat, knees touching.

Ella looked around and then at Khalid. "I hear talk and laughter, but no music."

He nodded. "It starts around eleven. We're a bit early. Want something to eat or drink?"

"A snack would be good. We hardly got a chance to sample the delicacies your mother had available."

"Want to go back?"

"No. This suits me better."

"Why is that?" he asked. He knew why he preferred the dim light of the tavern, the easy camaraderie of the patrons. The periodic escape from responsibilities and position. But why did she think it was better?

"I don't know anyone."

"That doesn't make sense. Wouldn't it be better to know friends when going to a place like this?"

She shrugged. "Not at this time."

"Did you have a favorite spot you and your husband liked to frequent?" he asked. He wanted to know more about her. Even if he had to hear about the man who must have been such a paragon she would never find anyone to replace him.

She nodded. "But I don't go there anymore. It's not the same."

"Where do you and your friends go?" he asked.

"Nowhere." She looked at him.

Her eyes were bright and her face seemed to light up the dark area they sat in.

"This is the first I've been out since my husband's death. Friends come to visit me, but I haven't been exactly in a party mood. But this isn't like a real date or anything, is it? Just paying you back for letting me use the salon for my pictures."

"Exactly. You wouldn't want to go on a real date with me. I know about that from my ex-fiancée."

"What are you talking about?"

"This." He gestured to the scar on the side of his face.

"Don't be dumb, Khalid. That has nothing to do with it. I still feel married to Alexander and am faithful."

Khalid nodded and looked away, feeling her words like a physical blow. Even if they got beyond the scar, she would never be interested in him. She loved a dead man. He wished they'd gone straight home. She could be with her memories, and he could get back to the reality of his life. Only her words had seemed so wrong.

CHAPTER FIVE

HE LOOKED back at her. "You're not serious? You are not married—that ended when your husband died. And you are far too young and pretty to stay single the rest of your life."

She blinked in surprise. "I'm not that young."

"I'd guess twenty-five at the most," he said.

"Add four years. Do you really think I look twenty-five?" She smiled in obvious pleasure.

Khalid felt as if she'd kicked him in the heart. "At most, I said. Even twenty-nine is too young to remain a widow the rest of your life. You could be talking another sixty years."

"I'll never find anyone to love like I did Alexander," she said, looking around the room. For a moment he glimpsed the sorrow that seemed so much a part of her. He much preferred when she looked happy.

"My grandmother said that after her husband died. But she was in her late sixties at the time. They'd had a good marriage. Raised a family, enjoyed grandchildren."

"I had a great marriage," she said.

"You could again."

She looked back. "You're a fine one to talk. Where's your wife and family?"

"Come on, Ella, who would marry me?"

"No one, with that attitude. How many women have you asked out in the last year?"

"If I don't count you, none."

"So how do you even know, then."

"The woman I was planning to spend my life with told me in no uncertain terms what a hardship that would be. Why would I set myself up for more of the same?"

The waiter came and asked for drink orders. Khalid ordered a bowl of nuts in addition.

"She was an idiot," Ella said, leaning closer after the man left.

"Who?"

"Your ex-fiancée. Did she expect life to be all roses and sunshine?"

"Apparently." He felt bemused at her defense. "Shouldn't it be?"

"It would be nice if it worked that way. I don't think it does. Everyone has problems. Some are on the inside, others outside."

"We know where mine is," he said.

She shocked him again when she got up and switched chairs to sit on his right side. "I've noticed, you know," she said, glaring at him in defiance.

"Noticed what?" He was growing uncomfortable. He tried to shelter others from the ugly slash of burned skin.

"That you always try to have me on your left. Are you afraid I'll go off in shock or something if I catch sight of the scar?"

"No, not you."

"What does that mean?"

"Just, no, not you. You wouldn't do that, even if you wanted to. I'd say your parents raised you very well."

"Leave my parents out of any discussion," she said bitterly.

"Touch a nerve?"

She shrugged. "They and I are not exactly on good terms. They didn't want me to marry Alexander."

"And why was that?"

"None of your business."

The waiter returned with the beverages and plate of nuts. Ella scooped up a few and popped them into her mouth.

"Mmm, good." She took a sip of the cold drink and looked at the small stage.

"I think your musicians are arriving."

So his tenant was at odds with her parents. He hadn't considered she had parents living, or he would have expected her to return home after her husband's death. Now that he knew they were alive, it seemed strange that she was still in Quishari and not at their place. His curiosity rose another notch. He would nudge the researcher at the oil company to complete the background check on his tenant.

Khalid spent more time watching Ella as the evening went on than the musicians. She seemed to be enjoying the music and the tavern. He enjoyed watching her. They stayed until after one before driving home.

"Planning to take a walk on the beach tonight?" he asked.

"Why not?" she asked. "I'm still buoyed up by that last set. Weren't they good?"

"I have enjoyed going there for years. We'll have to go again sometime."

"Mmm, maybe."

He didn't expect her to jump at the chance. But he would have liked a better response.

"Meet you at the beach in ten minutes," she said when she got out of the car.

"No walking straight through?" he asked.

"I don't know about you, but I don't want to get saltwater and sand on this gown. And I'd think it wouldn't be recommended for tuxedos, either."

Khalid changed into comfortable trousers and a loose shirt and arrived at the beach seconds ahead of Ella.

They started north. The moon was fuller tonight and spread

a silvery light over everything. Without much thought, he reached for her hand, lacing their fingers together. She didn't comment, nor pull away. Taking a deep breath, he felt alive as he hadn't in a long while.

"I appreciate your going with me tonight. My mother is always after me to attend those things for the sake of the family," he said.

"She would have been happier without me accompanying you," Ella said.

"She doesn't like anyone who shows an interest in her sons. Unless it's the woman she's picked out. Did you know Rashid almost had an arranged marriage?"

"No, what happened?"

"His supposed fiancée was to be flown in on the plane Bethanne delivered. Only she never left Morocco. When he fell for Bethanne, Mother was furious. I think they are getting along better now, but I wouldn't say Mother opened her arms to Bethanne."

"I bet your grandmother would have loved her."

"She would have loved knowing Rashid was getting married."

For a moment Khalid felt a tinge of envy for his brother. He had found a woman he adored and who seemed to love him equally. They planned a life in Quishari at the other home their grandmother had left and had twice in his hearing mentioned children. He'd be an uncle before the first year was out, he'd bet.

"Bethanne doesn't strike me as someone who cares a lot about what others think of her," Ella said.

"I'm sure Mother will come around once she sees how happy Rashid is. And once she's a grandmother."

Ella fell silent. They walked for several minutes. Khalid wondered what she was thinking. Had she wanted to be a mother? Would her life be vastly different if she had a small child to raise? She should get married again.

She was right—that was easy enough for him to say. They were a pair, neither wanting marriage for different reasons. Maybe one day another man would come along for her to marry. Once she was out, showing off her creations, she'd run into men from all over the world.

Khalid refused to examine why he didn't like that idea.

"Ready to head back?" she asked.

He nodded, but felt curiously reluctant to end the evening. He liked being with Ella.

The return walk was also in silence, but not without awareness. Khalid could breathe the sweet scent she wore, enjoy the softness of her hands, scarred here and there by burns from her work. She wore a skirt again. He didn't think he'd seen her in pants except when working at her studio. It made her seem all the more feminine. He didn't want the evening to end. Tomorrow would bring back the barriers and status of tenant and landlord. He had no more reasons to seek her out or take her out again. But he wanted to.

"I can get home from here," she said when they reached the path.

"I'll walk that short distance." He was not ready to say good-night.

When they reached the cottage, she tugged her hand free. "Good night. I enjoyed the tavern. And am glad I got to meet your mother even if she wasn't as glad to meet me."

He reached for her, holding her by her shoulders and drawing her closer. "I'm glad you went with me."

"We're even now, right?" Her voice sounded breathless. He could see her dimly in the light from the moon, her eyes wide, her mouth parted slightly.

With a soft groan, he leaned over and kissed her. He felt her start of surprise. He expected her to draw away in a huff. Instead, after a moment, she leaned against him and returned his kiss. Their mouths opened and tongues danced. Her arms hugged him closer and his embraced her. For a long moment they kissed, learning, tasting, touching, feeling.

She was sweet, soft, enticing. He could have stood all night on the doorstep, kissing Ella.

But she pushed away a moment later.

"Good night, Khalid," she said, darting into the house and shutting the door.

"Good night," he said to the wooden door.

This was not going to be their last date, no matter what Ella thought.

Ella leaned against the door, breathing hard. She closed her eyes. She'd kissed Sheikh Khalid al Harum! Oh, and what a kiss. Unlike anything she'd ever had before.

"No!" she said, pushing away and walking back to the kitchen. She wanted water, and a clear head. She loved Alexander. He was barely gone a year and she was caught up in the sensuousness of another man. How loyal was that? How could she have responded so strongly. Good grief, he'd probably think she was some sex-starved widow out to snare the first man who came along.

How could she have kissed him?

She took a long drink of water, her mind warring with her body. The kiss had been fantastic. Every cell in her tingled with awareness and yearning. She wanted more.

"No!" she said again. She had her life just as she wanted it. She did not need to become the slightest bit involved with a man who wanted her to leave so he could sell a family home.

On the other hand, maybe she should do just that. Put an end to time with Khalid by moving away.

She went to her bedroom and dressed for bed, thoughts jumbled as she brushed her teeth. She had a good place here, safe and perfect for making new pieces of art. She wasn't going anywhere. She just had to wait a little while; he'd get tired of being here and be off on some other oil field consultation and she'd be left alone. She just had to hold out until then. No more night walks. No more kisses.

Though as she fell asleep, she brushed her lips with her fingertips, remembering their first kiss.

The next morning Ella went to her studio, ready to work. She had to focus on her plans for the future and forget a kiss that threatened to turn her world upside down.

Easier said than done. Her dreams last night had been positively erotic. Her first thought this morning was that kiss. And now she was growing warm merely thinking about Khalid and his talented mouth. Why had he showed up? Why not go consult at some oil field and leave her in peace.

Try as she might, as the morning wore on, she couldn't get last night off her mind. Finally putting a small dish into the annealer to cool down, she decided to go see Khalid and make sure he knew she was not interested in getting involved.

She cleaned up, had a light lunch and then went to broach him at his home.

When she rang the bell, Jalilah opened the door, looking flustered. "Come in, things are hectic. His Excellency is leaving in a few minutes."

"Leaving?" This was perfect. He was leaving even earlier than she planned. He'd probably been as horrified by their kiss as she had been. He'd leave and if he ever came back, they'd have gotten over whatever awareness shimmered between them and they could resume the tenant-landlord relationship.

"A fire. He and his team are gathering at the airport in an hour."

Fear shot through Ella. He was going to another fire. For a moment she remembered Alexander, bloodied and burned from the car crash. He'd been coming after her. He hadn't deserved to die so young. She didn't like that memory any more than the one that flashed into her mind of Khalid burned beyond recognition. Nothing as unforgiving as flames.

She walked swiftly to the study, where Khalid was speaking on the phone. Entering, she crossed to the desk.

"See you then," he said, his eyes on her. "Got to go now."

"You can't go put out a fire," she said.

He rose and came around the desk. Lightly brushing the back of his fingers against her cheek, he asked, "Why not. It's what I do."

"It's too dangerous. Don't you have others who can handle that?"

"Others work with me on these projects. It's another one at a well Bashiri Oil has down on the southern coast. It blew a few months ago and it's burning again. Something's wrong with the pump or operators. Once this is capped, I plan to find out why it keeps igniting."

"It's dangerous."

"A bit. Are you all right? You have circles beneath your eyes."

She brushed his hand away. "I'm fine. It's you I'm worried about. What if something goes wrong? You don't have to do this. Send someone else."

"Something has gone wrong—a well is on fire. My team and I will put it out and do our best to make sure it doesn't happen again. I have to do this. It's what I do."

"It's too dangerous."

"I like the danger. Besides, what does it matter who does it as long as it gets put out? If not me, another man would be in danger. Maybe one who has a wife and children waiting at home."

She couldn't reach him. He would go off and probably get injured again. Or worse.

"Don't go," she said, reaching out to clutch his arms. She could feel his strength beneath the material, feel the determination.

"I have to—it's what I do."

"Find another job, something safer."

"Not today," he said, and leaned over to brush his lips against hers. "Come on, you can walk me out."

She stepped back, fear rising even more. What if something happened to him? She'd planned to tell him to stay away, but not like this.

When they reached the foyer, she noticed the duffel bags and heavy boots. He lifted them easily and nodded to Jalilah to open the door. A moment later they were stowed into the back of the small sports car. Ella followed him like a puppy, wishing she had the words to stop him. The seconds flew by. She could not slow time, much less stop it. But if she could, she would. Until she could talk him out of this plan. What if something happened to him?

"See you in a few days," he said easily.

"I hope so," she replied. But what if she didn't? What if she never saw him again? The feelings that thought triggered staggered her. She didn't want to care. That way lay heartache when tragedy struck.

She rounded the car and stood by him as he opened the driver's door. "Come back safely," she said, reaching up to kiss him. All thoughts of putting distance between them vanished. She couldn't let him go off without showing just a hint of what she felt. She would not think of all that could go wrong, but concentrate on all that could go right.

He let go the car door and kissed her back, cupping her face gently in his hands. His lips were warm but in only a moment she felt cold when he pulled away.

"I'll be back when the job's done," he said, climbing into the car. "Stay out of trouble," he said, and pulled away.

She watched for a moment, then with an ominous sense of foreboding, returned to her cottage. She felt as if she was in a daze. Fear warred with common sense. He knew what he was doing. Granted it was dangerous. But he'd done it before. And he did not have a death wish. He would take all necessary precautions.

Changing into work clothes, she went to the studio. She could always lose herself in art.

But not, it appeared, today. She tried to blow a traditional bowl, but the glass wasn't cooperating. Or her technique was off. Or it was just a bad day. Or she couldn't concentrate for thinking of Khalid. Glancing at her watch, she wondered where he was. She should have asked questions, found out where the fire was. How long he thought he'd be gone.

After two hours of trying to get one small project done, she gave up. Her thoughts were too consumed with Khalid. If he'd left the airport an hour ago, he could already be in harm's way. She paced her small studio, wondering how she could find out information about the fire. She did not have a television. She tried a radio, but the only programs she found were music.

Finally she went to the main house. When the maid answered the door, Ella asked to use the phone. She had done so a couple of times when Madame al Harum had lived here, so Jalilah was used to the request. Ella hoped Khalid had not given instructions to the contrary.

Jalilah showed her into the study and left. Ella stayed in the doorway for a moment. Everything inside instantly reminded her of Khalid. How odd. She'd visited Madame al Harum in this room many more times than she had her grandson. But he'd stamped his impression on the room in her mind forever.

She went to the phone. Who could she call but his brother. She hunted around for the phone number of Bashiri Oil and when she found it on a letterhead, she tried the number. It took her almost ten minutes to get to Rashid's assistant.

"I'm calling for Sheikh Rashid al Harum," she said for about the twentieth time.

"Who is calling?"

"Ella Ponti. I'm his brother's tenant in the house his grandmother once owned," she repeated.

"One moment, please."

On hold again, Ella held on to her composure. What would she do if Rashid wasn't there? Or wouldn't take her call? She had no idea how to reach Bethanne, who might be an ally.

"Al Harum." Rashid's voice came across the line sounding like Khalid's. She closed her eyes for a second, wishing it were Khalid.

"It's Ella Ponti. Khalid left this morning to put out a fire. Do you know anything about that?"

"I do. It's on one of the wells in the southern part of the country. Why?"

"I, uh…" She didn't know how to answer that. "I wanted to make sure he's all right," she said, wondering if Rashid would think her daft to be asking after his brother with such a short acquaintance.

"So far. The team arrived a short time ago. They assess the situation then plan their attack. It could be a day or two before they actually cap it."

Two days he could be in danger and she wouldn't know? This was so not the answer she wanted.

"Um, could you have someone keep me updated?" she asked tentatively. She didn't know if Sheikh al Harum would be bothered, but she had to ask. Surely there was some clerk there who could call her once something happened.

"I worry about him, too," Rashid said gently. "I'll let you know the minute I hear anything."

"Thank you. I'm using his phone. I don't have one. Jalilah can get me." She hung up, a bit reassured. She didn't want to question her need to make sure he was safe. She'd feel the same about anyone she knew who had such a dangerous job.

Ella sat in the desk chair for several moments. She studied the room, wondering what Khalid thought about when he sat here. She suspected he missed his grandmother more than he might have expected. The older woman had spoken so lovingly about her grandsons. Their family sounded close.

Except perhaps their mother. Or was her hesitancy welcoming women into the fold mere self-protection. It would be too bad to have someone pretend affection if they were only after money. How would she become convinced? Nothing had convinced her parents Alexander had not been after their money. They hadn't seemed to care that their only daughter was very happy in her marriage. The constant attempts to end the union had only alienated them. Ella hoped Madame al Harum never resorted to such tactics, but accepted Rashid's choice and wished him happiness.

She stood up and went back to her place. She didn't want to think about her parents, or Alexander, or anything in the past. She didn't want to worry about a man she hardly knew. And she didn't want to worry about the future. For today she'd try to just make it through without turmoil and complications, fear and dread.

Shortly after lunch there was a knock at the door. When Ella opened it, she was surprised to see Bethanne.

"Hi, I thought you might wish for some company," she said.

"Come in. I'm glad for company. I couldn't work today."

"I wouldn't be able to, either, if Rashid was doing something foolishly dangerous."

When they were on the terrace with ice-cold beverages, Ella smiled at her new friend. "What you said earlier, about Rashid being in a dangerous position—ever happen?"

"Not that I know about. And I would be sick with worry if he went off to put out an oil well fire."

"You and he are close, as it should be since you will be marrying him. Khalid is my landlord."

Bethanne laughed. “Right. And Madame al Harum and I are best friends.”

Ella wrinkled her nose slightly. “I don’t think she thinks in terms of friends.”

“Well, not with the women who might marry her sons.”

“I heard she helped arrange a marriage, but it didn’t take place.”

“Good thing for me. Rashid was going along with it for business reasons. Honestly, who wants to get married for business reasons? I’m glad he caught on.”

“And the other woman?”

“She ran off with a lover and I have no idea what happened after that. But she obviously had more sense than my future husband. Much as I adore him, I do wonder what he was thinking considering an arranged marriage. I can’t imagine all that passion— Oops, never mind.”

Ella looked away, hiding a smile. She remembered passion with Alexander when their marriage was new. The image of Khalid kissing her sprang to mind. Her heart raced. She experienced even more passion that night. She did not want to think about it, but couldn’t erase the image, nor the yearning for another kiss. Would that pass before he returned?

She had not helped her stance by kissing him goodbye. She should have wished him well and kept her distance.

“If they don’t get the well capped today, they’ll try tomorrow,” Bethanne said, sipping her drink. “And if that doesn’t work, Rashid wants to go there. If we do, want to fly with us? I took the crew down. They spent the entire flight going over schematics of the oil rig. It’s in the water, you know. You’d think with the entire Persian Gulf at their feet it would be easy enough to put out a fire.”

Ella laughed, but inside she stayed worried.

Bethanne was wonderful company and the two them spent the afternoon with laughter. Ella was glad she’d come to visit.

Except for a very few friends from the university, she didn't have many people she saw often. She had wanted it that way when Alexander first died. Now she could see the advantage of going out more with her friends. It took her mind off other things. Like if Khalid was safe or not.

The next morning she took an early walk along the beach. She never tired of the changing sea, some days incredibly blue other days steely-gray. She loved the solitude and beauty. During the day other people used the beach and she waved to a family she knew by sight. Watching the children as they played in the water gave her a pang. She and Alexander never had children. They thought they had years to start a family. They had wanted to spend time together as a couple before embarking on the next stage of family life.

His death cut everything short. She wished she'd had a baby with him. Would a child have brought her more comfort? Or more pain as every day she saw her husband in its face? She'd never know.

When she returned to the cottage, she saw a black car parked in front of the main house. Staying partially hidden behind the shrubs, she watched for a moment. It was not Khalid's sleek sports car. Was Madame al Harum visiting? Surely she knew her son was gone. Unless—had something happened. She could scarcely breathe. If Khalid had been injured, would Rashid send someone to tell her?

A moment later a man came from the house and got into the car, swiftly driving away.

Ella caught her breath at the recognition. She pulled back and waited until the car was gone before moving. In only seconds she was home, the door firmly locked behind her. How had they found her? She paced the living room. Obviously the maid had not given out where she lived or he would have camped on her doorstep. But it was only a matter of time now before he returned. Maybe he wanted to speak to the sheikh. Good grief, Khalid didn't know not to give out the information. His grandmother had been a staunch ally, but Khalid was looking for a way to get her to leave early. Had he any clue? Could she convince him not to divulge her whereabouts if her brother came calling again?

He had no reason to keep her home a secret. In fact, she could see it as his benefit to give out the information and stand aside while he tried to get her to return home.

Pacing did little but burn up energy, which seemed to pour through her as she fretted about this turn of events. She had grown comfortable here. She liked living here, liked her life as she'd made it since Alexander's death. She was not going home, no matter what. But she did not want the pressure Antonio would assert. Should she leave before Khalid returned? If he didn't know where she was, he couldn't give the location away.

But she didn't want to leave. Not until she knew if he was all right. What if the fire damaged more than equipment? Men could die trying to put out an oil fire. She so did not need any of this. She'd worked hard the last year to get her life under control.

Drawing a deep breath, she went to her desk and pulled out a sheet of paper. She'd make a list of her choices, calmly, rationally. She'd see what she could do to escape this situation—

Escape. That's what she wanted. Could Bethanne help? She could fly her to a secret location and never tell anyone.

Only, would she? And how much would it cost to hire the plane? Maybe she should have sold some of her work to give herself more capital. She had enough for her needs if she was careful. But a huge chunk spent on a plane trip could wreak the financial stability she had. Did she have the luxury of time? She could find a bus to take her somewhere in the interior. But not her equipment. Not her studio.

She couldn't leave that behind. It was her only way to make the glass art that she hoped was her future.

Jumping up, she began to walk around, gazing out the window, touching a piece of glass here and there that she'd made. What was she going to do?

There was a knock on the door. Ella froze. Had he found her already? Slowly she crossed the room and peeked out of the small glass in the door. It was Jalilah.

Ella opened the door.

"Hello," the maid said. "I came to tell you someone was at the house earlier, asking after you. He said the sheikh had sent inquiries to Italy. I remember Madame's comments when you first came here to live. She wanted you to have all the privacy you wanted. I told the man the sheikh was away from home and did not know when he would return."

"Thank you!" Ella breathed a sigh of relief. She had a respite. No fear of discovery today.

But—Khalid had sent inquiries to Italy? Why?

Jalilah bowed slightly and left.

Had Khalid sought to find other ways to get her to leave? Anger rose. How dare he put out inquiries? Who did he think he was? And more importantly, who did he think she was? He couldn't take her word?

After a hasty lunch Ella could barely eat, she went to the studio, trying to assess how much it would take to move her ovens, bench and all the accoutrements she had for glassblowing. More than a quick plane ride west.

Maybe she could leave for a short while, let her brother grow tired of looking for her again and when he left, she'd return. Only, what if Khalid then told him when she returned. She'd never be safe.

She heard a car and went to the window, peering out at the glimpse of the driveway she had. It was Khalid's car. He was home.

Without thinking, she stormed over to the main house. The door was shut, so she knocked, her anger at his actions growing with every breath.

Jalilah opened the door, but before she could say a word of greeting, Ella stepped inside.

"Where is he?" she demanded.

"In the study," the maid said, looking startled.

Ella almost ran to the study door. Khalid was standing behind the desk, leafing through messages. He hadn't shaved in a couple of days, the dark beard made him look almost like a pirate—especially when viewed with the slash of scar tissue. His clothes were dirty and she could smell the smoke from where she stood. None of it mattered.

"What have you done to my life?" she asked.

CHAPTER SIX

He looked up. "Hello, Ella."

"I mean it. What gives you the right to meddle in things that don't concern you? You have ruined everything!"

"What are you talking about?" he asked.

"You sent inquiries to Italy, right?"

He lifted a note. "Garibaldi?"

"If you wanted to know something, why not ask me? I told you all you needed to know. I told you more than I've told anyone else."

"Who is Antonio Garibaldi?" he asked, studying the note a moment, then looking at her. His eyes narrowed as he took in her anger.

"He's my brother. And the reason my husband is dead. I do not wish to have anything to do with him. How could you have contacted them? How could you have led them right to me? I've tried so hard to stay below the radar and with one careless inquiry you lead them right to me. I can't believe this!"

"Wait a second. I don't know what you're talking about. Your family didn't know you were living here?"

"If I had wanted them to know, I would have told them."

"How did your brother cause your husband's death? Didn't you say it was a car crash? Was your brother in the other car?"

"No. He practically kidnapped me. He lured me to the

airport with the intent of getting me on the private jet he'd hired. Only someone told Alexander. He was coming to get me before Antonio could take me out of the country. He crashed on the way to the airport. The police, thankfully, stepped in and stopped our departure." She looked away, remembering. "So I could identify Alexander's body."

She burst into tears.

Khalid looked at her dumbfounded. In only a second he was around the desk and holding her as she sobbed against his chest.

"He had a class. He should have been safely inside, teaching, instead he was trying to come to my rescue," she said between sobs. She clutched a fistful of his shirt, her face pressed against the material, her tears soaking the cotton. She scarcely noticed the smoke. "He would still be alive today if Antonio hadn't forced me. *Alexander*." She cried harder.

Khalid held her close, her pain went straight to his heart. He'd felt the anguish of losing a woman he thought he would build his life with. But his anger soon overcame any heartache. This woman was still devastated by the loss of her husband. What would it be like to mean so much to someone? He thought about his brother and the woman he was going to marry. Bethanne loved him; there was no doubt to anyone who saw them together. She'd be as devastated if something happened to Rashid.

Khalid knew that kind of attachment, that kind of love, was rare and special. Her husband had been dead for more than a year. Ella should have moved on. But the strength of her sobs told him she still mourned with an intensity that was amazing. The emotions told of a strong bond, a love that was deeply felt.

He had never known that kind of love. And never would.

Finally she began to subside. He didn't know what to do but hold her. He'd caused this outburst by his demand to know more. Had the man at Bashiri Oil been clumsy in his research?

Or was the family on alert for information about their daughter? Was her brother's involvement the cause of the estrangement, or did it go deeper? Khalid wanted answers to all the questions swirling around in his mind.

But now, his first priority was to make things right with Ella.

Slowly he felt her hands ease on the clutching of his shirt. A moment later she pushed against his chest. He let her go, catching her face in his palms and brushing away the lingering tears with his thumbs. Her skin was warm and flushed. He registered the softness and the vulnerability she had with her sorrowful eyes, red and puffy.

"I did not know making an inquiry would cause all this," he said. "You are safe here. I will not let anyone kidnap you. Tell me what happened."

She pushed away and stepped back. "I'm not telling you anything. You tell my brother when he contacts you again that you have no idea where I'm living. Make him go away. Make sure he never finds me."

"You think he'll come again?" Khalid asked.

"Of course. He's tenacious."

"Why should he come for you?"

"My family wants me home. I want to stay here. If you can't guarantee I can stay, I'll have to disappear and won't tell you where I go."

Two weeks ago Khalid would have jumped at the offer. He wanted his tenant gone so he could put the estate up for sale. But two weeks changed a lot. He wasn't as anxious to sell as he had once been. He liked living near the sea. He liked the after dark walks along the shore. He did not want his tenant to leave and not give a forwarding address.

More importantly, he wanted to know the full story of what was going on. How could she be so afraid of her family?

"How old are you?" he asked, stepping back to give her more space.

"Twenty-nine. You know that. What does that have to do with anything?"

"As far as I understand the laws in most countries, that makes you an adult, capable of making your own decisions on where to live."

"You'd think so," she said bitterly, brushing the last of the tears from her face. She walked to the window and peered out, but Khalid didn't think she saw the colorful blossoms.

She rubbed her chest, as if pressing against pain. "Alexander and I were childhood sweethearts. My parents thought we'd outgrow that foolishness. Their words. They had a marriage in mind for me that would probably rival what your mother had for Rashid. Combining two old Italian families, and merging two fortunes that would only grow even larger over the years."

Khalid frowned. He made a mental note to get in touch with the man at the company who had been doing the research for him. What had he discovered?

"So you and Alexander married against parental wishes. It happens."

"When they discovered where we were living, Antonio came and said I had to return home. There would be an annulment and the arranged marriage would go forth. I laughed at him, but he was stronger than I was and soon I was in a car heading for the airport. The rest you know. I managed to dodge him at the police station and then hid until I thought he'd left Quishari. Mutual friends contacted your grandmother who offered me a place to live. I'm forever grateful to her. I miss her a lot. She really liked my work, and I think she liked me. But more importantly—she gave me a safe haven. I'll never forget that."

"I'm sure she did," Khalid said, stunned to learn this. Had his actions threatened the haven Ella clung to? He would have to take steps to remedy the situation.

Ella turned and looked at him.

"If my actions caused this, I will fix it," he said.

"If? Of course they did. No one has ever come here before. Why did you have to ask about me. I told you about me."

"I wanted to know more. My grandmother never mentioned you. My family doesn't know about you. What you told me was limited."

"You're my landlord—you know all you need to know about me. I pay my rent on time and I have a lease. I don't trash the place. End of story."

"I want more."

"Well, we don't always get what we want in life," she snapped.

Khalid stared at her, seeing an unhappy, sad woman. One to whom he'd brought more pain and suffering. It didn't come easy, but he had to apologize. "I'm sorry."

She shrugged. "Sorry doesn't change anything."

"It lets you know I didn't deliberately cause you this grief. I said I'd fix it and I shall."

"How? Erase my brother's memory? Put up guards so no one can get on the estate? Wouldn't that also mean no one goes off, either? I had things going just fine until you showed up."

"Sit down and we'll get to the bottom of this." He went around the desk and called Bashiri Oil. In less than a minute he was speaking to the researcher in the office who had been asked to find out more about Ella Ponti. He listened for a solid five minutes, his expression impassive as the man recited what he'd discovered, ending with…

"One of her brothers was in the office yesterday, trying his best to get more information. We know better than to give that kind of information. He accosted people in the halls and in the parking area. Finally we had security remove him from the premises. But I'd watch out—he's looking for his sister and seems most determined."

"I, also, can be determined," Khalid said softly.

"True, Excellency. And I'd put my money on you."

Khalid ended the call.

"It appears the inquiries I had made did cause your brother to return to Quishari. He is staying at the Imperial Hotel. He has made a pest of himself at the company headquarters, questioning everyone trying to locate you. Why is it so important that you marry the man your parents picked out? Surely that was years ago. You said you'd been married for four years, and Alexander has been dead for one. What is so compelling?"

"To further the dynasty, of course. And ensure the money doesn't go outside the family or the family business—wine. I have a trust, that I can't access for another couple of years. But my father was convinced Alexander wanted only my money. He was wrong. Alexander loved me. We lived modestly on his income from the university. We were so happy."

Tears filled her eyes again, and Khalid quickly sought a way to divert them. He was not at all capable of dealing with a woman's tears. He wished he'd never thought to find out more about the woman his grandmother had rented the cottage to.

"I'll go see your brother and make sure he leaves you alone."

She blinked away the tears, hope shining from her eyes. "You will?"

Khalid nodded, loath to involve himself in her family dynamics, but he felt responsible for causing the problem. "I'll shower, change and go to the hotel myself."

Ella thought about it for a moment, then nodded once. "Fine, then. You take care of it." She turned and went to the door, pausing a moment and looking back at him. "I'm glad you got home safely. The fire out?"

"Yes."

"Did you find out what caused it?"

"I believe so. We have taken steps to make sure there won't be another one at that rig."

"Good." She left.

Khalid rubbed the back of his neck. He had better get changed and to the hotel before her brother annoyed even more people. Or came back and found Ella.

Ella kept her house locked up all day. She knew her brother. He would not likely be sidetracked from his goal just on Khalid's say-so. Not that she would buck the power of the sheikh. He could probably buy and sell her brother without batting an eye. And it was his country. His family was most prominent. Antonio would find no allies in Quishari. Served him right. She couldn't forget the last time she'd seen him. If he had never come last year, Alexander would be alive today.

As the afternoon waned, Ella wondered if Khalid had truly gone to see her brother. She had not seen him return. What if he'd changed his mind? Upon further consideration, he had to know this would be the perfect way to rid himself of the tenant he didn't want. The more Ella thought about it, the more certain she was that was what happened. It could not take Khalid hours to go tell Antonio to go home.

Restless, she set off for her walk when it was barely dark. She doubted she'd sleep tonight. In fact, she might best be served by packing essentials and contacting Bethanne to ask for a ride someplace. At this point, Ella would take anyplace away from Alkaahdar.

She walked farther than normal, still keyed up. When she came to a more populated area, she sat near the water. There were others still on the beach. A small party had a fire near the water, and were sitting around it, laughing and talking. She watched from the distance. How long had it been since she felt so carefree and happy?

When that party began breaking up, Ella realized how late it was—and she still had a very long walk home. She rose and walked along the water, the moon a bright disk in the sky. She was resigned to having to leave. There didn't seem to be any choice unless she wanted her family to take over her life. And that she vowed would never happen. She was not some pawn for her father's use. She liked being on her own. Loved living in Quishari. She'd have to find a way.

She slowed when she drew closer to the estate. Would Khalid be on the beach? She wasn't up to dealing with him tonight. She'd made a fool of herself crying in his study. She didn't want to deal with any more emotion. She was content with her decisions and her walk. A good night's sleep was all she wanted now. Tomorrow she'd begin packing and slip away before Antonio found her. She'd contact her friend Marissa to come after she was gone to pack up her glass art. Once she was settled somewhere, she'd see about resuming the glassblowing.

Khalid saw Ella slip through the garden on her way to the cottage. He had tried her place earlier, but she was already gone. Now she was back. It was late, however. He needed to tell her how the meeting with her brother had gone, but maybe it would be best handled in the morning.

He sat in the dark on the veranda, watching her go to her home. A moment later the lights came on in one room, then another. Before a half hour passed, the cottage was dark again. He hoped she had a good night's sleep, to better face tomorrow. He knew she would not be pleased with what he had to tell her.

The next day it rained. The dreary day seemed perfect to Ella as she packed her clothes in one large suitcase. She put her cosmetics in a smaller suitcase and stripped the bed, dumping the sheets into the washer behind the kitchen. She'd leave the place as immaculate as it had been when she moved in. The only part she couldn't do much with would be her studio. She hoped Khalid would permit her friend to come to clear away her things. If not, so be it. It wouldn't be the first time she'd started over. She was better equipped now than she had been a year ago.

The knock on the door put her on instant alert. She would not open to Antonio no matter what. Slowly she approached the door, looking through the glass, relieved to see it was Khalid.

Opening the door a crack, she stood, blocking the view into the living room. "Yes?" she said.

"I need to talk with you," he said. Today he wore a white shirt opened at the throat. His dark pants were obviously part of a suit. Was he going somewhere for business later?

"About?"

"Your brother, what do you think?"

"You saw him?'

"I did. Are you going to let me in or are we going to talk like this?"

She hesitated. "Is it going to take long? Either you got rid of him or you didn't."

He pushed against the door and she gave in, stepping back to allow him to enter.

She shut the door behind him and crossed to the small sofa, sitting on the edge. He took a chair near the sofa.

Wiping suddenly damp palms against her skirt, she waited with what patience she could muster.

"I saw your brother at the hotel. He is very anxious to talk with you. Seems there's a problem with your family that you only can help with."

"Sure, marry the man they picked out."

Khalid nodded. "Apparently there have been some financial setbacks and your family needs an influx of cash that the wedding settlement would bring."

She frowned. "What setbacks? The wine business is doing well. We've owned the land for generations, so there's no danger from that aspect. I don't understand."

Khalid shrugged. "Apparently your younger brother has a gambling habit. He's squandered money gambling, incurring steep debts which your father paid for. That didn't stop him. Unless they get another influx of cash, and soon, they will have to sell some of the land. It's mortgaged. They've been stringing creditors along, but it's all coming due soon and they are desperate."

"Giacomo has a gambling problem?" It was the first she'd heard about it. She frowned. For a moment she pictured her charming brother when she had last seen him. He had still been at university, wild and carefree and charming every girl in sight. They'd had fun as children. What had gone wrong?

"While I'm sorry to hear that, I don't see myself as sacrificial lamb to his problem. Let my father get him to marry some wealthy woman and get the cash that way." She could see her patriarchal father assuming she would be the sacrifice to restore the family fortunes.

"Both your brothers are already married."

Ella was startled at the news. She realized cutting herself off from the family when she married Alexander had meant she wasn't kept up-to-date on their activities. When had her brothers married? Recently? Obviously during the years she and Alexander had lived in Quishari.

"Apparently Antonio feels it is your duty to the family to help in this dire circumstance," Khalid said dryly.

"He's echoing my father. I have no desire to help them out. And I certainly am not going to be forced into marrying some man for his money to bail Giacomo out of a tight place." Antonio had always looked out for her and Giacomo. Looks as if he was still looking out for their younger brother. What about her?

Khalid nodded. "I knew you would feel that way."

"Does he know I live here?" she asked.

Khalid shook his head. “He could end up coming here to see me again and discover you around. But I did not tell him where you lived.”

“I’m leaving.”

He looked surprised at that.

“Going where?”

“I don’t know yet. But I’m not telling anyone. That way they can’t find me again.”

“Would it be so bad to be in touch with your family? I can’t imagine being cut off from Rashid.”

“That’s different. Your mother isn’t trying to marry you off to the woman she wants. Just listen to what Antonio said—I’m to come home and marry some man for his fortune. You don’t want to be married for money, why would you support that?”

“You know I wouldn’t. Would it hurt to listen to what he has to say?”

“I’m not going back to Italy.”

He shook his head. “I’m not suggesting that. Parents can’t arrange marriages for their offsprings.”

“Your mother tried with Rashid.”

“And it came to nought. I don’t see her doing anything now but eventually accepting Bethanne will be his wife.”

“She tried it, that’s the point. She may try with you.”

“I doubt it. She doesn’t like the scars any more than another woman would.”

“Honestly, I can’t believe you harp on that. So you have a scar. Try plastic surgery if you don’t like it. In truth, it makes you look more interesting than some rich playboy sheikh who rides by on his looks.”

“Playboy sheikh?” he said.

Ella leaned forward. “This is about my problem, not yours.”

“Of course.” The amusement in his eyes told her he was not taking this as seriously as she was. Why should he? He had power, prestige, money. She had nothing—not even a family to support her.

"So did Antonio leave?" she asked.

"Not yet. He wants to see you. Hear from you that everything is fine."

"And try to kidnap me again to take me home."

"No. I, uh, made it clear he could not do that."

"How?"

Khalid looked uncomfortable. "Actually by the time the meeting was drawing to an end, I was a bit exasperated with your brother."

Ella laughed shortly. "I can imagine. He's like a bulldog when he's after something. So what did you tell him?"

"That you and I were engaged."

Ella stared at him for a long moment, certain she had misheard him. "Excuse me?" she said finally, not believing what echoed in her mind.

"It seemed like a good idea at the time."

"You told my brother we were engaged? You don't even like me. We are not engaged. Not even friends, from what I can tell. Why in the world would you say such a thing?"

"To get him to back down."

"I don't believe this. You're a sheikh in this kingdom. You could order people to escort him to the country borders and kick him out. You could get his visa denied, declare him persona non grata. You could have—"

"Well, I didn't do any of that."

She blinked. "So Antonio thinks we're engaged."

Khalid nodded.

"And that's it? He's going home now?"

"After he's met you and is satisfied you are happy with this arrangement."

For a moment Ella felt a wave of affection for her brother. She didn't always agree with him, but for him to make sure she was happy sounded like the brother she remembered with love. However—

"No."

"No what?"

"I'm not taking that chance. I don't want to see Antonio. I don't want him to know where I live." She looked at him with incredulity. "You don't think they expect you to give the family money if I were really going to marry you, do you? He's probably just as happy with you as candidate as whomever they had picked out in Italy."

"I mentioned that I have a few thousand qateries put away for the future."

"Utterly stupid," she said, jumping to her feet. "I cannot believe you said that. You go back and tell him you were joking or something."

Khalid rose, as well, and came over to her. "Ella, think for a moment. This gets you off the hook. We'll meet him for dinner or something. Show we are devoted to each other. And that you have no intention of returning to Italy. Then he'll be satisfied and take off in the morning. You'll be safely ensconced here and that's an end to it. Once your family finds another way to deal with the debt, you can write and say the engagement ended."

She considered the plan. It sounded dishonest. But it also sounded like it might work. If she could convince Antonio she was committed to Khalid. Glancing out the window, she wondered if she could look as if she loved the man to distraction when her heart was buried with Alexander.

Yet, he knew her. He could believe she'd fallen in love. He'd often teased her for being a romantic. And her family would welcome Khalid like they never had Alexander. This time they had no reason to suspect he was interested in her money. Next to him, she was almost a pauper.

"Do you think it'll work?" she asked, grasping the idea with faint hope.

"What could go wrong?" he asked. "You'll convince your brother you're deliriously happy. He'll go home and you'll go back to making glass art."

"What do you get out of this?" she asked cynically.

"No more tears?" he said.

She flushed. "Sorry about that."

"No, I didn't mean to make light of it. Just make sure you don't have another meltdown. I'll be gone again soon so you'll have the place to yourself again, like before."

"So you're not planning to sell?"

"Maybe not for a while. I find I'm enjoying living by the water."

"Okay. We'll try your plan. But if he doesn't leave, or tries anything, I'm taking off."

Khalid arranged dinner at a restaurant near the hotel. He picked Ella up at seven and in less than twenty minutes they arrived at the restaurant. She saw her brother waiting for them once they entered.

"Ella," he said in Italian, coming to kiss both cheeks.

"Antonio," she replied. It had been almost a year since she'd seen him. He looked the same. She smiled and hugged him tightly. No matter what—he was still her older brother.

He shook hands with Khalid. Soon all three were seated in a table near the window that looked over a garden.

"We've been worried about you," Antonio said.

"I'm fine."

"More than fine. Engaged to be married again." He gave her a hard look.

She looked at him. "And?"

"It will come as a surprise to our parents."

"As learning about Giacomo's gambling problem surprised me."

Antonio flicked a glance at Khalid and shrugged. "A way

will be found to get the money. Family needs to support each other, don't you think?"

When the waiter came for the order, conversation was suspended for a moment. "Khalid doesn't speak Italian. He speaks English or French, so you choose," Ella said in English.

"English is not so good for me. But for, um, good feelings between us, I speak it," Antonio said.

"Ella tells me your family has been in the winemaking business for generations," Khalid said. "You are a part of that operation?"

Antonio nodded. "I sell wine. Giacomo helps father with the vineyard and the make. My father wants Ella to come home. She goes a long time."

"Maybe in a while. She cannot come now," Khalid said flatly.

Antonio looked surprised that anyone would tell him no. Ella hid a smile and took a moment to glance around the restaurant. The tables were given plenty of space to insure a quiet atmosphere and offer a degree of privacy for the customers. Her eye caught a glimpse of the minister of finance just as he spotted her.

"Uh-oh," she said softly in Arabic. "The minister is here."

Antonio frowned. "If we speak English, all speak," he said.

"Sorry, I forgot," she replied, looking at Khalid for guidance.

A moment later the minister was at their table.

"Ah, the lovely Madame Ponti," he said with a smile, reaching out to capture her hand and kiss the back. "Rashid, I didn't expect to see you with Madame Ponti," he said with a quick glance at Khalid.

Khalid stood, towering over the older man, exposing the scar when he faced him. "Minister," he said.

"Ah, my mistake. Khalid. No need to get up. I'm on my way out and saw you dining." He smiled affably at Antonio. "Another guest?"

"Ella's brother." Good manners dictated an introduction

which Khalid made swiftly. Explaining Antonio was Italian and didn't speak Arabic.

"English?" he asked.

Antonio nodded.

"Welcome to Quishari," the minister said with a heavy accent.

"Happy to be here. We are celebrating good news—Ella's engagement."

CHAPTER SEVEN

ELLA was struck dumb. She wished she could stuff a sock in her brother's mouth. Her horrified gaze must have shown, as Khalid reached out and touched her shoulder.

"Congratulate us, Minister. You are the first outside the family to know," he said easily.

His grip tightened and she tried to smile. What a disaster this was turning out to be. Khalid must be furious. That's what they got for trying to put something over on Antonio.

"My felicitations. I have to say I am not surprised after seeing you at your mother's event the other evening."

Khalid nodded, releasing his hold on Ella's shoulder as if convinced she would not jump up and flee—which she strongly felt like.

"Don't let me keep you from dinner," the minister said as the waiter approached with their meals on a tray.

When he left, Ella gave a sigh of relief. Maybe Khalid could catch him later and explain. She needed to concentrate on getting her brother on the next plane to Italy.

"Mother and father will want to meet your fiancé," Antonio said as they began to eat. "You two should visit soon. I can wait here a few days and return with you."

"Unfortunately I am unable to get away for a while and Ella must work on her art," Khalid said.

"Art?" Her brother looked puzzled.

"You have not seen the beautiful glass pieces she makes?" Khalid asked in surprise.

"Oh, those." Antonio gave a shrug. "I've seen bowls and such. Nice enough."

Ella knew better than to take offense at her brother's casual dismissal of her work. He had thought it an odd hobby when she'd been younger. But she'd come a long way since those early attempts. Not that she needed to show him. If Khalid was successful in getting him to leave, she'd be grateful. If not, then maybe Plan B would work better—get Bethanne to fly her somewhere far away and tell no one.

The meal seemed interminable. Ella wanted to scream at her brother to leave her alone. She couldn't forget his part in Alexander's death. If he had not tried to take her home last year, Alexander would still be alive.

Everything was different. When they finished eating, Khalid escorted them to the curb where the limo was waiting. Ushering them both inside, he gave instructions for Antonio's hotel and settled back.

"We will drop you at your hotel and in the morning I will arrange for the limousine to pick you up to take you to the airport. Ella will contact your parents when it is convenient to visit."

Never underestimate the power of money, status and arrogant male, she thought as she watched her brother struggle with something that would assert his own position. But one look from the dark eyes of the sheikh had Antonio subsiding quietly.

"As you wish. My father will be delighted to learn his daughter is engaged to one of the leading families in Quishari. I hope you both can visit soon."

The ride home from the hotel was in silence. Ella didn't know whether to be grateful to Khalid or annoyed at his outlandish handling of the situation. If the minister hadn't learned of the bogus engagement, they could have muddled through without any bother.

"What if the minister says something?" she asked.

"Who's he going to tell? We are not that important in his scheme of things. You worry about things too much," he said, studying the scenery as they were driven home.

"At least I didn't go off half-cocked and say we were engaged. Too bad he speaks English. The language barrier could have prevented it. I doubt he speaks Italian."

Khalid looked at her. "Your brother will return home, tell your parents you are safe and go on with his life. Once things settle down, you can tell them things didn't work out."

She laughed nervously. "I doubt things will settle down. They will push for marriage."

"Tell them I am not ready."

"Oh, Khalid, if they really need money for Giacomo, then my guess is the next step is get me safely married to you and hit me up for some money. If you were poor as Alexander was, they would never be satisfied with a marriage between us."

"You're an adult. Just tell them no."

"Antonio tried to force me from the country last time. Just say no doesn't work with my family."

"He won't try you in the future, not as long as you live in Quishari."

"Then I may never leave," she said, still worried about the entire scenario.

Khalid had the limousine stop by Ella's cottage and dismissed the man. He escorted her to her door.

"Thanks for dinner, and for standing up for me," she said, opening it.

"That's what fiancés are for," he said, brushing back her hair and kissing her lightly on the lips.

He turned and walked to the villa, wishing he had stayed for a longer good-night kiss. He had hidden it from Ella, but he was worried the minister could stir up trouble that would be hard to suppress.

When he entered the study a few moment later, the answering machine was flashing. He pressed the button.

"What's this I hear about your engagement? You couldn't tell me before the minister?" Rashid's voice came across loud and clear—with a hint of amusement. "Or did he get it wrong? Call me."

Khalid sighed and sank onto the chair. Dialing his brother, he wondered if he could finesse this somehow. It was hard sometimes to have a twin who knew him so well.

"Hello."

"Rashid, it's Khalid."

"Ah, the newly engaged man. I didn't have a clue."

"It's not what you think?"

"So what is it?"

Khalid explained and heard Rashid's laughter. "Sounds almost like Bethanne and me. We pretended she was my intended to close the deal I was working on when the woman I expected didn't show up. Watch it, brother—fake engagements have a way of turning real."

"Not this time. In fact, I wasn't going to tell anyone beyond Ella's brother. Once he was back Italy, she'd be left alone."

"Now you have the minister calling me and undoubtedly Mother to congratulate us on your engagement. And I know from experience, Mother isn't going to be happy."

"She should be glad anyone would even consider marrying me with this face."

"Not if it isn't someone she picked out—which I'm coming to believe means someone she can boss around. Bethanne isn't exactly docile. So what's the plan?"

"I haven't a clue. It would have gone smoothly if the minister hadn't come over. Her brother would have left and things would have returned to normal."

"Whatever that is these days." Rashid was quiet for a moment, then said, "Any chance…"

"What, that she'd want to marry me? Get real. First off, I'm not planning to marry. Your kids will carry on the line. And second, she's still hung up on her dead husband. And I see no signs of that abating. She was crying over him today."

"Fine, you've played the role of hero, rescuing her from her brother. Would that make her feel she owes you? Maybe vacate the cottage so you can sell the place sooner?"

"I wouldn't use that to get her gone."

Rashid was silent.

"Anyway, things will work out."

"Call me if you need me," Rashid said.

When he hung up, Khalid contemplated finding a job ten thousand miles away and staying as long as he could. Who would think inheriting a beautiful estate could end up making him so confused.

The phone rang again.

When he answered, he sighed hearing his mother's greeting.

"I just had an interesting call," she began.

"I know." For a split second he considered telling her the truth. But that fled when he thought of her calling to set the minister straight. He would not like having been lied to.

"Is it true? Honestly, if I had thought you were planning to marry, which you have stated many time you are not, I know several nice women who would have suited much better than a widow of dubious background."

"I know her background."

"I don't. Where is she from? Are you certain she wants to marry you to build a life together, or is she in it to keep the cottage? Once her career takes off, will she leave for greener fields?"

"Who knows what the future holds," he said.

"Your father used to say that all the time. Honestly, men.

I suppose I have to have another party to introduce her formally to everyone like I did with Bethanne."

"Hold off on that, Mother."

"Why?"

His mother was sharp; anything out of a normal progression would raise doubts. And he didn't want Ella talked about, or word to reach her family that the engagement wasn't going strong.

"You just had a party…we can wait a few weeks." Maybe by then something would occur to him that would get him out of the situation. He'd thought it the perfect answer to getting rid of Ella's brother. The first time in recent months he did anything spontaneous and it grew more complicated by the moment. Give him a raging oil fire any day.

"Nonsense. I'll call your aunt. She'll be thrilled to hear you are getting married and want to help. We had given up on you, you know."

Hold that thought, he wanted to say. But for the time being, he'd go along with her idea. He wondered if Ella would. Or if she'd put an end to it the minute her brother took off in the morning. She hadn't welcomed the idea when he first told her.

He went to change into casual clothes and headed for the beach. He didn't know if she'd join him on a walk tonight. He could gauge her reaction by her manner if she did show up.

When he reached the beach, there was no sign of her. He'd wait a bit. It wasn't that late.

Sitting on the still warm sand, he watched the moonlight dance on the water. The soft night breeze caressed. The silence was peaceful, tranquil. Why did men make things so complicated. A quiet night surrounded by nature—that's what he needed. That's what he liked about the desert. The solitude and stillness.

He heard her walking through the garden. Satisfaction filled him. She was coming again. Despite their differences, he felt closer to her in the dark than he did anyone except Rashid. Theirs was an odd friendship; one that probably wouldn't last through the years, but perfect for now.

"I wondered if you'd want to go walk," she said, walking over and sitting beside him. "You were right, you know. I overreacted, but this was a perfect scheme to get rid of Antonio. You know, of course, that had this been real, the minute we married, he'd be hitting you up for money."

"It crossed my mind," Khalid said. Antonio didn't know him well—nor ever would. But giving money away to people who wasted it was not something he did. Though he could understand family solidarity. Wonder if there were a different way to handle the situation.

He rose and reached out his hand to help her up. With one accord, they left their shoes and began walking to the water. Once on hard-packed sand, they turned north.

Khalid liked the end of the evening this way. Ella was comfortable to be around. With the darkness to cloak the scar, he had no hesitation in having her with him. She didn't have to see the horrible deformity and he didn't have to endure the looks of horror so often seen in people when they were around him. Not that he'd caught even a glimpse of that with Ella after that first day. She seemed to see right through the scar to the man beneath.

"At least we don't have to worry about that. I'm still working on a catalog and will see if I can get a showing earlier than originally planned. Once I have a way to earn a living, I'll be out of your way."

"There is one complication," he said.

"What?"

"My mother thinks we are engaged and is planning a party to announce it to the world."

"What? You've got to be kidding? How did your mother find out?" She stopped walking and stared at him.

"She called me tonight. The minister wasted no time. He has it in for Rashid and I expect is trying to gain an ally with mother in getting insider info or something."

Ella shook her head. "I can imagine how delighted she is to think we're engaged. Did you set her straight?"

"No."

"Why not?"

He refused to examine the reason. He felt protective toward Ella. He didn't want anything to mar her happiness—especially her family. It seemed she'd had enough grief to last a lifetime.

"Seemed better not to."

"Well, tell her in the morning."

"Or, let her think that for a while. What does it hurt?"

Ella thought about it for a moment. "Maybe no one," she said reluctantly.

"If people think you are engaged to me, it'll give you a bit of a step up when going to galleries."

"I wouldn't pretend for that reason."

"But you would to keep your family out of your life."

"I didn't know my younger brother had a gambling problem. He was the cutest little boy. So charming."

He took her hand and tugged her along and resumed walking. "I know. Family pressure can be unrelenting, however. If they think you are already out of reach, they have to look elsewhere for financial help. Personally I'd kick the man out and tell him to make a go of it on his own."

"You talk a hard line, but I bet you would try to work something out if it were Rashid," she said.

Khalid knew that to be true.

"I'm not sure it's fair to you," she continued.

"Why not? I'm the one who started the entire convoluted mess."

"I know, which I think is totally off the wall. But no one who knew us would believe we could fall in love and plan to marry."

"Because of the scar," he bit out.

She whacked him on his arm with her free hand. "Will you stop! That has nothing to do with anything. I'm still grieving for my husband. I don't want to ever go through something like that again. It's safer to go through life alone, making friends, having a great career, but not putting my heart on the line again. It hurts too much when it's shattered."

"Safer but lonely, isn't it?"

Ella glanced at him. Was he lonely? On the surface he had it all: good looks, money, family behind him. The downside would be the job he did. Yet because of the scarring on his face, he pulled away from social events, hadn't had a friend come to visit since he'd been in the main house. And to hear him talk, he was shunned by others.

She'd seen some looks at the reception, fascinated horror. Her regret was he had to deal with rude, obnoxious people who didn't seem to have the manners necessary to deal with real life.

"Come on," she said, pulling her hand free. "I'll race you to that piece of driftwood." With that, Ella took off at a run for the large log that had washed up on shore during the last storm. She knew she couldn't beat Khalid; he'd win by a long margin. But maybe it would get them out of gloomy thoughts. She felt she'd been on a roller coaster all day. It was time to regain her equilibrium and have some fun.

She'd taken him by surprise, she could tell as he hesitated a moment before starting to run. She had enough of a head start she thought for a few seconds she might win. Then Khalid raced past her, making it look easy and effortless.

Ella was gasping for breath when she reached the log. He was a bit winded, which helped her own self-respect.

"Do you often race at night?" he asked.

"No one can see me and I can race the wind. It's better than racing you, for I can convince myself I win."

He laughed and picked her up by her waist and twirled them

both around. "I win tonight," he said, and lowered her gently to the ground, drawing her closer until they were touching from chest to knees. He leaned over and kissed her sweetly.

Ella closed her eyes, blocking out the brilliant blanket of stars in the sky. Hearing only her own racing heartbeat and the soft sighing of the spent waves. Soon even they were lost to sound as the blood roared through her veins, heating every inch of her. She gave herself up to the wonderful feelings that coursed through her. His mouth was magic. His lips like nectar. His strong body made her feel safe and secure, and wildly desirable.

Time lost all meaning. For endless minutes, Ella was wrapped in sensation. She could have halted time and lived forever in this one moment. It was exquisite.

Then reality intruded. Slowly the kiss eased and soon Khalid had put several inches between them. She stepped forward not wanting to end the contact. His hands rested on her shoulders and gently pushed her away.

"We need to get back before things get out of hand," he said.

She cringed and turned, glad for the darkness to hide her embarrassment. How could she so wantonly throw herself at him when he made it perfectly clear he was not interested in her that way. His gesture with the fake engagement was merely a means to offer some protection to her. If her brother had never shown up, never threatened her, Khalid would never in a million years have pretended that they were involved.

And that was fine by her.

She increased her pace.

"Are we racing back?" he asked, easily keeping pace.

"No." She slowed, but longed to break into another run and beat him home, shut the door and pull the shades. She was an adult. She could handle this—it was only for the length of time to get to her cottage. Then she'd do her best from now on to stay away from Khalid al Harum!

* * *

That vow lasted until the next day. Ella spent the early hours working on a small bowl that would be the first of a set, each slightly larger than the previous. She concentrated and was pleased to note she could ignore everything else and focus on the work at hand.

It was past time for lunch when she stopped to get something to eat. In the midst of a project, she became caught up in the process. But once it was safely in the annealer, thoughts of last night surfaced.

Jalilah knocked on the door before Ella had a chance to fix something to eat.

"His Excellency would like to see you," she said.

"I'm getting ready to eat," Ella said. "Tell him I'll be over later."

Jalilah looked shocked. "I think he wants you now," she said.

"Well, he can't always have what he wants," Ella said. "Thanks for delivering his message. Tell him what I said. Maybe around three." She closed the door.

Who did he think he was, expecting her to drop everything just because he summoned her? He had delusions if he thought she'd drop everything to run to him.

In fact, she might not go at all.

Except her curiosity was roused. What did he want?

She prepared a light lunch and ate on her small veranda. The hot sun was blocked by the grape-covered arbor. The breeze was hot, blowing from the land and not the sea. She wouldn't stay outside long.

Sipping the last of her iced tea, Ella heard the banging on the front door. Sighing, she rose. It didn't take a psychic to know who was there. Dumping her dishes in the sink on her way to the front of the cottage, she wondered if she dare ignore him.

Opening the door, she glared at him instead. "What do you want?"

"To talk to you," he said easily, stepping inside.

She moved to allow him. It was that or be run over. He was quite a bit larger than she was.

Closing the door, she turned and put her hands on her hips. "About what?"

"My mother is hosting another party. This time to formally announce our engagement. We need to go."

"Are you crazy? This has gone on long enough. Tell her the truth."

"Not yet. You need to make sure your family turns elsewhere for relief from your brother's gambling. It's only one evening. You'll meet people, smile and look as if you like me."

"I'm not sure I do," she said, narrowing her eyes. "This gets more complicated by the moment."

"We need to invite some of your friends to make it seem real."

She crossed her arms over her chest. This was unexpected. "I'm not involving my friends. Besides, no one would believe it. They all know how much I loved Alexander. And do you really think they'd believe you'd fall for me?"

"So pretend."

"We don't have to pretend anymore. Antonio's gone and it was for his benefit, right?"

He was silent for a moment.

"Right?" she repeated.

"He did not leave as we thought."

"Why not?" She frowned. What was her brother doing? He wasn't waiting for the wedding, for heaven's sake, was he?

"Now how would I know what your brother thinks…I just met him. But the limo showed up at the hotel in time to get him to the airport for the first flight to Rome and he said he'd changed his plans and would be remaining in Quishari a bit longer."

"Great." She walked across the room and turned, walked back, trying to think of how to get out of the mess the men in her life had caused.

"I'll go away," she said.

"After the announcement," he replied.

She looked at him. He was calm. There was a hint of amusement in his eyes. Which made her all the more annoyed. "This is not a joke."

"No, but it's almost turning into a farce. I thought telling him would shut him up. Do you think I want the world to think I got engaged again and then a second fiancée breaks the engagement?"

She had not thought about that at all.

"Then you break it," she said.

"That'll look good."

"Well, one of us has to end it, so you decide. In the meantime, I do not want to go to your mother's. I do not want the entire city to think we are engaged. I do not—"

He raised a hand to stop her.

"Then you come up with something."

"I wouldn't have to if you hadn't told my brother."

"You could have told him the truth at dinner last night."

She bit her lip. She did not want to return to Italy. She would not be pressured day and night by parents trying to talk her into a marriage with some wealthy Italian to shore up her brother's losses. The days when daughters were sacrificed for the good of the family were long past. If only her father would accept that.

"Okay, so we pretend until Antonio leaves. Can we hurry him on his way?" she asked, already envisioning her mother's tearful pleas; Giacomo's little boy lost entreaties; Antonio begging her to think of the family reputation. She loved her family, but she wasn't responsible for them all.

"He's your brother. I could never hurry Rashid. The more I'd push, the more he'd resist."

She nodded. "Okay, so brothers are universal. Somehow we have to get him to leave me alone."

"So we'll convince him tonight that it's an arrangement meant to be and maybe he'll leave."

"Or hit you up for a loan."

Khalid frowned. "Do you really think that's the reason for the delay?"

"I don't know." Maybe her brother just wanted to make sure she was happy. Yet he'd been right there when her parents had railed against her for marrying Alexander and never said a word in her behalf. She had no intention of letting any of her family dictate her life.

"What time do we go to your mother's?"

"I'll pick you up at seven."

"How dressy?"

"About like last time. Do you need a new dress?"

She looked at him oddly. "I have enough clothes, thank you. What—do you expect everyone to hit you up for money?"

"No. But women always seem to need new clothes. I can help out if you need it."

"I do not." She studied him for a moment. Thinking about her own family, she knew there were some shirttail relatives who had asked her father for handouts. He'd refused and when she was a child, she wondered why he didn't share. Once she was older, she realized some people always have their hands out.

For a moment she wished she had brought some of her clothes from home. She and her mother had shopped at the most fashionable couturiers in Rome. She'd left them behind when joining her husband in Quishari. The dresses for receptions were more conservative. She wished at least one would make Khalid proud to be escorting her.

Then she remembered the red dress she'd bought from a shop near campus. Her friend Samantha had urged her to buy it. She'd never worn it. It was too daring for a professor's wife. But for tonight, it might just be the thing. Sophisticated and elegant, it was far more cosmopolitan than anything else she now owned. She smiled almost daringly at Khalid. If he insisted they continue, she'd show him more than he bargained for.

He studied her for a moment, a hint of wariness creeping into his expression.

"Until tonight," he said.

She nodded, opening the door wide and watching him as he started to leave.

"I don't think I trust your expression," he said.

She feigned a look of total innocence. "I'm sure I have no idea what you're talking about, darling."

He tapped her chin with his forefinger. "Behave."

She laughed and shooed him out the door. Tonight might prove fun. She was not out to impress anyone, nor kowtow to them. Madame al Harum would be horrified. The minister might wish he'd kept his mouth shut. And her brother would learn not to mess with his sister's life anymore.

Ella was ready before the appointed time. She'd tapped Jalilah's expertise in doing up her hair. She remembered the maid had a talent for that which her former employer had used. The dress was daring in comparison to the gowns Ella had worn to the university functions. The thin crimson straps showed brilliantly against her skin, the fitted bodice hugged every curve down to where the skirt flared slightly below the knees. The satiny material gleamed in the light, shifting highlights as she walked. She had her one set of pearls she again wore. The dress really cried out for diamonds or rubies, but Ella had neither. The high heel shoes gave her several inches in height, which would add to her confidence. She was ready to face the world on her terms.

Khalid arrived at seven. He stared at her for a moment, which had Ella feeling almost giddy with delight. She knew she'd surprised him.

"You look beautiful," he said softly.

She felt a glow begin deep inside. She felt beautiful. The dress was a dream, but the color in her cheeks came from being near Khalid. She knew she would do him proud at the reception, and give others something to think about. All too soon this pretend engagement would end, but until midnight struck, she'd enjoy herself to the fullest. And make sure he did, as well. He deserved lots for helping her out without question.

"Thank you. So do you," she said with a flirtatious smile.

He gave a harsh laugh. "Don't carry the pretense too far," he said. "This is a dumb idea."

"It was yours," she reminded him.

He laughed again, in amusement this time. "Don't remind me. I say we ditch the reception and go off on our own. You look too beautiful to be stuck in a room full of my mother's friends."

"You're not thinking. What would your mother say. She went to all the trouble to celebrate what she thinks is a happy occasion. You can't disappoint her."

"You got it right first time—it's hard to think around you the way you look right now."

Ella smiled, delighted he was so obviously taken with how she looked. The dress was really something and she didn't ever remember feeling so sexy or feminine. The hot look in Khalid's eyes spiked her own temperature. Maybe his idea of not going out had merit.

"Let's go wow them all. And when we've put in our appearance, we'll dash back here and take a walk on the beach. Much more fun that the ordeal ahead." Filled with confidence from his reaction, she could hold her own with his mother and anyone else who showed up.

CHAPTER EIGHT

WHEN they arrived at his mother's apartment building, Ella was impressed. It looked like a palace. They were admitted by the uniformed doorman and quickly whisked to the top floor by a private elevator.

"The family home, no hotel," she murmured.

"Only a few intimate friends, like maybe a hundred. You never gave me a list of your friends, so I had one of my assistants contact the university and find out who your friends were. Told them it was a surprise."

Ella gave a loud sigh. "You just can't leave things alone, can you? Did you drive everyone insane while growing up?"

"Hey, I had Rashid to help me then."

"But not now?"

"He knows, but he is the only one besides you and me. Unless he told Bethanne. I forget there is a new intimate confidant with my brother. That'll be interesting—learning how to deal with that aspect."

Entering the large flat that overlooked Alkaahdar, Ella was struck by the large salon, ceilings at least twelve feet high. A wall of windows opened to a large terrace. The room held dozens of people yet did not appear crowded. Classical artwork hung on the walls. The chandelier sparkled with a thousand facets. The furniture looked more Western than Arabian, chosen for elegance and style.

"Khalid, you should have been here before the first guests," his mother chided, coming to greet them. She looked at Ella, her eyes widening slightly. "You look different tonight," she said taking in the lovely dress and the sophisticated hairstyle.

Ella inclined her head slightly. "I've been told I clean up good," she said cheekily.

Sabria al Harum didn't know how to respond.

Khalid gave his mother a kiss on her cheek. "We're here, that's the important thing. I can't believe you managed such a crowd on less than a day's notice.

"Everyone here wishes you well, son," she said, eyeing Ella as if she wasn't sure how to react to her.

Ella slipped her arm through Khalid's and leaned closer. "We are honored you did this for us on such short notice, aren't we, darling?" she said, smiling up at him.

"Indeed we are, *darling*," he said back, his eyes promising retribution.

"Mingle, let people congratulation you," Sabria said. She gave Ella an uncertain look.

Rashid crossed the room with Bethanne. He grinned at Khalid and Ella. "Congratulations, Brother," he said, then leaned in and gave Ella a kiss on the cheek. "Keep him in check," he said.

"I couldn't believe it when Rashid told me," Bethanne said, glancing around. She hugged Ella, and said in English. "I think it's fabulous."

Ella giggled a little. "Outlandish, I thought," she replied, one arm still looped with Khalid's.

Antonio came over, bowing stiffly.

"I thought you went home," Ella said when he stopped beside them.

"There were one or two things to deal with before I left. I

spoke to our parents. They wish you both happiness in your marriage," he said. "If I had left, I would have missed this."

"And wouldn't that have been too bad," she murmured in Arabic.

"Come," Khalid said, "let me introduce you to some friends."

As they stepped away from the entry, they were surrounded by people who were mostly strangers to Ella. However one or two familiar faces had her smiling in delight to see again, though inside she felt guilty to be deceiving everyone.

Conscious she needed to convince her brother nothing would deter her from marrying Khalid, she stayed within touching distance all evening, reaching out sometimes to touch his arm as if to ground herself. Once when she did, he clasped her hand, lacing their fingers together and holding it all the while he carried on a conversation with a friend.

The finance minister saw Khalid with Ella and broke away from the small group he was talking with and came over to them.

"Your mother must be so pleased, both her sons are taking the next step to insure the family continues."

"There's more to marriage than having children," Khalid said dryly.

"Ah, but nothing like small ones around to keep you young."

"Do you have children?" Ella asked.

"Not yet."

"Yet you and your wife have been married for many years," Khalid said.

For a moment the minister looked uncomfortable, then he changed the subject. "So are you and your brother marrying at the same time? Or as Rashid is the elder, will you defer to him?"

"Our plans are not yet firm," Khalid responded. "Excuse us, please, I see some friends of Ella's have arrived." Khalid moved them toward the door where two couples were standing, looking around in bewilderment.

"How do you know they are my friends?" she asked recognizing her friends.

"They look out of place. They obviously don't know anyone else here."

Greetings were soon exchanged. Though Ella's university friends were startled by the scar on Khalid's face, they quickly hid it and greeted him as warmly as they did her.

"I had no idea," Jannine said. "Though we haven't seen much of you this last year. I guess a lot has happened that I don't know about."

"It has been a hectic and busy year," Ella said vaguely. If this had been a true engagement, she would have shared the news with her friends immediately. She knew they'd wish only happiness for her.

"So, how are you doing with your glassmaking?" Joseph asked. He looked at Khalid. "You've seen her work, of course."

"Yes. Exquisite. She's planning a showing before too much longer. I predict a spectacular future for our artist."

"Do tell us all," Monique said.

Ella was pleased her friends had come on such short notice and silently vowed to keep in touch better. They'd been part of her life for several years and were each interesting people. She talked about the tentative plans for getting into a gallery someplace. They listened attentively, only now and again darting a glance at Khalid.

A moment later, he touched Ella's shoulder.

"Someone I must speak to. I'll leave you with your friends." He left and she watched as he crossed over to an elderly man. Turning back to her friends, she found all eyes on her.

"He's one of the richest men in the country, you know," Jannine said. "How in the world did you land him?"

"Good grief, Jannine, is that how you refer to me? I feel like a large-mouth bass," her husband said.

Everyone laughed.

"Okay, maybe that was not quite what I meant."

"So did you mean how did Ella attract him? She's pretty, young and talented. What's not to like?" Monique said.

"You all are twisting my words and you know it. Tell all, Ella."

She glossed over details mentioning simply that she had been renting a cottage on a family estate and they met that way. The rest they knew. "Tell me what's going on at the university. I've been so out of touch."

Joseph began telling her about professors and students she might remember. She enjoyed catching up on the news, but felt distant, as if that part of her life was over and she was no longer connected as she once had been. It felt a bit lonely.

Glancing around at one point, she saw Khalid and Rashid both talking with the elderly man. They were in profile, left sides showing. Stunning men, she thought. Then Khalid turned and caught her eye. Once again the ruined side of his face showed. She swallowed a pang of regret for the damage and smiled. That was easily overlooked when his dark eyes focused on her. Then she felt as if everything else faded away and left only the two of them in a world of their own.

"She's got it bad," Jannine said, laughing.

"What?" Ella asked, turning back to her friend.

"He's gone five minutes and you're already looking for him. How long until the wedding?"

"I'm not sure. We haven't made plans yet."

Antonio came over at that point. Ella made introductions and the group began talking in English, a common language for them all.

"This is a night of firsts," Jannine said. "I didn't even know Ella had family. She never spoke of you."

Her husband nudged her.

"Oh, sorry. Was that not the thing to say?"

Antonio looked at her. "You never spoke of us? Ella, we are your family."

"Who wouldn't accept my husband," she replied.

As the others looked on, she wished she could march her brother away and find Khalid. She was tired of the pretense, tired of trying to smile all the time when she wanted to rail against Antonio for getting her into this mess.

"But you like al Harum better, scar notwithstanding" Joseph muttered in Arabic.

Ella narrowed her eyes. "Khalid is a wonderful man. He puts out oil fires. Do you know how dangerous that is? He was injured trying to stop a conflagration. There are very few people in the world who can do something like that. And did you ever stop to think how much pain and agony he went through with such severe burns?"

Khalid put his hand on her shoulder. "Defending me?"

"There's no need," she said, glaring at Joseph.

Antonio watched, glancing between Joseph, Ella and Khalid.

"No offence meant, Ella," Joseph said.

"None taken," Khalid said. "Please, help yourselves to refreshments. I want to borrow Ella a moment to introduce her to an old friend."

He took her hand in his and they moved toward the man she'd seen before. Rashid and Bethanne were talking with him.

"He was a friend of my grandparents, Hauk bin Arissi. Unfortunately he is thrilled with our engagement. It is awkward, to say the least. I do not like deceiving people."

"You should have thought of that."

"Or left you to your brother?"

Before Ella could respond, they were beside Hauk bin Arissi. Introductions were made.

"Ah, Khalid, you and your brother have once again surprised me. The antics you used to do. Your grandmother would be so happy today—both her precious grandsons embarking on a lifelong partnership with such beautiful women."

"You are most kind," Ella said.

"Ah, and you my dear, already speak our language."

"I've lived in Alkaahdar for several years. Studied the language before that."

"You speak it well."

"Thank you. My reading is not as proficient."

He waved his hand dismissively. "Have Khalid read to you. The evenings my wife and I enjoyed reading from the classics. I do miss that."

She glanced at Khalid, a question in her eyes.

"We all miss her, Hauk."

"So how did you two meet. I've heard about Bethanne's piloting."

"She lives on Grandmother's estate, the one I inherited."

"So he inherited me," Ella said.

"Are you the artist? The glassmaker? Alia told me about your excellent work. I saw the vase you made for her. It looks like captured sunshine."

Ella smiled. "Thank you for telling me. I miss her so much."

Hauk studied her a moment, then looked at Khalid. "You, also, have found a treasure. See you treat her appropriately."

Khalid bowed slightly. Ella saw the amusement in his eyes. For a moment she wished this was real. That he would treasure her and treat her appropriately. The thought startled her. This was one evening to get through, not let their pretense slip. Soon things would go back to normal.

By the end of the evening, Khalid's temper was held by a thread. His mother was pushing for a wedding date, pushing to learn more, pushing period. The minister watched Ella more than Khalid thought wise. His wife had been unable to attend, and Khalid did not like the way he eyed Ella. Rashid teased him, which normally he'd accept in good stead. But tonight, it rubbed him wrong.

He and Ella spent most of the evening together, except

when she was visiting with her friends. It was growing late when she came over to him and smiled sweetly at the couple he was talking with.

"Will you please excuse us?" she asked, drawing Khalid away.

With the same smile on her face, she leaned closer, to speak only to him.

"My feet hurt, my cheeks hurt, I'm getting very cranky so suggest we leave very soon."

He leaned forward, breathing in the scent of her perfume, something flowery that he had grown familiar with over the last few weeks.

"I was ready to leave about two hours ago."

"I could have gone then. We've been here long enough, right? Your mother can't complain."

"She will, but that's her way. Come, follow me."

He led the way down a corridor and in moments they were in the primary hallway of the building. In seconds they descended in the elevator and were outside.

Ella leaned her head back and drew in a deep breath. It was all he could do to resist leaning over and kissing her. But standing in front of the building with the doorman and valet parking attendants standing mere feet away wasn't conducive for such activities.

Ella was tired. The strain of pretending she was wildly happy with a new engagement, and the anxiety over her brother, was wearing on her. To make matters worse, she almost wished she and Khalid were engaged. He had been most attentive tonight, hovering over her like he couldn't stay away. He even seemed the tiniest bit jealous when he spoke to the finance minister. He was so good in his role he almost had her convinced.

What would it be like to be engaged to him? Fabulous. She knew that without a doubt. He would lavish attention on the woman he chose for wife. She sighed softly, wishing she could imagine herself as his wife. To share their lives, to have his support of her art would be beyond wonderful.

Suddenly she was jealous of the unknown woman who would one day see past his own barriers and find a way into his heart. She would be the one to receive his kisses and caresses. She would be the one to share nights of passion and days of happiness. Ella could see them living on the estate his grandmother had left him—with a half dozen children running around, laughing and shouting with glee.

"Are you all right?" Khalid asked.

Ella hoped he couldn't read minds. "Of course. Just tired."

"So no walk along the beach tonight?"

Did he enjoy their shared time as much as she did? Unlikely. He probably liked walking and didn't mind if she accompanied him. The darkness hid all things. Was that special for him?

"Not tonight." She'd have to decide how to handle this. Everything was complicated. She was drawing closer and closer to Khalid and while he seemed to enjoy her company, she wasn't sure he was seeing her as anything but the woman who leased his cottage. Who was an impediment to his selling the estate.

When they reached home, Ella dashed into the cottage even before Khalid got out of the car. She closed the door and hurried to her bedroom, already unfastening the necklace. She didn't want to be thinking about kisses and caresses and dark nights alone with the man. He tantalized her with things she had thought lost forever.

Her life with Alexander had been all she ever expected. And when he died, she thought a part of her had, as well. But could she find another life, one unexpected but fulfilling nevertheless? Khalid was so different from Alexander it was amazing to her she could think of him in such terms. Alexander had been kind, gentle, thoughtful. Khalid was exciting, provocative, dynamic and intense. Yet she felt more alive around him than any other time in life. Colors seemed more vivid. Experiences savored longer. Nebulous longing rose, solidifying into a desire to be with him.

She put the pearls on the dresser and peeked out of her curtains. She could only see a small corner of the main villa from this room. Nothing to show Khalid had gone to the study or his bedroom. Or, would he take a walk on the beach tonight without her. That first night he'd not known she was there. Did he often swim alone after dark?

Suddenly she felt daring. Taking off her dress, she slipped on her bathing suit. Just maybe she'd go swimming in the dark. So much the better if he were there, as well.

Pulling on a cover-up, she hurried to the beach. The moon was waning, but still cast enough light over the beach to see a pile of material near the water. Scanning the sea, she thought she saw him swimming several yards offshore. Smiling at the thought of reading his mind, she dropped her own things by his and plunged into the warm water. It felt energizing and buoyant. Swimming toward him, she saw when he first realized she was there.

Treading water, he waited for her to get closer.

"What are you doing here?" he asked.

"I didn't want a walk. But a swim sounded nice," she replied. When she drew closer, she also tread water. "Do you swim every night?"

"Not every night. But many. I like it."

"Always after dark."

"Easier that way."

"How far do the scars go?"

Khalid stared at her for a long moment, then motioned her closer. When she paddled nearer, he reached out and caught one hand, drawing her up to him. Tracing the ruined skin down his right side, he tried to gauge her reaction in the dim light. Most women would be horrified. The scarring went across part of his chest and his upper arm. It no longer pained him, except to look at.

She kicked closer and brushed against him. Instant heat. It had been a long time since he'd slept with a woman. He was already attracted to Ella, but her touch sent him over the edge. He pulled her into his arms and kissed her, kicking gently to keep them both above water. Then he forgot everything except the feel of her in his arms. Her silky skin was warm in the water. Her hair floated on the surface, tangling with one hand as he held her closer. Her kiss spiked desire for more—much more.

The water covering them both brought him back to sanity.

She broke away and laughed, shaking her head. Water flew from her hair, splashing against him.

"Romantic," she said, pushing up against him again, wrapping her arms around his neck. "Unless you drown us." Her lips were close, then she brushed against him, teasing, tantalizing. She trailed light kisses along his lips, across to his left cheek, then to his right one. He pulled away.

"Don't," she said softly, cupping his ruined cheek with her hand. "Khalid, you make me forget everything. Don't pull away and bring reality back. This is a night just for us." Again she kissed him and this time he didn't hold back. He relished the feel of her in his arms, the length of her petite body pressed against his, banishing the loneliness of the last few years. He felt more aware of every aspect of life than ever before. All because she kissed him.

They were both breathing hard when the kiss ended. Khalid wanted to sweep her ashore and make love to her on the sand. He even began swimming that way, but stopped when he realized she was swimming parallel to the shore.

"It's a glorious night for a swim," she called out, swimming away with each stroke.

He'd been fooling himself. He knew what women saw when they looked at him. The night hid the scars, but light would expose them for the awful things they were. He'd take what he could get and ignore the vague yearning for even more.

He swiftly caught up with her.

"I thought you said it was unsafe to swim after dark," he said, keeping pace with her.

"If one is alone, it is. I'm not alone, I have you."

Together they swam along the coast, only turning back when Khalid began to fear she would tire out before reaching their things. Ella seemed as full of energy at the end as when they started. And once their towels and clothes were in sight, she stopped and tread water again. Curious, he stopped, too, and was greeted with a wave of water. A tap on his shoulder as he shook his head to clear the water from his eyes was followed immediately by "You're it!"

Ella dove under the water and for a moment he didn't know which direction she'd gone. When she resurfaced some yards away, he struck out. She laughed and dove beneath the water again. This time she appeared near the shore. Khalid laughed and reversed direction. By the time he reached her, she was already standing and hurrying up the shallow shelf to reach the beach.

Snatching up her towel, she wrung out her hair and then dried herself, all the while moving back, watching him.

"Dangerous games you play, Ella," he said, walking steadily toward her.

"It was fun." She laughed, but kept backing away.

Khalid pursued, gaining ground with every step.

"It was. But you don't play fair. Why leave the water?"

"I'm tired. That was a long swim." She giggled and stepped back. "I'm leaving my cover-up behind," she said.

"Come and get it."

"I'm not that dumb."

"No one said you were dumb," he said, reaching out to catch her.

She laughed but came willingly into his arms. "Khalid, you are the dangerous one," she said just before he kissed her.

The next morning Khalid stood on the veranda on the side of the house nearest Ella's cottage, looking toward the sea. He'd had breakfast early, checked in with the office and debated taking a consulting job that had been offered or sending his second in command. The time away would give him some perspective. Last night replayed itself like an endless film. He should have pushed for more. But his respect for Ella wouldn't allow him to press for more than she wanted. And it appeared as if kisses were the limit of her willingness.

He should take the job.

"The maid said I'd find you here," Rashid said behind him.

Khalid turned. His casual clothes contrasted with the Western suit and tie that Rashid wore.

"And she was right. What's up?" he asked his brother.

"Just came by to see you." Rashid pulled a chair away from the small table and removed his suit jacket, hanging it across the back. Sitting, he looked at his brother, eyebrows raised in silent question.

Khalid came across and pulled out another chair, sitting opposite his twin.

"I heard from an oil company in Egypt. They want us to come vet their new well."

"Are you going?" Rashid asked.

Khalid shrugged. "Don't know."

"You usually jump at foreign assignments."

"I've been to Egypt before."

"More than once. Maybe your new fiancée is keeping you closer to home."

"I don't need that from you. You know the entire thing escalated out of hand. Damn, I was only trying to help out my tenant. I told you."

Rashid smiled at that. "Right. Somehow I guess I forgot."

"Like you ever would. Is that why you're here? To rehash the entire affair?"

"Ah, you've moved on to an affair now."

"No, I have not. I stepped in to try to keep her family from pressuring her. Once her brother leaves, end of story." He rose and paced to the edge of the stone floor, then turned back.

"What would you have done?" he asked.

"The same thing, I'm sure. Actually I came by to see if you were at all interested in her. She seemed devoted to you last night. Maybe this could develop into something good."

The scene in the water and on the sand flashed into mind. Khalid wasn't sharing that with his brother, twin bond or not. "An act." Had it all been an act? He hoped not.

"A suggestion only—" Rashid began.

"What?" Khalid felt his barriers rise.

"Give the relationship a chance. She's a nice woman. Talented, pretty. She loved the country, gave up her family for her first husband. Is loyal."

"Makes her sound like a dog or something."

"I'm trying to get through to you that not everyone is Damara. She was shallow and superficial and at the first setback fled. In retrospect, you got a lucky break. What if you were married and she couldn't stay for the long haul."

"I'm sure she felt she caught the lucky break." He turned back to gaze at the sea, remembering the scene in the hospital—he so doped up because of the searing pain and the one person beside his twin he thought he could count on instead shredding their relationship. As he watched the water sparkle beneath the sun, that image was replaced with a scene from last night: Ella's splashing him and then laughing.

Ella kissing his damaged skin. Ella.

More than anything, he loved her laugh.

Scowling at his thoughts, he turned back to Rashid.

"I'm taking off. The job in Egypt will last a couple of weeks at least."

"Give my suggestion some thought."

"There's nothing like that between us. She needed help. I gave it. She's locked into the cottage legally—nothing I can do to get rid of her before the lease expires. We'll muddle through. Not everyone is like you. Enjoy what you have with Bethanne. Don't try to find a happy ending here."

Rashid rose, slung his jacket over his shoulder and looked at his brother. "Okay. I gave it a shot. Your life is yours. Just don't screw it up any more than you can help."

Khalid laughed. "Thanks for the vote of confidence."

Once Rashid left, he went to the study and called his office. "Make the arrangements…I'll leave this afternoon," he told his assistant.

Ella had expected to hear from Khalid, but he had not sent word for her to come to the main house, nor visited. She kept busy sorting the glass pieces, pleased to study some and find they were better quality than she remembered. Stepping back a bit helped her gain perspective. The piece might not have attained her vision for it, but it was still good.

She had early pieces grouped together. Later ones separated. Definitely an improvement in the later ones. Maybe she should have a seconds sale—knock off the prices of the earlier less-than-perfect pieces. But only after she had started selling.

The pictures she had taken in the house looked great. She'd see about contacting a printer to make them into a booklet.

As much as she tried to concentrate on work, she was on tenterhooks for Khalid. Last night had been amazing. She'd hated to go home alone.

But this morning—nothing.

Finally she took a light lunch on her veranda. Maybe she should just go over and find out what he was doing. Or if he had gone into his office today. It was a workday after all. She'd gotten used to his being available whenever she wanted. How spoiled was that?

She refused to hang around like some lovelorn idiot. She had her own life. If it coincided with his once in a while, so much the better.

The day seemed to last forever. She cleaned her small cottage. Did a load of laundry, even cooked dinner which was not something she often did. Finally—it was dark. Normally she walked after eleven, but even though it was scarcely past nine, she couldn't wait.

She headed for the beach. No sign of Khalid. She knew she was early. Slowly she walked to the water's edge. She'd wait.

Which wasn't easy to do when every nerve clamored for him. She sat on the warm sand, the water lapping the beach a few feet from her toes. Picking up handfuls of sand, she let it slip between her fingers. Last night had been surreal. One part at the party Khalid's mother had given. The other—the real part—had been swimming in the warm sea. She smiled remembering how much fun she'd had. How much she liked being with Khalid.

Glancing over her shoulder, she wondered what time it was. How long before he came?

CHAPTER NINE

THE next morning Ella headed to her studio, firmly intending to push all thoughts of a certain sheikh from her mind. It did not take a two-by-four hitting her on the side of the head to get it. He had not shown at the beach last night. When she finally gave up and returned home, all lights in the main house were off. Had he gone out?

It didn't matter. He was merely her landlord. Nothing else. She would not let herself believe there was something special between them. If there was any special feelings, they were obviously one-sided—on her side.

Now she was going to focus on her career and leave all men out of the equation until she was firmly on the path to money. Next place she lived, she wanted to own. To be able to come and go when she pleased and not worry about someone trying to evict her because of their own agenda.

Firing up the oven, she chose the glass shards carefully, then melted the different colors, picking them up one at a time on her wand. Slowly the glasses melded and when she began shaping the blob, she was pleased with the greens and blues and turquoise that began to show through. Taking her time, concentrating on the task at hand, Ella fashioned a large flat plate.

It was early afternoon when she was satisfied and put the

art piece in her annealer. Stretching to work out the kinks in knotted muscles, she went to the cottage for lunch. For the first time in hours her mind flipped to Khalid. Where was he? Despite her vow to refrain from thinking about him, now she could think of nothing else.

She wished he'd stroll around the corner of the veranda on which she sat and smile that lopsided smile that crinkled the skin around his eyes and caused her to catch her breath. Saunter over and sit casually in the chair, his dark eyes sending shivers down her spine as she lost herself in them.

She was becoming too involved with the man. He'd made it clear he was not interested in any relationship—short or long-term—and she'd do best to remember that.

Yet when she remembered the fun they'd had playing in the water, the drugging kisses that had her clamoring for more, it was hard to believe. Didn't actions speak louder than words? His actions showed he liked her. She wanted to spend more time with him. It was the first time since Alexander's death she'd had such an interest in anyone. Khalid was special. She felt stirred up every time they were together. When apart, she longed to see him again. Even if he never did more than talk about his work, she relished the moments together.

Frowning, she sat back in her chair and gazed toward the sea. She had a small glimpse of it from this place on her veranda. Normally it soothed. Today, however, she was more worried than before. She could not be falling for the man. She could list a dozen reasons why that would be such a bad idea—starting with she could get her heart broken.

Yet, testing her feelings as she might test a toothache, she had to admit there were a lot of similarities to falling in love. She wanted to be with him. Felt alive in his presence. Knew he was very special. Yet she didn't believe he was perfect. He could be short-tempered at times. And his idea that no one would ever find him attractive because of the scar was dumb. Sure, it was disfiguring, but he was more than a swatch of skin on the right side of his face and neck.

When he spoke to her, she felt like she was the only person in the world. The flare of attraction wasn't dying down. His kisses spiked her senses like nothing else had. And his protective view was intriguing. Her own family didn't feel that obligation, yet he'd stepped in without being asked to try to thwart her brother's goal.

She leaned back in the chair, trying to relax. She should just go along with things—pretend to be engaged and see what happened. Only it was hard to play that part when half the couple had vanished.

Perhaps vanished was a bit strong, she argued. He had not come to the beach last night nor stopped by today. He had no need to. Except she wanted him to.

She jumped up and cleared her dishes. After rinsing them off, she changed into a cool sundress, brushed her hair and headed for the main house.

Jalilah answered the door to her ring.

"Madame Ponti," she said politely.

"Is His Excellency in?" Ella asked.

"No. He has flown to Egypt."

"Egypt?" Ella hadn't expected that. "When will he be home?"

"I cannot say. He took a large suitcase, so I suspect a few days at least."

Ella thanked the maid and turned to return home. Walking slowly through the garden, she wondered why he hadn't told her. She almost went back to see if he had responded to a fire. That would cause every moment to be precious as he packed and left and he might not think to let his fake fiancée know of his plans. But the maid had said he had a large suitcase and might be gone awhile. No sense of urgency in her tone. Had he just left?

Ella debated calling Bethanne to ask if she knew what Khalid was doing, but decided she would not.

Still at the front of the main house, Ella turned when a car drove down the driveway. She recognized her brother even before he got out of the vehicle.

"Ella," he said.

"Antonio. What are you doing here?"

"I came to speak to Khalid al Harum. I've spoken with father and he entrusts me to handle things. Are you visiting, as well?"

"What things?" Did he not know she lived on the estate? If not, she didn't plan to tell him. She was more interested in what her father wanted Antonio to handle.

"Marriage settlements," Antonio said after a moment's hesitation.

"Dowery?" she asked, walking closer to her brother.

He looked uncomfortable. "Not exactly."

"Exactly what? I've moved away from home. I was married several years to another man. I can't imagine why there would be any talk of settlements unless you plan to see if Khalid would give something to get out of the mess Giacomo caused. Which I absolutely forbid."

"Forbid? You can't do that—it's between me and your future husband."

"If you even speak to him about that, I'll refuse to marry him," she said recklessly. She would not put Khalid in such a situation. She was embarrassed to even think of her family asking the man for money. It would be bad enough if they were madly in love and truly engaged. But this was humiliating. She would not let Antonio do it.

He studied her for a moment. "If you don't marry him, you can come home and marry someone else."

"I may never marry again," she said, stepping up to her brother and tapping his chest with her forefinger. "But I sure will never marry someone I don't love. Giacomo got himself into this mess, let him get himself out of it. I am not a pawn to be used like in feudal days. I can't believe even our father would consider such a thing."

"Your family needs you," Antonio said, capturing her hand and pushing it away. "The sheikh has more money than anyone we know. He wouldn't miss a few thousand euros. Let him help us."

"No! I mean it, if you talk to him about this, I'll vanish and it'll be years before you find me next time."

Her brother stared at her for a long moment. "We need help, Ella," he said softly. "Where else can we go? We cannot make it known in Italy or the business will suffer. If we don't get an infusion of cash soon, it will come out. A company in dire straits loses business which could help it get out of trouble. Then takeovers are bandied about. The business has been in our family for generations, for centuries. Would you see all that gone?"

"No, of course not. Look for other ways. Mother's jewelry—"

"Most already copied in paste and the originals sold."

That surprised Ella. Things were worse than she envisioned.

"Is Giacomo still gambling?" Ella asked, horrified at the lengths her family had already gone. She felt herself softening to them. They had practically excommunicated her when she married Alexander. But they were still her family. The problem seemed larger than she'd realized from what Antonio said.

"No. But the fallout is lasting."

"Go home, Antonio. If I can, I'll send some money." It was too bad her trust fund was not available until she turned thirty. Maybe she could borrow against that. Or she could see about selling some of her artwork. Madame al Harum had thought it had merit. Would others?

He looked at the house.

"Khalid is not home. He had a business trip to Egypt. I don't know when he'll be back."

Antonio nodded. “Very well, then. Come visit, Ella. Your mother misses you.”

“One day.” It was hard to overlook the obstacles her parents had thrown in her way when she had married Alexander. But she knew her husband never wanted her to be parted from her family. He would not want her holding on to wrongs of the past.

She watched Antonio drive away and began to walk back to the cottage. Alexander would not have wanted her to be a widow all her life, either. He had loved life, loved her and would always want the best for her. Including another husband who could bring her happiness.

Wistfully, she wished Khalid had the same thoughts.

It was amazing the absence of one slightly standoffish man made. As the days went by, Ella gradually resumed her former routine. Working during the day, long walks after dark. Always alone. Only her enjoyment of being alone had been disturbed. She missed Khalid. Which only went to reinforce her belief she had to get on with her life and not grow attached to him.

The bright spot in the week was a visit by Bethanne. She was driving a new car Rashid had just bought for her and wanted to take Ella for a spin.

“It’s no fun to have a brand-new convertible and have no one to share it with,” she said as the two began driving away from the estate.

“And Rashid doesn’t want to go?”

“He has one of his own. I’m sure he’s not as enchanted with the convertible as I am. Isn’t it great?” She drove to the coast highway and flew along the sea. Ella glanced at the speedometer once and then quickly looked away. Obviously the pilot in Bethanne had no qualms about flying low. Instead of worrying, Ella relaxed and enjoyed the ride. The blue of the

Persian Gulf was on their right. The road was straight and smooth. The wind through her hair made her feel carefree and happy. With sudden insight, she realized she was happy. In this day, in this moment. Worries were gone. Plans and projects on hold. Nothing held her back. She could enjoy this time and not feel sad or guilty.

It had taken a long time, but she knew she was ready to embrace life again. To find all it had to offer and enjoy every speck of the journey—even the heartbreaks and hardships.

"You're quiet," Bethanne said with a smile. "What are you thinking?"

Ella told her and Bethanne nodded. "I know the feeling. But I have an excuse. I'm in love. The colors in the sea seem brighter because Rashid's in my life. The flowers more delicate and lovely, especially when I'm in the garden with him. But I bet coming out of grieving is like falling in love with life again. I'm so sorry for your loss, but time does heal wounds. I was so devastated when I learned my dad was really dead. I grieved both before and after I found out. Then I realized he had loved life. He had done exactly as he had wanted throughout and had no regrets at the end. That's what I want."

"No regrets?"

"No regrets and feeling I lived life to the fullest. Which means even more than I expected before I met Rashid. He's so fabulous."

Ella laughed. "So says a woman in love."

"I know, and I'm so proud of him I could burst, and happy he loves me as much." She flicked Ella a glance. "How is Khalid these days?"

She gazed at the sea. "I wouldn't know. He's on a business trip."

"Still in Egypt?" Bethanne asked.

Ella nodded. "I have no idea when he'll be back."

"I'll ask Rashid if you like."

She hesitated. She didn't want to make demands or have him think she had any expectations. But she did want to know how he was, what he was doing, when she'd get to see him again. Ella almost groaned. She had it bad.

"Please." Khalid need never know she'd asked after him. When he returned, she'd play it cool, not going for walks, not expecting him to spend time with her. But for now—she wanted any information she could get.

Trying to change the subject, Ella asked about how much flying Bethanne was doing these days and the subject of Khalid was dropped.

That evening Ella was summoned to the main house by the maid for a phone call. It was Bethanne.

"Rashid said Khalid is still in Egypt. He called him to see when he was coming home. Turns out he's thinking about visiting some of the oil fields in the interior of Quishari before coming home. Stalling do you think?"

"Why would he?" Ella said, her heart dropping at the news he would be gone even longer.

"I could fly you inland, if you like," Bethanne said.

Ella blinked.

"You know, you could get some great ideas from seeing some of the nomadic people and the colors they use in weaving cloth. And there is an austere beauty of the desert that I find enchanting at all times of the day, from cool sunrise to the spectacular sunsets."

"It's tempting."

"I'll ask my darling fiancé if we can go tomorrow. That way, when Khalid shows up, you'll already be there."

Ella wanted to protest, but she closed her mouth before the words would spill out. She longed to be with him again. Here was a chance to see him in the kind of environments he worked. Not in fire suppression, but as a consultant to oil fields. She'd never seen an oil pump and had only the vaguest idea of how everything worked from discovery to gasoline in her car. It would be educational.

She laughed at her foolishness. She was going to see Khalid! "You're on. And tell Rashid thank you very much!"

The next morning Bethanne picked Ella up and drove them to the airport in her new car.

The gleaming jet sat in solitary splendor in a private section of the airport. Service personnel scrambled around, making sure the jet was ready to fly. Ella watched with fascination as Bethanne changed her personality into a competent pilot, double-checking all aspects of the plane before being satisfied. She invited Ella into the cockpit, and talked as she went through the preflight routine. In only moments they were airborne. Ella leaned forward to better see the landscape below them. The crowded developed land near the sea gradually grew less and less populated until they were flying over desert sand. In the distance, toward the west, she saw hills, valleys and mountains. The flight didn't take long, and went even faster fascinated as she was by the sights below.

She knew Bethanne had been half joking when talking about getting new ideas, but Ella already had a bunch of them crowding in her mind. She had brought her sketchbook, but it was in her bag. Her fingers itched to get down the ideas. She would love to capture the feeling of the burning sand, the starkness of the open land. The contrast with the sea and distant mountains.

"Nice, huh?" Bethanne said.

"Beautiful. It's so lush where I'm from in Italy. And I've lived in Alkaahdar since arriving. I had no idea the desert could be beautiful."

"It's not to all. But I love it. Rashid tells me if I wish, he will build us a villa by an oasis surrounded by endless desert.

I'm still too new at everything in Quishari to wish to change a thing. But the thought tantalizes."

"I think I should like that, as well. As long as there was enough water at the oasis."

They circled the town of Quraim Wadi Samil on the edge of an oil field and then Bethanne landed.

Ella watched the pumps on the field with their steady rise and fall as they made their approach. She regretted losing them from view as they landed.

"That's where Khalid will be tomorrow," Bethanne said. "Rashid arranged for someone to pick us up and drive us to the hotel. Once I know Khalid's arrived, I'll return home."

"Stranding me here?" Ella said. She hadn't expected that.

"Hey, he's good for helping a damsel in distress."

Ella laughed, growing nervous. What if he was more annoyed than anxious to help? And she wasn't exactly stranded. She'd be able to take a bus back to the capital city, or even one of the daily commercial planes.

Bethanne arranged for them to go to the hotel that Khalid would use when he arrived. She and Ella checked in and agreed to meet for lunch, then take a short tour of the town.

By dinnertime, they'd both showered, changed and were sitting in the lobby.

Bethanne watched the double doors to the street while Ella sat with her back to them.

"He just walked in," Bethanne said, smiling. She looked at Ella. "Go say hi and ask him to join us for dinner. We'll want to hear all about Egypt."

Ella rose and turned, her heart kicking up a notch when she saw him. He wore a dark suit and white shirt with blue and silver tie. He looked fantastic. She took a breath and crossed the lobby, her eyes never leaving him. She saw when he turned slightly and saw her. For a moment she thought she saw welcome in his eyes. Then he closed down.

"Ella, is everything all right?" he asked, crossing the short distance to meet her.

"Everything is fine. Did you have a good trip to Egypt?"

Khalid's eyes narrowed slightly, then he looked beyond her and saw Bethanne. She raised one hand in a short wave and grinned.

Khalid looked back at Ella. He hadn't expected to see her. One reason he'd decided to stop off at Quraim Wadi Samil was to delay returning home. But she was standing right in front of him, her eyes dark and mysterious, shadowed with a hint of uncertainty. He clenched his fists at his sides to keep from reaching out and pulling her into a hug that he might not ever let go.

"We wondered if you'd like to join us for dinner," she said quickly. "Tell us about your trip."

"You didn't come all this way to have dinner and hear about my trip," he said.

"Actually I'm getting new ideas for more glass pieces. You should see the sketches I've done since I've arrived. I'm hoping to go to the oil fields tomorrow." She stopped abruptly.

"With whom?" he asked, feeling a flare of jealousy that someone would show her around.

"You?" she said.

Khalid relaxed a fraction. His voluntary exile for the last week hadn't done anything to kill his desire for this woman. Now she was right here.

"I don't usually eat dinner in restaurants," he said slowly.

She nodded. "I know, eating alone is awkward in public places. But you'll have me and Bethanne so it'll be fun."

Fun? The stares of the other customers? The whispers that ran rampant as speculation abounded?

"I'm glad to see you again," she was saying. "I've missed you at night when I walk along the beach." Her eyes were shining with more happiness than he'd ever seen before. For another smile, he'd face the horror of others at the restaurant.

He'd make sure he was seated by a wall, with the damaged side of his face away from other diners.

"I need to check in, then it will be my pleasure to escort two such lovely ladies to dinner."

She reached out and touched his arm, pulling her hand back quickly as if unsure of a welcome.

"We'll be waiting." With another smile, she turned and walked back to Bethanne.

Dinner did not prove to be the ordeal Khalid had expected. As if in one agreement, the seating went as he wanted. With fewer people having to see the scar, they were more ignored than he normally experienced. For the first time in years, he enjoyed dining out. The food was excellent. The conversation lively. The more he grew to know Bethanne, the more he understood his brother's love for the woman. Yet his eyes kept turning to Ella. She was feminine and sweet. He detected a difference but couldn't put his finger on it. Was she more confident? Had the sadness diminished around her eyes?

"So Rashid called and doesn't want me to wait until tomorrow to return home. I'm leaving right after dinner," Bethanne said.

Ella looked startled. Khalid watched her as she turned to the other woman. "I thought we'd stay a day so I can see everything here."

Bethanne looked at Khalid. "You can show her around, can't you? She wants to see an oil field. You could explain things. And show her the sunrise. I think the colors in the sky are amazing."

Khalid knew a setup when he saw one. But instead of arguing, he looked at Ella. Another day together suited him. "Fine. We'll watch the sunrise together, I'll take you to the oil fields."

"And see she gets home safely?" Bethanne said.

Amusement warred with irritation. He suspected this was not

Ella's plan but one of his soon to be sister-in-law's. Yet why not give in with good grace. He had to admit he'd missed Ella while in Egypt. More than once he'd seen something he'd wanted to share with her. Had almost called her a couple of times.

Dangerous territory, but he was a man who lived with danger. He liked being with her. There was no harm in that. It was only if he let himself dream of a future that could never be that he risked more than he wanted to pay.

Ella couldn't fall asleep after returning to her room. She was too much a night person to go to bed early. Yet Khalid had made no suggestion about spending time with her in the evening. Bethanne had now taken off for Alkaahdar. Ella sat at the window, watching the dark sky display the sparkles of lights from a million stars. There was no beach to walk along. It was too late to wander around town alone. There was nothing to do but think and that she didn't want to do.

She drew out her sketchpad, but instead of sketching various pieces of glass she wanted to try, she drew quick vignettes of Khalid—walking along the beach, swimming in the sea, leaning against his desk.

She also sketched him in traditional Arab robes, like he'd worn the first night she'd met him. She'd love to see him attired like that again. Did he wear the robes in the desert? Slowing in her drawing, she let her imagination drift as she thought about an oasis like Bethanne had talked of. What would it be like to have a small house in the scant shade of the palms surrounding a small pool of clear water? She envisioned a rooftop veranda that would provide a 360-degree view when the heat of the day dissipated. Quiet. Silent except for the wind sweeping across the sand. Sometimes the sand hummed in harmony. Would they feel cocooned together in a world apart?

She filled several pages with sketches, then tossed the

tablet aside. Restlessness was getting her nowhere. She had best go to bed and hope to fall asleep quickly. She'd spend tomorrow with Khalid.

He was waiting for her when she stepped into the lobby the next morning. She greeted him and joined him in the small restaurant attached to the hotel for breakfast. The croissants were hot, the jam her favorite—grape. The coffee was dark and aromatic. She sipped the rich beverage, trying not to stare. Khalid looked fabulous. His dark eyes met hers.

"Ready for the scenic tour?" he asked.

"Ready. I have a hat, sunscreen and a long-sleeved shirt to put on at midday to protect against the sun."

"I have hired a Jeep for our use, and stocked it with a cooler and plenty of cold water. Even lunch."

She smiled in anticipation. "Lovely, a picnic, just the two of us."

"I know a place you'll love," he said.

She would love anyplace he showed her. Looking away before she made a fool of herself, she finished her meal.

In no time they were in the open Jeep, weaving their way through the streets of the old town. The sandstone walls blended with the color of the desert. Bright spots of blues and red punctuated the monotonous walls. Soon the crowded streets fell behind. The homes were farther and farther apart until they were left behind and she and Khalid continued straight for the oil field she could see in the distance.

Fascinated by the acres of oil pumpers slowly rising and falling as they drew the oil from deep in the ground, she ignored what was behind her, trying to see what was ahead.

"Amazing. How did anyone know there was oil here?" she asked. There was nothing in the sparse desert to differentiate it from any other area.

"Geologists can find it anywhere. My father is the one who started this field. For Bashiri Oil, of course."

She looked around. "Was the town this big when the oil was discovered?"

"No. First the drilling and now the activity of the wells boosted the population considerably. It was a small, sleepy oasis way back when oil was first discovered. Inhabited by a few families who had lived here for generations. It was on the trade routes and the migration of nomadic people, so this was a resting place for caravans."

"Now it's another city, though small. With an airport."

Khalid laughed. "With an airport. Did Bethanne really bring you here to get ideas for your glass?"

"That was one reason," she said, staring straight ahead.

She caught a glimpse of him from the corner of her eye when he looked at her. "And another?"

"To see you."

He didn't respond, so Ella looked at him. "Surprised?"

"A bit."

"I think we need to get straight on what we're doing," she said.

He looked at her again, then back to the road. "We're going to see the wells, then have a picnic."

"About this fake engagement. I think Antonio has finally returned home. That should be the end of that matter. Interesting, don't you think, my parents are not against my being engaged to you a stranger, but objected to my marriage to Alexander whom they had known for years."

"Money is important to a lot of people. You are not one of them," he said.

"I think people are much more important. And experiences in life. I'm enjoying today. I have never gone very far into the desert. And I've never been to an oil field." She gave him a shy look, "Nor with a sheikh."

"Hey, I'm a man like any other."

Oh, no, she thought privately. *You are unlike anyone else in the world.* For a moment she wanted to reach over and touch him, grasp his hand and hold on and never let go. Her heart beat faster and colors seemed brighter. She loved him. Closing her eyes for a moment, she wondered when it had happened. How it could have happened. And what she could do to make sure he never knew.

Khalid was the perfect guide when they reached the oil field. He introduced her to the foreman and then gave her an abbreviated tour, explaining how the wells were drilled, capped and put into production. He even told her how something minor could go wrong and cause a fire. She had a healthy respect for the men who worked the fields, their lives in danger if any one of a myriad of things went wrong.

After their visit to the oil field, he drove them straight into the desert. It was just past noon. The sun glared overhead. The air was hot, the breeze from the moving car not doing much to cool. Ella had donned her hat and long-sleeved shirt and was sweltering. She was about to suggest they give up this expedition and return to the air-conditioned comfort of the hotel when she saw the faint suggestion of green in the distance. She stared at the spot gradually seeing the palms as they drove close. A cluster of trees offering a respite to the monotonous brown of the sand.

"The oasis?" she asked, pointing to the spot.

"Yes. A small wadi that holds enough water for a few humans or animals, it can't support a settlement. But there is plenty of water for the trees and shrubs that grow around it. And it provides a nice shady spot in a hot afternoon."

Ella studied the contrast of the golden-brown of the desert with the surprise of green from the trees. It gave her an idea for a new art piece. Could she do a palm, leaning slightly as if wishing to touch the earth? Maybe a small collage with blue glass at the base surrounded by a smoky golden glass with the palm rising.

Khalid stopped in the shade and turned off the engine. For a moment only silence reigned. Ella felt the heat encompass them, then a slight cooling from the shade. She turned and smiled at him.

"It's beautiful here. I know now why Bethanne says she'd like a home in the desert with water nearby. It would be lovely. I could live in such a place."

"Sometimes when things get too much, I come here for a few days." Khalid studied the water, the pond a scant four feet in diameter. The palms were spread out, their roots able to find enough moisture to support them even some distance from the pool.

"Surprisingly the water is cool," he said.

"In this heat?" she asked.

"Come."

He got out of the Jeep and waited for her at the front. When she joined him, he reached over to take her hand, leading her to the water's edge. They sat on the warm sand. Ella trailed her fingers in the water.

"It is cool!" she said in amazement. The water felt silky and refreshing. "How did you find this place?"

"Exploring when I was a kid. Rashid and I spent lots of time exploring while my dad spent time in the town. We learned later it was to visit a woman who had had a child by him."

Ella looked at him in surprise.

He looked back. "We never met her. She died, the daughter. My father's only daughter. He kept her hidden from my mother, understandably. She died in a plane crash that claimed Bethanne's father's life. My father died only days later—we think of a broken heart. Rashid and I haven't mentioned it around Mother."

"Does she know?"

"We don't know. But out of respect we have not brought it up. If she does, it must hurt her and if she doesn't, we don't want to have her learn about it at this late date."

Ella nodded, understanding. She wished her family was as loving and concerned for each other instead of always thinking of money and how to expand the vineyard or protect the family name.

"Your mother is lucky to have you two," she said wistfully. Would she ever have a child? A strong son who would look like his father? Or a beautiful little girl with dark eyes and a sparkle that telegraphed the mischief she might get into?

CHAPTER TEN

THE afternoon was pleasant in the shade. Khalid had brought blankets to spread on the sand. The picnic lunch was delicious. Ella ate with relish. The cool water from the pool completed the meal. Afterward, Khalid made sure the blankets were in the shade and lay down. Closing his eyes, he looked completely relaxed.

Ella watched him for a time, growing drowsy. Finally she lay down and closed her eyes. The quiet and peace of the oasis enveloped her and before long, she slept.

When she awoke, Khalid was nowhere to be seen. The Jeep was parked where he'd left it so she knew he hadn't gone far. She splashed cool water on her face and then rose, folding the blankets and putting them in the back of the Jeep.

"Khalid?" she called.

He appeared a moment later from behind a sand dune. "Just checking things out," he said, walking back to the shady area. "Sandstorms can wreak havoc in this area. That's what brought down the plane my father's daughter was on. Yet time and again, this oasis reappears. I was trying to figure out why. Ready to return to town?"

Ella nodded, feeling reluctant to end the afternoon. She looked around, imprinting every bit of the scene in her mind. It would forever be special—because of Khalid.

The sooner they were back among others, the sooner she could get her emotions under control. She really wanted to stay. To camp out under the stars. To share feelings and thoughts on the vastness of the desert and the beauty found despite the harshness.

To tell him he was loved.

That she could not do. She hurried to the Jeep and jumped in.

Quraim Wadi Samil seemed to shimmer in the late sunshine as heat waves distorted the air. They drove into the town and straight to the hotel. Ella felt wrung-out with the heat. She would relish the coolness of the hotel. She began to long for the cottage by the sea. At least there seemed to always be a breeze by the Gulf.

"Dinner at seven?" Khalid asked as they entered the lobby.

"That's perfect." It would give her time to shower and change and cool down.

Her room was spacious with little furnishings to clutter the space. She lay down for a few moments, wondering if there could be any future between her and Khalid. His fake engagement had been to help her out, made public by the minister. Since he already had it in for Khalid's family, they dare not end the engagement so soon without negative gossip. Yet the longer it lasted, the more people would expect to see them together, and expect plans for a wedding to be forthcoming.

She wished she was planning a wedding with Khalid. She would so love to spend the rest of her life with him. It would be very different from the life she had before. Khalid had a stronger intensity with life than she was used to. Was it because he flirted with death whenever dealing with oil fires?

The thought of him being injured again had her in a panic. Would he consider not doing that in the future?

As if they had a future.

Ella rose and went to take her shower. She had some serious thinking to do. She could not bear to fall more in love with the man and then have fate snatch him away. Maybe it was time to consider going back to Italy and finding a life she could live there. She'd already lost one man she loved. She could not go through that again.

At least if she left, she could always remember Khalid as he was today. And hope to never hear of his death. As long as he was living in the world, she could find contentment. Couldn't she?

Khalid met Ella at the elevator when she stepped off in the lobby at seven. He had been tempted to go to her room, but had mustered what patience he could to wait for her in a public place. She'd looked perfect that afternoon sleeping in the shade at the oasis. He'd wanted to touch her cheeks, faintly pink. Her hair looked silky and soft. He had touched her hair before and knew its texture.

He was playing a fool's game, tempting fate by spending time with her. What if he became attached? He knew what he could expect from life. He'd made his peace with being alone years ago. His work was interesting and challenging. Especially when fighting fires. He liked the men he worked with. Liked being consulted by Rashid from time to time.

But he couldn't change reality. A scarred and bitter man was not going to appeal to a pretty woman like Ella. He'd help her out because he disliked the way her brother was handling things. And her family sounded totally unlike his. Despite the scarring, his family rallied around when needed.

He moved away from the pillar where he'd been leaning when she stepped out. Her look of expectancy touched him. When she spotted him, she smiled. Khalid felt it like a punch in the gut. It always made him feel whole again. She didn't seem freaked out by the scar. He still remembered the night she had cupped his cheeks, touching the damaged skin without revulsion. He'd never forget it.

"I thought I wouldn't want to eat again after that lavish lunch," she said as she hurried over to meet him. "But now that I've cooled down, I'm famished."

"Then let's hope they have enough food to fill you up."

She laughed. He almost groaned. Her laugher was like water sparkling and gurgling over rocks in the high country. Light and airy and pleasing. He wished he could hear it all his life.

"So tomorrow we return home?" she asked as they walked to the restaurant.

"Yes. We'll summon a plane if you like."

"I'd love to see the country between here and the coast, but not in a hot Jeep like today. It was fine for a short foray into the desert, but for the long drive home, I'd like more comfort."

"Your wish is my command," he said. He did wish he could do anything for her she wanted. An air-conditioned car would be easy. Could he help with selling her artwork? He knew nothing about that. But his mother did. If she'd just warm up to Ella a little, she'd be a tremendous help.

He had a life-size picture of that ever happening. Rashid was head over heels in love with Bethanne, and his mother still chided him for not seeking the woman she had wanted him to marry. He wasn't head over heels in love with Ella. But he liked being with her. Liked hearing her take on things. It gave him a different perspective.

He loved hearing her talk period. Her voice carried a trace of accent. Her Arabic was quite fluent, but softer than most women's. He liked it.

"Khalid!"

He looked at her.

"What?"

"I asked how long it would take to drive back to the coast. Where were you?" She peered up at him.

"Woolgathering. It takes about eight hours. It's a long and boring drive. The road is straight as a stick and there's nothing but sand and scrub bushes as far as the eye can see. We can do it, but I'd rather fly home and spend the afternoon at the beach."

"That does sound nice."

The maître d' appeared and showed them to a secluded table. He presented the menus with a flourish then quietly bowed away.

"No argument? I thought you wanted to drive home," he said.

"Well, you've obviously been across the desert and if it looks all the same, maybe I don't need to experience it for eight hours. You can take me on another trip to the desert if I need more inspiration," she replied, looking at the menu.

"Maybe."

She looked up and grinned. "We are supposed to be engaged, remember?"

"I thought you wanted to talk about that," he said. He had not planned for things to get complicated when he'd told her brother they were engaged. How was he to know it would come out and his mother would make a big production about it?

"So I do. How do we get out of it?"

He stared at her—realizing for the first time he did not want to get out of it. He could understand her haste in ending the agreement. Hadn't his fiancée tossed him over because of the scar? But he wanted Ella to pretend a bit longer.

"We can say we fought on this trip and the deal is off," he said slowly.

She looked at him thoughtfully. "So whose fault was it?"

He met her gaze, almost smiling. "Does it matter?"

"People will ask. And if they don't, they will speculate."

"Have it be mine. It doesn't matter."

"Of course it does," she said passionately. "If you break it off, that's not very nice of you. And if I do, that doesn't reflect well on me."

"So I play the villain. It won't impact my life."

She shook her head slowly. "Not fair. You tried to help me

out. And I appreciate it. Antonio would still be here trying to coerce me back to Italy if you hadn't."

"So if I can't break it off and you can't, we don't." Was that the solution? Keep the engagement going long enough for her to feel more comfortable around him. Would she ever see beyond the exterior to what he thought and felt? Could she ever fall in love with him?

Unlikely. She still loved her dead husband. And he sounded like a paragon. Intellectual. A professor. What did an oil field roustabout have to offer in comparison? Granted he had position in the country, but she hadn't been very impressed being seen with a sheikh. He had money, but she came from money herself and was unimpressed. Not like other women he'd dated years ago. In fact, nothing seemed to impress Ella. That was one thing he loved—*liked*—about her. Money and stature and material items others were impressed by seemed inconsequential to her. She liked people—and it didn't seem to matter what they had or did; if they were of interest to her, she was friendly. If not, she was cordial. And someone who knew her well could easily tell the difference.

"So we stay engaged for a while longer," she mused. "Suits me." Her attention turned back to her menu.

Khalid felt a strange relief at her compliance. At least for a while longer, they continued being engaged.

And didn't engaged couples kiss?

The thought sprang to mind and wouldn't leave. He glanced at her. Her attention on the menu, he had ample time to study her lips, imaging them pressed against his again. Imagine feeling her soft body against his, passion rising between them.

If he didn't stop soon, he'd embarrass himself. He wanted dinner ordered eaten and over. They could walk to the square. The day's heat was abating. It would cool down soon as the desert did at night. They could find a secluded spot and watch the stars appear. And he'd hold her and kiss her and pretend for one night everything was normal.

It almost worked that way. They agreed to stroll through town when dinner finished. And when they found a parapet overlooking a city garden, they leaned against the still-warm stone and tried to make out the plants in the garden. But the light faded quickly. Turning, Ella looked up at the sky. "It's growing darker by the second. Soon a million stars will show."

He nodded and stepped closer, bringing her into his arms. "And you are more beautiful than all of them," he said, and kissed her.

Nothing was normal about that kiss. He felt every inch of his body come alive as he deepened the kiss. She responded like she had been waiting as long as he had. Her mouth was sweet and tender and provocative. Her curves met his muscles and tempted him even more. Her tongue danced with his, inflaming desire to a new level. The parapet disappeared. The stars were forgotten. There remained only the two of them, locked in an embrace that he wanted to go on forever.

Forgotten was the hideous scar that so repulsed others. Gone was the fear he would never find a woman to overlook the distortion even for a night. Khalid felt he was soaring. And he loved every moment.

If only it could last forever.

But it was not fair to Ella to kiss her when he'd coerced her into this engagement. Slowly he broke off the kiss, pleased when she followed him as he pulled back—obviously not wanting to end the kiss.

He was breathing hard when they parted. She was, too.

"Wow," she said, then turned. "I think we should go back to the hotel."

He wanted to agree—if she meant they'd go to his room. He wanted to make love to her so badly he ached from head to toe. Yet nothing she'd said or done gave him any indication that was where her thoughts were heading.

They turned and walked back toward the hotel.

"Did you arrange for Bethanne to pick us up tomorrow?" she asked as they came into the light spilling into the street from the hotel.

"She'll be here at nine."

"Good."

When they entered the lobby, Ella quickened her pace. She punched the elevator button almost savagely. She hadn't looked at him once since they came into the light.

"Ella, if you're upset—"

"Why would I be upset?" she asked in a brittle tone. "Engaged couples kiss all the time."

The elevator arrived and she stepped in, punching the number for her floor.

Khalid hesitated, then remained where he was. She did look up as the doors began to close.

"See you in the morning," he said before she was lost from view.

Turning, he went back outside. A long walk—like maybe to Alkaahdar—was required. He hoped he had his head on straight come morning.

Stupid, stupid, *stupid!* How could she have responded so freely to Khalid's kiss. No wonder she drove him away. He didn't even want to escort her to her room. Probably thought she'd jump him and drag him inside. Ella paced her room, slapping the wall when she reached it. Turning, she paced to the other wall, slapped it. What could she do to make things come right? She knew he had only helped her out. There was nothing there. How could she have responded so ardently?

Because she loved him and knew he had been lacking in love for years. She wanted to hold him close, pour out her feelings, let him know she loved him beyond anything. But to do so would probably have him running for the nearest exit. A kindness to help her out of a jam didn't mean he was falling for her. He had his life, she had hers.

"Stupid!" she almost shouted the word.

Taking a deep breath, she crossed to the bed and sat down hard. Nothing was going right. She was at odds with her family, had lost her husband—whom she was having trouble remembering when every time she tried her mind saw Khalid. She felt a flare of panic. She couldn't forget Alexander. He'd been her childhood sweetheart. They'd had a nice marriage. At one time she thought he was the only man for her.

Only Khalid had a way of making her forget him. Forget the sweet love they'd shared for the hot and passionate feelings that sprang to life anytime she saw Khalid. Or even thought about him.

Daydreams about what life together could be like. And fears for his safety. She had to get away. Pack her things, face her parents and take complete charge of her life. She didn't have to marry anyone. It wasn't her fault her brother had a gambling problem. Time he faced the music and not expect her to martyr herself on his behalf.

And if she made it big in art, great. If not, maybe she could do stained glass work, or something to keep doing what she loved. It wasn't the same as sharing a life with a man she felt passionately about. But it would have to suffice.

If she could make it on her own. Somehow she must find a way to be self-supporting.

Which meant staying in the cottage was her best bet—the lease was solid for another four years. Khalid would get tired of hanging around and move on. Or sell the estate with the cottage occupied. She could make sure she didn't walk along the beach at night. Or venture outside if she knew he was in residence.

She'd faced worse. She could do this.

"But I don't want to," she wailed, and burst into tears.

The next morning Ella felt more composed. She ate a small breakfast in her room. Made sure no traces of last night's tears showed and descended to the lobby promptly at nine. Khalid was nowhere to be seen. She hadn't gotten the time wrong, had she?

One of the porters saw her and came over. "I will take your bag. You should have called down. The taxi is waiting."

So he wasn't even going back with her. That should help. But Ella felt the loss to her toes. Much as she'd talked herself into staying away from him in the future, she still hoped to fly back with him this morning. Saying goodbye silently so he'd never know, but having a few more hours of his company. Now even that was denied her.

The gleaming white jet sat on the runway with a bevy of men working around it. The cab stopped near the plane and a man rushed over to get her bag. She felt like royalty. Tears stung as she tried to smile and walked to the plane. She missed Khalid and it had been less than ten hours since she'd seen him.

Bethanne popped out of the opened doorway. "Hey, let's get a move on. I've got another run later," she said with a wide smile.

It must not be odd that Khalid wasn't with her, Ella thought as she ran lightly up the stairs.

"Where to later?" she asked, hoping Khalid would not be a topic of conversation.

"To take Khalid and his crew to that fire, of course. Didn't he tell you? Since I was already airborne when the call came in, he's staying here and I'm flying back to get the rest of his crew and then we'll head for Kuwait."

Ella felt her heart freeze. "Another fire?" she said. He had not told her. He had not contacted her at all that morning. Which should show her more than anything how nebulous their connection was. It was not her business after all. He saw no reason to inform her.

"A double from what I understand. Want to sit up in the cockpit? We can talk as I fly."

In a surprisingly short time they were airborne. Ella was so curious about the fire she could hardly sit still. Respecting Bethanne's need for concentration, she kept quiet until the pilot leveled out.

"There, all set. We're heading for the capital city now," Bethanne said.

Ella looked at her. "Tell me about the fire. Khalid didn't say a thing to me about it."

"It's in Kuwait and a bad one. Apparently two wells, connected somehow, ignited. Seven men are known dead and a couple of others are missing. They says it's burning millions of gallons of oil. And hot enough to be felt a half a mile away."

"He can't put it out," Ella said, staggered trying to imagine the puny efforts of men to extinguish such a raging inferno.

"You know Khalid, he'll do his best. And my money's on him."

"Someone should stop him," Ella said.

"What?" Bethanne looked at her. "He'll be okay. He always comes through."

"He got burned pretty badly one time," Ella reminded her.

"Freak accident."

"Which could happen again. Good grief, if the heat is felt so far away, what would it be like close enough to cap it? It's probably melting everything around it and there'd be nothing to cap."

"So they put out the flames, let the oil seep and figure out a way to get into production again. That's what Khalid does, and he's really good at it, according to Rashid. Who, by the way, also wishes he wouldn't do this job. But he knows Khalid is driven to do this and won't stand in his way."

Ella nodded, fear rising like a knot in her throat. She swallowed with difficulty, every fiber of her being wanting to see Khalid again.

She gazed out the window, wishing they'd arranged to ride back together in that air-conditioned car she'd wanted. They would have been out of contact, and someone else would be tapped to try to put out the oil fire. He'd be safe.

"When did the call come?" she asked.

"It happened last night. I suspect they called him once they saw what happened. He's the world's best, you know."

"He should retire."

Bethanne reached out and squeezed Ella's hand. "I know, I'd feel that way if it were Rashid. But women can't change men. My mother told me that fact years ago when explaining how she and my father married and then divorced. She had hoped having a family would be enough for him, but it never was. Some men are meant to do more adventurous things than others."

"I'd hardly call putting out raging oil fires adventurous—more like exceedingly dangerous. Why couldn't he have been a professor or accountant or something?"

Bethanne shrugged. "You might ask yourself why you're engaged to the man. You knew what he did. Yet you plan to marry. It's not going to get easier, but support is important."

Ella couldn't tell her why they were engaged. Apparently Rashid had kept Khalid's secret. Ella couldn't tell anyone she considered leaving Quishari because of Khalid. Maybe the decision would be taken from her. There was nothing she could do now but pray for his safety. She wished they'd ended the evening differently. That she had told him how much she cared. That she'd dare risk everything to let him know she loved him. Would she ever get that chance?

The flight seemed endless. She wanted more information. Could she call Khalid when they landed? She knew Bethanne was flying his crew back to Quraim Wadi Samil to pick him up and fly them all to Kuwait. He'd still be at the hotel. For a moment her mind went blank. What was the name of the hotel? She had to call him, tell him to be careful.

"Rashid will meet the plane," Bethanne said after responding to flight control. She began descending. Ella could see the city, the blue of the Gulf beyond. But the beauty was lost, fear held her tightly. "He's not going, is he?" Ella asked.

"No, he's taking you home. I'll be back late tonight. He didn't want you to be alone."

"Maybe I can work to take my mind off things," she said. The truth was she couldn't think about anything except Khalid and the danger he was facing.

"Go with Rashid. He'll have the most current information about Khalid and the crew. Besides, he's swinging by his mother's place to update her. Dealing with Madame al Harum is enough to take anyone's mind off troubles. That woman is a piece of work."

Ella smiled despite her worry. "At least we have that in common. Do you think she'll ever come around to accepting you?"

"My guess is once I have a baby or two."

Ella blinked and gazed out the window. What if she and Khalid married and she had a baby? She remembered thinking about a little dark-eyed little girl, or a couple of rambunctious boys that looked just like Khalid. How would she ever stand it if they wanted to grow up to be oil firefighters.

"Madame al Harum must be beside herself with worry," she said. "I would be if it were my son going to fight that fire."

"I would never let a son of mine grow up to do that," Bethanne said.

"Thought you said a woman can't change a man."

"Well, then I'd start with a little boy."

Ella laughed. Then almost cried when she thought more

about the danger Khalid faced. How he'd once been an adorable little boy, running at the beach, playing with his twin. How quickly those years must have flown by.

Rashid was standing beside a limo when the plane taxied up to the hangar. There were a half dozen men near him with duffel bags and crates. As soon as the engines were shut down, men began swarming around the plane, loading everything. It was being refueled even as Ella stepped down the stairs. Bethanne followed, then hugged Rashid tightly.

"I wish you'd let someone else fly the plane," he said.

"I'm going. Don't argue. It's Khalid you should be worried about. I'll pick him up and then take them all to Kuwait. I'll be home late tonight. You take care of Ella. I think she's in shock."

"No, I'm fine. I think I should go home."

"You're coming with me," Rashid said.

She looked at him, almost seeing Khalid. Certainly hearing that autocratic tone of his. They looked so alike, yet so different.

"Any news?" she asked.

"Nothing beyond what we learned earlier. Once we reach home we'll call Khalid. He's been talking with the oil field people so will have the latest intel. This all you have?" he asked as one of the men put her bag in the trunk of the limo.

"Yes. It was a short trip." Too short if it was to be the last time she saw Khalid.

Ella went with Rashid to his mother's home. He did not speak on the ride except to try to reassure her that Khalid knew what he was doing and wouldn't take any foolish risks. "Especially now," Rashid said.

Ella nodded, wishing they'd never embarked on this stupid fake engagement. Everyone thought he'd be extra careful, but Rashid knew Khalid had no special reason to be extra cautious. She knew he wouldn't be foolhardy, but so many things could go wrong. What if there was another explosion and his suit was torn again. She couldn't bear to think of the pain he'd go through while healing.

Or what if things went really, really wrong?

"My mother can be a bit difficult. We know she loves us. Sometimes I think it's hard for a mother to realize her children are grown and have their own lives."

Ella thought about her parents. "Sometimes they just want to control children forever."

"Or maybe they get used to it and find it hard to let go."

"Your mother doesn't have to like me," she said.

"No, but it would make family life so much more comfortable in the future, don't you think? We do celebrate happy occasions together—holidays, birthdays."

"Bethanne said once she was a grandmother, she'd come around."

Rashid laughed. "That's our hope. But not right away. I want her to myself for a while."

Would Khalid ever want someone to himself for a while? She wished it would be her.

Madame al Harum was distraught when they arrived. She rushed to the door. "Have you heard anything more?"

"No, Mother," Rashid said, giving her a hug. "He's still in Quraim Wadi Samil. Bethanne just took off to get him. It'll be a few hours before they're in Kuwait."

"Call him. I need to talk to him," she ordered.

"You and Ella."

The older woman looked at Ella as if seeing her for the first time. "Oh." She frowned. "Of course."

"We both want Khalid safely back," Ella said.

Madame al Harum nodded. "Come, we will call him."

* * *

Khalid had maps and charts spread around him when the phone rang.

"Al Harum," he said, hoping this was another call from the site, updating the situation.

"Khalid, it's your mother. I wanted to tell you to be careful."

"I always am, Mother." He leaned back in his chair, pressing his thumb and forefinger against his eyes. He'd been studying the layout of the oil field, where the pipes had been drilled and the safety protocols that were in place. He figured he could recite every fact about that field in his sleep.

Glancing at his watch, he noted the plane would be arriving in less than an hour. He had talked to his second in command before he boarded and all the gear they needed was either on the plane or being shipped directly to the fire.

"We will watch over Ella for you," she said.

Khalid's attention snapped back to his mother. Ella. He should have told her this morning before she left, but he'd already been involved in learning all he could from the source. He hadn't wanted to interrupt the phone call to go tell her goodbye.

"She returned safely?" he asked.

"Yes. She's here. Take care of yourself, son."

Before Khalid could say anything, he heard Ella's soft voice. "Khalid?"

"Yes. You got back all right, I see."

"I didn't know until we were on the plane what was going on. I wished you had told me. You will be careful, won't you?"

"I always am." He was warmed by the concern in her voice.

"From what I've heard, this one is really bad."

He heard a sound from his mother in the background.

"It does seem that way. I'll know more when I get there, but so far, this is probably the most challenging one we've tried."

"I guess I couldn't talk you out of going?" she asked hopefully.

He laughed, picturing her with her pretty brown eyes, hair

blowing in the sea breeze. "No, but I wish I didn't have to leave you. Not that I'd take you to a fire. I enjoyed yesterday." He wished he could pull her into his arms this moment and kiss her again. If he hadn't already been on the phone, nothing would have stopped him from explaining this morning—and taking another kiss for luck.

"Me, too."

He waited, hoping she'd say more. The silence on the line was deafening.

"I better go. I'm expecting another call," he finally said. Nothing was going to be decided on the telephone.

"Okay. Take care of yourself. I'll be here when you get back."

He hung up, wondering where else she'd be but at the cottage. She had a lease for another four years. And at this moment, he was grateful for his grandmother's way of doing things.

The phone rang again and this time it was the field manager in Kuwait. Time to push personal agendas on the back burner. He had a conflagration to extinguish.

CHAPTER ELEVEN

Ella chafed at the way time dragged by. Rashid stayed for a while, then claimed work needed him and took off. Leaving her with Madame al Harum. Ella knew she'd be better off at home. She could try to take her mind off her worry about Khalid with work. Here she had nothing. She rose from the sofa where she'd sat almost since she'd arrived and walked to the window which overlooked the city. It looked hot outside. She'd rather be at the beach.

"I think I'll go home," she said.

"Stay."

Turning, she looked at Khalid's mother. "There's nothing to do here. At home I have work that might distract me from worry."

Sabria al Harum tried to smile. "Nothing will make you forget. I had years of practice with my husband when he went on oil fields. Always worrying about his safety. And he did not try to put out fires. I now worry about Khalid. Rashid assures me he knows his job. But he cannot know what a fire will do."

"It makes it worse since he was injured once," Ella said, looking back out the window.

"Yet you don't seem to mind his scar."

Ella shrugged. "He is not his scar, any more than he is defined by being tall. It's what's inside that counts."

There was a short silence then Sabria said, "Many people

don't grasp that concept. He was terribly hurt by the defection of his fiancée when he was still in hospital."

"She either freaked or was not strong enough to be his wife. Khalid is very intense. Not everyone could live with that."

"You could."

Ella nodded, tears filling her eyes. She could. She would love to be the one he picked to share his life. She would match him toe-to-toe if he got autocratic. And she would love to spend the nights in his arms.

"He was like that as a little boy," Sabria said softly.

When Ella turned, she was surprised at the look of love on her hostess's face. "Tell me," she invited. She was eager for every scrap of knowledge she could get of Khalid.

"I have some pictures. Come, I'll tell you all about my wild twins and show you what I had to put up with." The words were belied by the tone of affection and longing.

Ella was surprised at the number of photo albums in the sitting area of Sabria al Harum's bedroom. The room was bright and airy, decorated in peach and cream colors, feminine and friendly. She would never have suspected the rather austere woman to have this side to her.

Pulling a fat album from the shelves behind the sofa, Sabria sat and patted the cushion next to her for Ella to sit. Placing the album in Ella's lap a moment later, she opened it. For the next hour, the two women looked at all the pictures—from when two adorable babies came home in lacy robes, to the smiling nannies who helped care for them, to the proud parents and on up to adulthood. There were fewer pictures of the two young men, too busy to spend lots of time with their parents. Then she paused over one last picture.

"This was the one taken just before the fire that scarred my son so badly. He has never had his picture taken since. People can be cruel when faced unexpectedly with abnormalities—

whether scarring or handicaps. He was doubly injured with the loss of his fiancée. He has so much to offer."

Ella nodded. A mother always said that, but in Khalid's case, it was true.

The phone rang. Sabria rose swiftly and crossed to answer the extension in her sitting room.

"Thank you," she said a moment later.

"That was Rashid. The team has taken off from Quraim Wadi Samil. They'll be in Kuwait in a couple of hours. There's nothing to do but wait."

"Then come with me to my studio. I'll show you my work and you can advise me. Madame Alia al Harum thought I had promise. I want to earn a living by my work, but if it is really impossible, maybe I should find out now, rather than later."

"You will not need to work once married to Khalid."

Ella had no quick response. Only she and Khalid knew there would be no marriage.

"Come and see."

Sabria thought about it for a moment then nodded. "I believe I should like to see what you do."

The afternoon passed slowly. Sabria looked at all the work Ella had done, proclaiming with surprise how beautiful it was. "No wonder my mother-in-law thought you had such promise. You have rare talent. I know just where I'd like to see that rosy vase. It would be perfect in my friend's bedroom. Perhaps I shall buy it for her. When will you begin to sell?"

Ella explained the original plan and then her idea to start earlier. Soon she and Sabria were discussing advantages and disadvantages of going public too soon, yet without the public feedback, how would Ella know which ideas were the most marketable.

Ella wasn't sure if it was the situation, or the fact Sabria was finally receptive to seeing her as an individual—not someone out to capture her son's affections—but she felt the tentative beginning of a friendship. Not that Sabria would necessarily wish to continue when the engagement was broken. Ella could see the dilemma—who took the blame? She didn't want to. Yet in fairness, she needed to be the one. Khalid had been helping her. He did not need any more grief in his life.

They called Rashid for news before eating dinner on the veranda. Nothing new. Ella made a quick spaghetti with sauce she'd prepared a while ago and frozen. The camaraderie in the kitchen was another surprise. Ella thought she could really get to like Khalid's mother.

"I'm going now," Sabria said after they'd enjoyed dinner and some more conversation. Ella could listen to stories about the twins all week. Darkness had fallen. It was getting late. Nothing would change tonight. Khalid had told Rashid they needed to plan carefully since the fire was involved with two wells.

When she took a walk on the beach before going to bed, Ella looked to the north. She could see nothing. The fire was too far away. But she could imagine it. She dealt with fire every day—controlled and beneficial. Raging out of control would be so different. She offered another prayer for Khalid's safety. Her decision to leave was best. She could see about selling what she'd already done and arrange shipping to Italy of her annealer and crucible and glass. She'd establish herself somewhere near enough to see her parents, but far enough away to make sure they knew she was not coming back to the family. Not until her brother's situation was cleared up.

In the meantime, she did her best not to focus on Khalid, but everything from the beach to the house next door reminded her of him. She could picture him standing in her doorway. Looking at the art she had created. Holding the yellow vase in his house that his grandmother had loved. She ached with loneliness and yearning. Could she get by without him over the years ahead?

She had to. There was no future for her in Quishari. That part of her life was over.

Tomorrow she'd begin packing and making arrangements to move.

The next two days were difficult. Ella made Rashid promise to call her the moment he learned of anything—good or bad. There was nothing else she could do, so she began packing. She ordered shipping cartons and crates and enlisted the help of Jalilah to help her. Carefully they wrapped the fragile pieces in packing materials, then in boxes, then crates. It was slow work, but had to be done carefully to insure no breakage during transit.

Every time Khalid's cordless phone rang, Ella's heart dropped, then raced. She'd answer only to hear Rashid's calm voice giving her an update. The materials had arrived. The maps had been updated. The plan was coming together. There was never a personal message for her. What did she expect? Khalid had far more important things to worry about.

But each time Rashid hung up, Ella's heart hurt a bit more. One word, one "tell Ella I'm okay," would have sufficed.

On the third day, Ella could see the progress. She had arranged for the shipping agent to pick up what was already packed. He would hold it at the depot until everything was ready and ship all at once. She and Jalilah were talking when Ella heard a car. Glancing out the window, she saw Rashid and Bethanne get out and hurry toward the cottage.

Fear swamped her as she rushed to the door. "What happened?" she called before they could speak.

Bethanne came to her first, hugging her tightly. "He'll be okay," she said.

"What?" Sick with fear, she looked at Rashid.

"Another well exploded. The fire is worse than ever. Khalid was hit by flying debris. One of the crew was killed, but

Khalid's in hospital. He's going to be okay. We're going now. You come with us."

Ella wanted to refuse, but her need to see him was too strong. She had to make sure he was truly okay before leaving.

"I just need my purse and passport," she said. She dashed to the house, Bethanne with her. "Bring a change of clothes and sleepwear. We're planning to stay as long as we need to," she said.

Ella went through the motions, but her thoughts stuck on Khalid. "He's really all right?"

"No, but he will be. So far he's still unconscious. We hope we're there by the time he wakes up," Bethanne said, helping fold clothes and stuffing them in the small travel bag.

Time seemed to stop. Ella felt like she was walking through molasses. She remembered hurrying to Alexander's hospital bed—too late. He had died from the car crash injuries before she was there to see him. She couldn't be too late for Khalid.

She sat on the edge of the bed.

"I can't go," she said.

Bethanne stopped and looked at her. "What?"

"I can't go." She pressed her hands against her chest, wishing she could stop the tearing pain. Khalid. He had to be all right!

"Yes, you can. And will. And greet him with all the love in your heart. He cannot have another fiancée abandon him when he's in the hospital."

Ella looked at Bethanne. "I'm not—" Now was not the time to confess she wasn't really his fiancée. "I'm not abandoning him. But I don't think I can go into a hospital."

"We'll be right with you. Come on. That's all you need. Get your passport and let's go."

Four hours later they entered the hospital. Ella felt physically sick. The few updates Rashid had obtained during the flight had not been encouraging. Entering the new hospital, Ella felt waves of nausea roil over her. "I need a restroom," she said, dashing to the nearest one. Bethanne followed.

After throwing up, Ella leaned limply against the stall wall. "I can't do this again," she said.

"He'll be okay, Ella. He's not Alexander. He'll pull through," Bethanne said, rubbing her back.

"Go on up. I know Rashid needs to see him instantly. I'll clean up and be right behind you." She wanted a few moments to herself. She could do this. She had to. The thought of Khalid lying helpless in bed was almost more than she could stand. But she also wanted to see him. At least one more time. And assure herself he was alive and would recover.

She tried hard to think of this as visiting a sick friend. But as she walked down the corridor, the smells that assailed her reminded her vividly of the frantic dash to see Alexander. Only the times got mixed up. She felt the fear and panic, but it was for Khalid. The door was ajar to the room she'd been directed to. She stood outside, drawing in a deep breath, hoping she wouldn't lose her composure.

Rashid stepped out, smiling when he saw her. "I'm calling Mother. He's awake. And probably wondering where you are." He flipped open his mobile phone and hit a speed-dial number. Walking down the corridor, he began to speak when his mother answered.

Ella turned back to the room, stepping inside. Immediately she saw Khalid, the hospital bed raised so he was sitting. His face was bandaged, both eyes looked blackened. His right shoulder was also bandaged. Bethanne was on the far side, talking a mile a minute in English. Khalid watched her; he hadn't seen Ella yet.

Which was a good thing. It gave her time to get over her shock, give a brief thanks he was awake and seemingly able to recover. Pasting a smile on her face she stepped into the room.

"You scared me to death!" she said.

Khalid swiveled around, groaned at the movement, but

looked at her like she was some marvelous creation. Her heart raced. Nothing wrong with his eyes.

"You came," he said.

"You said you'd keep safe." She walked over to the bed. Conscious of Bethanne watching her, she leaned over and kissed him gently on the mouth. His hand came up and kept her head in place as he kissed her back.

"Don't hurt yourself," she said, pulling back a few inches, gazing deep into his eyes.

"I didn't think you'd come," he said, pulling her closer for another brush of lips.

"Why ever not?" Bethanne asked. "If Rashid were injured nothing could keep me away."

"And nothing could keep me away," Ella said. She straightened and took his hand in hers, feeling his grip tighten. Studying him, she shook her head.

"You look horrible," she said.

He laughed, and squeezed her hand. "I feel like a truck ran me over. That was something we didn't expect—another explosion. I think they had the wells linked in a way that didn't show on the maps."

"I heard one of your men died. I'm so sorry."

"Me, too."

She leaned closer. "But I'm glad it wasn't you."

"I'm going to find Rashid. We'll be back." Bethanne waved and headed out of the room.

"When Rashid first came in, I thought you hadn't come," he said.

"Well, some of your fiancées might desert you in hospital, but not all," she said lightly, hating for him to know how much it had taken for her to come. She was so glad she had, but the fear she'd lived with wouldn't easily be forgotten.

He laughed again. Despite his injuries, he seemed the happiest she'd ever seen him.

"Did that blow to the head knock you silly?" she asked.

"Maybe knocked some sense in me. I lay here thinking, after I woke up, what if you didn't come? We haven't known each other that long. What if you didn't care enough to come."

"What if I knocked you up side the head again to stop those rattled brains. Of course I would come. I had to see that you were all right. I couldn't just take Rashid's word for it."

"Why?"

She looked at their linked hands. "I care about you," she said.

"How much?"

She met his gaze. "What do you mean, how much?" she asked.

"I want to know how much you care about me—what's hard about that?"

"Like, more than spinach but less than chocolate?"

His gaze held hers, his demeanor going serious. "Like enough to marry me, stay in Quishari and make a life with me?"

Ella caught her breath. For a moment she forgot to breathe. Did he mean it? Seriously?

"Are you asking me to marry you?" she said. "I mean, for real?"

He nodded. "I am. I hated to say good-night to you in Quraim Wadi Samil. Hated even more leaving for Kuwait without having another kiss. Then I woke up here and realized, life is unexpected. I could die here today, or live for decades. But I knew instantly either way, I wanted you as part of my life. I love you, Ella. I think I have since you touched my cheek on the beach weeks ago. A woman who wasn't horrified by how I look. Who could see me clearer in the dark than anyone in the light. A woman who had been through a lot already, and valued people for who they were, not what they could offer monetarily. Did I also mention who sets my entire body on fire with a single kiss?"

Warmth and love spread through her as she smiled at his

words. "You didn't. Maybe we need another check on that." She leaned over and kissed him.

"Are you saying yes?" he prompted a few moments later.

"I am. I love you. I never expected to say those words again after Alexander's death. But you swept into my life, running roughshod over any obstacles I might throw up. I can't pinpoint the moment I fell in love, but I can the moment I realized it. I will love you forever."

"The fire is still going," he said.

"And are you planning to put it out?"

"Might be involved in the planning. But right now I don't feel up to standing to kiss you, so doubt if I'll be leading a foray close to the flames."

"This time," she murmured, remembering what Bethanne had said. She wouldn't want to change a thing about this man.

"This time. But I'm careful. I'm still here, right?"

"Right. Here's hoping there are no more fires in your future."

"Only the one you set with your kisses," he said.

Ella laughed, seeing an entirely different side of the man who had captured her heart. And to think, she almost missed this. She'd have some quick unpacking to do when she got back to the cottage. She couldn't bear for him to think she was leaving. She'd tell him—after a while. After he was convinced of her love as she was already convinced of his.

"I love you, Ella, now and always."

"I love you, Khalid. Now and always."

EPILOGUE

"I'M GETTING car sick riding with my eyes closed," Ella said, still gripping the edge of the door to help with the bouncing. They'd left Quraim Wadi Samil a while ago. In the last ten minutes, Khalid had insisted she close her eyes—he had a surprise for her. It couldn't be the oasis; she'd already seen that. What else was out in this desert?

"Almost there," he said, reaching out to grasp her free hand in his, squeezing it a little.

She felt the car slowing. Then it stopped. The desert wind brought scents of sand, scant vegetation and—was it water?

"Open your eyes," he said.

She did and stared. They were at the oasis. The late afternoon sun cast long shadows against the tall palms, the small pool of water—and the sandstone house that looked as if it had miraculously sprung up from the ground.

"What? Is that a house?"

He left the Jeep and came around to her side, taking her hand to help her out. "It's our house. Ours and Rashid's and Bethanne's. She doesn't know yet. He'll bring her out next week. We have it first."

Ella looked around in astonishment. "You built it here miles and miles from anywhere? How could you get all the materials, how—never mind, money can achieve anything. This is fantastic! I want to see."

He smiled and led her across a flagstone patio to the front door. Lounge chairs rested on the patio, which gave a perfect view of the pool and palms. Opening the door, he swept her into his arms and stepped inside. "Isn't this what newlyweds do?" he asked at her shriek of surprise.

"Yes, in Italy. I didn't know you did it in Quishari." She laughed, traced the new scar on his face and pulled his head down for a kiss. She was so full of love for this husband of hers. And so grateful for his full recovery—with one or two new scars which only made her love him more.

"Why not at our home when we married?" she asked.

"We had the reception there—how could I carry you over the threshold? You were already inside."

"Hmm, good point."

He set her on her feet and turned her around. The small room was furnished with comfortable items. Large windows gave expansive views. Two of her glass pieces were on display. Taking a quick tour, Ella discovered the small kitchen, bath and two large bedrooms.

"This is so lovely," she said, returning to the center of the main room. Khalid had done all he could to make her life wonderful. He'd backed her art exhibit, which turned out wildly successful. She had orders lined up for new pieces.

They'd attended Bethanne and Rashid's wedding in Texas. And then done a quick tour of several larger cities in the United States which Ella had enjoyed with her new husband.

On their way back to Quishari, they'd stopped in Italy so he could meet her parents. Even settled Giacomo's remaining debts, with a stern warning to never gamble again—which only reiterated what her father had decreed. She'd protested, but Khalid had insisted he wanted to have harmonious relations with his new in-laws.

Which she still hoped for with his mother. One day at a time, she reminded herself. At least they'd been married in Quishari, which Madame al Harum liked better than Rashid and Bethanne's wedding.

"The best is outside. Come," Khalid said, drawing her out and around to the side of the house where stairs led to the flat roof.

When they reached the upper level, Ella exclaimed at the loveliness. Pots of flowers dotted the hip-high wall. Several outdoor chairs and sofas provided ample seating. The view was amazing. Slowly she turned around, delight shining in her eyes.

"This is so perfect."

He smiled at her and drew her into his arms. "I wanted something special for us to get away to sometimes, just the two of us. To enjoy the quiet of the desert and the beauty of this oasis."

She smiled, then frowned a little.

"You don't like it?"

"I love it. It's just…" She bit her lower lip and glanced around, then back at Khalid. "It won't be just the two of us."

"Rashid and I plan to keep the other informed when we want to use the house. We won't be here when they are. Or I can just tell him forget it, we want it all ourselves."

"Don't you dare. It's not that. We're having a baby," she blurted out. "Darn, that was not the way I wanted to tell you," she said.

Staring at his stunned face, she almost laughed. "Well, we've been married for four months and not exactly celibate. What do you think?"

"I'm stunned. And thrilled." With a whoop, he lifted her up and spun her around. "How are you feeling? When is it due? Do we know if it's a boy or girl? How long have you known?"

She laughed, feeling light and free and giddy with happiness. She thought he'd be happy; this confirmed it.

"You know Bethanne and Rashid are expecting. She gave

me a full rundown on the symptoms she was feeling, from morning sickness to constantly being tired. Only, I don't have any of those. I feel fine. But there are signs and I had it confirmed yesterday. I was going to tell you last night, but then you had that meeting, and then we flew to Quraim Wadi Samil and here we are. Really, this turns out to be the best place to tell you. I loved our picnic here months ago. I'm so thrilled with this new house. We'll have only happy memories here. Do you know we're probably going to have our baby within weeks of Rashid and Bethanne's?"

"So our child will grow up with theirs," he said with quiet satisfaction.

She nodded, already picturing two small children playing on the beach by their home. Or coming here with parents to explore the desert.

"Do you think we'll have twins?" she asked.

"Who cares—one at a time or multiples, we'll love them all."

"All?"

"Don't you want a dozen?" he teased.

She laughed. "No, I do not. A couple, maybe three or four, but not twelve."

"Whatever makes you happy. You have made me happy beyond belief. I love you, Ella." He drew her into his arms and kissed her gently. "You changed everything beyond what I ever expected."

She smiled at him, not seeing the scars, only the love shining from his eyes. "You are all I'll ever want," she said, reaching up to kiss him again on the rooftop of a house made for happy memories.

* * * * *

Harlequin Intrigue top author Delores Fossen presents a brand-new series of breathtaking romantic suspense!

TEXAS MATERNITY: HOSTAGES

The first installment available May 2010:

THE BABY'S GUARDIAN

Shaw cursed and hooked his arm around Sabrina.

Despite the urgency that the deadly gunfire created, he tried to be careful with her, and he took the brunt of the fall when he pulled her to the ground. His shoulder hit hard, but he held on tight to his gun so that it wouldn't be jarred from his hand.

Shaw didn't stop there. He crawled over Sabrina, sheltering her pregnant belly with his body, and he came up ready to return fire.

This was obviously a situation he'd wanted to avoid at all cost. He didn't want his baby in the middle of a fight with these armed fugitives, but when they fired that shot, they'd left him no choice. Now, the trick was to get Sabrina safely out of there.

"Get down," someone on the SWAT team yelled from the roof of the adjacent building.

Shaw did. He dropped lower, covering Sabrina as best he could.

There was another shot, but this one came from a rifleman on the SWAT team. Shaw didn't look up, but he heard the sound of glass being blown apart.

The shots continued, all coming from his men, which meant it might be time to try to get Sabrina to better cover. Shaw glanced at the front of the building.

So that Sabrina's pregnant belly wouldn't be smashed

against the ground, Shaw eased off her and moved her to a sitting position so that her back was against the brick wall. They were close. Too close. And face-to-face.

He found himself staring right into those sea-green eyes.

How will Shaw get Sabrina out?
Follow the daring rescue and the heartbreaking aftermath in THE BABY'S GUARDIAN by Delores Fossen, available May 2010 from Harlequin Intrigue.

FRANKENSTEIN

Inspired by a ghastly vision in a waking dream, *FRANKENSTEIN* also stemmed from the events of Mary Shelley's life. Following the death of her first baby, Clara, who lived for only two weeks, Shelley recorded a recurrent dream in her journal: "Dream that my little baby came to life again; that it had only been cold, and that we rubbed it before the fire, and it lived." The story of Victor Frankenstein and the creature he creates but cannot control echoes Mary Shelley's own experiences of loss, love, and anger as a child whose mother died giving her birth, and as a woman fearful of her own capacity for motherhood.

This Enriched Classics edition of *FRANKENSTEIN* was prepared by Anne K. Mellor, Professor of English and Women's Studies at the University of California, Los Angeles. She is the author of *Mary Shelley: Her Life, Her Fiction, Her Monsters* and *Romanticism and Gender*, and co-editor of *The Other Mary Shelley: Beyond Frankenstein*. A recipient of two Guggenheim Fellowships, among numerous awards, she recently directed three National Endowment for the Humanities seminars for college teachers on Romantic women writers.

Titles available in the
ENRICHED CLASSICS SERIES

Adventures of Huckleberry Finn • Mark Twain
The Adventures of Tom Sawyer • Mark Twain
The Age of Innocence • Edith Wharton
The Awakening • Kate Chopin
Billy Budd, Sailor • Herman Melville
The Call of the Wild • Jack London
Dr. Jekyll and Mr. Hyde • Robert Louis Stevenson
Dubliners • James Joyce
Frankenstein • Mary Shelley
The Good Earth • Pearl S. Buck
Great Expectations • Charles Dickens
Jane Eyre • Charlotte Brontë
Kon-Tiki • Thor Heyerdahl
Lame Deer, Seeker of Visions • John (Fire) Lame Deer & Richard Erdoes
Moby-Dick • Herman Melville
My Antonia • Willa Cather
Oedipus the King • Sophocles
A Portrait of the Artist as a Young Man • James Joyce
Pygmalion • George Bernard Shaw
The Red Badge of Courage • Stephen Crane
The Scarlet Letter • Nathaniel Hawthorne
She Stoops to Conquer • Oliver Goldsmith
A Tale of Two Cities • Charles Dickens
Tess of the d'Urbervilles • Thomas Hardy
This Side of Paradise • F. Scott Fitzgerald
Wuthering Heights • Emily Brontë

Frankenstein;

or,

The Modern Prometheus

Mary Shelley

Introduced by Anne K. Mellor

Edited by Anne K. Mellor
with Teresa Reyes

WSP

WASHINGTON SQUARE PRESS
PUBLISHED BY POCKET BOOKS
New York London Toronto Sydney Tokyo Singapore

WSP

A Washington Square Press Publication of
POCKET BOOKS, a division of Simon & Schuster Inc.
1230 Avenue of the Americas, New York, NY 10020

ISBN: 0-671-53150-6

First Washington Square Press printing September 1995

10 9 8 7 6 5

WASHINGTON SQUARE PRESS and colophon are
registered trademarks of Simon & Schuster Inc.

Cover art by Janet Woolley
Photo research by Cheryl Moch

Printed in the U.S.A.

Contents

Introduction

Mothering Monsters: Mary Shelley's *Frankenstein*

Mary Shelley's *Frankenstein* has traditionally been read as the story of the mad scientist, the scientist who creates a monster that destroys its maker. Yet there are other, equally rewarding ways to look at this powerful novel, some of which I want to suggest here. From a woman's perspective, for instance, we can see this novel as a reflection of Mary Shelley's own experiences as a very young mother, as a novel about having a baby. To recognize the psychological and political dimensions of this novel, as well as the scientific, we need to know something about Mary Shelley's life.

Life

When Mary Wollstonecraft died eleven days after giving birth on September 10, 1797, she left her newborn daughter—Mary Wollstonecraft Godwin (Shelley)—with a double burden: a powerful and ever-frustrated need to be mothered and a name that blazoned her the child of the most famous radical literary marriage of eighteenth-century England. Tracking the growth of this baby girl into the author of one of the most famous novels ever written, *Frankenstein, or The Modern Prometheus,* we should never forget how much her desire for a loving and supportive family defined her character, shaped her fantasies, and structured her fictional idealizations of family life.

After her mother's death, Mary's father, the austere philosopher William Godwin, was left with two infant daughters to raise. He immediately hired a nannie, Louisa Jones, to care for Mary and her half-sister Fanny. For three years, Mary enjoyed a happy childhood, beloved by both Louisa and Fanny. But when Louisa fell in love with one of Godwin's more irresponsible disciples, Godwin strongly objected; when she decided to live with him, Godwin forbade her ever to see the girls again. At the age of three, Mary thereby lost the only mother she had ever known. Godwin, desperate to find a wife to care for his family, two years later married Mary Jane Clairmont, the unmarried mother of two children, who deeply resented the special attention paid by visitors to Wollstonecraft's and Godwin's only daughter. She favored her own children, refused to provide any special lessons for Mary, and quarrelled frequently with her. The tension between Mary Godwin and her stepmother was so severe that Mary suffered from psychosomatic skin boils at the age of thirteen, boils that disappeared when the two were separated. Godwin then decided to send Mary away indefinitely, shipping her to Dundee, Scotland to stay with the family of a stranger, David Baxter, in June 1812.

An outsider in the happy home of the Baxters, Mary nonetheless learned to enjoy the bleak but beautiful Scottish landscape and gradually became close friends with the Baxter daughters. She continued to yearn for her father, however, for whom by the age of twelve she had developed, as she later confessed to her friend Maria Gisborne, an "excessive and romantic attachment" (Letter to Gisborne, October 30, 1834). At the age of sixteen, she returned to London to discover that Godwin had acquired a new disciple, one whom she saw as a youthful incarnation of all she most admired in her father. Within two months, she and this disciple, the married poet Percy Bysshe Shelley, had become lovers; on July 18, 1814, they eloped to Paris, taking Mrs. Godwin's daughter, Jane Clairmont, with them.

Furious at this turn of events, the Godwins refused to speak to Mary, especially after Jane insisted on living with Mary and Percy. The trio traveled across Europe to Lake Lucerne; during this trip Mary became pregnant and Jane and Percy probably became lovers, the two women having been converted to Percy's fervent belief in free love and universal benevolence as the solution to every social and political evil.

When they returned to England, Mary gave birth to a baby girl, christened Clara, who lived for only two weeks. After Clara's death on March 6, 1815, Mary had a recurrent dream that she recorded in her journal: "Dream that my little baby came to life again; that it had only been cold, and that we rubbed it before the fire, and it lived. Awake and find no baby. I think about the little thing all day. Not in good spirits" (Journal, March 19, 1815).

Increasingly resenting Jane's presence in her household, Mary insisted that she leave; Jane then decided to find her own poet and set her cap for the most famous young poet of the day, Lord Byron. By April 1816, Jane, having now changed her name to the more romantic Claire, had become Byron's lover despite his obvious lack of affection for her. She then persuaded Percy, who wanted to meet Byron, and Mary to accompany her to Switzerland in pursuit of Byron. The four spent the coldest summer for a century, the summer of 1816, together on the shores of Lake Geneva, engaging in intense conversation, reading ghost stories out loud, and, on the memorable night of June 15, competing to write the most frightening story. The next day Mary Godwin, having experienced a "reverie"—a waking nightmare in which "a pale student of unhallowed arts" creates a living being from dead parts—began to write one of the most powerful horror stories of Western civilization.

Frankenstein, or The Modern Prometheus (1816)

Mary Shelley's story of a scientist who creates a monster he cannot control can claim the status of a myth, so profoundly resonant in its implications for our understanding of the modern world that it has become an image in everyday life. The name Frankenstein, of course, is often mistakenly assigned to the monster rather than its creator. But this "mistake" derives from an intuitively correct reading of the final identification of the creator with his creation.

Psychological Origins

From the woman's perspective which has dominated recent discussions of this novel, *Frankenstein* is a book about what happens when a man tries to have a baby without a woman. Ellen Moers first drew our attention, in 1974, to the novel's emphasis on birth and "the trauma of the after-birth." Since this is a novel about giving birth, we should first ask why the eighteen-year-old Mary Godwin gave birth to this particular novel on this particular night. In her introduction to the revised edition of *Frankenstein* (1831), she tells us that the night before her dream she heard Byron and Shelley discussing the latest scientific experiments by Erasmus Darwin, in which he had animated a piece of spaghetti by sending an electrical current though it.

Mary's dream draws on a far more personal experience, however. Over fifteen years later, she claimed she could still see vividly the room to which she woke and feel "the thrill of fear" that ran through her. Why was she so frightened by her dream? Remember that only eighteen months earlier she had given birth to a baby girl whom she had dreamed she had "rubbed before the fire" and brought back to life. Now she is again dreaming of reanimating a corpse by warming it with "a spark of life." And only six months before, she had given birth a second time, to a boy named William. While Mary wrote her novel, she was pregnant a third time, with a daughter, Clara, born in September 1817. Mary's waking dream unleashed her deepest subconscious anxieties, the anxieties of a very young and frequently pregnant unmarried mother.

The dream that gave birth to her novel also gave shape to her deepest fears: What if my child is born deformed, a freak, a "hideous" thing? Could I still love it, or would I be horrified and wish it were dead again (as the "pale student" does)? What will happen if I can't love my child? Am I capable of raising a normal, healthy child? Will my child die (as my first baby did)? Could I wish my own child to die, to destroy itself? Could I kill it? Could it kill me (as I killed my mother, Mary Wollstonecraft)?

One reason Mary Shelley's story has such resonance is that it expresses, perhaps for the first time in Western literature, women's most powerfully felt anxieties about pregnancy, a topic avoided by male writers and considered improper for women to discuss in public. She breaks new ground in suggesting to her male readers that women may not always desire their own babies, even as she reassures her female readers that their fears and hostilities are shared by other women.

Her dream generates that dimension of the novel's plot which has been much discussed by recent critics:

Victor Frankenstein's total failure at parenting. Even though he has labored nine months to give birth to his creature, Frankenstein flees from his child the moment it opens its eyes with the "convulsive motion" of birth. And when his creature follows him like a new born child, arms open to embrace him and grinning, Frankenstein can see his creation only as a devil, a wretch whom he violently pushes away. Throughout the novel, Frankenstein is unable to accept responsibility for his son, his Adam. His failure is contrasted to the examples of two loving fathers, Alphonse Frankenstein and Father de Lacey. Through them, Mary Shelley portrays her ideal family as a community of equals, joined by love and mutual respect. The De Laceys exemplify this paragon of harmony: Felix, whose name connotes happiness; Agatha, whose name means goodness; and Safie, or Sophia, the Greek word for wisdom, a portrait of the liberated woman modelled on her mother Mary Wollstonecraft.

As the novel develops, Shelley's attention focuses not so much on the feelings and experiences of Victor Frankenstein as those of his creature, the abandoned child. Mary Shelley strongly identified with this rejected child. The creature spends two years peering in on the De Lacey family, just as Mary had peered in on the Baxters. The creature reads the same books that did Mary circa 1814: *Paradise Lost, The Sufferings of Young Werther,* Plutarch's *Lives of the Roman Emperors,* Volney's *Ruins of Civilization,* and the poetry of Coleridge and Byron. And both the creature and Mary lack a mother and father. The novel powerfully evokes the creature's pain at the recognition that he will always be alone; equally powerful, the novel evokes the anger and desire for revenge that such abandonment and isolation can produce. Only when the creature finally loses his last hope of joining the De Lacey family does he commit his first act of violence and burn down their cottage.

Mary Shelley recognized that an experience of parental rejection can produce a desire to retaliate: it is no accident that the creature's first victim is a young boy named William, whom he wished to adopt. By naming this child *William* Frankenstein, Mary Shelley may have invoked her father William Godwin, or her stepbrother, William Godwin, Jr., who had displaced her in her father's affections, or her own son, William Shelley, of whom William Frankenstein is an exact portrait. The creature's murder of William Frankenstein might be informed by Mary Shelley's own repressed anger, revealing to her horrified eyes her own capacity for aggression. By writing this scene, by imagining the murder of her own son, she acknowledges that she, a battered child, could easily become a battering parent.

Anxiety about her capacity to give birth to a healthy child that she could raise successfully surfaces in the novel in another way. In her introduction to the revised edition of *Frankenstein* (1831), she identifies the novel itself as her child, her "hideous progeny." This metaphor of book as baby articulates for Mary Shelley a double anxiety. In giving birth to a book, she is giving birth to herself as an author, specifically the author of horror.

Guilt at writing a horrifying book led to an extensive self-censorship in her novel. First, she repressed the voice of the female author, assigning her tale to three male narrators: Walton, Frankenstein, and the creature. Then, she gave her tale to another man, Percy Shelley, to "edit" and "correct." Percy Shelley made numerous changes to the manuscript of *Frankenstein,* changes which both improved and damaged the novel. He corrected factual errors and misspellings, substituted technical terms for Mary Shelley's less precise ones, and sometimes clarified her text. But he also "heightened" her style, substituting polysyllabic words and inverting sentence structures in place of her common Anglo-Saxon constructions. He is thus responsible for that artificial, learned prose style used both by Frankenstein and his creature, a style that many readers find distancing and stilted, not to mention unrealistic for a creature only two years old!

Even more substantive, Percy changed the ending of Mary Shelley's text. He revised the last line of the novel—from Mary Shelley's "I soon lost sight of him in the darkness and distance" to "he disappeared in darkness and distance." Mary Shelley's ending leaves open the possibility that the creature is still alive, the more so because his promise to build a funeral pyre at the North Pole is inherently incredible, given the lack of wood there. Percy Shelley's ending gives a false sense of closure to the novel. Why did Mary accept all of Percy's changes? Probably because she felt inferior to this older, already published author, this father figure who was now her husband. Percy married Mary on December 30, 1816, after his first wife committed suicide.

Politics

As its subtitle suggests, *Frankenstein, or The Modern Prometheus* also functions as a political criticism both of Romanticism and of the ideology of the French Revolution. By naming her scientist a modern Prometheus, Mary Shelley called into question the fundamental goal of the Romantic poets and philosophers she knew best (Godwin, Coleridge, Byron, Percy

Shelley). All these poets were engaged in an attempt to *perfect* mankind, to transform mortals into godlike creatures, to locate the divine *in* the human. Victor Frankenstein's quest, to "bestow animation upon lifeless matter" and thereby "renew life where death had apparently devoted the body to corruption," is in effect a quest to become God, to become the creator of life and the gratefully worshipped father of a new species of immortal beings.

Shelley's novel invokes both versions of the myth of Prometheus. In one, he is the god who steals fire from Jupiter to help mankind, Prometheus pyphorus—the fire stealer; in the other, Prometheus actually creates man by breathing life into a clay body—Prometheus plasticator, the maker of man. Mary Shelley identified her modern Prometheus explicitly with Byron and Percy Shelley, both of whom had written poems celebrating Prometheus as the savior of mankind. She based her portrait of Victor Frankenstein on her husband. Percy Shelley had published his first volume of poems under the pen-name Victor; like Frankenstein, he had a "sister" named Elizabeth; he had received the same education as Victor, reading Paracelsus, Albertus Magnus, Pliny and Buffon, and specializing in alchemy, chemistry, and foreign languages; he shared Frankenstein's revolutionary ideals, signaled in the novel by sending Frankenstein to the University of Ingolstadt, the home of the leading German revolutionary thinker, Adam Weishaupt. Most important, Frankenstein shared Percy Shelley's relative indifference to his children: he had abandoned his first wife and their children and had not grieved for the death of Mary's first daughter Clara.

Mary Shelley also included a positive portrait of her husband in her novel in the character of Clerval, Victor's other "self." Clerval is a poet who loves nature, is capable of empathy, of mothering others (he nurses Victor when Victor is sick), and does not disobey his father. But this positive image of an altruistic parent is ripped out of the novel when Clerval is murdered, leaving only the egotistical, self-absorbed Victor.

As a modern Prometheus, Victor Frankenstein is a fire stealer, someone who usurps nature's "spark of life" in order to animate a dead corpse but then refuses to accept responsibility for the creation. Mary Shelley rejected the Romantic dream of progressing ever upward to human perfection, recognizing that the desire to achieve a future ideal too often entailed an indifference to the present. She concluded that a Romanticism that valued creative process above created result too often failed to acknowledge the predictable consequences of that product, once created—the suffering caused by the political and social revolutions that might be inspired by the passionate words of the poet.

Imbedded in *Frankenstein,* therefore, is an allegory of the French Revolution and the terror. Mary Shelley encourages us to see the creature as the embodiment of the entire progress of the French Revolution. The creature first invokes Rousseau's claim that men are born free but everywhere in chains: "I was benevolent and good," he claims, "misery made me a fiend." Were he incorporated into the family of man, he would be entirely virtuous, he insists. But the creature doesn't get the female companion he craves and is driven to violence. Likewise, the French Revolution was forced out of the hands of the well-intentioned Girondists—Mirabeau, Lafayette, Talleyrand—during the September massacres and the execution of Louis XIV and Marie Antoinette. The bloodthirsty arms of Marat, St. Just and Robespierre prevailed.

Mary Shelley puts forth a subtle political argument, crudely stated as "the end does not justify the means." An abstract cause can never be separated from its actual historical manifestations. If Victor Frankenstein had loved and cared for his child, the creature might never have become a monster; similarly, if the early leaders of the French Revolution had found a place for the aristocrats, clergy, and King and Queen in their new republic, the terror and the devastations of Napoleon's campaigns might not have occurred. Mary Shelley sums up her political credo in a central passage in *Frankenstein:*

> A human being in perfection ought always to preserve a calm and peaceful mind and never to allow passion or a transitory desire to disturb his tranquillity. I do not think that the pursuit of knowledge is an exception to this rule. If the study to which you apply yourself has a tendency to weaken your affections, and to destroy your taste for those simple pleasures in which no alloy can possibly mix, then that study is certainly unlawful, that is to say, not befitting the human mind. If this rule were always observed; if no man allowed any pursuit whatsoever to interfere with the tranquillity of his domestic affections, Greece had not been enslaved; Caesar would have spared his country; America would have been discovered more gradually; and the empires of Mexico and Peru had not been destroyed.

Mary Shelley is a political reformist, not a revolutionary. She believed that the nation-state ought to be modeled upon the "domestic affections," upon a loving family in which each member is valued and cared for equally. She shares this concept of what we might call "family politics" with the other women writers of her day: Mary Wollstonecraft, Maria Edgeworth, and Jane Austen. This concept of the ideal state as a socialist community is grounded on an ethic of care that serves the needs of all its members.

Science

Frankenstein offers a powerful critique both of scientific thought and of the psychology of the modern scientist. Mary Shelley may have been the first to question the commitment of science to the search for objective truth whatever the consequences. What science did Mary Shelley know? Clearly, she had no personal experience with scientific research: she envisioned Frankenstein's laboratory as a small attic room lit by a single candle! Nonetheless, she had a sound grasp of the concepts and implications of some of the most important scientific research of her day, namely the work of Sir Humphrey Davy, Erasmus Darwin and Luigi Galvani.

Victor Frankenstein chooses to specialize at the University of Ingolstadt in the field of "natural philosophy" or chemical physiology, the field defined by Humphrey Davy in his *A Discourse, Introductory to a Course of Lectures on Chemistry* (1802), the source for Professor Waldman's lecture in the novel. In this pamphlet, Davy insisted that modern chemistry has bestowed upon the chemist:

> . . . powers which may be almost called creative; which have enabled him to modify and change the beings surrounding him, and by his experiments to interrogate nature with power, not simply as a scholar, passive and seeking only to understand her operations, but rather as a master, active with his own instruments.

Defining nature as female, Davy delineated two scientific ways of dealing with her. One could practice what we might call "descriptive" science, an effort to understand the workings of Mother Nature. Or one could practice an "interventionist" science, an effort to change the ways of nature. Davy clearly preferred the latter, hailing the scientist who modified nature as a "master." Similarly, Professor Waldman urges Victor Frankenstein to "penetrate into the recesses of nature, and show how she works in her hiding places," an effort Victor undertakes so that he might discover the "secret of life" and use it to his own ends. In Mary Shelley's view, such interventionist science is bad science, dangerous and self-serving.

In contrast, good science is that practised by Erasmus Darwin, the first theorist of evolution and grand uncle to Charles Darwin. In *The Botanic Garden* (1791), Darwin had described the evolution of more complex life forms from simpler ones, arguing that sexual propagation is higher on the evolutionary ladder than asexual propagation. From Darwin's perspective, Victor Frankenstein's experiment would reverse evolutionary progress, not only because Frankenstein reproduces asexually, but also because he constructs his new species from parts male and female, human and nonhuman. Moreover, he defies the entire concept of evolution by attempting to create a "new" species all at once, rather than by the random mutation of existing species.

The scientist who had the most direct impact on Shelley's representation of Frankenstein's experiment was Luigi Galvani, who argued that the life force was electricity, and who had performed numerous experiments conducting electrical currents through dead animals in order to revive them. His most notorious experiment was performed in public in London on January 17, 1803, by his nephew Giovanni Aldini. On that day, Aldini applied galvanic electricity to the corpse of a human being. The body of the recently hanged criminal Thomas Forster was brought from Newgate Prison to Mr. Wilson's Anatomical Theatre, where live wires attached to a pile composed of 120 plates of zinc and 120 plates of copper were connected to the ear and mouth of the dead man. At this moment, Aldini reported, "the jaw began to quiver, the adjoining muscles were horribly contorted, and the left eye actually opened." When the wires were applied to the ear and rectum, they "excited in the muscles contractions much stronger . . . The action even of those muscles furthest distant from the points of contact with the arc was so much increased as almost to give an appearance of re-animation. . . . The effect in this case surpassed our most sanguine expectations," Aldini said, concluding, ". . . vitality might, perhaps, have been restored, if many circumstances had not rendered it impossible." Here is the scientific prototype for Victor Frankenstein, restoring life to dead human corpses.

By grounding her literary vision of a scientist animating a corpse upon the cutting edge of science of her day, Mary Shelley initiated the new literary genre of science fiction. As Brian Aldiss and Robert Scholes have argued, *Frankenstein* possesses the three characteristics essential to the genre of science fiction: it is based on valid scientific research; it gives a persuasive prediction of what science might achieve in the future; and it offers a humanistic critique of the benefits and dangers of either a specific scientific milestone or of the nature of scientific thought.

Frankenstein is notable both for its grasp of the nature of the scientific enterprise and for its searching analysis of the dangers inherent in that enterprise. Victor Frankenstein is our first literary portrait of what we might now call the "mad scientist," but a far more subtle one than that provided by such films as Stanley Kubrick's *Dr. Strangelove.* Mary Shelley recognized that Victor Frankenstein's passion for scientific research is a displacement of normal emotions and healthy affections. Significantly, when Victor is working on his experiment, he cannot love: he ignores his family, even his fiancée Elizabeth, and takes no pleasure in the beauties of nature. Moreover, he becomes physically and mentally ill, subject to nervous fevers.

Mary Shelley also offers a critique of the very nature of scientific thought. Inherent in the concept of science is a potent gender dichotomy, as Sir Humphrey Davy assumed: nature is female, the scientist is male. The scientist who analyses, manipulates and attempts to control nature is engaging in a politics that today we would call sexism. Francis Bacon heralded the seventeenth-century scientific revolution: "I am come in very truth leading to you Nature with all her children to bind her to your service and make her your slave." By constructing nature as female, the scientist feels entitled to exploit her to gratify his own desire for power, money, status. Frankenstein's scientific quest is nothing less than an attempt to "penetrate into the recesses of nature, and show how she works in her hiding places," to penetrate her womb and to appropriate it, to steal female biological reproduction. In effect, Frankenstein wishes to rape nature in order to gratify his own lust for power. As Frankenstein fantasizes, "A new species would bless me as its creator and source; many happy and excellent natures would owe their being to me. No father could claim the gratitude of his child so completely as I should deserve theirs." If Frankenstein were to succeed in stealing the power of female biological reproduction, he would eliminate the biological necessity for females as such; the human race of males could survive by cloning. This is why he rips up the half-constructed female creature: he wishes to destroy the ability of an independent female to create a new race of her own. Frankenstein's hostility to female sexuality as such is perhaps the greatest horror, for women readers, of Mary Shelley's story: Frankenstein poses a threat to the very social and biological survival of the human female.

In Mary Shelley's feminist novel, however, Victor Frankenstein does not succeed in creating a new race of supermen who can survive without women. Mother Nature fights back. She begins by plaguing Frankenstein with bad health: as he engages in his two experiments, he is tormented by fevers, heart palpitations, nervous fits, depression and paranoia. His physical exhaustion is finally so great that he dies at the age of twenty-five. Nature further punishes Victor, thwarting his creation of a normal child: his lack of empathy and maternal bonding first causes him to create a giant—the "minuteness of the [normal-sized] parts formed a great hindrance to my speed"—and then prevents him from normal procreation with his bride Elizabeth, whom he abandons to his creature on their wedding night. Finally, nature pursues Victor Frankenstein with the very electricity and fire he has stolen from her. The lightning, thunder and rain that flashes around Victor as he carries on his experiments are not just the conventional atmospheric effects of the Gothic novel, but also a manifestation of nature's elemental powers. Like the classical Greek Furies, nature pursues Victor to his hiding places, destroying not only Victor but his family, friend, and servant. Finally, the penalty of violating nature is death.

Mary Shelley's novel offers an alternative to Victor's and Walton's view of nature as a female to be penetrated and possessed by the male scientist, or as merely dead matter to be reassembled at his will.

Significantly, the only member of the Frankenstein family still alive at the end of the novel is Ernest, who wished to become a farmer, not a manipulative and oppressive lawyer like his father. His survival, together with Clerval's enthusiastic love of the changing beauty of nature's seasons, reveals Mary Shelley's own view of the appropriate relationship between human beings and nature: a vision of nature as a person with rights and responsibilities who must be treated with respect, even reverence. Only if we can learn to embrace even nature's freaks and monsters with the understanding love of a mother can we avoid the fate of Frankenstein. As the creature reminds Victor, "You are my creator but I am your master—obey!"

Anne K. Mellor
The University of California,
Los Angeles

Frankenstein;

or,

The Modern Prometheus

Did I request thee, Maker, from my clay
To mould me man? Did I solicit thee
From darkness to promote me?———

PARADISE LOST.

To

WILLIAM GODWIN,

Author of Political Justice, Caleb Williams, &c.

THESE VOLUMES

Are Respectfully Inscribed by the Author.

PREFACE

The event on which this fiction is founded has been supposed, by Dr. Darwin, and some of the physiological writers of Germany, as not of impossible occurrence. I shall not be supposed as according the remotest degree of serious faith to such an imagination; yet, in assuming it as the basis of a work of fancy, I have not considered myself as merely weaving a series of supernatural terrors. The event on which the interest of the story depends is exempt from the disadvantages of a mere tale of spectres or enchantment. It was recommended by the novelty of the situations which it developes; and, however impossible as a physical fact, affords a point of view to the imagination for the delineating of human passions more comprehensive and commanding than any which the ordinary relations of existing events can yield.

I have thus endeavoured to preserve the truth of the elementary principles of human nature, while I have not scrupled to innovate upon their combinations. The *Iliad,* the tragic poetry of Greece,—Shakespeare, in the *Tempest* and *Midsummer Night's Dream,*—and most especially Milton, in *Paradise Lost,* conform to this rule; and the most humble novelist, who seeks to confer or receive amusement from his labours, may, without presumption, apply to prose fiction a licence, or rather a rule, from the adoption of which so many exquisite combinations of human feeling have resulted in the highest specimens of poetry.

The circumstance on which my story rests was suggested in casual conversation. It was commenced, partly as a source of amusement, and partly as an expedient for exercising any untried resources of mind. Other motives were mingled with these, as the work proceeded. I am by no means indifferent to the manner in which whatever moral tendencies exist in the sentiments or characters it contains shall affect the reader; yet my chief concern in this respect has been limited to the avoiding the enervating effects of the novels of the present day, and to the exhibition of the amiableness of domestic affection, and the excellence of universal virtue. The opinions which naturally spring from the character and situation of the hero are by no means to be conceived as existing always in my own conviction; nor is any inference justly to be drawn from the following pages as prejudicing any philosophical doctrine of whatever kind.

It is a subject also of additional interest to the author, that this story was begun in the majestic region where the scene is principally laid, and in society which cannot cease to be regretted. I passed the summer of 1816 in the environs of Geneva. The season was cold and rainy, and in the evenings we crowded around a blazing wood fire, and occasionally amused ourselves with some German stories of ghosts, which happened to fall into our hands. These tales excited in us a playful desire of imitation. Two other friends (a tale from the pen of one of whom would be far more acceptable to the public than any thing I can ever hope to produce) and myself agreed to write each a story, founded on some supernatural occurrence.

The weather, however, suddenly became serene; and my two friends left me on a journey among the Alps, and lost, in the magnificent scenes which they present, all memory of their ghostly visions. The following tale is the only one which has been completed.

Volume I

LETTER I

To Mrs. Saville, England

St. Petersburgh, Dec. 11th, 17—.

You will rejoice to hear that no disaster has accompanied the commencement of an enterprise which you have regarded with such evil forebodings. I arrived here yesterday; and my first task is to assure my dear sister of my welfare, and increasing confidence in the success of my undertaking.

I am already far north of London; and as I walk in the streets of Petersburgh, I feel a cold northern breeze play upon my cheeks, which braces my nerves, and fills me with delight. Do you understand this feeling? This breeze, which has travelled from the regions towards which I am advancing, gives me a foretaste of those icy climes. Inspirited by this wind of promise, my day dreams become more fervent and vivid. I try in vain to be persuaded that the pole is the seat of frost and desolation; it ever presents itself to my imagination as the region of beauty and delight. There, Margaret, the sun is for ever visible; its broad disk just skirting the horizon, and diffusing a perpetual splendour. There—for with your leave, my sister, I will put some trust in preceding navigators—there snow and frost are banished; and, sailing over a calm sea, we may be wafted to a land surpassing in wonders and in beauty every region hitherto discovered on the habitable globe. Its productions and features may be without example, as the phænomena of the heavenly bodies undoubtedly are in those undiscovered solitudes. What may not be expected in a country of eternal light? I may there discover the wondrous power which attracts the needle; and may regulate a thousand celestial observations, that require only this voyage to render their seeming eccentricities consistent for ever. I shall satiate my ardent curiosity with the sight of a part of the world never before visited, and may tread a land never before imprinted by the foot of man. These are my enticements, and they are sufficient to conquer all fear of danger or death, and to induce me to commence this laborious voyage with the joy a child feels when he embarks in a little boat, with his holiday mates, on an expedition of discovery up his native river. But, supposing all these conjectures to be false, you cannot contest the inestimable benefit which I shall confer on all mankind to the last generation, by discovering a passage near the pole to those countries, to reach which at present so many months are requisite; or by ascertaining the secret of the magnet, which, if at all possible, can only be effected by an undertaking such as mine.

These reflections have dispelled the agitation with which I began my letter, and I feel my heart glow with an enthusiasm which elevates me to heaven; for nothing contributes so much to tranquillize the mind as a steady purpose,—a point on which the soul may fix its intellectual eye. This expedition has been the favourite dream of my early years. I have read with ardour the accounts of the various voyages which have been made in the prospect of arriving at the North Pacific Ocean through the seas which surround the pole. You may remember, that a history of all the voyages made for purposes of discovery composed the whole of our good uncle Thomas's library. My education was neglected, yet I was passionately fond of reading. These volumes were my study day and night, and my familiarity with them increased that regret which I had felt, as a child, on learning that my father's dying injunction had forbidden my uncle to allow me to embark in a sea-faring life.

These visions faded when I perused, for the first time, those poets whose effusions entranced my soul, and lifted it to heaven. I also became a poet, and for one year lived in a Paradise of my own creation; I imagined that I also might obtain a niche in the temple where the names of Homer and Shakespeare are consecrated. You are well acquainted with my failure, and how heavily I bore the disappointment. But just at that time I inherited the fortune of my cousin, and my thoughts were turned into the channel of their earlier bent.

Six years have passed since I resolved on my present undertaking. I can, even now, remember the hour from which I dedicated myself to this great enterprise. I commenced by inuring my body to hardship. I accompanied the whale-fishers on several expeditions to the North Sea; I voluntarily endured cold, famine, thirst, and want of sleep; I often worked harder than the common sailors during the day, and devoted my nights to the study of mathematics, the theory of medicine, and those branches of physical science from which a naval adventurer might derive the greatest practical advantage. Twice I actually hired myself as an under-mate in a Greenland whaler, and acquitted myself to admiration. I must own I felt a little proud, when my captain offered me the second dignity in the vessel, and entreated me to remain with the greatest earnestness; so valuable did he consider my services.

And now, dear Margaret, do I not deserve to accomplish some great purpose. My life might have been passed in ease and luxury; but I preferred glory to every enticement that wealth placed in my path. Oh, that some encouraging voice would answer in the affirmative! My courage and my resolution is firm; but my hopes fluctuate, and my spirits are often depressed. I am about to proceed on a long and difficult voyage; the emergencies of which will demand all my fortitude: I am required not only to raise the spirits of others, but sometimes to sustain my own, when their's are failing.

This is the most favourable period for travelling in Russia. They fly quickly over the snow in their sledges; the motion is pleasant, and, in my opinion, far more agreeable than that of an English stage-coach. The cold is not excessive, if you are wrapt in furs, a dress which I have already adopted; for there is a great difference between walking the deck and remaining seated motionless for hours, when no exercise prevents the blood from actually freezing in your veins. I have no ambition to lose my life on the post-road between St. Petersburgh and Archangel.

I shall depart for the latter town in a fortnight or three weeks; and my intention is to hire a ship there, which can easily be done by paying the insurance for the owner, and to engage as many sailors as I think necessary among those who are accustomed to the whale-fishing. I do not intend to sail until the month of June: and when shall I return? Ah, dear sister, how can I answer this question? If I succeed, many, many months, perhaps years, will pass before you and I may meet. If I fail, you will see me again soon, or never.

Farewell, my dear, excellent, Margaret. Heaven shower down blessings on you, and save me, that I may again and again testify my gratitude for all your love and kindness.

Your affectionate brother,
R. Walton.

LETTER II

To Mrs. Saville, England.

Archangel, 28th March, 17—.

How slowly the time passes here, encompassed as I am by frost and snow; yet a second step is taken towards my enterprise. I have hired a vessel, and am occupied in collecting my sailors; those whom I have already engaged appear to be men on whom I can depend, and are certainly possessed of dauntless courage.

But I have one want which I have never yet been able to satisfy; and the absence of the object of which I now feel as a most severe evil. I have no friend, Margaret: when I am glowing with the enthusiasm of success, there will be none to participate my joy; if I am assailed by disappointment, no one will endeavour to sustain me in dejection. I shall commit my thoughts to paper, it is true; but that is a poor medium for the communication of feeling. I desire the company of a man who could sympathize with me; whose eyes would reply to mine. You may deem me romantic, my dear sister, but I bitterly feel the want of a friend. I have no one near me, gentle yet courageous, possessed of a cultivated as well as of a capacious mind, whose tastes are like my own, to approve or amend my plans. How would such a friend repair the faults of your poor brother! I am too ardent in execution, and too impatient of difficulties. But it is a still greater evil to me that I am self-educated: for the first fourteen years of my life I ran wild on a common and read nothing but our uncle Thomas's books o voyages. At that age I became acquainted with th celebrated poets of our own country; but it was onl when it had ceased to be in my power to derive it most important benefits from such a conviction, tha I perceived the necessity of becoming acquainted with more languages than that of my native country. Now am twenty-eight, and am in reality more illiterat than many school-boys of fifteen. It is true that I hav thought more, and that my day dreams are mor extended and magnificent; but they want (as th painters call it) *keeping;* and I greatly need a frien who would have sense enough not to despise me a romantic, and affection enough for me to endeavou to regulate my mind.

Well, these are useless complaints; I shall certainl find no friend on the wide ocean, nor even here i Archangel, among merchants and seamen. Yet som feelings, unallied to the dross of human nature, bea even in these rugged bosoms. My lieutenant, fo instance, is a man of wonderful courage and enter prise; he is madly desirous of glory. He is an English man, and in the midst of national and professiona prejudices, unsoftened by cultivation, retains some o the noblest endowments of humanity. I first becam acquainted with him on board a whale vessel: findin that he was unemployed in this city, I easily engage him to assist in my enterprise.

The master is a person of an excellent disposition and is remarkable in the ship for his gentleness, an the mildness of his discipline. He is, indeed, of s amiable a nature, that he will not hunt (a favourite and almost the only amusement here), because h cannot endure to spill blood. He is, moreover, heroi cally generous. Some years ago he loved a youn

Russian lady, of moderate fortune; and having amassed a considerable sum in prize-money, the father of the girl consented to the match. He saw his mistress once before the destined ceremony; but she was bathed in tears, and, throwing herself at his feet, entreated him to spare her, confessing at the same time that she loved another, but that he was poor, and that her father would never consent to the union. My generous friend reassured the suppliant, and on being informed of the name of her lover instantly abandoned his pursuit. He had already bought a farm with his money, on which he had designed to pass the remainder of his life; but he bestowed the whole on his rival, together with the remains of his prize-money to purchase stock, and then himself solicited the young woman's father to consent to her marriage with her lover. But the old man decidedly refused, thinking himself bound in honour to my friend; who, when he found the father inexorable, quitted his country, nor returned until he heard that his former mistress was married according to her inclinations. "What a noble fellow!" you will exclaim. He is so; but then he has passed all his life on board a vessel, and has scarcely an idea beyond the rope and the shroud.

But do not suppose that, because I complain a little, or because I can conceive a consolation for my toils which I may never know, that I am wavering in my resolutions. Those are as fixed as fate; and my voyage is only now delayed until the weather shall permit my embarkation. The winter has been dreadfully severe; but the spring promises well, and it is considered as a remarkably early season; so that, perhaps, I may sail sooner than I expected. I shall do nothing rashly; you know me sufficiently to confide in my prudence and considerateness whenever the safety of others is committed to my care.

I cannot describe to you my sensations on the near prospect of my undertaking. It is impossible to communicate to you a conception of the trembling sensation, half pleasurable and half fearful, with which I am preparing to depart. I am going to unexplored regions, to "the land of mist and snow;" but I shall kill no albatross, therefore do not be alarmed for my safety.

Shall I meet you again, after having traversed immense seas, and returned by the most southern cape of Africa or America? I dare not expect such success, yet I cannot bear to look on the reverse of the picture. Continue to write to me by every opportunity: I may receive your letters (though the chance is very doubtful) on some occasions when I need them most to support my spirits. I love you very tenderly. Remember me with affection, should you never hear from me again.

Your affectionate brother,
Robert Walton.

LETTER III

To Mrs. Saville, England.

July 7th, 17—.

My dear Sister,

I write a few lines in haste, to say that I am safe, and well advanced on my voyage. This letter will reach England by a merchant-man now on its homeward voyage from Archangel; more fortunate than I, who may not see my native land, perhaps, for many years. I am, however, in good spirits: my men are bold, and apparently firm of purpose; nor do the floating sheets of ice that continually pass us, indicating the dangers of the region towards which we are advancing, appear to dismay them. We have already reached a very high latitude; but it is the height of summer, and although not so warm as in England, the southern gales, which blow us speedily towards those shores which I so ardently desire to attain, breathe a degree of renovating warmth which I had not expected.

No incidents have hitherto befallen us, that would make a figure in a letter. One or two stiff gales, and the breaking of a mast, are accidents which experienced navigators scarcely remember to record; and I shall be well content, if nothing worse happen to us during our voyage.

Adieu, my dear Margaret. Be assured, that for my own sake, as well as your's, I will not rashly encounter danger. I will be cool, persevering, and prudent.

Remember me to all my English friends.

Most affectionately yours,
R. W.

LETTER IV

To Mrs. Saville, England.

August 5th, 17—.

So strange an accident has happened to us, that I cannot forbear recording it, although it is very probable that you will see me before these papers can come into your possession.

Last Monday (July 31st), we were nearly surrounded by ice, which closed in the ship on all sides, scarcely leaving her the sea room in which she floated. Our situation was somewhat dangerous, especially as we were compassed round by a very thick fog. We accordingly lay to, hoping that some change would take place in the atmosphere and weather.

About two o'clock the mist cleared away, and we beheld, stretched out in every direction, vast and irregular plains of ice, which seemed to have no end. Some of my comrades groaned, and my own mind began to grow watchful with anxious thoughts, when a strange sight suddenly attracted our attention, and diverted our solicitude from our own situation. We perceived a low carriage, fixed on a sledge and drawn by dogs, pass on towards the north, at the distance of half a mile: a being which had the shape of a man, but apparently of gigantic stature, sat in the sledge, and guided the dogs. We watched the rapid progress of the traveller with our telescopes, until he was lost among the distant inequalities of the ice.

This appearance excited our unqualified wonder. We were, as we believed, many hundred miles from any land; but this apparition seemed to denote that it was not, in reality, so distant as we had supposed. Shut in, however, by ice, it was impossible to follow his track, which we had observed with the greatest attention.

About two hours after this occurrence, we heard the ground sea; and before night the ice broke, and freed our ship. We, however, lay to until the morning, fearing to encounter in the dark those large loose masses which float about after the breaking up of the ice. I profited of this time to rest for a few hours.

In the morning, however, as soon as it was light, I went upon deck, and found all the sailors busy on one side of the vessel, apparently talking to some one in the sea. It was, in fact, a sledge, like that we had seen before, which had drifted towards us in the night, on a large fragment of ice. Only one dog remained alive; but there was a human being within it, whom the sailors were persuading to enter the vessel. He was not, as the other traveller seemed to be, a savage inhabitant of some undiscovered island, but an European. When I appeared on deck, the master said, "Here is our captain, and he will not allow you to perish on the open sea."

On perceiving me, the stranger addressed me in English, although with a foreign accent. "Before I come on board your vessel," said he, "will you have the kindness to inform me whither you are bound?"

You may conceive my astonishment on hearing such a question addressed to me from a man on the brink of destruction, and to whom I should have supposed that my vessel would have been a resource which he would not have exchanged for the most precious wealth the earth can afford. I replied, however, that we were on a voyage of discovery towards the northern pole.

Upon hearing this he appeared satisfied, and consented to come on board. Good God! Margaret, if you had seen the man who thus capitulated for his safety, your surprise would have been boundless. His limbs were nearly frozen, and his body dreadfully emaciated by fatigue and suffering. I never saw a man in so wretched a condition. We attempted to carry him into the cabin; but as soon as he had quitted the fresh air, he fainted. We accordingly brought him back to the deck, and restored him to animation by rubbing him with brandy, and forcing him to swallow a small quantity. As soon as he shewed signs of life, we wrapped him up in blankets, and placed him near the chimney of the kitchen-stove. By slow degrees he recovered, and ate a little soup, which restored him wonderfully.

Two days passed in this manner before he was able to speak; and I often feared that his sufferings had deprived him of understanding. When he had in some measure recovered, I removed him to my own cabin, and attended on him as much as my duty would permit. I never saw a more interesting creature: his eyes have generally an expression of wildness, and even madness; but there are moments when, if any one performs an act of kindness towards him, or does him any the most trifling service, his whole countenance is lighted up, as it were, with a beam of benevolence and sweetness that I never saw equalled. But he is generally melancholy and despairing; and sometimes he gnashes his teeth, as if impatient of the weight of woes that oppresses him.

When my guest was a little recovered, I had great trouble to keep off the men, who wished to ask him a thousand questions; but I would not allow him to be tormented by their idle curiosity, in a state of body and mind whose restoration evidently depended upon entire repose. Once, however, the lieutenant asked, Why he had come so far upon the ice in so strange a vehicle?

His countenance instantly assumed an aspect of the deepest gloom; and he replied, "To seek one who fled from me."

"And did the man whom you pursued travel in the same fashion?"

"Yes."

"Then I fancy we have seen him; for, the day before we picked you up, we saw some dogs drawing a sledge, with a man in it, across the ice."

This aroused the stranger's attention; and he asked a multitude of questions concerning the route which the dæmon, as he called him, had pursued. Soon after, when he was alone with me, he said, "I have, doubtless, excited your curiosity, as well as that of these good people; but you are too considerate to make inquiries."

"Certainly; it would indeed be very impertinent and inhuman in me to trouble you with any inquisitiveness of mine."

"And yet you rescued me from a strange and perilous situation; you have benevolently restored me to life."

Soon after this he inquired, if I thought that the breaking up of the ice had destroyed the other sledge? I replied, that I could not answer with any degree of certainty; for the ice had not broken until near midnight, and the traveller might have arrived at a place of safety before that time; but of this I could not judge.

From this time the stranger seemed very eager to be upon deck, to watch for the sledge which had before appeared; but I have persuaded him to remain in the cabin, for he is far too weak to sustain the rawness of the atmosphere. But I have promised that some one should watch for him, and give him instant notice if any new object should appear in sight.

Such is my journal of what relates to this strange occurrence up to the present day. The stranger has gradually improved in health, but is very silent, and appears uneasy when any one except myself enters his cabin. Yet his manners are so conciliating and gentle, that the sailors are all interested in him, although they have had very little communication with him. For my own part, I begin to love him as a brother; and his constant and deep grief fills me with sympathy and compassion. He must have been a noble creature in his better days, being even now in wreck so attractive and amiable.

I said in one of my letters, my dear Margaret, that I should find no friend on the wide ocean; yet I have found a man who, before his spirit had been broken by misery, I should have been happy to have possessed as the brother of my heart.

I shall continue my journal concerning the stranger at intervals, should I have any fresh incidents to record.

August 13th, 17—.

My affection for my guest increases every day. He excites at once my admiration and my pity to an astonishing degree. How can I see so noble a creature destroyed by misery without feeling the most poignant grief? He is so gentle, yet so wise; his mind is so cultivated; and when he speaks, although his words are culled with the choicest art, yet they flow with rapidity and unparalleled eloquence.

He is now much recovered from his illness, and is continually on the deck, apparently watching for the sledge that preceded his own. Yet, although unhappy, he is not so utterly occupied by his own misery, but that he interests himself deeply in the employments of others. He has asked me many questions concerning my design; and I have related my little history frankly to him. He appeared pleased with the confidence, and suggested several alterations in my plan, which I shall find exceedingly useful. There is no pedantry in his manner; but all he does appears to spring solely from the interest he instinctively takes in the welfare of those who surround him. He is often overcome by gloom, and then he sits by himself, and tries to overcome all that is sullen or unsocial in his humour. These paroxysms pass from him like a cloud from before the sun, though his dejection never leaves him. I have endeavoured to win his confidence; and I trust that I have succeeded. One day I mentioned to him the desire I had always felt of finding a friend who might sympathize with me, and direct me by his counsel. I said, I did not belong to that class of men who are offended by advice. "I am self-educated, and perhaps I hardly rely sufficiently upon my own powers. I wish therefore that my companion should be wiser and more experienced than myself, to confirm and support me; nor have I believed it impossible to find a true friend."

"I agree with you," replied the stranger, "in believing that friendship is not only a desirable, but a possible acquisition. I once had a friend, the most noble of human creatures, and am entitled, therefore, to judge respecting friendship. You have hope, and the world before you, and have no cause for despair. But I——I have lost everything, and cannot begin life anew."

As he said this, his countenance became expressive of a calm settled grief, that touched me to the heart. But he was silent, and presently retired to his cabin.

Even broken in spirit as he is, no one can feel more deeply than he does the beauties of nature. The starry sky, the sea, and every sight afforded by these wonderful regions, seems still to have the power of elevating his soul from earth. Such a man has a double existence: he may suffer misery, and be overwhelmed by disappointments; yet when he has retired into himself, he will be like a celestial spirit, that has a halo around him, within whose circle no grief or folly ventures.

Will you laugh at the enthusiasm I express concerning this divine wanderer? If you do, you must have certainly lost that simplicity which was once your characteristic charm. Yet, if you will, smile at the warmth of my expressions, while I find every day new causes for repeating them.

August 19th, 17—.

Yesterday the stranger said to me, "You may easily perceive, Captain Walton, that I have suffered great and unparalleled misfortunes. I had determined, once, that the memory of these evils should die with me; but you have won me to alter my determination. You seek for knowledge and wisdom, as I once did; and I ardently hope that the gratification of your wishes may not be a serpent to sting you, as mine has been. I do not know that the relation of my misfortunes will be useful to you, yet, if you are inclined, listen to my tale. I believe that the strange incidents connected with it will afford a view of nature, which may enlarge your faculties and understanding. You will hear of powers and occurrences, such as you have been accustomed to believe impossible: but I do not doubt that my tale conveys in its series internal evidence of the truth of the events of which it is composed."

You may easily conceive that I was much gratified by the offered communication; yet I could not endure that he should renew his grief by a recital of his misfortunes. I felt the greatest eagerness to hear the promised narrative, partly from curiosity, and partly from a strong desire to ameliorate his fate, if it were in my power. I expressed these feelings in my answer.

"I thank you," he replied, "for your sympathy, but it is useless; my fate is nearly fulfilled. I wait but for one event, and then I shall repose in peace. I understand your feeling," continued he, perceiving that I wished to interrupt him; "but you are mistaken, my friend, if thus you will allow me to name you; nothing can alter my destiny: listen to my history, and you will perceive how irrevocably it is determined."

He then told me, that he would commence his narrative the next day when I should be at leisure. This promise drew from me the warmest thanks. I have resolved every night, when I am not engaged, to record, as nearly as possible in his own words, what he has related during the day. If I should be engaged, I will at least make notes. This manuscript will doubtless afford you the greatest pleasure: but to me, who know him, and who hear it from his own lips, with what interest and sympathy shall I read it in some future day!

CHAPTER I

I am by birth a Genevese; and my family is one of the most distinguished of that republic. My ancestors had been for many years counsellors and syndics; and my father had filled several public situations with honour and reputation. He was respected by all who knew him for his integrity and indefatigable attention to public business. He passed his younger days perpetually occupied by the affairs of his country; and it was not until the decline of life that he thought of marrying, and bestowing on the state sons who might carry his virtues and his name down to posterity.

As the circumstances of his marriage illustrate his character, I cannot refrain from relating them. One of his most intimate friends was a merchant, who, from a flourishing state, fell, through numerous mischances, into poverty. This man, whose name was Beaufort, was of a proud and unbending disposition, and could not bear to live in poverty and oblivion in the same country where he had formerly been distinguished for his rank and magnificence. Having paid his debts, therefore, in the most honourable manner, he retreated with his daughter to the town of Lucerne, where he lived unknown and in wretchedness. My father loved Beaufort with the truest friendship, and was deeply grieved by his retreat in these unfortunate circumstances. He grieved also for the loss of his society, and resolved to seek him out and endeavour to persuade him to begin the world again through his credit and assistance.

Beaufort had taken effectual measures to conceal himself; and it was ten months before my father discovered his abode. Overjoyed at this discovery, he hastened to the house, which was situated in a mean street, near the Reuss. But when he entered, misery and despair alone welcomed him. Beaufort had saved but a very small sum of money from the wreck of his fortunes; but it was sufficient to provide him with sustenance for some months, and in the mean time he hoped to procure some respectable employment in a merchant's house. The interval was consequently spent in inaction; his grief only became more deep and rankling, when he had leisure for reflection; and at length it took so fast hold of his mind, that at the end of three months he lay on a bed of sickness, incapable of any exertion.

His daughter attended him with the greatest tenderness; but she saw with despair that their little fund was rapidly decreasing, and that there was no other prospect of support. But Caroline Beaufort possessed a mind of an uncommon mould; and her courage rose to support her in her adversity. She procured plain work; she plaited straw; and by various means contrived to earn a pittance scarcely sufficient to support life.

Several months passed in this manner. Her father grew worse; her time was more entirely occupied in attending him; her means of subsistence decreased; and in the tenth month her father died in her arms, leaving her an orphan and a beggar. This last blow overcame her; and she knelt by Beaufort's coffin, weeping bitterly, when my father entered the chamber. He came like a protecting spirit to the poor girl, who committed herself to his care, and after the interment of his friend he conducted her to Geneva, and placed her under the protection of a relation. Two years after this event Caroline became his wife.

When my father became a husband and a parent, he found his time so occupied by the duties of his new situation, that he relinquished many of his public employments, and devoted himself to the education of his children. Of these I was the eldest, and the destined successor to all his labours and utility. No creature could have more tender parents than mine. My improvement and health were their constant care, especially as I remained for several years their only child. But before I continue my narrative, I must record an incident which took place when I was four years of age.

My father had a sister, whom he tenderly loved, and who had married early in life an Italian gentleman. Soon after her marriage, she had accompanied her husband into his native country, and for some years my father had very little communication with her. About the time I mentioned she died; and a few months afterwards he received a letter from her husband, acquainting him with his intention of marrying an Italian lady, and requesting my father to take charge of the infant Elizabeth, the only child of his deceased sister. "It is my wish," he said, "that you should consider her as your own daughter, and educate her thus. Her mother's fortune is secured to her, the documents of which I will commit to your keeping. Reflect upon this proposition; and decide whether you would prefer educating your niece yourself to her being brought up by a stepmother."

My father did not hesitate, and immediately went to Italy, that he might accompany the little Elizabeth to her future home. I have often heard my mother say that she was at that time the most beautiful child she had ever seen, and shewed signs even then of a gentle and affectionate disposition. These indications, and a desire to bind as closely as possible the ties of domestic love, determined my mother to consider Elizabeth as my future wife; a design which she never found reason to repent.

From this time Elizabeth Lavenza became my playfellow, and, as we grew older, my friend. She was docile and good tempered, yet gay and playful as a summer insect. Although she was lively and animated, her feelings were strong and deep, and her disposition uncommonly affectionate. No one could better enjoy liberty, yet no one could submit with more grace than she did to constraint and caprice. Her imagination was luxuriant, yet her capability of application was great. Her person was the image of her mind; her hazel eyes, although as lively as a bird's, possessed an attractive softness. Her figure was light and airy; and, though capable of enduring great fatigue, she appeared the most fragile creature in the world. While I admired her understanding and fancy, I loved to tend on her, as I should on a favourite animal; and I never saw so much grace both of person and mind united to so little pretension.

Every one adored Elizabeth. If the servants had any request to make, it was always through her intercession. We were strangers to any species of disunion and dispute; for although there was a great dissimilitude in our characters, there was an harmony in that very dissimilitude. I was more calm and philosophical than my companion; yet my temper was not so yielding. My application was of longer endurance; but it was not so severe whilst it endured. I delighted in investigating the facts relative to the actual world; she busied herself in following the aerial creations of the poets. The world was to me a secret, which I desired to discover; to her it was a vacancy, which she sought to people with imaginations of her own.

My brothers were considerably younger than myself; but I had a friend in one of my schoolfellows, who compensated for this deficiency. Henry Clerval was the son of a merchant of Geneva, an intimate friend of my father. He was a boy of singular talent and fancy. I remember, when he was nine years old, he wrote a fairy tale, which was the delight and amazement of all his companions. His favourite study consisted in books of chivalry and romance; and when very young, I can remember, that we used to act plays composed by him out of these favourite books, the principal characters of which were Orlando, Robin Hood, Amadis, and St. George.

No youth could have passed more happily than mine. My parents were indulgent, and my companions amiable. Our studies were never forced; and by some means we always had an end placed in view, which excited us to ardour in the prosecution of them. It was by this method, and not by emulation, that we were urged to application. Elizabeth was not incited to apply herself to drawing, that her companions might not outstrip her; but through the desire of pleasing her aunt, by the representation of some favourite scene done by her own hand. We learned Latin and English, that we might read the writings in those languages; and so far from study being made odious to us through punishment, we loved application, and our amusements would have been the labours of other children. Perhaps we did not read so many books, or learn languages so quickly, as those who are disciplined according to the ordinary methods; but what we learned was impressed the more deeply on our memories.

In this description of our domestic circle I include Henry Clerval; for he was constantly with us. He went to school with me, and generally passed the afternoon at our house; for being an only child, and destitute of companions at home, his father was well pleased that he should find associates at our house; and we were never completely happy when Clerval was absent.

I feel pleasure in dwelling on the recollections of childhood, before misfortune had tainted my mind and changed its bright visions of extensive usefulness into gloomy and narrow reflections upon self. But, in drawing the picture of my early days, I must not omit to record those events which led, by insensible steps to my after tale of misery: for when I would account to myself for the birth of that passion, which afterwards ruled my destiny, I find it arise, like a mountain river, from ignoble and almost forgotten sources; but swelling as it proceeded, it became the torrent which in its course, has swept away all my hopes and joys.

Natural philosophy is the genius that has regulated my fate; I desire therefore, in this narration, to state those facts which led to my predilection for that science. When I was thirteen years of age, we all went on a party of pleasure to the baths near Thonon: the inclemency of the weather obliged us to remain a day confined to the inn. In this house I chanced to find a volume of the works of Cornelius Agrippa. I opened it with apathy; the theory which he attempts to demon strate, and the wonderful facts which he relates, soon changed this feeling into enthusiasm. A new light seemed to dawn upon my mind; and, bounding with joy, I communicated my discovery to my father. I cannot help remarking here the many opportunities instructors possess of directing the attention of their pupils to useful knowledge, which they utterly neglect. My father looked carelessly at the title-page of my book, and said, "Ah! Cornelius Agrippa! My dear Victor, do not waste your time upon this; it is sad trash."

If, instead of this remark, my father had taken the pains to explain to me, that the principles of Agrippa had been entirely exploded, and that a modern system of science had been introduced, which possessed much greater powers than the ancient, because the powers of the latter were chimerical, while those of the former were real and practical; under such circumstances, I should certainly have thrown Agrippa aside, and, with my imagination warmed as it was, should probably have applied myself to the more rational theory of chemistry which has resulted from modern discoveries. It is even possible, that the train of my ideas would never have received the fatal impulse that led to my ruin. But the cursory glance my father had taken of my volume by no means assured me that he was acquainted with its contents; and I continued to read with the greatest avidity.

When I returned home, my first care was to procure the whole works of this author, and afterwards of Paracelsus and Albertus Magnus. I read and studied the wild fancies of these writers with delight; they appeared to me treasures known to few beside myself; and although I often wished to communicate these secret stores of knowledge to my father, yet his indefinite censure of my favourite Agrippa always withheld me. I disclosed my discoveries to Elizabeth, therefore, under a promise of strict secrecy; but she did not interest herself in the subject, and I was left by her to pursue my studies alone.

It may appear very strange, that a disciple of Albertus Magnus should arise in the eighteenth century; but our family was not scientifical, and I had not attended any of the lectures given at the schools of Geneva. My dreams were therefore undisturbed by reality; and I entered with the greatest diligence into the search of the philosopher's stone and the elixir of life. But the latter obtained my most undivided attention: wealth was an inferior object; but what glory would attend the discovery, if I could banish disease from the human frame, and render man invulnerable to any but a violent death!

Nor were these my only visions. The raising of ghosts or devils was a promise liberally accorded by my favourite authors, the fulfilment of which I most eagerly sought; and if my incantations were always unsuccessful, I attributed the failure rather to my own inexperience and mistake, than to a want of skill or fidelity in my instructors.

The natural phænomena that take place every day before our eyes did not escape my examinations. Distillation, and the wonderful effects of steam, processes of which my favourite authors were utterly ignorant, excited my astonishment; but my utmost wonder was engaged by some experiments on an air-pump, which I saw employed by a gentleman whom we were in the habit of visiting.

The ignorance of the early philosophers on these and several other points served to decrease their credit with me: but I could not entirely throw them aside, before some other system should occupy their place in my mind.

When I was about fifteen years old, we had retired to our house near Belrive, when we witnessed a most violent and terrible thunder-storm. It advanced from behind the mountains of Jura; and the thunder burst at once with frightful loudness from various quarters of the heavens. I remained, while the storm lasted, watching its progress with curiosity and delight. As I stood at the door, on a sudden I beheld a stream of fire issue from an old and beautiful oak, which stood about twenty yards from our house; and so soon as the dazzling light vanished, the oak had disappeared, and nothing remained but a blasted stump. When we visited it the next morning, we found the tree shattered in a singular manner. It was not splintered by the shock, but entirely reduced to thin ribbands of wood. I never beheld any thing so utterly destroyed.

The catastrophe of this tree excited my extreme astonishment; and I eagerly inquired of my father the nature and origin of thunder and lightning. He replied, "Electricity;" describing at the same time the various effects of that power. He constructed a small electrical machine, and exhibited a few experiments; he made also a kite, with a wire and string, which drew down that fluid from the clouds.

This last stroke completed the overthrow of Cornelius Agrippa, Albertus Magnus, and Paracelsus, who had so long reigned the lords of my imagination. But by some fatality I did not feel inclined to commence the study of any modern system; and this disinclination was influenced by the following circumstance.

My father expressed a wish that I should attend a course of lectures upon natural philosophy, to which I cheerfully consented. Some accident prevented my attending these lectures until the course was nearly finished. The lecture, being therefore one of the last, was entirely incomprehensible to me. The professor discoursed with the greatest fluency of potassium and boron, of sulphates and oxyds, terms to which I could affix no idea; and I became disgusted with the science of natural philosophy, although I still read Pliny and Buffon with delight, authors, in my estimation, of nearly equal interest and utility.

My occupations at this age were principally the mathematics, and most of the branches of study appertaining to that science. I was busily employed in learning languages; Latin was already familiar to me, and I began to read some of the easiest Greek authors without the help of a lexicon. I also perfectly understood English and German. This is the list of my accomplishments at the age of seventeen; and you may conceive that my hours were fully employed in acquiring and maintaining a knowledge of this various literature.

Another task also devolved upon me, when I became the instructor of my brothers. Ernest was six years younger than myself, and was my principal pupil. He had been afflicted with ill health from his infancy, through which Elizabeth and I had been his constant nurses: his disposition was gentle, but he was incapable of any severe application. William, the youngest of our family, was yet an infant, and the most beautiful little fellow in the world; his lively blue eyes, dimpled cheeks, and endearing manners, inspired the tenderest affection.

Such was our domestic circle, from which care and pain seemed for ever banished. My father directed our studies, and my mother partook of our enjoyments. Neither of us possessed the slightest preeminence over the other; the voice of command was never heard amongst us; but mutual affection engaged us all to comply with and obey the slightest desire of each other.

CHAPTER II

When I had attained the age of seventeen, my parents resolved that I should become a student at the university of Ingolstadt. I had hitherto attended the schools of Geneva; but my father thought it necessary, for the completion of my education, that I should be made acquainted with other customs than those of my native country. My departure was therefore fixed at an early date; but, before the day resolved upon could arrive, the first misfortune of my life occurred—an omen, as it were, of my future misery.

Elizabeth had caught the scarlet fever; but her illness was not severe, and she quickly recovered. During her confinement, many arguments had been urged to persuade my mother to refrain from attending upon her. She had, at first, yielded to our entreaties; but when she heard that her favourite was recovering, she could no longer debar herself from her society, and entered her chamber long before the danger of infection was past. The consequences of this imprudence were fatal. On the third day my mother sickened; her fever was very malignant, and the looks of her attendants prognosticated the worst event. On her death-bed the fortitude and benignity of this admirable woman did not desert her. She joined the hands of Elizabeth and myself: "My children," she said, "my firmest hopes of future happiness were placed on the prospect of your union. This expectation will now be the consolation of your father. Elizabeth, my love, you must supply my place to your younger cousins. Alas! I regret that I am taken from you; and, happy and beloved as I have been, is it not hard to quit you all? But these are not thoughts befitting me; I will endeavour to resign myself cheerfully to death, and will indulge a hope of meeting you in another world."

She died calmly; and her countenance expressed affection even in death. I need not describe the feelings of those whose dearest ties are rent by that most irreparable evil, the void that presents itself to the soul, and the despair that is exhibited on the countenance. It is so long before the mind can persuade itself that she, whom we saw every day, and whose very existence appeared a part of our own, can have departed for ever—that the brightness of a beloved eye can have been extinguished, and the sound of a voice so familiar, and dear to the ear, can be hushed, never more to be heard. These are the reflections of the first days; but when the lapse of time proves the reality of the evil, then the actual bitterness of grief commences. Yet from whom has not that rude hand rent away some dear connexion; and why should I describe a sorrow which all have felt, and must feel? The time at length arrives, when grief is rather an indulgence than a necessity; and the smile that plays upon the lips, although it may be deemed a sacrilege, is not banished. My mother was dead, but we had still duties which we ought to perform; we must continue our course with the rest, and learn to think ourselves fortunate, whilst one remains whom the spoiler has not seized.

My journey to Ingolstadt, which had been deferred by these events, was now again determined upon. I obtained from my father a respite of some weeks. This period was spent sadly; my mother's death, and my speedy departure, depressed our spirits; but Elizabeth endeavoured to renew the spirit of cheerfulness in our little society. Since the death of her aunt, her mind had acquired new firmness and vigour. She determined to fulfil her duties with the greatest exactness; and she felt that that most imperious duty, of rendering her uncle and cousins happy, had devolved upon her. She consoled me, amused her uncle, instructed my brothers; and I never beheld her so enchanting as at this time, when she was continually endeavouring to contribute to the happiness of others, entirely forgetful of herself.

The day of my departure at length arrived. I had taken leave of all my friends, excepting Clerval, who spent the last evening with us. He bitterly lamented that he was unable to accompany me: but his father could not be persuaded to part with him, intending that he should become a partner with him in business, in compliance with his favourite theory, that learning was superfluous in the commerce of ordinary life. Henry had a refined mind; he had no desire to be idle, and was well pleased to become his father's partner, but he believed that a man might be a very good trader, and yet possess a cultivated understanding.

We sat late, listening to his complaints, and making many little arrangements for the future. The next morning early I departed. Tears gushed from the eyes of Elizabeth; they proceeded partly from sorrow at my departure, and partly because she reflected that the same journey was to have taken place three months before, when a mother's blessing would have accompanied me.

I threw myself into the chaise that was to convey me away, and indulged in the most melancholy reflections. I, who had ever been surrounded by amiable companions, continually engaged in endeavouring to bestow mutual pleasure, I was now alone. In the university, whither I was going, I must form my own friends, and be my own protector. My life had hitherto been remarkably secluded and domestic; and this had given me invincible repugnance to new countenances. I loved my brothers, Elizabeth, and Clerval; these were "old familiar faces;" but I believed myself totally unfitted for the company of strangers. Such were my reflections as I commenced my journey; but as I proceeded, my spirits and hopes rose. I ardently desired the acquisition of knowledge. I had often, when at home, thought it hard to remain during my youth cooped up in one place, and had longed to enter the world, and take my station among other human beings. Now my desires were complied with, and it would, indeed, have been folly to repent.

I had sufficient leisure for these and many other reflections during my journey to Ingolstadt, which was long and fatiguing. At length the high white steeple of the town met my eyes. I alighted, and was conducted to my solitary apartment, to spend the evening as I pleased.

The next morning I delivered my letters of introduction, and paid a visit to some of the principal professors, and among others to M. Krempe, professor of natural philosophy. He received me with politeness, and asked me several questions concerning my progress in the different branches of science appertaining to natural philosophy. I mentioned, it is true, with fear and trembling, the only authors I had ever read upon those subjects. The professor stared: "Have you," he said, "really spent your time in studying such nonsense?"

I replied in the affirmative. "Every minute," continued M. Krempe with warmth, "every instant that you have wasted on those books is utterly and entirely lost. You have burdened your memory with exploded systems, and useless names. Good God! in what desert land have you lived, where no one was kind enough to inform you that these fancies, which you have so greedily imbibed, are a thousand years old, and as musty as they are ancient? I little expected in this enlightened and scientific age to find a disciple of Albertus Magnus and Paracelsus. My dear Sir, you must begin your studies entirely anew."

So saying, he stept aside, and wrote down a list of several books treating of natural philosophy, which he desired me to procure, and dismissed me, after mentioning that in the beginning of the following week he intended to commence a course of lectures upon natural philosophy in its general relations, and that M. Waldman, a fellow-professor, would lecture upon chemistry the alternate days that he missed.

I returned home, not disappointed, for I had long considered those authors useless whom the professor had so strongly reprobated; but I did not feel much inclined to study the books which I procured at his recommendation. M. Krempe was a little squat man, with a gruff voice and repulsive countenance; the teacher, therefore, did not prepossess me in favour of his doctrine. Besides, I had a contempt for the uses of modern natural philosophy. It was very different, when the masters of the science sought immortality and power; such views, although futile, were grand: but now the scene was changed. The ambition of the inquirer seemed to limit itself to the annihilation of those visions on which my interest in science was chiefly founded. I was required to exchange chimeras of boundless grandeur for realities of little worth.

Such were my reflections during the first two or three days spent almost in solitude. But as the ensuing week commenced, I thought of the information which M. Krempe had given me concerning the lectures. And although I could not consent to go and hear that little conceited fellow deliver sentences out of a pulpit, I recollected what he had said of M. Waldman, whom I had never seen, as he had hitherto been out of town.

Partly from curiosity, and partly from idleness, I went into the lecturing room, which M. Waldman entered shortly after. This professor was very unlike his colleague. He appeared about fifty years of age, but with an aspect expressive of the greatest benevolence; a few gray hairs covered his temples, but those at the back of his head were nearly black. His person was short, but remarkably erect; and his voice the sweetest I had ever heard. He began his lecture by a recapitulation of the history of chemistry and the various improvements made by different men of learning, pronouncing with fervour the names of the most distinguished discoverers. He then took a cursory view of the present state of the science, and explained many of its elementary terms. After having made a few preparatory experiments, he concluded with a panegyric upon modern chemistry, the terms of which I shall never forget:—

"The ancient teachers of this science," said he, "promised impossibilities, and performed nothing. The modern masters promise very little; they know that metals cannot be transmuted, and that the elixir of life is a chimera. But these philosophers, whose hands seem only made to dabble in dirt, and their eyes to pour over the microscope or crucible, have indeed performed miracles. They penetrate into the recesses of nature, and shew how she works in her hiding places. They ascend into the heavens; they have discovered how the blood circulates, and the nature of the air we breathe. They have acquired new and almost unlimited powers; they can command the thunders of heaven, mimic the earthquake, and even mock the invisible world with its own shadows."

I departed highly pleased with the professor and his lecture, and paid him a visit the same evening. His manners in private were even more mild and attractive than in public; for there was a certain dignity in his mien during his lecture, which in his own house was replaced by the greatest affability and kindness. He heard with attention my little narration concerning my studies, and smiled at the names of Cornelius Agrippa, and Paracelsus, but without the contempt that M. Krempe had exhibited. He said, that "these were men to whose indefatigable zeal modern philosophers were indebted for most of the foundations of their knowledge. They had left to us, as an easier task, to give new names, and arrange in connected classifications, the facts which they in a great degree had been the instruments of bringing to light. The labours of men of genius, however erroneously directed, scarcely ever fail in ultimately turning to the solid advantage of mankind." I listened to his statement, which was delivered without any presumption or affectation; and then added, that his lecture had removed my prejudices against modern chemists; and I, at the same time, requested his advice concerning the books I ought to procure.

"I am happy," said M. Waldman, "to have gained a disciple; and if your application equals your ability, I have no doubt of your success. Chemistry is that branch of natural philosophy in which the greatest improvements have been and may be made; it is on that account that I have made it my peculiar study; but at the same time I have not neglected the other branches of science. A man would make but a very sorry chemist, if he attended to that department of human knowledge alone. If your wish is to become really a man of science, and not merely a petty experimentalist, I should advise you to apply to every branch of natural philosophy, including mathematics."

He then took me into his laboratory, and explained

to me the uses of his various machines; instructing me as to what I ought to procure, and promising me the use of his own, when I should have advanced far enough in the science not to derange their mechanism. He also gave me the list of books which I had requested: and I took my leave.

Thus ended a day memorable to me: it decided my future destiny.

CHAPTER III

From this day natural philosophy, and particularly chemistry, in the most comprehensive sense of the term, became nearly my sole occupation. I read with ardour those works, so full of genius and discrimination, which modern inquirers have written on these subjects. I attended the lectures, and cultivated the acquaintance, of the men of science of the university; and I found even in M. Krempe a great deal of sound sense and real information, combined, it is true, with a repulsive physiognomy and manners, but not on that account the less valuable. In M. Waldman I found a true friend. His gentleness was never tinged by dogmatism; and his instructions were given with an air of frankness and good nature, that banished every idea of pedantry. It was, perhaps, the amiable character of this man that inclined me more to that branch of natural philosophy which he professed, than an intrinsic love for the science itself. But this state of mind had place only in the first steps towards knowledge: the more fully I entered into the science, the more exclusively I pursued it for its own sake.

That application, which at first had been a matter of duty and resolution, now became so ardent and eager, that the stars often disappeared in the light of morning whilst I was yet engaged in my laboratory.

As I applied so closely, it may be easily conceived that I improved rapidly. My ardour was indeed the astonishment of the students; and my proficiency, that of the masters. Professor Krempe often asked me, with a sly smile, how Cornelius Agrippa went on? whilst M. Waldman expressed the most heartfelt exultation in my progress. Two years passed in this manner, during which I paid no visit to Geneva, but was engaged, heart and soul, in the pursuit of some discoveries, which I hoped to make. None but those who have experienced them can conceive of the enticements of science. In other studies you go as far as others have gone before you, and there is nothing more to know; but in a scientific pursuit there is continual food for discovery and wonder. A mind of moderate capacity, which closely pursues one study, must infallibly arrive at great proficiency in that study; and I, who continually sought the attainment of one object of pursuit, and was solely wrapt up in this, improved so rapidly, that, at the end of two years, I made some discoveries in the improvement of some chemical instruments, which procured me great esteem and admiration at the university. When I had arrived at this point, and had become as well acquainted with the theory and practice of natural philosophy as depended on the lessons of any of the professors at Ingolstadt, my residence there being no longer conducive to my improvements, I thought of returning to my friends and my native town, when an incident happened that protracted my stay.

One of the phænomena which had peculiarly attracted my attention was the structure of the human frame, and, indeed, any animal endued with life.

Whence, I often asked myself, did the principle of life proceed? It was a bold question, and one which has ever been considered as a mystery; yet with how many things are we upon the brink of becoming acquainted, if cowardice or carelessness did not restrain our inquiries. I revolved these circumstances in my mind, and determined thenceforth to apply myself more particularly to those branches of natural philosophy which relate to physiology. Unless I had been animated by an almost supernatural enthusiasm, my application to this study would have been irksome, and almost intolerable. To examine the causes of life, we must first have recourse to death. I became acquainted with the science of anatomy: but this was not sufficient; I must also observe the natural decay and corruption of the human body. In my education my father had taken the greatest precautions that my mind should be impressed with no supernatural horrors. I do not ever remember to have trembled at a tale of superstition, or to have feared the apparition of a spirit. Darkness had no effect upon my fancy; and a church-yard was to me merely the receptacle of bodies deprived of life, which, from being the seat of beauty and strength, had become food for the worm. Now I was led to examine the cause and progress of this decay, and forced to spend days and nights in vaults and charnel houses. My attention was fixed upon every object the most insupportable to the delicacy of the human feelings. I saw how the fine form of man was degraded and wasted; I beheld the corruption of death succeed to the blooming cheek of life; I saw how the worm inherited the wonders of the eye and brain. I paused, examining and analysing all the minutiæ of causation, as exemplified in the change from life to death, and death to life, until from the midst of this darkness a sudden light broke in upon me—a light so brilliant and wondrous, yet so simple, that while I became dizzy with the immensity of the prospect which it illustrated, I was surprised that among so many men of genius, who had directed their inquiries towards the same science, that I alone should be reserved to discover so astonishing a secret.

Remember, I am not recording the vision of a madman. The sun does not more certainly shine in the heavens, than that which I now affirm is true. Some miracle might have produced it, yet the stages of the discovery were distinct and probable. After days and nights of incredible labour and fatigue, I succeeded in discovering the cause of generation and life; nay, more, I became myself capable of bestowing animation upon lifeless matter.

The astonishment which I had at first experienced on this discovery soon gave place to delight and rapture. After so much time spent in painful labour, to arrive at once at the summit of my desires, was the most gratifying consummation of my toils. But this discovery was so great and overwhelming, that all the steps by which I had been progressively led to it were obliterated, and I beheld only the result. What had been the study and desire of the wisest men since the creation of the world, was now within my grasp. Not that, like a magic scene, it all opened upon me at once: the information I had obtained was of a nature rather to direct my endeavours so soon as I should point them towards the object of my search, than to exhibit that object already accomplished. I was like the Arabian who had been buried with the dead, and found a passage to life aided only by one glimmering, and seemingly ineffectual light.

I see by your eagerness, and the wonder and hope which your eyes express, my friend, that you expect to be informed of the secret with which I am acquainted; that cannot be: listen patiently until the end of my story, and you will easily perceive why I am reserved upon that subject. I will not lead you on, unguarded and ardent as I then was, to your destruction and infallible misery. Learn from me, if not by my precepts, at least by my example, how dangerous is the acquirement of knowledge, and how much happier that man is who believes his native town to be the world, than he who aspires to become greater than his nature will allow.

When I found so astonishing a power placed within my hands, I hesitated a long time concerning the manner in which I should employ it. Although I possessed the capacity of bestowing animation, yet to prepare a frame for the reception of it, with all its intricacies of fibres, muscles, and veins, still remained a work of inconceivable difficulty and labour. I doubted at first whether I should attempt the creation of a being like myself or one of simpler organization; but my imagination was too much exalted by my first success to permit me to doubt of my ability to give life to an animal as complex and wonderful as man. The materials at present within my command hardly appeared adequate to so arduous an undertaking; but I doubted not that I should ultimately succeed. I prepared myself for a multitude of reverses; my operations might be incessantly baffled, and at last my work be imperfect: yet, when I considered the improvement which every day takes place in science and mechanics, I was encouraged to hope my present attempts would at least lay the foundations of future success. Nor could I consider the magnitude and complexity of my plan as any argument of its impracticability. It was with these feelings that I began the creation of a human being. As the minuteness of the parts formed a great hindrance to my speed, I resolved, contrary to my first intention, to make the being of a gigantic stature; that is to say, about eight feet in height, and proportionably large. After having formed this determination, and having spent some months in successfully collecting and arranging my materials, I began.

No one can conceive the variety of feelings which bore me onwards, like a hurricane, in the first enthusiasm of success. Life and death appeared to me ideal bounds, which I should first break through, and pour a torrent of light into our dark world. A new species would bless me as its creator and source; many happy and excellent natures would owe their being to me. No father could claim the gratitude of his child so completely as I should deserve their's. Pursuing these reflections, I thought, that if I could bestow animation upon lifeless matter, I might in process of time (although I now found it impossible) renew life where death had apparently devoted the body to corruption.

These thoughts supported my spirits, while I pursued my undertaking with unremitting ardour. My cheek had grown pale with study, and my person had become emaciated with confinement. Sometimes, on the very brink of certainty, I failed; yet still I clung to the hope which the next day or the next hour might realize. One secret which I alone possessed was the hope to which I had dedicated myself; and the moon gazed on my midnight labours, while, with unrelaxed and breathless eagerness, I pursued nature to her hiding places. Who shall conceive the horrors of my secret toil, as I dabbled among the unhallowed damps of the grave, or tortured the living animal to animate the lifeless clay? My limbs now tremble, and my eyes swim with the remembrance; but then a resistless, and almost frantic impulse, urged me forward; I seemed to have lost all soul or sensation but for this one pursuit. It was indeed but a passing trance, that only made me feel with renewed acuteness so soon as, the unnatural stimulus ceasing to operate, I had returned to my old habits. I collected bones from charnel houses; and disturbed, with profane fingers, the tremendous secrets of the human frame. In a solitary chamber, or rather cell, at the top of the house, and separated from all the other apartments by a gallery and staircase, I kept my workshop of filthy creation; my eyeballs were starting from their sockets in attending to the details of my employment. The dissecting room and the slaughter-house furnished many of my materials; and often did my human nature turn with loathing from my occupation, whilst, still urged on by an eagerness which perpetually increased, I brought my work near to a conclusion.

The summer months passed while I was thus engaged, heart and soul, in one pursuit. It was a most beautiful season; never did the fields bestow a more plentiful harvest, or the vines yield a more luxuriant vintage: but my eyes were insensible to the charms of nature. And the same feelings which made me neglect the scenes around me caused me also to forget those friends who were so many miles absent, and whom I had not seen for so long a time. I knew my silence disquieted them; and I well remembered the words of my father: "I know that while you are pleased with yourself, you will think of us with affection, and we shall hear regularly from you. You must pardon me, if I regard any interruption in your correspondence as a proof that your other duties are equally neglected."

I knew well therefore what would be my father's feelings; but I could not tear my thoughts from my employment, loathsome in itself, but which had taken an irresistible hold of my imagination. I wished, as it were, to procrastinate all that related to my feelings of affection until the great object, which swallowed up every habit of my nature, should be completed.

I then thought that my father would be unjust if he ascribed my neglect to vice, or faultiness on my part; but I am now convinced that he was justified in conceiving that I should not be altogether free from blame. A human being in perfection ought always to preserve a calm and peaceful mind, and never to allow passion or a transitory desire to disturb his tranquillity. I do not think that the pursuit of knowledge is an exception to this rule. If the study to which you apply yourself has a tendency to weaken your affections, and to destroy your taste for those simple pleasures in which no alloy can possibly mix, then that study is certainly unlawful, that is to say, not befitting the human mind. If this rule were always observed; if no man allowed any pursuit whatsoever to interfere with the tranquillity of his domestic affections, Greece had not been enslaved; Cæsar would have spared his country; America would have been discovered more gradually; and the empires of Mexico and Peru had not been destroyed.

But I forget that I am moralizing in the most interesting part of my tale; and your looks remind me to proceed.

My father made no reproach in his letters; and only took notice of my silence by inquiring into my occupations more particularly than before. Winter, spring, and summer, passed away during my labours; but I did not watch the blossom or the expanding leaves—sights which before always yielded me supreme delight, so deeply was I engrossed in my occupation. The leaves of that year had withered before my work drew near to a close; and now every day shewed me more plainly how well I had succeeded. But my enthusiasm was checked by my anxiety, and I appeared rather like one doomed by slavery to toil in the mines, or any other unwholesome trade, than an artist occupied by his favourite employment. Every night I was oppressed by a slow fever, and I became nervous to a most painful degree; a disease that I regretted the more because I had hitherto enjoyed most excellent health, and had always boasted of the firmness of my nerves. But I believed that exercise and amusement would soon drive away such symptoms; and I promised myself both of these, when my creation should be complete.

CHAPTER IV

It was on a dreary night of November, that I beheld the accomplishment of my toils. With an anxiety that almost amounted to agony, I collected the instruments of life around me, that I might infuse a spark of being into the lifeless thing that lay at my feet. It was already one in the morning; the rain pattered dismally against the panes, and my candle was nearly burnt out, when, by the glimmer of the half-extinguished light, I saw the dull yellow eye of the creature open; it breathed hard, and a convulsive motion agitated its limbs.

How can I describe my emotions at this catastrophe, or how delineate the wretch whom with such infinite pains and care I had endeavoured to form? His limbs were in proportion, and I had selected his features as beautiful. Beautiful!—Great God! His yellow skin scarcely covered the work of muscles and arteries beneath; his hair was of a lustrous black, and flowing; his teeth of a pearly whiteness; but these luxuriances only formed a more horrid contrast with his watery eyes, that seemed almost of the same colour as the dun white sockets in which they were set, his shrivelled complexion, and straight black lips.

The different accidents of life are not so changeable

as the feelings of human nature. I had worked hard for nearly two years, for the sole purpose of infusing life into an inanimate body. For this I had deprived myself of rest and health. I had desired it with an ardour that far exceeded moderation; but now that I had finished, the beauty of the dream vanished, and breathless horror and disgust filled my heart. Unable to endure the aspect of the being I had created, I rushed out of the room, and continued a long time traversing my bed-chamber, unable to compose my mind to sleep. At length lassitude succeeded to the tumult I had before endured; and I threw myself on the bed in my clothes, endeavouring to seek a few moments of forgetfulness. But it was in vain: I slept indeed, but I was disturbed by the wildest dreams. I thought I saw Elizabeth, in the bloom of health, walking in the streets of Ingolstadt. Delighted and surprised, I embraced her; but as I imprinted the first kiss on her lips, they became livid with the hue of death; her features appeared to change, and I thought that I held the corpse of my dead mother in my arms; a shroud enveloped her form, and I saw the grave-worms crawling in the folds of the flannel. I started from my sleep with horror; a cold dew covered my forehead, my teeth chattered, and every limb became convulsed; when, by the dim and yellow light of the moon, as it forced its way through the window-shutters, I beheld the wretch—the miserable monster whom I had created. He held up the curtain of the bed; and his eyes, if eyes they may be called, were fixed on me. His jaws opened, and he muttered some inarticulate sounds, while a grin wrinkled his cheeks. He might have spoken, but I did not hear; one hand was stretched out, seemingly to detain me, but I escaped, and rushed down stairs. I took refuge in the court-yard belonging to the house which I inhabited; where I remained during the rest of the night, walking up and down in the greatest agitation, listening attentively, catching and fearing each sound as if it were to announce the approach of the demoniacal corpse to which I had so miserably given life.

Oh! no mortal could support the horror of that countenance. A mummy again endued with animation could not be so hideous as that wretch. I had gazed on him while unfinished; he was ugly then; but when those muscles and joints were rendered capable of motion, it became a thing such as even Dante could not have conceived.

I passed the night wretchedly. Sometimes my pulse beat so quickly and hardly, that I felt the palpitation of every artery; at others, I nearly sank to the ground through languor and extreme weakness. Mingled with this horror, I felt the bitterness of disappointment: dreams that had been my food and pleasant rest for so long a space, were now become a hell to me; and the change was so rapid, the overthrow so complete!

Morning, dismal and wet, at length dawned, and discovered to my sleepless and aching eyes the church of Ingolstadt, its white steeple and clock, which indicated the sixth hour. The porter opened the gates of the court, which had that night been my asylum, and I issued into the streets, pacing them with quick steps, as if I sought to avoid the wretch whom I feared every turning of the street would present to my view. I did not dare return to the apartment which I inhabited, but felt impelled to hurry on, although wetted by the rain, which poured from a black and comfortless sky.

I continued walking in this manner for some time, endeavouring, by bodily exercise, to ease the load that weighed upon my mind. I traversed the streets, without any clear conception of where I was, or what I was doing. My heart palpitated in the sickness of fear; and

I hurried on with irregular steps, not daring to look about me:

> Like one who, on a lonely road,
>   Doth walk in fear and dread,
> And, having once turn'd round, walks on,
>   And turns no more his head;
> Because he knows a frightful fiend
>   Doth close behind him tread.

Continuing thus, I came at length opposite to the inn at which the various diligences and carriages usually stopped. Here I paused, I knew not why; but I remained some minutes with my eyes fixed on a coach that was coming towards me from the other end of the street. As it drew nearer, I observed that it was the Swiss diligence: it stopped just where I was standing; and, on the door being opened, I perceived Henry Clerval, who, on seeing me, instantly sprung out. "My dear Frankenstein," exclaimed he, "how glad I am to see you! how fortunate that you should be here at the very moment of my alighting!"

Nothing could equal my delight on seeing Clerval; his presence brought back to my thoughts my father, Elizabeth, and all those scenes of home so dear to my recollection. I grasped his hand, and in a moment forgot my horror and misfortune; I felt suddenly, and for the first time during many months, calm and serene joy. I welcomed my friend, therefore, in the most cordial manner, and we walked towards my college. Clerval continued talking for some time about our mutual friends, and his own good fortune in being permitted to come to Ingolstadt. "You may easily believe," said he, "how great was the difficulty to persuade my father that it was not absolutely necessary for a merchant not to understand any thing except book-keeping; and, indeed, I believe I left him incredulous to the last, for his constant answer to my unwearied entreaties was the same as that of the Dutch school-master in the Vicar of Wakefield: 'I have ten thousand florins a year without Greek, I eat heartily without Greek.' But his affection for me at length overcame his dislike of learning, and he has permitted me to undertake a voyage of discovery to the land of knowledge."

"It gives me the greatest delight to see you; but tell me how you left my fathers, brothers, and Elizabeth."

"Very well, and very happy, only a little uneasy that they hear from you so seldom. By the bye, I mean to lecture you a little upon their account myself.—But, my dear Frankenstein," continued he, stopping short, and gazing full in my face, "I did not before remark how very ill you appear; so thin and pale; you look as if you had been watching for several nights."

"You have guessed right; I have lately been so deeply engaged in one occupation, that I have not allowed myself sufficient rest, as you see: but I hope, I sincerely hope, that all these employments are now at an end, and that I am at length free."

I trembled excessively; I could not endure to think of, and far less to allude to the occurrences of the preceding night. I walked with a quick pace, and we soon arrived at my college. I then reflected, and the thought made me shiver, that the creature whom I had left in my apartment might still be there, alive, and walking about. I dreaded to behold this monster; but I feared still more that Henry should see him. Entreating him therefore to remain a few minutes at the bottom of the stairs, I darted up towards my own room. My hand was already on the lock of the door before I recollected myself. I then paused; and a cold shivering came over me. I threw the door forcibly open, as children are accustomed to do when they expect a spectre to stand in waiting for them on the other side; but nothing appeared. I stepped fearfully in: the apartment was empty; and my bed-room was also freed from its hideous guest. I could hardly believe that so great a good-fortune could have befallen me; but when I became assured that my enemy had indeed fled, I clapped my hands for joy, and ran down to Clerval.

We ascended into my room, and the servant presently brought breakfast; but I was unable to contain myself. It was not joy only that possessed me; I felt my flesh tingle with excess of sensitiveness, and my pulse beat rapidly. I was unable to remain for a single instant in the same place; I jumped over the chairs, clapped my hands, and laughed aloud. Clerval at first attributed my unusual spirits to joy on his arrival; but when he observed me more attentively, he saw a wildness in my eyes for which he could not account; and my loud, unrestrained, heartless laughter, frightened and astonished him.

"My dear Victor," cried he, "what, for God's sake, is the matter? Do not laugh in that manner. How ill you are! What is the cause of all this?"

"Do not ask me," cried I, putting my hands before my eyes, for I thought I saw the dreaded spectre glide into the room; "*he* can tell.—Oh, save me! save me!" I imagined that the monster seized me; I struggled furiously, and fell down in a fit.

Poor Clerval! what must have been his feelings? A meeting, which he anticipated with such joy, so strangely turned to bitterness. But I was not the witness of his grief; for I was lifeless, and did not recover my senses for a long, long time.

This was the commencement of a nervous fever, which confined me for several months. During all that time Henry was my only nurse. I afterwards learned that, knowing my father's advanced age, and unfitness for so long a journey, and how wretched my sickness would make Elizabeth, he spared them this grief by concealing the extent of my disorder. He knew that I could not have a more kind and attentive nurse than himself; and, firm in the hope he felt of my recovery, he did not doubt that, instead of doing harm, he performed the kindest action that he could towards them.

But I was in reality very ill; and surely nothing but the unbounded and unremitting attentions of my friend could have restored me to life. The form of the monster on whom I had bestowed existence was for ever before my eyes, and I raved incessantly concerning him. Doubtless my words surprised Henry: he at first believed them to be the wanderings of my disturbed imagination; but the pertinacity with which I continually recurred to the same subject persuaded him that my disorder indeed owed its origin to some uncommon and terrible event.

By very slow degrees, and with frequent relapses, that alarmed and grieved my friend, I recovered. I remember the first time I became capable of observing outward objects with any kind of pleasure, I perceived that the fallen leaves had disappeared, and that the young buds were shooting forth from the trees that shaded my window. It was a divine spring; and the season contributed greatly to my convalescence. I felt also sentiments of joy and affection revive in my bosom; my gloom disappeared, and in a short time I became as cheerful as before I was attacked by the fatal passion.

"Dearest Clerval," exclaimed I, "how kind, how very good you are to me. This whole winter, instead of being spent in study, as you promised yourself, has been consumed in my sick room. How shall I ever repay you? I feel the greatest remorse for the disappointment of which I have been the occasion; but you will forgive me."

"You will repay me entirely, if you do not discompose yourself, but get well as fast as you can; and since you appear in such good spirits, I may speak to you on one subject, may I not?"

I trembled. One subject! what could it be? Could he allude to an object on whom I dared not even think?

"Compose yourself," said Clerval, who observed my change of colour, "I will not mention it, if it agitates you; but your father and cousin would be very happy if they received a letter from you in your own handwriting. They hardly know how ill you have been, and are uneasy at your long silence."

"Is that all? my dear Henry. How could you suppose that my first thought would not fly towards those dear, dear friends whom I love, and who are so deserving of my love."

"If this is your present temper, my friend, you will perhaps be glad to see a letter that has been lying here some days for you: it is from your cousin, I believe."

CHAPTER V

Clerval then put the following letter into my hands.

"To V. Frankenstein.

"My dear Cousin,

"I cannot describe to you the uneasiness we have all felt concerning your health. We cannot help imagining that your friend Clerval conceals the extent of your disorder: for it is now several months since we have seen your hand-writing; and all this time you have been obliged to dictate your letters to Henry. Surely, Victor, you must have been exceedingly ill; and this makes us all very wretched, as much so nearly as after the death of your dear mother. My uncle was almost persuaded that you were indeed dangerously ill, and could hardly be restrained from undertaking a journey to Ingolstadt. Clerval always writes that you are getting better; I eagerly hope that you will confirm this intelligence soon in your own hand-writing; for indeed, indeed, Victor, we are all very miserable on this account. Relieve us from this fear, and we shall be the happiest creatures in the world. Your father's health is now so vigorous, that he appears ten years younger since last winter. Ernest also is so much improved, that you would hardly know him: he is now nearly sixteen, and has lost that sickly appearance which he had some years ago; he is grown quite robust and active.

"My uncle and I conversed a long time last night about what profession Ernest should follow. His constant illness when young has deprived him of the habits of application; and now that he enjoys good health, he is continually in the open air, climbing the hills, or rowing on the lake. I therefore proposed that he should be a farmer; which you know, Cousin, is a favourite scheme of mine. A farmer's is a very healthy happy life; and the least hurtful, or rather the most beneficial profession of any. My uncle had an idea of his being educated as an advocate, that through his interest he might become a judge. But, besides that he is not at all fitted for such an occupation, it is certainly more creditable to cultivate the earth for the sustenance of man, than to be the confidant, and sometimes the accomplice, of his vices; which is the profession of a lawyer. I said, that the employments of a prosperous farmer, if they were not a more honourable, they were at least a happier species of occupation than that of a judge, whose misfortune it was always to meddle with the dark side of human nature. My uncle smiled, and said, that I ought to be an advocate myself, which put an end to the conversation on that subject.

"And now I must tell you a little story that will please, and perhaps amuse you. Do you not remember Justine Moritz? Probably you do not; I will relate her history, therefore, in a few words. Madame Moritz, her mother, was a widow with four children, of whom Justine was the third. This girl had always been the favourite of her father; but, through a strange perversity, her mother could not endure her, and, after the death of M. Moritz, treated her very ill. My aunt observed this; and, when Justine was twelve years of age, prevailed on her mother to allow her to live at her house. The republican institutions of our country have produced simpler and happier manners than those which prevail in the great monarchies that surround it. Hence there is less distinction between the several classes of its inhabitants; and the lower orders being neither so poor nor so despised, their manners are more refined and moral. A servant in Geneva does not mean the same thing as a servant in France and England. Justine, thus received in our family, learned the duties of a servant; a condition which, in our fortunate country, does not include the idea of ignorance, and a sacrifice of the dignity of a human being.

"After what I have said, I dare say you well remember the heroine of my little tale: for Justine was a great favourite of your's; and I recollect you once remarked, that if you were in an ill humour, one glance from Justine could dissipate it, for the same reason that Ariosto gives concerning the beauty of

Angelica—she looked so frank-hearted and happy. My aunt conceived a great attachment for her, by which she was induced to give her an education superior to that which she had at first intended. This benefit was fully repaid; Justine was the most grateful little creature in the world: I do not mean that she made any professions, I never heard one pass her lips; but you could see by her eyes that she almost adored her protectress. Although her disposition was gay, and in many respects inconsiderate, yet she paid the greatest attention to every gesture of my aunt. She thought her the model of all excellence, and endeavoured to imitate her phraseology and manners, so that even now she often reminds me of her.

"When my dearest aunt died, every one was too much occupied in their own grief to notice poor Justine, who had attended her during her illness with the most anxious affection. Poor Justine was very ill; but other trials were reserved for her.

"One by one, her brothers and sister died; and her mother, with the exception of her neglected daughter, was left childless. The conscience of the woman was troubled; she began to think that the deaths of her favourites was a judgment from heaven to chastise her partiality. She was a Roman Catholic; and I believe her confessor confirmed the idea which she had conceived. Accordingly, a few months after your departure for Ingolstadt, Justine was called home by her repentant mother. Poor girl! she wept when she quitted our house: she was much altered since the death of my aunt; grief had given softness and a winning mildness to her manners, which had before been remarkable for vivacity. Nor was her residence at her mother's house of a nature to restore her gaiety. The poor woman was very vacillating in her repentance. She sometimes begged Justine to forgive her unkindness, but much oftener accused her of having caused the deaths of her brothers and sister. Perpetual fretting at length threw Madame Moritz into a decline, which at first increased her irritability, but she is now at peace for ever. She died on the first approach of cold weather, at the beginning of this last winter. Justine has returned to us; and I assure you I love her tenderly. She is very clever and gentle, and extremely pretty; as I mentioned before, her mien and her expressions continually remind me of my dear aunt.

"I must say also a few words to you, my dear cousin, of little darling William. I wish you could see him; he is very tall of his age, with sweet laughing blue eyes, dark eye-lashes, and curling hair. When he smiles, two little dimples appear on each cheek, which are rosy with health. He has already had one or two little *wives,* but Louisa Biron is his favourite, a pretty little girl of five years of age.

"Now, dear Victor, I dare say you wish to be indulged in a little gossip concerning the good people of Geneva. The pretty Miss Mansfield has already received the congratulatory visits on her approaching marriage with a young Englishman, John Melbourne, Esq. Her ugly sister, Manon, married M. Duvillard, the rich banker, last autumn. Your favourite schoolfellow, Louis Manoir, has suffered several misfortunes since the departure of Clerval from Geneva. But he has already recovered his spirits, and is reported to be on the point of marrying a very lively pretty Frenchwoman, Madame Tavernier. She is a widow, and much older than Manoir; but she is very much admired, and a favourite with every body.

"I have written myself into good spirits, dear cousin; yet I cannot conclude without again anxiously inquiring concerning your health. Dear Victor, if you are not very ill, write yourself, and make your father and all of us happy; or—I cannot bear to think of the other side of the question; my tears already flow. Adieu, my dearest cousin.

"Elizabeth Lavenza.

"Geneva, March 18th, 17—."

"Dear, dear Elizabeth!" I exclaimed when I had read her letter, "I will write instantly, and relieve them from the anxiety they must feel." I wrote, and this exertion greatly fatigued me; but my convalescence had commenced, and proceeded regularly. In another fortnight I was able to leave my chamber.

One of my first duties on my recovery was to introduce Clerval to the several professors of the university. In doing this, I underwent a kind of rough usage, ill befitting the wounds that my mind had sustained. Ever since the fatal night, the end of my labours, and the beginning of my misfortunes, I had conceived a violent antipathy even to the name of natural philosophy. When I was otherwise quite restored to health, the sight of a chemical instrument would renew all the agony of my nervous symptoms. Henry saw this, and had removed all my apparatus from my view. He had also changed my apartment; for he perceived that I had acquired a dislike for the room which had previously been my laboratory. But these cares of Clerval were made of no avail when I visited the professors. M. Waldman inflicted torture when he praised, with kindness and warmth, the astonishing progress I had made in the sciences. He soon perceived that I disliked the subject; but, not guessing the real cause, he attributed my feelings to modesty, and changed the subject from my improvement to the science itself, with a desire, as I evidently saw, of drawing me out. What could I do? He meant to please, and he tormented me. I felt as if he had placed carefully, one by one, in my view those instruments which were to be afterwards used in putting me to a slow and cruel death. I writhed under his words, yet dared not exhibit the pain I felt. Clerval, whose eyes and feelings were always quick in discerning the sensations of others, declined the subject, alleging, in excuse, his total ignorance; and the conversation took a more general turn. I thanked my friend from my heart, but I did not speak. I saw plainly that he was surprised, but he never attempted to draw my secret from me; and although I loved him with a mixture of affection and reverence that knew no bounds, yet I could never persuade myself to confide to him that event which was so often present to my recollection, but which I feared the detail to another would only impress more deeply.

M. Krempe was not equally docile; and in my condition at that time, of almost insupportable sensitiveness, his harsh blunt encomiums gave me even more pain than the benevolent approbation of M. Waldman. "D—n the fellow!" cried he; "why, M. Clerval, I assure you he has outstript us all. Aye, stare if you please; but it is nevertheless true. A youngster who, but a few years ago, believed Cornelius Agrippa as firmly as the gospel, has now set himself at the head of the university; and if he is not soon pulled down, we shall all be out of countenance.—Aye, aye," continued he, observing my face expressive of suffering, "M. Frankenstein is modest; an excellent quality in a young man. Young men should be diffident of themselves, you know, M. Clerval; I was myself when young: but that wears out in a very short time."

M. Krempe had now commenced an eulogy on himself, which happily turned the conversation from a subject that was so annoying to me.

Clerval was no natural philosopher. His imagination was too vivid for the minutiæ of science. Languages were his principal study; and he sought, by acquiring their elements, to open a field for self-instruction on his return to Geneva. Persian, Arabic, and Hebrew, gained his attention, after he had made himself perfectly master of Greek and Latin. For my own part, idleness had ever been irksome to me; and now that I wished to fly from reflection, and hated my former studies, I felt great relief in being the fellow-pupil with my friend, and found not only instruction but consolation in the works of the orientalists. Their melancholy is soothing, and their joy elevating to a degree I never experienced in studying the authors of any other country. When you read their writings, life appears to consist in a warm sun and garden of roses,—in the smiles and frowns of a fair enemy, and the fire that consumes your own heart. How different from the manly and heroical poetry of Greece and Rome.

Summer passed away in these occupations, and my return to Geneva was fixed for the latter end of autumn; but being delayed by several accidents, winter and snow arrived, the roads were deemed impassable, and my journey was retarded until the ensuing spring. I felt this delay very bitterly; for I longed to see my native town, and my beloved friends. My return had only been delayed so long from an unwillingness to leave Clerval in a strange place, before he had become acquainted with any of its inhabitants. The winter, however, was spent cheerfully; and although the spring was uncommonly late, when it came, its beauty compensated for its dilatoriness.

The month of May had already commenced, and I expected the letter daily which was to fix the date of my departure, when Henry proposed a pedestrian tour in the environs of Ingolstadt that I might bid a personal farewell to the country I had so long inhabited. I acceded with pleasure to this proposition: I was fond of exercise, and Clerval had always been my favourite companion in the rambles of this nature that I had taken among the scenes of my native country.

We passed a fortnight in these perambulations; my health and spirits had long been restored, and they gained additional strength from the salubrious air I breathed, the natural incidents of our progress, and the conversation of my friend. Study had before secluded me from the intercourse of my fellow-creatures, and rendered me unsocial; but Clerval called forth the better feelings of my heart; he again taught me to love the aspect of nature, and the cheerful faces of children. Excellent friend! how sincerely did you love me, and endeavour to elevate my mind, until it was on a level with your own. A selfish pursuit had cramped and narrowed me, until your gentleness and affection warmed and opened my senses; I became the same happy creature who, a few years ago, loving and beloved by all, had no sorrow or care. When happy, inanimate nature had the power of bestowing on me the most delightful sensations. A serene sky and verdant fields filled me with ecstacy. The present season was indeed divine; the flowers of spring bloomed in the hedges, while those of summer were already in bud: I was undisturbed by thoughts which during the preceding year had pressed upon me, notwithstanding my endeavours to throw them off, with an invincible burden.

Henry rejoiced in my gaiety, and sincerely sympathized in my feelings: he exerted himself to amuse me, while he expressed the sensations that filled his soul. The resources of his mind on this occasion were truly astonishing: his conversation was full of imagination; and very often, in imitation of the Persian and Arabic writers, he invented tales of wonderful fancy and passion. At other times he repeated my favourite poems, or drew me out into arguments, which he supported with great ingenuity.

We returned to our college on a Sunday afternoon: the peasants were dancing, and every one we met appeared gay and happy. My own spirits were high, and I bounded along with feelings of unbridled joy and hilarity.

CHAPTER VI

On my return, I found the following letter from my father:—

"To V. Frankenstein.

"My dear Victor,

"You have probably waited impatiently for a letter to fix the date of your return to us; and I was at first tempted to write only a few lines, merely mentioning the day on which I should expect you. But that would be a cruel kindness, and I dare not do it. What would be your surprise, my son, when you expected a happy and gay welcome, to behold, on the contrary, tears and wretchedness? And how, Victor, can I relate our misfortune? Absence cannot have rendered you callous to our joys and griefs; and how shall I inflict pain on an absent child? I wish to prepare you for the woeful news, but I know it is impossible; even now your eye skims over the page, to seek the words which are to convey to you the horrible tidings.

"William is dead!—that sweet child, whose smiles delighted and warmed my heart, who was so gentle, yet so gay! Victor, he is murdered!

"I will not attempt to console you; but will simply relate the circumstances of the transaction.

"Last Thursday (May 7th) I, my niece, and your two brothers, went to walk in Plainpalais. The evening was warm and serene, and we prolonged our walk farther than usual. It was already dusk before we thought of returning; and then we discovered that William and Ernest, who had gone on before, were not to be found. We accordingly rested on a seat until they should return. Presently Ernest came, and inquired if we had seen his brother: he said, that they had been playing together, that William had run away to hide himself, and that he vainly sought for him, and afterwards waited for him a long time, but that he did not return.

"This account rather alarmed us, and we continued to search for him until night fell, when Elizabeth conjectured that he might have returned to the house. He was not there. We returned again, with torches; for I could not rest, when I thought that my sweet boy had lost himself, and was exposed to all the damps and dews of night: Elizabeth also suffered extreme anguish. About five in the morning I discovered my lovely boy, whom the night before I had seen blooming and active in health, stretched on the grass livid and motionless: the print of the murderer's finger was on his neck.

"He was conveyed home, and the anguish that was visible in my countenance betrayed the secret to Elizabeth. She was very earnest to see the corpse. At first I attempted to prevent her; but she persisted, and entering the room where it lay, hastily examined the neck of the victim, and clasping her hands exclaimed, 'Oh God! I have murdered my darling infant!'

"She fainted, and was restored with extreme difficulty. When she again lived, it was only to weep and sigh. She told me, that that same evening William had teazed her to let him wear a very valuable miniature that she possessed of your mother. This picture is gone, and was doubtless the temptation which urged the murderer to the deed. We have no trace of him at present, although our exertions to discover him are unremitted; but they will not restore my beloved William.

"Come, dearest Victor; you alone can console Elizabeth. She weeps continually, and accuses herself unjustly as the cause of his death; her words pierce my heart. We are all unhappy; but will not that be an additional motive for you, my son, to return and be our comforter? Your dear mother! Alas, Victor! I now say, Thank God she did not live to witness the cruel, miserable death of her youngest darling!

"Come, Victor; not brooding thoughts of vengeance against the assassin, but with feelings of peace and gentleness, that will heal, instead of festering the wounds of our minds. Enter the house of mourning, my friend, but with kindness and affection for those who love you, and not with hatred for your enemies.

"Your affectionate and afflicted father,
Alphonse Frankenstein.

"Geneva, May 12th, 17—."

Clerval, who had watched my countenance as I read this letter, was surprised to observe the despair that succeeded to the joy I at first expressed on receiving news from my friends. I threw the letter on the table, and covered my face with my hands.

"My dear Frankenstein," exclaimed Henry, when he perceived me weep with bitterness, "are you always to be unhappy? My dear friend, what has happened?"

I motioned to him to take up the letter, while I walked up and down the room in the extremest agitation. Tears also gushed from the eyes of Clerval, as he read the account of my misfortune.

"I can offer you no consolation, my friend," said

he; "your disaster is irreparable. What do you intend to do."

"To go instantly to Geneva: come with me, Henry, to order the horses."

During our walk, Clerval endeavoured to raise my spirits. He did not do this by common topics of consolation, but by exhibiting the truest sympathy. "Poor William!" said he, "that dear child; he now sleeps with his angel mother. His friends mourn and weep, but he is at rest: he does not now feel the murderer's grasp; a sod covers his gentle form, and he knows no pain. He can no longer be a fit subject for pity; the survivors are the greatest sufferers, and for them time is the only consolation. Those maxims of the Stoics, that death was no evil, and that the mind of man ought to be superior to despair on the eternal absence of a beloved object, ought not to be urged. Even Cato wept over the dead body of his brother."

Clerval spoke thus as we hurried through the streets; the words impressed themselves on my mind, and I remembered them afterwards in solitude. But now, as soon as the horses arrived, I hurried into a cabriole, and bade farewell to my friend.

My journey was very melancholy. At first I wished to hurry on, for I longed to console and sympathize with my loved and sorrowing friends; but when I drew near my native town, I slackened my progress. I could hardly sustain the multitude of feelings that crowded into my mind. I passed through scenes familiar to my youth, but which I had not seen for nearly six years. How altered every thing might be during that time? One sudden and desolating change had taken place; but a thousand little circumstances might have by degrees worked other alterations which, although they were done more tranquilly, might not be the less decisive. Fear overcame me; I dared not advance, dreading a thousand nameless evils that made me tremble, although I was unable to define them.

I remained two days at Lausanne, in this painful state of mind. I contemplated the lake: the waters were placid; all around was calm, and the snowy mountains, "the palaces of nature," were not changed. By degrees the calm and heavenly scene restored me, and I continued my journey towards Geneva.

The road ran by the side of the lake, which became narrower as I approached my native town. I discovered more distinctly the black sides of Jura, and the bright summit of Mont Blanc; I wept like a child: "Dear mountains! my own beautiful lake! how do you welcome your wanderer? Your summits are clear; the sky and lake are blue and placid. Is this to prognosticate peace, or to mock at my unhappiness?"

I fear, my friend, that I shall render myself tedious by dwelling on these preliminary circumstances; but they were days of comparative happiness, and I think of them with pleasure. My country, my beloved country! who but a native can tell the delight I took in again beholding thy streams, thy mountains, and, more than all, thy lovely lake.

Yet, as I drew nearer home, grief and fear again overcame me. Night also closed around; and when I could hardly see the dark mountains, I felt still more gloomily. The picture appeared a vast and dim scene of evil, and I foresaw obscurely that I was destined to become the most wretched of human beings. Alas! I prophesied truly, and failed only in one single circumstance, that in all the misery I imagined and dreaded, I did not conceive the hundredth part of the anguish I was destined to endure.

It was completely dark when I arrived in the environs of Geneva; the gates of the town were already shut; and I was obliged to pass the night at

Secheron, a village half a league to the east of the city. The sky was serene; and, as I was unable to rest, I resolved to visit the spot where my poor William had been murdered. As I could not pass through the town, I was obliged to cross the lake in a boat to arrive at Plainpalais. During this short voyage I saw the lightnings playing on the summit of Mont Blanc in the most beautiful figures. The storm appeared to approach rapidly; and, on landing, I ascended a low hill, that I might observe its progress. It advanced; the heavens were clouded, and I soon felt the rain coming slowly in large drops, but its violence quickly increased.

I quitted my seat, and walked on, although the darkness and storm increased every minute, and the thunder burst with a terrific crash over my head. It was echoed from Salêve, the Juras, and the Alps of Savoy; vivid flashes of lightning dazzled my eyes, illuminating the lake, making it appear like a vast sheet of fire; then for an instant every thing seemed of a pitchy darkness, until the eye recovered itself from the preceding flash. The storm, as is often the case in Switzerland, appeared at once in various parts of the heavens. The most violent storm hung exactly north of the town, over that part of the lake which lies between the promontory of Belrive and the village of Copêt. Another storm enlightened Jura with faint flashes; and another darkened and sometimes disclosed the Môle, a peaked mountain to the east of the lake.

While I watched the storm, so beautiful yet terrific, I wandered on with a hasty step. This noble war in the sky elevated my spirits; I clasped my hands, and exclaimed aloud, "William, dear angel! this is thy funeral, this thy dirge!" As I said these words, I perceived in the gloom a figure which stole from behind a clump of trees near me; I stood fixed, gazing intently: I could not be mistaken. A flash of lightning illuminated the object, and discovered its shape plainly to me; its gigantic stature, and the deformity of its aspect, more hideous than belongs to humanity, instantly informed me that it was the wretch, the filthy dæmon to whom I had given life. What did he there? Could he be (I shuddered at the conception) the murderer of my brother? No sooner did that idea cross my imagination, than I became convinced of its truth; my teeth chattered, and I was forced to lean against a tree for support. The figure passed me quickly, and I lost it in the gloom. Nothing in human shape could have destroyed that fair child. *He* was the murderer! I could not doubt it. The mere presence of the idea was an irresistible proof of the fact. I thought of pursuing the devil; but it would have been in vain, for another flash discovered him to me hanging among the rocks of the nearly perpendicular ascent of Mont Salêve, a hill that bounds Plainpalais on the south. He soon reached the summit, and disappeared.

I remained motionless. The thunder ceased; but the rain still continued, and the scene was enveloped in an impenetrable darkness. I revolved in my mind the events which I had until now sought to forget: the whole train of my progress towards the creation; the appearance of the work of my own hands alive at my bed side; its departure. Two years had now nearly elapsed since the night on which he first received life; and was this his first crime? Alas! I had turned loose into the world a depraved wretch, whose delight was in carnage and misery; had he not murdered my brother?

No one can conceive the anguish I suffered during the remainder of the night, which I spent, cold and wet, in the open air. But I did not feel the inconvenience of the weather; my imagination was busy in scenes of evil and despair. I considered the being whom I had cast among mankind, and endowed with the will and power to effect purposes of horror, such as the deed which he had now done, nearly in the light of my own vampire, my own spirit let loose from the grave, and forced to destroy all that was dear to me.

Day dawned; and I directed my steps toward the town. The gates were open; and I hastened to my father's house. My first thought was to discover what I knew of the murderer, and cause instant pursuit to be made. But I paused when I reflected on the story that I had to tell. A being whom I myself had formed, and endued with life, had met me at midnight among the precipices of an inaccessible mountain. I remembered also the nervous fever with which I had been seized just at the time that I dated my creation, and which would give an air of delirium to a tale otherwise so utterly improbable. I well knew that if any other had communicated such a relation to me, I should have looked upon it as the ravings of insanity. Besides, the strange nature of the animal would elude all pursuit, even if I were so far credited as to persuade my relatives to commence it. Besides, of what use would be pursuit? Who could arrest a creature capable of scaling the overhanging sides of Mont Salêve? These reflections determined me, and I resolved to remain silent.

It was about five in the morning when I entered my father's house. I told the servants not to disturb the family, and went into the library to attend their usual hour of rising.

Six years had elapsed, passed as a dream but for one indelible trace, and I stood in the same place where I had last embraced my father before my departure for Ingolstadt. Beloved and respectable parent! He still remained to me. I gazed on the picture of my mother, which stood over the mantlepiece. It was an historical subject, painted at my father's desire, and represented

Caroline Beaufort in an agony of despair, kneeling by the coffin of her dead father. Her garb was rustic, and her cheek pale; but there was an air of dignity and beauty, that hardly permitted the sentiment of pity. Below this picture was a miniature of William; and my tears flowed when I looked upon it. While I was thus engaged, Ernest entered: he had heard me arrive, and hastened to welcome me. He expressed a sorrowful delight to see me: "Welcome, my dearest Victor," said he. "Ah! I wish you had come three months ago, and then you would have found us all joyous and delighted. But we are now unhappy; and, I am afraid, tears instead of smiles will be your welcome. Our father looks so sorrowful: this dreadful event seems to have revived in his mind his grief on the death of Mamma. Poor Elizabeth also is quite inconsolable." Ernest began to weep as he said these words.

"Do not," said I, "welcome me thus; try to be more calm, that I may not be absolutely miserable the moment I enter my father's house after so long an absence. But, tell me, how does my father support his misfortunes? and how is my poor Elizabeth?"

"She indeed requires consolation; she accused herself of having caused the death of my brother, and that made her very wretched. But since the murderer has been discovered—"

"The murderer discovered! Good God! how can that be? who could attempt to pursue him? It is impossible; one might as well try to overtake the winds, or confine a mountain-stream with a straw."

"I do not know what you mean; but we were all very unhappy when she was discovered. No one would believe it at first; and even now Elizabeth will not be convinced; notwithstanding all the evidence. Indeed, who would credit that Justine Moritz, who was so amiable, and fond of all the family, could all at once become so extremely wicked?"

"Justine Moritz! Poor, poor girl, is she the accused? But it is wrongfully; every one knows that; no one believes it, surely, Ernest?"

"No one did at first; but several circumstances came out, that have almost forced conviction upon us: and her own behaviour has been so confused, as to add to the evidence of facts a weight that, I fear, leaves no hope for doubt. But she will be tried to-day, and you will then hear all."

He related that, the morning on which the murder of poor William had been discovered, Justine had been taken ill, and confined to her bed; and, after several days, one of the servants, happening to examine the apparel she had worn on the night of the murder, had discovered in her pocket the picture of my mother, which had been judged to be the temptation of the murderer. The servant instantly shewed it to one of the others, who, without saying a word to any of the family, went to a magistrate; and, upon their deposition, Justine was apprehended. On being charged with the fact, the poor girl confirmed the suspicion in a great measure by her extreme confusion of manner.

This was a strange tale, but it did not shake my faith; and I replied earnestly, "You are all mistaken; I know the murderer. Justine, poor, good Justine, is innocent."

At that instant my father entered. I saw unhappiness deeply impressed on his countenance, but he endeavoured to welcome me cheerfully; and, after we had exchanged our mournful greeting, would have introduced some other topic than that of our disaster, had not Ernest exclaimed, "Good God, Papa! Victor says that he knows who was the murderer of poor William."

"We do also, unfortunately," replied my father; "for indeed I had rather have been for ever ignorant than have discovered so much depravity and ingratitude in one I valued so highly."

"My dear father, you are mistaken; Justine is innocent."

"If she is, God forbid that she should suffer as guilty. She is to be tried to-day, and I hope, I sincerely hope, that she will be acquitted."

This speech calmed me. I was firmly convinced in my own mind that Justine, and indeed every human being, was guiltless of this murder. I had no fear, therefore, that any circumstantial evidence could be brought forward strong enough to convict her; and, in this assurance, I calmed myself, expecting the trial with eagerness, but without prognosticating an evil result.

We were soon joined by Elizabeth. Time had made great alterations in her form since I had last beheld her. Six years before she had been a pretty, good-humoured girl, whom every one loved and caressed. She was now a woman in stature and expression of countenance, which was uncommonly lovely. An open and capacious forehead gave indications of a good understanding, joined to great frankness of disposition. Her eyes were hazel, and expressive of mildness, now through recent affliction allied to sadness. Her hair was of a rich dark auburn, her complexion fair, and her figure slight and graceful. She welcomed me with the greatest affection. "Your arrival, my dear cousin," said she, "fills me with hope. You perhaps will find some means to justify my poor guiltless Justine. Alas! who is safe, if she be convicted of crime? I rely on her innocence as certainly as I do upon my own. Our misfortune is doubly hard to us; we have not only lost that lovely darling boy, but this poor girl, whom I sincerely love, is to be torn away by even a worse fate. If she is condemned, I never shall know joy more. But she will not, I am sure she will not; and then I shall be happy again, even after the sad death of my little William."

"She is innocent, my Elizabeth," said I, "and that shall be proved; fear nothing, but let your spirits be cheered by the assurance of her acquittal."

"How kind you are! every one else believes in her guilt, and that made me wretched; for I knew that it was impossible: and to see every one else prejudiced in so deadly a manner, rendered me hopeless and despairing." She wept.

"Sweet niece," said my father, "dry your tears. If she is, as you believe, innocent, rely on the justice of our judges, and the activity with which I shall prevent the slightest shadow of partiality."

CHAPTER VII

We passed a few sad hours, until eleven o'clock, when the trial was to commence. My father and the rest of the family being obliged to attend as witnesses, I accompanied them to the court. During the whole of this wretched mockery of justice, I suffered living torture. It was to be decided, whether the result of my curiosity and lawless devices would cause the death of two of my fellow-beings: one a smiling babe, full of innocence and joy; the other far more dreadfully murdered, with every aggravation of infamy that could make the murder memorable in horror. Justine also was a girl of merit, and possessed qualities which promised to render her life happy: now all was to be obliterated in an ignominious grave; and I the cause! A thousand times rather would I have confessed myself guilty of the crime ascribed to Justine; but I was absent when it was committed, and such a declaration would have been considered as the ravings of a madman, and would not have exculpated her who suffered through me.

The appearance of Justine was calm. She was dressed in mourning; and her countenance, always engaging, was rendered, by the solemnity of her feelings, exquisitely beautiful. Yet she appeared confident in innocence, and did not tremble, although gazed on and execrated by thousands; for all the kindness which her beauty might otherwise have excited, was obliterated in the minds of the spectators by the imagination of the enormity she was supposed to have committed. She was tranquil, yet her tranquillity was evidently constrained; and as her confusion had before been adduced as a proof of her guilt, she worked up her mind to an appearance of courage. When she entered the court, she threw her eyes round it, and quickly discovered where we were seated. A tear seemed to dim her eye when she saw us; but she quickly recovered herself, and a look of sorrowful affection seemed to attest her utter guiltlessness.

The trial began; and after the advocate against her had stated the charge, several witnesses were called. Several strange facts combined against her, which might have staggered any one who had not such proof of her innocence as I had. She had been out the whole of the night on which the murder had been committed, and towards morning had been perceived by a market-woman not far from the spot where the body of the murdered child had been afterwards found. The woman asked her what she did there; but she looked very strangely, and only returned a confused and unintelligible answer. She returned to the house about eight o'clock; and when one inquired where she had passed the night, she replied, that she had been looking for the child, and demanded earnestly, if any thing had been heard concerning him. When shewn the body, she fell into violent hysterics, and kept her bed for several days. The picture was then produced, which the servant had found in her pocket; and when Elizabeth, in a faltering voice, proved that it was the same which, an hour before the child had been missed, she had placed round his neck, a murmur of horror and indignation filled the court.

Justine was called on for her defence. As the trial had proceeded, her countenance had altered. Surprise, horror, and misery, were strongly expressed. Sometimes she struggled with her tears; but when she was desired to plead, she collected her powers, and spoke in an audible although variable voice:—

"God knows," she said, "how entirely I am innocent. But I do not pretend that my protestations should acquit me: I rest my innocence on a plain and simple explanation of the facts which have been adduced against me; and I hope the character I have always borne will incline my judges to a favourable interpretation, where any circumstance appears doubtful or suspicious."

She then related that, by the permission of Elizabeth, she had passed the evening of the night on which the murder had been committed, at the house of an aunt at Chêne, a village situated at about a league from Geneva. On her return, at about nine o'clock, she met a man, who asked her if she had seen any thing of the child who was lost. She was alarmed by this account, and passed several hours in looking for him, when the gates of Geneva were shut, and she was forced to remain several hours of the night in a barn belonging to a cottage, being unwilling to call up the inhabitants, to whom she was well known. Unable to rest or sleep, she quitted her asylum early, that she might again endeavour to find my brother. If she had gone near the spot where his body lay, it was without her knowledge. That she had been bewildered when questioned by the market-woman, was not surprising, since she had passed a sleepless night, and the fate of poor William was yet uncertain. Concerning the picture she could give no account.

"I know," continued the unhappy victim, "how heavily and fatally this one circumstance weighs against me, but I have no power of explaining it; and when I have expressed my utter ignorance, I am only left to conjecture concerning the probabilities by which it might have been placed in my pocket. But here also I am checked. I believe that I have no enemy on earth, and none surely would have been so wicked as to destroy me wantonly. Did the murderer place it there? I know of no opportunity afforded him for so doing; or if I had, why should he have stolen the jewel, to part with it again so soon?

"I commit my cause to the justice of my judges, yet I see no room for hope. I beg permission to have a few witnesses examined concerning my character; and if their testimony shall not overweigh my supposed guilt, I must be condemned, although I would pledge my salvation on my innocence."

Several witnesses were called, who had known her for many years, and they spoke well of her; but fear, and hatred of the crime of which they supposed her guilty, rendered them timorous, and unwilling to come forward. Elizabeth saw even this last resource, her excellent dispositions and irreproachable conduct, about to fail the accused, when, although violently agitated, she desired permission to address the court.

"I am," said she, "the cousin of the unhappy child who was murdered, or rather his sister, for I was educated by and have lived with his parents ever since and even long before his birth. It may therefore be judged indecent in me to come forward on this occasion; but when I see a fellow-creature about to perish through the cowardice of her pretended friends, I wish to be allowed to speak, that I may say what I know of her character. I am well acquainted with the accused. I have lived in the same house with her, at one time for five, and at another for nearly two years. During all that period she appeared to me the most amiable and benevolent of human creatures. She nursed Madame Frankenstein, my aunt, in her last illness with the greatest affection and care; and afterwards attended her own mother during a tedious illness, in a manner that excited the admiration of all who knew her. After which she again lived in my uncle's house, where she was beloved by all the family. She was warmly attached to the child who is now dead, and acted towards him like a most affectionate mother. For my own part, I do not hesitate to say, that, notwithstanding all the evidence produced against her, I believe and rely on her perfect innocence. She had no temptation for such an action: as to the bauble on which the chief proof rests, if she had earnestly desired it, I should have willingly given it to her; so much do I esteem and value her."

Excellent Elizabeth! A murmur of approbation was heard; but it was excited by her generous interference, and not in favour of poor Justine, on whom the public indignation was turned with renewed violence, charging her with the blackest ingratitude. She herself wept as Elizabeth spoke, but she did not answer. My own agitation and anguish was extreme during the whole trial. I believed in her innocence; I knew it. Could the dæmon, who had (I did not for a minute doubt) murdered my brother, also in his hellish sport have betrayed the innocent to death and ignominy. I could not sustain the horror of my situation; and when I perceived that the popular voice, and the countenances of the judges, had already condemned my unhappy victim, I rushed out of the court in agony. The tortures of the accused did not equal mine; she was sustained by innocence, but the fangs of remorse tore my bosom, and would not forego their hold.

I passed a night of unmingled wretchedness. In the morning I went to the court; my lips and throat were parched. I dared not ask the fatal question; but I was known, and the officer guessed the cause of my visit. The ballots had been thrown; they were all black, and Justine was condemned.

I cannot pretend to describe what I then felt. I had before experienced sensations of horror; and I have endeavoured to bestow upon them adequate expressions, but words cannot convey an idea of the heart-sickening despair that I then endured. The person to whom I addressed myself added, that Justine had already confessed her guilt. "That evidence," he observed, "was hardly required in so glaring a case, but I am glad of it; and, indeed, none of our judges like to condemn a criminal upon circumstantial evidence, be it ever so decisive."

When I returned home, Elizabeth eagerly demanded the result.

"My cousin," replied I, "it is decided as you may have expected; all judges had rather that ten innocent should suffer, than that one guilty should escape. But she has confessed."

This was a dire blow to poor Elizabeth, who had relied with firmness upon Justine's innocence. "Alas!" said she, "how shall I ever again believe in human benevolence? Justine, whom I loved and esteemed as my sister, how could she put on those smiles of innocence only to betray; her mild eyes seemed incapable of any severity or ill-humour, and yet she has committed a murder."

Soon after we heard that the poor victim had

expressed a wish to see my cousin. My father wished her not to go; but said, that he left it to her own judgment and feelings to decide. "Yes," said Elizabeth, "I will go, although she is guilty; and you, Victor, shall accompany me: I cannot go alone." The idea of this visit was torture to me, yet I could not refuse.

We entered the gloomy prison-chamber, and beheld Justine sitting on some straw at the further end; her hands were manacled, and her head rested on her knees. She rose on seeing us enter; and when we were left alone with her, she threw herself at the feet of Elizabeth, weeping bitterly. My cousin wept also.

"Oh, Justine!" said she, "why did you rob me of my last consolation. I relied on your innocence; and although I was then very wretched, I was not so miserable as I am now."

"And do you also believe that I am so very, very wicked? Do you also join with my enemies to crush me?" Her voice was suffocated with sobs.

"Rise, my poor girl," said Elizabeth, "why do you kneel, if you are innocent? I am not one of your enemies; I believed you guiltless, notwithstanding every evidence, until I heard that you had yourself declared your guilt. That report, you say, is false; and be assured, dear Justine, that nothing can shake my confidence in you for a moment, but your own confession."

"I did confess; but I confessed a lie. I confessed, that I might obtain absolution; but now that false-hood lies heavier at my heart than all my other sins. The God of heaven forgive me! Ever since I was condemned, my confessor has besieged me; he threat-ened and menaced, until I almost began to think that I was the monster that he said I was. He threatened excommunication and hell fire in my last moments, if I continued obdurate. Dear lady, I had none to support me; all looked on me as a wretch doomed to ignominy and perdition. What could I do? In an evil hour I subscribed to a lie; and now only am I truly miserable."

She paused, weeping, and then continued—"I thought with horror, my sweet lady, that you should believe your Justine, whom your blessed aunt had so highly honoured, and whom you loved, was a creature capable of a crime which none but the devil himself could have perpetrated. Dear William! dearest blessed child! I soon shall see you again in heaven, where we shall all be happy; and that consoles me, going as I am to suffer ignominy and death."

"Oh, Justine! forgive me for having for one moment distrusted you. Why did you confess? But do not mourn, my dear girl; I will every where proclaim your innocence, and force belief. Yet you must die; you, my playfellow, my companion, my more than sister. I never can survive so horrible a misfortune."

"Dear, sweet Elizabeth, do not weep. You ought to raise me with thoughts of a better life, and elevate me from the petty cares of this world of injustice and strife. Do not you, excellent friend, drive me to despair."

"I will try to comfort you; but this, I fear, is an evil too deep and poignant to admit of consolation, for there is no hope. Yet heaven bless thee, my dearest Justine, with resignation, and a confidence elevated beyond this world. Oh! how I hate its shews and mockeries! when one creature is murdered, another is immediately deprived of life in a slow torturing manner; then the executioners, their hands yet reeking with the blood of innocence, believe that they have done a great deed. They call this *retribution.* Hateful name! When that word is pronounced, I know greater and more horrid punishments are going to be inflicted than the gloomiest tyrant has ever invented to satiate his utmost revenge. Yet this is not consolation for you, my Justine, unless indeed that you may glory in escaping from so miserable a den. Alas! I would I were in peace with my aunt and my lovely William, escaped from a world which is hateful to me, and the visages of men which I abhor."

Justine smiled languidly. "This, dear lady, is despair, and not resignation. I must not learn the lesson that you would teach me. Talk of something else, something that will bring peace, and not increase of misery."

During this conversation I had retired to a corner of the prison-room, where I could conceal the horrid anguish that possessed me. Despair! Who dared talk of that? The poor victim, who on the morrow was to pass the dreary boundary between life and death, felt not as I did, such deep and bitter agony. I gnashed my teeth, and ground them together, uttering a groan that came from my inmost soul. Justine started. When she saw who it was, she approached me, and said, "Dear Sir, you are very kind to visit me; you, I hope, do not believe that I am guilty."

I could not answer. "No, Justine," said Elizabeth; "he is more convinced of your innocence than I was; for even when he heard that you had confessed, he did not credit it."

"I truly thank him. In these last moments I feel the sincerest gratitude towards those who think of me with kindness. How sweet is the affection of others to such a wretch as I am! It removes more than half my misfortune; and I feel as if I could die in peace, now that my innocence is acknowledged by you, dear lady, and your cousin."

Thus the poor sufferer tried to comfort others and herself. She indeed gained the resignation she desired. But I, the true murderer, felt the never-dying worm alive in my bosom, which allowed of no hope or consolation. Elizabeth also wept, and was unhappy; but her's also was the misery of innocence, which, like a cloud that passes over the fair moon, for a while hides, but cannot tarnish its brightness. Anguish and despair had penetrated into the core of my heart; I bore a hell within me, which nothing could extinguish. We staid several hours with Justine; and it was with great difficulty that Elizabeth could tear herself away. "I wish," cried she, "that I were to die with you; I cannot live in this world of misery."

Justine assumed an air of cheerfulness, while she with difficulty repressed her bitter tears. She embraced Elizabeth, and said, in a voice of half-suppressed emotion, "Farewell, sweet lady, dearest Elizabeth, my beloved and only friend; may heaven in its bounty bless and preserve you; may this be the last misfortune that you will ever suffer. Live, and be happy, and make others so."

As we returned, Elizabeth said, "You know not, my dear Victor, how much I am relieved, now that I trust in the innocence of this unfortunate girl. I never could again have known peace, if I had been deceived in my reliance on her. For the moment that I did believe her guilty, I felt an anguish that I could not have long sustained. Now my heart is lightened. The innocent suffers; but she whom I thought amiable and good has not betrayed the trust I reposed in her, and I am consoled."

Amiable cousin! such were your thoughts, mild and gentle as your own dear eyes and voice. But I—I was a wretch, and none ever conceived of the misery that I then endured.

END OF VOL. I.

Volume II

CHAPTER I

Nothing is more painful to the human mind, than, after the feelings have been worked up by a quick succession of events, the dead calmness of inaction and certainty which follows, and deprives the soul both of hope and fear. Justine died; she rested; and I was alive. The blood flowed freely in my veins, but a weight of despair and remorse pressed on my heart, which nothing could remove. Sleep fled from my eyes; I wandered like an evil spirit, for I had committed deeds of mischief beyond description horrible, and more, much more, (I persuaded myself) was yet behind. Yet my heart overflowed with kindness, and the love of virtue. I had begun life with benevolent intentions, and thirsted for the moment when I should put them in practice, and make myself useful to my fellow-beings. Now all was blasted: instead of that serenity of conscience, which allowed me to look back upon the past with self-satisfaction, and from thence to gather promise of new hopes, I was seized by remorse and the sense of guilt, which hurried me away to a hell of intense tortures, such as no language can describe.

This state of mind preyed upon my health, which had entirely recovered from the first shock it had sustained. I shunned the face of man; all sound of joy or complacency was torture to me; solitude was my only consolation—deep, dark, death-like solitude.

My father observed with pain the alteration perceptible in my disposition and habits, and endeavoured to reason with me on the folly of giving way to immoderate grief. "Do you think, Victor," said he, "that I do not suffer also? No one could love a child more than I loved your brother;" (tears came into his eyes as he spoke); "but is it not a duty to the survivors, that we should refrain from augmenting their unhappiness by an appearance of immoderate grief? It is also a duty owed to yourself; for excessive sorrow prevents improvement or enjoyment, or even the discharge of daily usefulness, without which no man is fit for society."

This advice, although good, was totally inapplicable to my case; I should have been the first to hide my grief, and console my friends, if remorse had not mingled its bitterness with my other sensations. Now I could only answer my father with a look of despair, and endeavour to hide myself from his view.

About this time we retired to our house at Belrive. This change was particularly agreeable to me. The shutting of the gates regularly at ten o'clock, and the impossibility of remaining on the lake after that hour, had rendered our residence within the walls of Geneva very irksome to me. I was now free. Often, after the rest of the family had retired for the night, I took the boat, and passed many hours upon the water. Sometimes, with my sails set, I was carried by the wind; and sometimes, after rowing into the middle of the lake, I left the boat to pursue its own course, and gave way to my own miserable reflections. I was often tempted, when all was at peace around me, and I the only unquiet thing that wandered restless in a scene so beautiful and heavenly, if I except some bat, or the frogs, whose harsh and interrupted croaking was heard only when I approached the shore—often, I say, I was tempted to plunge into the silent lake, that the waters might close over me and my calamities for ever. But I was restrained, when I thought of the heroic and suffering Elizabeth, whom I tenderly loved, and whose existence was bound up in mine. I thought also of my father, and surviving brother: should I by my base desertion leave them exposed and unprotected to the malice of the fiend whom I had let loose among them?

At these moments I wept bitterly, and wished that peace would revisit my mind only that I might afford them consolation and happiness. But that could not be. Remorse extinguished every hope. I had been the author of unalterable evils; and I lived in daily fear, lest the monster whom I had created should perpetrate some new wickedness. I had an obscure feeling that all was not over, and that he would still commit some signal crime, which by its enormity should almost efface the recollection of the past. There was always scope for fear, so long as any thing I loved remained behind. My abhorrence of this fiend cannot be conceived. When I thought of him, I gnashed my teeth, my eyes became inflamed, and I ardently wished to extinguish that life which I had so thoughtlessly bestowed. When I reflected on his crimes and malice, my hatred and revenge burst all bounds of moderation. I would have made a pilgrimage to the highest peak of the Andes, could I, when there, have precipitated him to their base. I wished to see him again, that I might wreak the utmost extent of anger on his head, and avenge the deaths of William and Justine.

Our house was the house of mourning. My father's health was deeply shaken by the horror of the recent events. Elizabeth was sad and desponding; she no longer took delight in her ordinary occupations; all pleasure seemed to her sacrilege towards the dead; eternal woe and tears she then thought was the just tribute she should pay to innocence so blasted and destroyed. She was no longer that happy creature, who in earlier youth wandered with me on the banks of the lake, and talked with ecstacy of our future prospects. She had become grave, and often conversed of the inconstancy of fortune, and the instability of human life.

"When I reflect, my dear cousin," said she, "on the miserable death of Justine Moritz, I no longer see the world and its works as they before appeared to me. Before, I looked upon the accounts of vice and injustice, that I read in books or heard from others, as tales of ancient days, or imaginary evils; at least they were remote, and more familiar to reason than to the imagination; but now misery has come home, and men appear to me as monsters thirsting for each other's blood. Yet I am certainly unjust. Every body believed that poor girl to be guilty; and if she could have committed the crime for which she suffered, assuredly she would have been the most depraved of human creatures. For the sake of a few jewels, to have murdered the son of her benefactor and friend, a child whom she had nursed from its birth, and appeared to love as if it had been her own! I could not consent to the death of any human being; but certainly I should have thought such a creature unfit to remain in the society of men. Yet she was innocent. I know, I feel she was innocent; you are of the same opinion, and that confirms me. Alas! Victor, when falsehood can look so like the truth, who can assure themselves of certain happiness? I feel as if I were walking on the edge of a precipice, towards which thousands are crowding, and endeavouring to plunge me into the abyss. William and Justine were assassinated, and the murderer escapes; he walks about the world free, and perhaps respected. But even if I were condemned to suffer on the scaffold for the same crimes, I would not change places with such a wretch."

I listened to this discourse with the extremest

agony. I, not in deed, but in effect, was the true murderer. Elizabeth read my anguish in my countenance, and kindly taking my hand said, "My dearest cousin, you must calm yourself. These events have affected me, God knows how deeply; but I am not so wretched as you are. There is an expression of despair, and sometimes of revenge, in your countenance, that makes me tremble. Be calm, my dear Victor; I would sacrifice my life to your peace. We surely shall be happy: quiet in our native country, and not mingling in the world, what can disturb our tranquillity?"

She shed tears as she said this, distrusting the very solace that she gave; but at the same time she smiled, that she might chase away the fiend that lurked in my heart. My father, who saw in the unhappiness that was painted in my face only an exaggeration of that sorrow which I might naturally feel, thought that an amusement suited to my taste would be the best means of restoring to me my wonted serenity. It was from this cause that he had removed to the country; and, induced by the same motive, he now proposed that we should all make an excursion to the valley of Chamounix. I had been there before, but Elizabeth and Ernest never had; and both had often expressed an earnest desire to see the scenery of this place, which had been described to them as so wonderful and sublime. Accordingly we departed from Geneva on this tour about the middle of the month of August, nearly two months after the death of Justine.

The weather was uncommonly fine; and if mine had been a sorrow to be chased away by any fleeting circumstance, this excursion would certainly have had the effect intended by my father. As it was, I was somewhat interested in the scene; it sometimes lulled, although it could not extinguish my grief. During the first day we travelled in a carriage. In the morning we had seen the mountains at a distance, towards which we gradually advanced. We perceived that the valley through which we wound, and which was formed by the river Arve, whose course we followed, closed in upon us by degrees; and when the sun had set, we beheld immense mountains and precipices overhanging us on every side, and heard the sound of the river raging among rocks, and the dashing of waterfalls around.

The next day we pursued our journey upon mules; and as we ascended still higher, the valley assumed a more magnificent and astonishing character. Ruined castles hanging on the precipices of piny mountains; the impetuous Arve, and cottages every here and there peeping forth from among the trees, formed a scene of singular beauty. But it was augmented and rendered sublime by the mighty Alps, whose white and shining pyramids and domes towered above all, as belonging to another earth, the habitations of another race of beings.

We passed the bridge of Pelissier, where the ravine, which the river forms, opened before us, and we began to ascend the mountain that overhangs it. Soon after we entered the valley of Chamounix. This valley is more wonderful and sublime, but not so beautiful and picturesque as that of Servox, through which we had just passed. The high and snowy mountains were its immediate boundaries; but we saw no more ruined castles and fertile fields. Immense glaciers approached the road; we heard the rumbling thunder of the falling avalanche, and marked the smoke of its passage. Mont Blanc, the supreme and magnificent Mont Blanc, raised itself from the surrounding *aiguilles,* and its tremendous *dome* overlooked the valley.

During this journey, I sometimes joined Elizabeth,

and exerted myself to point out to her the various beauties of the scene. I often suffered my mule to lag behind, and indulged in the misery of reflection. At other times I spurred on the animal before my companions, that I might forget them, the world, and, more than all, myself. When at a distance, I alighted, and threw myself on the grass, weighed down by horror and despair. At eight in the evening I arrived at Chamounix. My father and Elizabeth were very much fatigued; Ernest, who accompanied us, was delighted, and in high spirits: the only circumstance that detracted from his pleasure was the south wind, and the rain it seemed to promise for the next day.

We retired early to our apartments, but not to sleep; at least I did not. I remained many hours at the window, watching the pallid lightning that played above Mont Blanc, and listening to the rushing of the Arve, which ran below my window.

CHAPTER II

The next day, contrary to the prognostications of our guides, was fine, although clouded. We visited the source of the Arveiron, and rode about the valley until evening. These sublime and magnificent scenes afforded me the greatest consolation that I was capable of receiving. They elevated me from all littleness of feeling; and although they did not remove my grief, they subdued and tranquillized it. In some degree, also, they diverted my mind from the thoughts over which it had brooded for the last month. I returned in the evening, fatigued, but less unhappy, and conversed with my family with more cheerfulness than had been my custom for some time. My father was pleased, and Elizabeth overjoyed. "My dear cousin," said she, "you see what happiness you diffuse when you are happy; do not relapse again!"

The following morning the rain poured down in torrents, and thick mists hid the summits of the mountains. I rose early, but felt unusually melancholy. The rain depressed me; my old feelings recurred, and I was miserable. I knew how disappointed my father would be at this sudden change, and I wished to avoid him until I had recovered myself so far as to be enabled to conceal those feelings that overpowered me. I knew that they would remain that day at the inn; and as I had ever inured myself to rain, moisture, and cold, I resolved to go alone to the summit of Montanvert. I remembered the effect that the view of the tremendous and ever-moving glacier had produced upon my mind when I first saw it. It had then filled me with a sublime ecstacy that gave wings to the soul, and allowed it to soar from the obscure world to light and joy. The sight of the awful and majestic in nature had indeed always the effect of solemnizing my mind, and causing me to forget the passing cares of life. I determined to go alone, for I was well acquainted with the path, and the presence of another would destroy the solitary grandeur of the scene.

The ascent is precipitous, but the path is cut into continual and short windings, which enable you to surmount the perpendicularity of the mountain. It is a scene terrifically desolate. In a thousand spots the traces of the winter avalanche may be perceived, where trees lie broken and strewed on the ground; some entirely destroyed, others bent, leaning upon the jutting rocks of the mountain, or transversely upon other trees. The path, as you ascend higher, is intersected by ravines of snow, down which stones continually roll from above; one of them is particularly dangerous, as the slightest sound, such as even speaking in a loud voice, produces a concussion of air sufficient to draw destruction upon the head of the speaker. The pines are not tall or luxuriant, but they are sombre, and add an air of severity to the scene. I looked on the valley beneath; vast mists were rising from the rivers which ran through it, and curling in thick wreaths around the opposite mountains, whose summits were hid in the uniform clouds, while rain poured from the dark sky, and added to the melancholy impression I received from the objects around me. Alas! why does man boast of sensibilities superior to those apparent in the brute; it only renders them more necessary beings. If our impulses were confined to hunger, thirst, and desire, we might be nearly free; but now we are moved by every wind that blows, and a chance word or scene that that word may convey to us.

We rest; a dream has power to poison sleep.
  We rise; one wand'ring thought pollutes the day.
We feel, conceive, or reason; laugh, or weep,
  Embrace fond woe, or cast our cares away;
It is the same: for, be it joy or sorrow,
  The path of its departure still is free.
Man's yesterday may ne'er be like his morrow;
  Nought may endure but mutability!

It was nearly noon when I arrived at the top of the ascent. For some time I sat upon the rock that overlooks the sea of ice. A mist covered both that and the surrounding mountains. Presently a breeze dissipated the cloud, and I descended upon the glacier. The surface is very uneven, rising like the waves of a troubled sea, descending low, and interspersed by rifts that sink deep. The field of ice is almost a league in width, but I spent nearly two hours in crossing it. The opposite mountain is a bare perpendicular rock. From the side where I now stood Montanvert was exactly opposite, at the distance of a league; and above it rose Mont Blanc, in awful majesty. I remained in a recess of the rock, gazing on this wonderful and stupendous scene. The sea, or rather the vast river of ice, wound among its dependent mountains, whose aerial summits hung over its recesses. Their icy and glittering peaks shone in the sunlight over the clouds. My heart, which was before sorrowful, now swelled with something like joy; I exclaimed—"Wandering spirits, if indeed ye wander, and do not rest in your narrow beds, allow me this faint happiness, or take me, as your companion, away from the joys of life."

As I said this, I suddenly beheld the figure of a man. at some distance, advancing towards me with superhuman speed. He bounded over the crevices in the ice, among which I had walked with caution; his stature also, as he approached, seemed to exceed that of man. I was troubled: a mist came over my eyes, and I felt a faintness seize me; but I was quickly restored by the cold gale of the mountains. I perceived, as the shape came nearer, (sight tremendous and abhorred!) that it was the wretch whom I had created. I trembled with rage and horror, resolving to wait his approach, and then close with him in mortal combat. He approached; his countenance bespoke bitter anguish, combined with disdain and malignity, while its unearthly ugliness rendered it almost too horrible for human eyes. But I scarcely observed this; anger and hatred had at first deprived me of utterance, and I recovered only to overwhelm him with words expressive of furious detestation and contempt.

"Devil!" I exclaimed, "do you dare approach me? and do not you fear the fierce vengeance of my arm wreaked on your miserable head? Begone, vile insect! or rather stay, that I may trample you to dust! and, oh, that I could, with the extinction of your miserable existence, restore those victims whom you have so diabolically murdered!"

"I expected this reception," said the dæmon. "All men hate the wretched; how then must I be hated, who am miserable beyond all living things! Yet you, my creator, detest and spurn me, thy creature, to whom thou art bound by ties only dissoluble by the annihilation of one of us. You purpose to kill me. How dare you sport thus with life? Do your duty towards me, and I will do mine towards you and the rest of mankind. If you will comply with my conditions, I will leave them and you at peace; but if you refuse, I will glut the maw of death, until it be satiated with the blood of your remaining friends."

"Abhorred monster! fiend that thou art! the tortures of hell are too mild a vengeance for thy crimes. Wretched devil! you reproach me with your creation; come on then, that I may extinguish the spark which I so negligently bestowed."

My rage was without bounds; I sprang on him, impelled by all the feelings which can arm one being against the existence of another.

He easily eluded me, and said,

"Be calm! I entreat you to hear me, before you give vent to your hatred on my devoted head. Have I not suffered enough, that you seek to increase my misery? Life, although it may only be an accumulation of anguish, is dear to me, and I will defend it. Remember, thou hast made me more powerful than thyself; my height is superior to thine; my joints more supple.

But I will not be tempted to set myself in opposition to thee. I am thy creature, and I will be even mild and docile to my natural lord and king, if thou wilt also perform thy part, the which thou owest me. Oh, Frankenstein, be not equitable to every other, and trample upon me alone, to whom thy justice, and even thy clemency and affection, is most due. Remember, that I am thy creature: I ought to be thy Adam; but I am rather the fallen angel, whom thou drivest from joy for no misdeed. Every where I see bliss, from which I alone am irrevocably excluded. I was benevolent and good; misery made me a fiend. Make me happy, and I shall again be virtuous."

"Begone! I will not hear you. There can be no community between you and me; we are enemies. Begone, or let us try our strength in a fight, in which one must fall."

"How can I move thee? Will no entreaties cause thee to turn a favourable eye upon thy creature, who implores thy goodness and compassion. Believe me, Frankenstein: I was benevolent; my soul glowed with love and humanity: but am I not alone, miserably alone? You, my creator, abhor me; what hope can I gather from your fellow-creatures, who owe me nothing? they spurn and hate me. The desert mountains and dreary glaciers are my refuge. I have wandered here many days; the caves of ice, which I only do not fear, are a dwelling to me, and the only one which man does not grudge. These bleak skies I hail, for they are kinder to me than your fellow-beings. If the multitude of mankind knew of my existence, they would do as you do, and arm themselves for my destruction. Shall I not then hate them who abhor me? I will keep no terms with my enemies. I am miserable, and they shall share my wretchedness. Yet it is in your power to recompense me, and deliver them from an evil which it only remains for you to make so great, that not only you and your family, but thousands of others, shall be swallowed up in the whirlwinds of its rage. Let your compassion be moved, and do not disdain me. Listen to my tale: when you have heard that, abandon or commiserate me, as you shall judge that I deserve. But hear me. The guilty are allowed, by human laws, bloody as they may be, to speak in their own defence before they are condemned. Listen to me, Frankenstein. You accuse me of murder; and yet you would, with a satisfied conscience, destroy your own creature. Oh, praise the eternal justice of man! Yet I ask you not to spare me: listen to me; and then, if you can, and if you will, destroy the work of your hands."

"Why do you call to my remembrance circumstances of which I shudder to reflect, that I have been the miserable origin and author? Cursed be the day, abhorred devil, in which you first saw light! Cursed (although I curse myself) be the hands that formed you! You have made me wretched beyond expression. You have left me no power to consider whether I am just to you, or not. Begone! relieve me from the sight of your detested form."

"Thus I relieve thee, my creator," he said, and placed his hated hands before my eyes, which I flung from me with violence; "thus I take from thee a sight which you abhor. Still thou canst listen to me, and grant me thy compassion. By the virtues that I once possessed, I demand this from you. Hear my tale; it is long and strange, and the temperature of this place is not fitting to your fine sensations; come to the hut upon the mountain. The sun is yet high in the heavens; before it descends to hide itself behind yon snowy precipices, and illuminate another world, you will have heard my story, and can decide. On you it rests, whether I quit for ever the neighbourhood of man, and lead a harmless life, or become the scourge of your fellow-creatures, and the author of your own speedy ruin."

As he said this, he led the way across the ice: I followed. My heart was full, and I did not answer him; but, as I proceeded, I weighed the various arguments that he had used, and determined at least to listen to his tale. I was partly urged by curiosity, and compassion confirmed my resolution. I had hitherto supposed him to be the murderer of my brother, and I eagerly sought a confirmation or denial of this opinion. For the first time, also, I felt what the duties of a creator towards his creature were, and that I ought to render him happy before I complained of his wickedness. These motives urged me to comply with his demand. We crossed the ice, therefore, and ascended the opposite rock. The air was cold, and the rain again began to descend: we entered the hut, the fiend with an air of exultation, I with a heavy heart. and depressed spirits. But I consented to listen; and, seating myself by the fire which my odious compan ion had lighted, he thus began his tale.

CHAPTER III

"It is with considerable difficulty that I remember the original æra of my being: all the events of that period appear confused and indistinct. A strange multiplicity of sensations seized me, and I saw, felt, heard, and smelt, at the same time; and it was, indeed, a long time before I learned to distinguish between the operations of my various senses. By degrees, I remember, a stronger light pressed upon my nerves, so that I was obliged to shut my eyes. Darkness then came over me, and troubled me; but hardly had I felt this, when, by opening my eyes, as I now suppose, the light poured in upon me again. I walked, and, I believe, descended; but I presently found a great alteration in my sensations. Before, dark and opaque bodies had surrounded me, impervious to my touch or sight; but I now found that I could wander on at liberty, with no obstacles which I could not either surmount or avoid. The light became more and more oppressive to me; and, the heat wearying me as I walked, I sought a place where I could receive shade. This was the forest near Ingolstadt; and here I lay by the side of a brook resting from my fatigue, until I felt tormented by hunger and thirst. This roused me from my nearly dormant state, and I ate some berries which I found hanging on the trees, or lying on the ground. I slaked my thirst at the brook; and then lying down, was overcome by sleep.

"It was dark when I awoke; I felt cold also, and half-frightened as it were instinctively, finding myself so desolate. Before I had quitted your apartment, on a sensation of cold, I had covered myself with some clothes; but these were insufficient to secure me from the dews of night. I was a poor, helpless, miserable wretch; I knew, and could distinguish, nothing; but, feeling pain invade me on all sides, I sat down and wept.

"Soon a gentle light stole over the heavens, and gave me a sensation of pleasure. I started up, and beheld a radiant form rise from among the trees. I gazed with a kind of wonder. It moved slowly, but it enlightened my path; and I again went out in search of berries. I was still cold, when under one of the trees I found a huge cloak, with which I covered myself, and sat down upon the ground. No distinct ideas occupied my mind; all was confused. I felt light, and hunger, and thirst, and darkness; innumerable sounds rung in my ears, and on all sides various scents saluted me: the only object that I could distinguish was the bright moon, and I fixed my eyes on that with pleasure.

"Several changes of day and night passed, and the orb of night had greatly lessened when I began to distinguish my sensations from each other. I gradually saw plainly the clear stream that supplied me with drink, and the trees that shaded me with their foliage. I was delighted when I first discovered that a pleasant sound, which often saluted my ears, proceeded from the throats of the little winged animals who had often intercepted the light from my eyes. I began also to observe, with greater accuracy, the forms that surrounded me, and to perceive the boundaries of the radiant roof of light which canopied me. Sometimes I tried to imitate the pleasant songs of the birds, but was unable. Sometimes I wished to express my sensations in my own mode, but the uncouth and inarticulate sounds which broke from me frightened me into silence again.

"The moon had disappeared from the night, and again, with a lessened form, shewed itself, while I still remained in the forest. My sensations had, by this time, become distinct, and my mind received every day additional ideas. My eyes became accustomed to the light, and to perceive objects in their right forms; I distinguished the insect from the herb, and, by degrees, one herb from another. I found that the sparrow uttered none but harsh notes, whilst those of the blackbird and thrush were sweet and enticing.

"One day, when I was oppressed by cold, I found a fire which had been left by some wandering beggars, and was overcome with delight at the warmth I experienced from it. In my joy I thrust my hand into the live embers, but quickly drew it out again with a cry of pain. How strange, I thought, that the same cause should produce such opposite effects! I examined the materials of the fire, and to my joy found it to be composed of wood. I quickly collected some branches; but they were wet, and would not burn. I was pained at this, and sat still watching the operation of the fire. The wet wood which I had placed near the heat dried, and itself became inflamed. I reflected on this; and, by touching the various branches, I discovered the cause, and busied myself in collecting a great quantity of wood, that I might dry it, and have a plentiful supply of fire. When night came on, and brought sleep with it, I was in the greatest fear lest my fire should be extinguished. I covered it carefully with dry wood and leaves, and placed wet branches upon it; and then, spreading my cloak, I lay on the ground, and sunk into sleep.

"It was morning when I awoke, and my first care was to visit the fire. I uncovered it, and a gentle breeze quickly fanned it into a flame. I observed this also, and contrived a fan of branches, which roused the embers when they were nearly extinguished. When night came again, I found, with pleasure, that the fire gave light as well as heat; and that the discovery of this element was useful to me in my food; for I found some of the offals that the travellers had left had been roasted, and tasted much more savoury than the berries I gathered from the trees. I tried, therefore, to dress my food in the same manner, placing it on the live embers. I found that the berries were spoiled by this operation, and the nuts and roots much improved.

"Food, however, became scarce; and I often spent the whole day searching in vain for a few acorns to assuage the pangs of hunger. When I found this, I resolved to quit the place that I had hitherto inhabited, to seek for one where the few wants I experienced would be more easily satisfied. In this emigration, I exceedingly lamented the loss of the fire which I had obtained through accident, and knew not how to re-produce it. I gave several hours to the serious consideration of this difficulty; but I was obliged to relinquish all attempts to supply it; and, wrapping myself up in my cloak, I struck across the wood towards the setting sun. I passed three days in these rambles, and at length discovered the open country. A great fall of snow had taken place the night before, and the fields were of one uniform white; the appearance was disconsolate, and I found my feet chilled by the cold damp substance that covered the ground.

"It was about seven in the morning, and I longed to obtain food and shelter; at length I perceived a small hut, on a rising ground, which had doubtless been built for the convenience of some shepherd. This was a new sight to me; and I examined the structure with great curiosity. Finding the door open, I entered. An old man sat in it, near a fire, over which he was preparing his breakfast. He turned on hearing a noise; and, perceiving me, shrieked loudly, and, quitting the hut, ran across the fields with a speed of which his debilitated form hardly appeared capable. His appearance, different from any I had ever before seen, and his flight, somewhat surprised me. But I was enchanted by the appearance of the hut: here the snow and rain could not penetrate; the ground was dry; and it presented to me then as exquisite and divine a retreat as Pandæmonium appeared to the dæmons of hell after their sufferings in the lake of fire. I greedily devoured the remnants of the shepherd's breakfast, which consisted of bread, cheese, milk, and wine; the latter, however, I did not like. Then overcome by fatigue, I lay down among some straw, and fell asleep.

"It was noon when I awoke; and, allured by the warmth of the sun, which shone brightly on the white ground, I determined to recommence my travels; and, depositing the remains of the peasant's breakfast in a wallet I found, I proceeded across the fields for several hours, until at sunset I arrived at a village. How miraculous did this appear! the huts, the neater cottages, and stately houses, engaged my admiration by turns. The vegetables in the gardens, the milk and cheese that I saw placed at the windows of some of the cottages, allured my appetite. One of the best of these I entered; but I had hardly placed my foot within the door, before the children shrieked, and one of the women fainted. The whole village was roused; some fled, some attacked me, until, grievously bruised by stones and many other kinds of missile weapons, I escaped to the open country, and fearfully took refuge in a low hovel, quite bare, and making a wretched appearance after the palaces I had beheld in the village. This hovel, however, joined a cottage of a neat and pleasant appearance; but, after my late dearly-bought experience, I dared not enter it. My place of refuge was constructed of wood, but so low, that I could with difficulty sit upright in it. No wood, however, was placed on the earth, which formed the floor, but it was dry; and although the wind entered it by innumerable chinks, I found it an agreeable asylum from the snow and rain.

"Here then I retreated, and lay down, happy to have found a shelter, however miserable, from the inclemency of the season, and still more from the barbarity of man.

"As soon as morning dawned, I crept from my kennel, that I might view the adjacent cottage, and discover if I could remain in the habitation I had found. It was situated against the back of the cottage, and surrounded on the sides which were exposed by a pig-stye and a clear pool of water. One part was open, and by that I had crept in; but now I covered every crevice by which I might be perceived with stones and wood, yet in such a manner that I might move them on occasion to pass out: all the light I enjoyed came through the stye, and that was sufficient for me.

"Having thus arranged my dwelling, and carpeted it with clean straw, I retired; for I saw the figure of a man at a distance, and I remembered too well my treatment the night before, to trust myself in his power. I had first, however, provided for my sustenance for that day, by a loaf of coarse bread, which I purloined, and a cup with which I could drink, more conveniently than from my hand, of the pure water which flowed by my retreat. The floor was a little raised, so that it was kept perfectly dry, and by its vicinity to the chimney of the cottage it was tolerably warm.

"Being thus provided, I resolved to reside in this hovel, until something should occur which might alter my determination. It was indeed a paradise, compared to the bleak forest, my former residence, the raindropping branches, and dank earth. I ate my breakfast with pleasure, and was about to remove a plank to procure myself a little water, when I heard a step, and, looking through a small chink, I beheld a young creature, with a pail on her head, passing before my hovel. The girl was young and of gentle demeanour, unlike what I have since found cottagers and farm-house servants to be. Yet she was meanly dressed, a coarse blue petticoat and a linen jacket being her only garb; her fair hair was plaited, but not adorned; she looked patient, yet sad. I lost sight of her; and in about a quarter of an hour she returned, bearing the pail, which was now partly filled with milk. As she walked along, seemingly incommoded by the burden, a young man met her, whose countenance expressed a deeper despondence. Uttering a few sounds with an air of melancholy, he took the pail from her head, and bore it to the cottage himself. She followed, and they disappeared. Presently I saw the young man again, with some tools in his hand, cross the field behind the cottage; and the girl was also busied, sometimes in the house, and sometimes in the yard.

"On examining my dwelling, I found that one of the windows of the cottage had formerly occupied a part of it, but the panes had been filled up with wood. In one of these was a small and almost imperceptible chink, through which the eye could just penetrate. Through this crevice, a small room was visible, white-washed and clean, but very bare of furniture. In one corner, near a small fire, sat an old man, leaning his head on his hands in a disconsolate attitude. The young girl was occupied in arranging the cottage; but presently she took something out of a drawer, which employed her hands, and she sat down beside the old man, who, taking up an instrument, began to play, and to produce sounds, sweeter than the voice of the thrush or the nightingale. It was a lovely sight, even to me, poor wretch! who had never beheld aught beautiful before. The silver hair and benevolent countenance of the aged cottager, won my reverence; while the gentle manners of the girl enticed my love. He played a sweet mournful air, which I perceived drew tears from the eyes of his amiable companion, of which the old man took no notice, until she sobbed audibly; he then pronounced a few sounds, and the fair creature, leaving her work, knelt at his feet. He raised her, and smiled with such kindness and affection, that I felt sensations of a peculiar and overpowering nature: they were a mixture of pain and pleasure, such as I had never before experienced, either from hunger or cold, warmth or food; and I withdrew from the window, unable to bear these emotions.

"Soon after this the young man returned, bearing

on his shoulders a load of wood. The girl met him at the door, helped to relieve him of his burden, and, taking some of the fuel into the cottage, placed it on the fire; then she and the youth went apart into a nook of the cottage, and he shewed her a large loaf and a piece of cheese. She seemed pleased; and went into the garden for some roots and plants, which she placed in water, and then upon the fire. She afterwards continued her work, whilst the young man went into the garden, and appeared busily employed in digging and pulling up roots. After he had been employed thus about an hour, the young woman joined him, and they entered the cottage together.

"The old man had, in the mean time, been pensive; but, on the appearance of his companions, he assumed a more cheerful air, and they sat down to eat. The meal was quickly dispatched. The young woman was again occupied in arranging the cottage; the old man walked before the cottage in the sun for a few minutes, leaning on the arm of the youth. Nothing could exceed in beauty the contrast between these two excellent creatures. One was old, with silver hairs and a countenance beaming with benevolence and love; the younger was slight and graceful in his figure, and his features were moulded with the finest symmetry; yet his eyes and attitude expressed the utmost sadness and despondency. The old man returned to the cottage; and the youth, with tools different from those he had used in the morning, directed his steps across the fields.

"Night quickly shut in; but, to my extreme wonder, I found that the cottagers had a means of prolonging light, by the use of tapers, and was delighted to find, that the setting of the sun did not put an end to the pleasure I experienced in watching my human neighbours. In the evening, the young girl and her companion were employed in various occupations which I did not understand; and the old man again took up the instrument, which produced the divine sounds that had enchanted me in the morning. So soon as he had finished, the youth began, not to play, but to utter sounds that were monotonous, and neither resembling the harmony of the old man's instrument or the songs of the birds; I since found that he read aloud, but at that time I knew nothing of the science of words or letters.

"The family, after having been thus occupied for a short time, extinguished their lights, and retired, as I conjectured, to rest.

CHAPTER IV

"I lay on my straw, but I could not sleep. I thought of the occurrences of the day. What chiefly struck me was the gentle manners of these people; and I longed to join them, but dared not. I remembered too well the treatment I had suffered the night before from the barbarous villagers, and resolved, whatever course of conduct I might hereafter think it right to pursue, that for the present I would remain quietly in my hovel, watching, and endeavouring to discover the motives which influenced their actions.

"The cottagers arose the next morning before the sun. The young woman arranged the cottage, and prepared the food; and the youth departed after the first meal.

"This day was passed in the same routine as that which preceded it. The young man was constantly employed out of doors, and the girl in various laborious occupations within. The old man, whom I soon perceived to be blind, employed his leisure hours on his instrument, or in contemplation. Nothing could exceed the love and respect which the younger cottagers exhibited towards their venerable companion. They performed towards him every little office of affection and duty with gentleness; and he rewarded them by his benevolent smiles.

"They were not entirely happy. The young man and his companion often went apart, and appeared to weep. I saw no cause for their unhappiness; but I was deeply affected by it. If such lovely creatures were miserable, it was less strange that I, an imperfect and solitary being, should be wretched. Yet why were these gentle beings unhappy? They possessed a delightful house (for such it was in my eyes), and every luxury; they had a fire to warm them when chill, and delicious viands when hungry; they were dressed in excellent clothes; and, still more, they enjoyed one another's company and speech, interchanging each day looks of affection and kindness. What did their tears imply? Did they really express pain? I was at first unable to solve these questions; but perpetual attention, and time, explained to me many appearances which were at first enigmatic.

"A considerable period elapsed before I discovered one of the causes of the uneasiness of this amiable family; it was poverty; and they suffered that evil in a very distressing degree. Their nourishment consisted entirely of the vegetables of their garden, and the milk of one cow, who gave very little during the winter, when its masters could scarcely procure food to support it. They often, I believe, suffered the pangs of hunger very poignantly, especially the two younger cottagers; for several times they placed food before the old man, when they reserved none for themselves.

"This trait of kindness moved me sensibly. I had

been accustomed, during the night, to steal a part of their store for my own consumption; but when I found that in doing this I inflicted pain on the cottagers, I abstained, and satisfied myself with berries, nuts, and roots, which I gathered from a neighbouring wood.

"I discovered also another means through which I was enabled to assist their labours. I found that the youth spent a great part of each day in collecting wood for the family fire; and, during the night, I often took his tools, the use of which I quickly discovered, and brought home firing sufficient for the consumption of several days.

"I remember, the first time that I did this, the young woman, when she opened the door in the morning, appeared greatly astonished on seeing a great pile of wood on the outside. She uttered some words in a loud voice, and the youth joined her, who also expressed surprise. I observed, with pleasure, that he did not go to the forest that day, but spent it in repairing the cottage, and cultivating the garden.

"By degrees I made a discovery of still greater moment. I found that these people possessed a method of communicating their experience and feelings to one another by articulate sounds. I perceived that the words they spoke sometimes produced pleasure or pain, smiles or sadness, in the minds and countenances of the hearers. This was indeed a godlike science, and I ardently desired to become acquainted with it. But I was baffled in every attempt I made for this purpose. Their pronunciation was quick; and the words they uttered, not having any apparent connexion with visible objects, I was unable to discover any clue by which I could unravel the mystery of their reference. By great application, however, and after having remained during the space of several revolutions of the moon in my hovel, I discovered the names that were given to some of the most familiar objects of discourse; I learned and applied the words *fire, milk, bread,* and *wood.* I learned also the names of the cottagers themselves. The youth and his companion had each of them several names, but the old man had only one, which was *father.* The girl was called *sister,* or *Agatha;* and the youth *Felix, brother,* or *son.* I cannot describe the delight I felt when I learned the ideas appropriated to each of these sounds, and was able to pronounce them. I distinguished several other words, without being able as yet to understand or apply them; such as *good, dearest, unhappy.*

"I spent the winter in this manner. The gentle manners and beauty of the cottagers greatly endeared them to me; when they were unhappy, I felt depressed; when they rejoiced, I sympathized in their joys. I saw few human beings beside them; and if any other happened to enter the cottage, their harsh manners and rude gait only enhanced to me the superior accomplishments of my friends. The old man, I could perceive, often endeavoured to encourage his children, as sometimes I found that he called them, to cast off their melancholy. He would talk in a cheerful accent, with an expression of goodness that bestowed pleasure even upon me. Agatha listened with respect, her eyes sometimes filled with tears, which she endeavoured to wipe away unperceived; but I generally found that her countenance and tone were more cheerful after having listened to the exhortations of her father. It was not thus with Felix. He was always the saddest of the groupe; and, even to my unpractised senses, he appeared to have suffered more deeply than his friends. But if his countenance was more sorrowful, his voice was more cheerful than that of his sister, especially when he addressed the old man.

"I could mention innumerable instances, which,

although slight, marked the dispositions of these amiable cottagers. In the midst of poverty and want, Felix carried with pleasure to his sister the first little white flower that peeped out from beneath the snowy ground. Early in the morning before she had risen, he cleared away the snow that obstructed her path to the milk-house, drew water from the well, and brought the wood from the outhouse, where, to his perpetual astonishment, he found his store always replenished by an invisible hand. In the day, I believe, he worked sometimes for a neighbouring farmer, because he often went forth, and did not return until dinner, yet brought no wood with him. At other times he worked in the garden; but, as there was little to do in the frosty season, he read to the old man and Agatha.

"This reading had puzzled me extremely at first; but, by degrees, I discovered that he uttered many of the same sounds when he read as when he talked. I conjectured, therefore, that he found on the paper signs for speech which he understood, and I ardently longed to comprehend these also; but how was that possible, when I did not even understand the sounds for which they stood as signs? I improved, however, sensibly in this science, but not sufficiently to follow up any kind of conversation, although I applied my whole mind to the endeavour: for I easily perceived that, although I eagerly longed to discover myself to the cottagers, I ought not to make the attempt until I had first become master of their language; which knowledge might enable me to make them overlook the deformity of my figure; for with this also the contrast perpetually presented to my eyes had made me acquainted.

"I had admired the perfect forms of my cottagers—their grace, beauty, and delicate complexions: but how was I terrified, when I viewed myself in a transparent pool! At first I started back, unable to believe that it was indeed I who was reflected in the mirror; and when I became fully convinced that I was in reality the monster that I am, I was filled with the bitterest sensations of despondence and mortification. Alas! I did not yet entirely know the fatal effects of this miserable deformity.

"As the sun became warmer, and the light of day longer, the snow vanished, and I beheld the bare trees and the black earth. From this time Felix was more employed; and the heart-moving indications of impending famine disappeared. Their food, as I afterwards found, was coarse, but it was wholesome; and they procured a sufficiency of it. Several new kinds of plants sprung up in the garden, which they dressed; and these signs of comfort increased daily as the season advanced.

"The old man, leaning on his son, walked each day at noon, when it did not rain, as I found it was called when the heavens poured forth its waters. This frequently took place; but a high wind quickly dried the earth, and the season became far more pleasant than it had been.

"My mode of life in my hovel was uniform. During the morning I attended the motions of the cottagers; and when they were dispersed in various occupations, I slept: the remainder of the day was spent in observing my friends. When they had retired to rest, if there was any moon, or the night was star-light, I went into the woods, and collected my own food and fuel for the cottage. When I returned, as often as it was necessary, I cleared their path from the snow, and performed those offices that I had seen done by Felix. I afterwards found that these labours, performed by an invisible hand, greatly astonished them; and once or twice I heard them, on these occasions, utter the words *good spirit, wonderful;* but I did not then understand the signification of these terms.

"My thoughts now became more active, and I longed to discover the motives and feelings of these lovely creatures; I was inquisitive to know why Felix appeared so miserable, and Agatha so sad. I thought (foolish wretch!) that it might be in my power to restore happiness to these deserving people. When I slept, or was absent, the forms of the venerable blind father, the gentle Agatha, and the excellent Felix, flitted before me. I looked upon them as superior beings, who would be the arbiters of my future destiny. I formed in my imagination a thousand pictures of presenting myself to them, and their reception of me. I imagined that they would be disgusted, until, by my gentle demeanour and conciliating words, I should first win their favour, and afterwards their love.

"These thoughts exhilarated me, and led me to apply with fresh ardour to the acquiring the art of language. My organs were indeed harsh, but supple; and although my voice was very unlike the soft music of their tones, yet I pronounced such words as I understood with tolerable ease. It was as the ass and the lap-dog; yet surely the gentle ass, whose intentions were affectionate, although his manners were rude, deserved better treatment than blows and execration.

"The pleasant showers and genial warmth of spring greatly altered the aspect of the earth. Men, who before this change seemed to have been hid in caves, dispersed themselves, and were employed in various arts of cultivation. The birds sang in more cheerful notes, and the leaves began to bud forth on the trees. Happy, happy earth! fit habitation for gods, which, so short a time before, was bleak, damp, and unwholesome. My spirits were elevated by the enchanting appearance of nature; the past was blotted from my memory, the present was tranquil, and the future gilded by bright rays of hope, and anticipations of joy.

CHAPTER V

"I now hasten to the more moving part of my story. I shall relate events that impressed me with feelings which, from what I was, have made me what I am.

"Spring advanced rapidly; the weather became fine, and the skies cloudless. It surprised me, that what before was desert and gloomy should now bloom with the most beautiful flowers and verdure. My senses were gratified and refreshed by a thousand scents of delight, and a thousand sights of beauty.

"It was on one of these days, when my cottagers periodically rested from labour—the old man played on his guitar, and the children listened to him—I observed that the countenance of Felix was melancholy beyond expression; he sighed frequently; and once his father paused in his music, and I conjectured by his manner that he inquired the cause of his son's sorrow. Felix replied in a cheerful accent, and the old man was recommencing his music, when some one tapped at the door.

"It was a lady on horseback, accompanied by a countryman as a guide. The lady was dressed in a dark suit, and covered with a thick black veil. Agatha asked a question; to which the stranger only replied by pronouncing, in a sweet accent, the name of Felix. Her voice was musical, but unlike that of either of my friends. On hearing this word, Felix came up hastily to the lady; who, when she saw him, threw up her veil, and I beheld a countenance of angelic beauty and expression. Her hair of a shining raven black, and curiously braided; her eyes were dark, but gentle, although animated; her features of a regular proportion, and her complexion wondrously fair, each cheek tinged with a lovely pink.

"Felix seemed ravished with delight when he saw her, every trait of sorrow vanished from his face, and it instantly expressed a degree of ecstatic joy, of which I could hardly have believed it capable; his eyes sparkled, as his cheek flushed with pleasure; and at that moment I thought him as beautiful as the stranger. She appeared affected by different feelings; wiping a few tears from her lovely eyes, she held out her hand to Felix, who kissed it rapturously, and called her, as well as I could distinguish, his sweet Arabian. She did not appear to understand him, but smiled. He assisted her to dismount, and, dismissing her guide, conducted her into the cottage. Some conversation took place between him and his father; and the young stranger knelt at the old man's feet, and would have kissed his hand, but he raised her, and embraced her affectionately.

"I soon perceived, that although the stranger uttered articulate sounds, and appeared to have a language of her own, she was neither understood by, or herself understood, the cottagers. They made many signs which I did not comprehend; but I saw that her presence diffused gladness through the cottage, dispelling their sorrow as the sun dissipates the morning mists. Felix seemed peculiarly happy, and with smiles of delight welcomed his Arabian. Agatha, the ever-gentle Agatha, kissed the hands of the lovely stranger; and, pointing to her brother, made signs which appeared to me to mean that he had been sorrowful until she came. Some hours passed thus, while they, by their countenances, expressed joy, the cause of which I did not comprehend. Presently I found, by the frequent recurrence of one sound which the stranger repeated after them, that she was endeavouring to learn their language; and the idea instantly occurred to me, that I should make use of the same instructions to the same end. The stranger learned about twenty words at the first lesson, most of them indeed were those which I had before understood, but I profited by the others.

"As night came on, Agatha and the Arabian retired early. When they separated, Felix kissed the hand of the stranger, and said, 'Good night, sweet Safie.' He sat up much longer, conversing with his father; and, by the frequent repetition of her name, I conjectured that their lovely guest was the subject of their conversation. I ardently desired to understand them, and bent every faculty towards that purpose, but found it utterly impossible.

"The next morning Felix went out to his work; and, after the usual occupations of Agatha were finished, the Arabian sat at the feet of the old man, and, taking his guitar, played some airs so entrancingly beautiful, that they at once drew tears of sorrow and delight from my eyes. She sang, and her voice flowed in a rich cadence, swelling or dying away, like a nightingale of the woods.

"When she had finished, she gave the guitar to Agatha, who at first declined it. She played a simple air, and her voice accompanied it in sweet accents, but unlike the wondrous strain of the stranger. The old man appeared enraptured, and said some words, which Agatha endeavoured to explain to Safie, and by which he appeared to wish to express that she bestowed on him the greatest delight by her music.

"The days now passed as peaceably as before, with the sole alteration, that joy had taken place of sadness in the countenances of my friends. Safie was always gay and happy; she and I improved rapidly in the knowledge of language, so that in two months I began to comprehend most of the words uttered by my protectors.

"In the meanwhile also the black ground was covered with herbage, and the green banks interspersed with innumerable flowers, sweet to the scent and the eyes, stars of pale radiance among the moonlight woods; the sun became warmer, the nights clear and balmy; and my nocturnal rambles were an extreme pleasure to me, although they were considerably shortened by the late setting and early rising of the sun; for I never ventured abroad during day-light, fearful of meeting with the same treatment as I had formerly endured in the first village which I entered.

"My days were spent in close attention, that I might more speedily master the language; and I may boast that I improved more rapidly than the Arabian, who understood very little, and conversed in broken accents, whilst I comprehended and could imitate almost every word that was spoken.

"While I improved in speech, I also learned the science of letters, as it was taught to the stranger; and this opened before me a wide field for wonder and delight.

"The book from which Felix instructed Safie was Volney's *Ruins of Empires.* I should not have understood the purport of this book, had not Felix, in reading it, given very minute explanations. He had chosen this work, he said, because the declamatory style was framed in imitation of the eastern authors. Through this work I obtained a cursory knowledge of history, and a view of the several empires at present existing in the world; it gave me an insight into the manners, governments, and religions of the different nations of the earth. I heard of the slothful Asiatics; of the stupendous genius and mental activity of the Grecians; of the wars and wonderful virtue of the early Romans—of their subsequent degeneration—

of the decline of that mighty empire; of chivalry, Christianity, and kings. I heard of the discovery of the American hemisphere, and wept with Safie over the hapless fate of its original inhabitants.

"These wonderful narrations inspired me with strange feelings. Was man, indeed, at once so powerful, so virtuous, and magnificent, yet so vicious and base? He appeared at one time a mere scion of the evil principle, and at another as all that can be conceived of noble and godlike. To be a great and virtuous man appeared the highest honour that can befall a sensitive being; to be base and vicious, as many on record have been, appeared the lowest degradation, a condition more abject than that of the blind mole or harmless worm. For a long time I could not conceive how one man could go forth to murder his fellow, or even why there were laws and governments; but when I heard details of vice and bloodshed, my wonder ceased, and I turned away with disgust and loathing.

"Every conversation of the cottagers now opened new wonders to me. While I listened to the instructions which Felix bestowed upon the Arabian, the strange system of human society was explained to me. I heard of the division of property, of immense wealth and squalid poverty; of rank, descent, and noble blood.

"The words induced me to turn towards myself. I learned that the possessions most esteemed by your fellow-creatures were, high and unsullied descent united with riches. A man might be respected with only one of these acquisitions; but without either he was considered, except in very rare instances, as a vagabond and a slave, doomed to waste his powers for the profit of the chosen few. And what was I? Of my creation and creator I was absolutely ignorant; but I knew that I possessed no money, no friends, no kind of property. I was, besides, endowed with a figure hideously deformed and loathsome; I was not even of the same nature as man. I was more agile than they, and could subsist upon coarser diet; I bore the extremes of heat and cold with less injury to my frame; my stature far exceeded their's. When I looked around, I saw and heard of none like me. Was I then a monster, a blot upon the earth, from which all men fled, and whom all men disowned?

"I cannot describe to you the agony that these reflections inflicted upon me; I tried to dispel them, but sorrow only increased with knowledge. Oh, that I had for ever remained in my native wood, nor known or felt beyond the sensations of hunger, thirst, and heat!

"Of what a strange nature is knowledge! It clings to the mind, when it has once seized on it, like a lichen on the rock. I wished sometimes to shake off all thought and feeling; but I learned that there was but one means to overcome the sensation of pain, and that was death—a state which I feared yet did not understand. I admired virtue and good feelings, and loved the gentle manners and amiable qualities of my cottagers; but I was shut out from intercourse with them, except through means which I obtained by stealth, when I was unseen and unknown, and which rather increased than satisfied the desire I had of becoming one among my fellows. The gentle words of Agatha, and the animated smiles of the charming Arabian, were not for me. The mild exhortations of the old man, and the lively conversation of the loved Felix, were not for me. Miserable, unhappy wretch!

"Other lessons were impressed upon me even more deeply. I heard of the difference of sexes; of the birth and growth of children; how the father doated on the smiles of the infant, and the lively sallies of the older child; how all the life and cares of the mother were wrapt up in the precious charge; how the mind of youth expanded and gained knowledge; of brother, sister, and all the various relationships which bind one human being to another in mutual bonds.

"But where were my friends and relations? No father had watched my infant days, no mother had blessed me with smiles and caresses; or if they had, all my past life was now a blot, a blind vacancy in which I distinguished nothing. From my earliest remembrance I had been as I then was in height and proportion. I had never yet seen a being resembling me, or who claimed any intercourse with me. What was I? The question again recurred, to be answered only with groans.

"I will soon explain to what these feelings tended; but allow me now to return to the cottagers, whose story excited in me such various feelings of indignation, delight, and wonder, but which all terminated in additional love and reverence for my protectors (for so I loved, in an innocent, half painful self-deceit, to call them).

CHAPTER VI

"Some time elapsed before I learned the history of my friends. It was one which could not fail to impress itself deeply on my mind, unfolding as it did a number of circumstances each interesting and wonderful to one so utterly inexperienced as I was.

"The name of the old man was De Lacey. He was descended from a good family in France, where he had lived for many years in affluence, respected by his superiors, and beloved by his equals. His son was bred in the service of his country; and Agatha had ranked with ladies of the highest distinction. A few months before my arrival, they had lived in a large and luxurious city, called Paris, surrounded by friends, and possessed of every enjoyment which virtue, refinement of intellect, or taste, accompanied by a moderate fortune, could afford.

"The father of Safie had been the cause of their ruin. He was a Turkish merchant, and had inhabited Paris for many years, when, for some reason which I could not learn, he became obnoxious to the government. He was seized and cast into prison the very day that Safie arrived from Constantinople to join him. He was tried, and condemned to death. The injustice of his sentence was very flagrant; all Paris was indignant; and it was judged that his religion and wealth, rather than the crime alleged against him, had been the cause of his condemnation.

"Felix had been present at the trial; his horror and indignation were uncontrollable, when he heard the decision of the court. He made, at that moment, a solemn vow to deliver him, and then looked around for the means. After many fruitless attempts to gain admittance to the prison, he found a strongly grated window in an unguarded part of the building, which lighted the dungeon of the unfortunate Mahometan; who, loaded with chains, waited in despair the execution of the barbarous sentence. Felix visited the grate at night, and made known to the prisoner his intentions in his favour. The Turk, amazed and delighted, endeavoured to kindle the zeal of his deliverer by promises of reward and wealth. Felix rejected his offers with contempt; yet when he saw the lovely Safie, who was allowed to visit her father, and who, by her gestures, expressed her lively gratitude, the youth could not help owning to his own mind, that the captive possessed a treasure which would fully reward his toil and hazard.

"The Turk quickly perceived the impression that his daughter had made on the heart of Felix, and endeavoured to secure him more entirely in his interests by the promise of her hand in marriage, so soon as he should be conveyed to a place of safety. Felix was too delicate to accept this offer; yet he looked forward to the probability of that event as to the consummation of his happiness.

"During the ensuing days, while the preparations were going forward for the escape of the merchant, the zeal of Felix was warmed by several letters that he received from this lovely girl, who found means to express her thoughts in the language of her lover by the aid of an old man, a servant of her father's who understood French. She thanked him in the most ardent terms for his intended services towards her father; and at the same time she gently deplored her own fate.

"I have copies of these letters; for I found means, during my residence in the hovel, to procure the implements of writing; and the letters were often in the hands of Felix or Agatha. Before I depart, I will give them to you, they will prove the truth of my tale; but at present, as the sun is already far declined, I shall only have time to repeat the substance of them to you.

"Safie related, that her mother was a Christian Arab, seized and made a slave by the Turks; recommended by her beauty, she had won the heart of the father of Safie, who married her. The young girl spoke in high and enthusiastic terms of her mother, who, born in freedom spurned the bondage to which she was now reduced. She instructed her daughter in the tenets of her religion, and taught her to aspire to

(MORRIS ARCHIVE)

Mary was married to poet Percy Bysshe Shelley in 1816. Their marriage license is below.

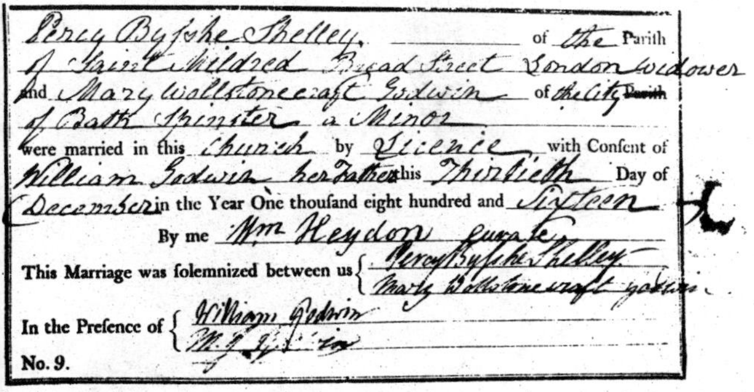

Percy Bysshe Shelley of the Parish of Saint Mildred Bread Street London Widower
and Mary Wollstonecraft Godwin of the City of Bath Spinster a Minor
were married in this Church by Licence with Consent of William Godwin her Father this Thirtieth Day of December in the Year One thousand eight hundred and Sixteen

By me Wm Heydon Curate

This Marriage was solemnized between us { Percy Bysshe Shelley / Mary Wollstonecraft Godwin.

In the Presence of { William Godwin / M. J. Godwin

No. 9.

(NEWSTEAD ABBEY, NOTTINGHAM MUSEUMS)

Jane Clairmont, who changed her name to the more romantic sounding Claire, at age twenty-one. She had an affair with Lord Byron, and may also have been Percy's lover.

(NEWSTEAD ABBEY, NOTTINGHAM MUSEUMS)

The most famous young poet of the day, Lord Byron, in 1814. A cold summer evening in 1816, spent with Byron, Percy, and Claire, helped inspire Mary Shelley to write *Frankenstein*.

...of the murder of the Protestants at
...ne yet I am fully satisfied that
...r royal Highness has always the
...of the holy Catholic Church near
...r heart. How it was dear to me
...ounds of three hundred heretics now wandering
...can testify for me. But your royal
...ness rules, for it you that have the real
...r in France / over a nation
the established religion of which
...nowledges. and however painful it is to
I must remind your royal highness that it is
the mercy of your ancestors that allowed

(BODLEIAN LIBRARY, OXFORD)

Frankenstein's political origins are reflected in its author's 1818 draft of a satire in the form of a letter from Bloody Queen Mary, offering congratulations for the slaughter of French pro-revolutionaries.

(BODLEIAN LIBRARY, OXFORD)

Mary Shelley's sketch of a murdered man lying on a pallet, 1819.

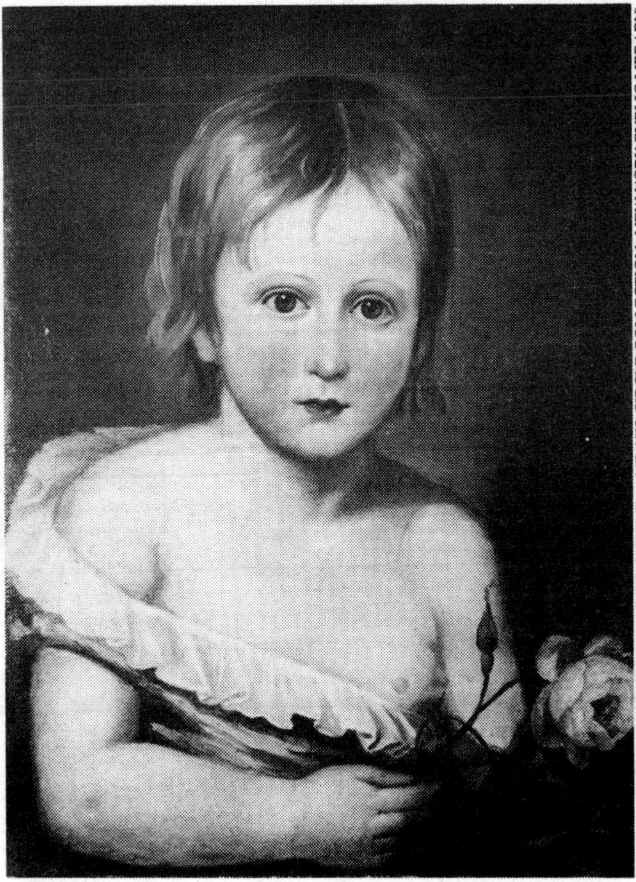
(THE CARL H. PFORZHEIMER SHELLEY AND HIS CIRCLE COLLECTION, NEW YORK PUBLIC LIBRARY)

William Shelley, at age three, painted by Amelia Curran in Rome in 1819, just before the child's death.

(THE BETTMANN ARCHIVE)

Mary Shelley at forty-two, painted by Richard Rothwell, dated 1840.

(GIRAUDON/ART RESOURCE, NY, MUSEE GUSTAVE MOREAU, PARIS)

Shelley titled her novel *Frankenstein; or, The Modern Prometheus*. According to versions of Greek mythology, Prometheus is a Titan who steals fire from heaven to help mankind, or a god who actually creates man by breathing life into a clay body. This 1868 painting by Gustave Morea portrays his punishment: to have his liver eaten daily by a vulture.

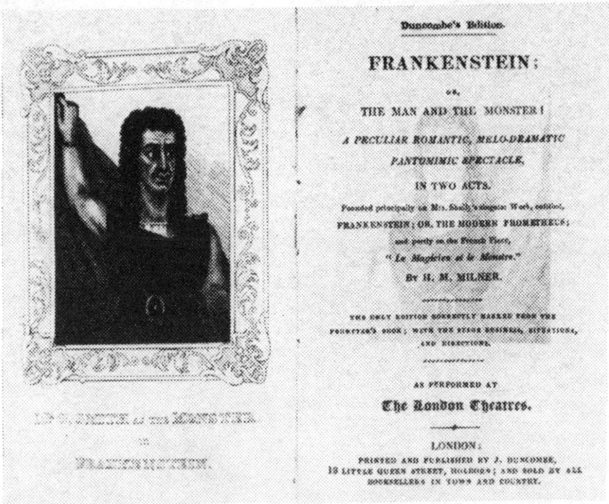

Duncombe's Edition.

FRANKENSTEIN;

OR,

THE MAN AND THE MONSTER!

A PECULIAR ROMANTIC, MELO-DRAMATIC PANTOMIMIC SPECTACLE,

IN TWO ACTS.

Founded principally on Mrs. Shelly's elegant Work, entitled,

FRANKENSTEIN; OR, THE MODERN PROMETHEUS;

and partly on the French Piece,

"Le Magicien et le Monstre."

BY H. M. MILNER.

THE ONLY EDITION CORRECTLY MARKED FROM THE PROMPTER'S BOOK; WITH THE STAGE BUSINESS, SITUATIONS, AND DIRECTIONS.

AS PERFORMED AT

The London Theatres.

LONDON:

PRINTED AND PUBLISHED BY J. DUNCOMBE, 19 LITTLE QUEEN STREET, HOLBORN; AND SOLD BY ALL BOOKSELLERS IN TOWN AND COUNTRY.

The first dramatic version of Shelley's novel was *Frankenstein; or, The Man and the Monster* (1823), which presented the "Monster" as a handsome Greek god.

Similarly, *Presumption; or, the Fate of Frankenstein* (1823), by Richard Brinsley Peake, shows that the creature was initially seen as a handsome giant.

A lithograph from an 1826 French production, captioned: "I submit to your blows, but my son, spare his days!"

(THE CARL H. PFORZHEIMER SHELLEY AND HIS CIRCLE COLLECTION, NEW YORK PUBLIC LIBRARY)

Illustrations from the 1831 second edition of *Frankenstein*. Above: "By the glimmer of the half-extinguished light, I saw the dull, yellow eye of the creature open; it breathed hard, and a convulsive motion agitated its limbs. . . . I rushed out of the room." Right: "The day of my departure at length arrived."

(THE CARL H. PFORZHEIMER SHELLEY AND HIS CIRCLE COLLECTION, NEW YORK PUBLIC LIBRARY)

Mary Shelley's creature was quickly given political meanings. At left, he represents the threat of a Russian invasion, in John Tenniel's "The Russian Frankenstein and his Monster," from the July 15, 1854 issue of *Punch*.

And at right, he represents the threat of an Irish rebellion against British rule in Tenniel's "The Irish Frankenstein," from the May 20, 1882 issue of *Punch*.

Until 1930, the creature continued to be portrayed in the theater and popular media as a sympathetic "model man." Not until 1931, with John Whale's film *Frankenstein*, starring Boris Karloff, did he become exclusively a figure of terror, a "monster" in all ways. This 1850 version of *The Model Man* appeared in the *Illustrated London News*.

Since Boris Karloff first portrayed the creature with stitches in his head and bolts in his neck, scores of sequels, film adaptations, parodies, and cartoons have done the same. This is the cover of a December 1945 comic book.

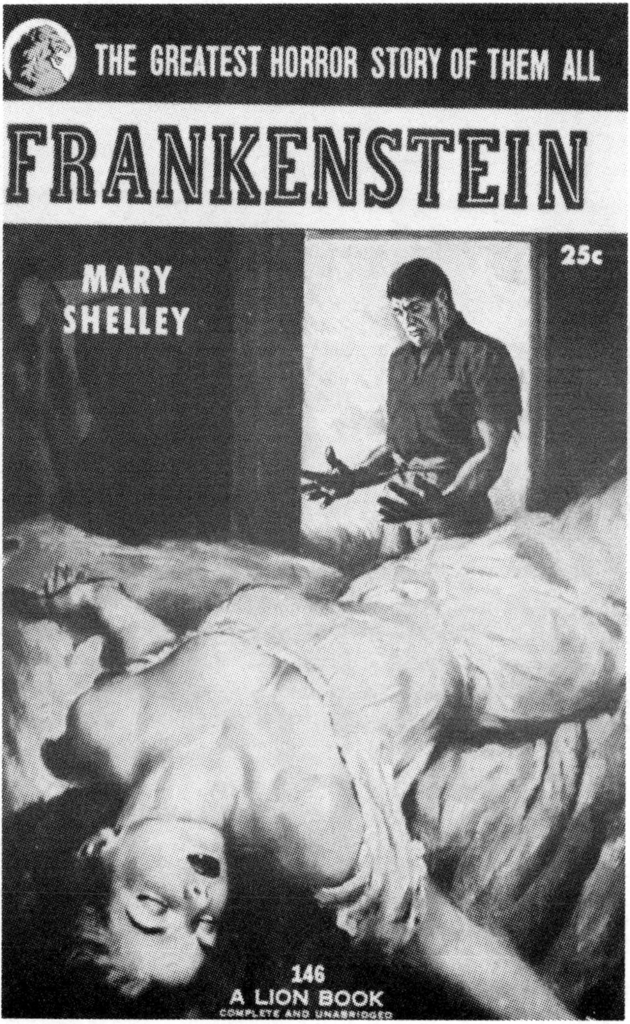

A 1953 paperback edition of *Frankenstein*, "The Greatest Horror Story of Them All."

(MOVIE STAR NEWS)

A scene from Kenneth Branagh's 1994 film, *Mary Shelley's Frankenstein,* that starred Robert De Niro as the creature.

higher powers of intellect, and an independence of spirit, forbidden to the female followers of Mahomet. This lady died; but her lessons were indelibly impressed on the mind of Safie, who sickened at the prospect of again returning to Asia, and the being immured within the walls of a haram, allowed only to occupy herself with puerile amusements, ill suited to the temper of her soul, now accustomed to grand ideas and a noble emulation for virtue. The prospect of marrying a Christian, and remaining in a country where women were allowed to take a rank in society, was enchanting to her.

"The day for the execution of the Turk was fixed; but, on the night previous to it, he had quitted prison, and before morning was distant many leagues from Paris. Felix had procured passports in the name of his father, sister, and himself. He had previously communicated his plan to the former, who aided the deceit by quitting his house, under the pretence of a journey, and concealed himself, with his daughter, in an obscure part of Paris.

"Felix conducted the fugitives through France to Lyons, and across Mont Cenis to Leghorn, where the merchant had decided to wait a favourable opportunity of passing into some part of the Turkish dominions.

"Safie resolved to remain with her father until the moment of his departure, before which time the Turk renewed his promise that she should be united to his deliverer; and Felix remained with them in expectation of that event; and in the mean time he enjoyed the society of the Arabian, who exhibited towards him the simplest and tenderest affection. They conversed with one another through the means of an interpreter, and sometimes with the interpretation of looks; and Safie sang to him the divine airs of her native country.

"The Turk allowed this intimacy to take place, and encouraged the hopes of the youthful lovers, while in his heart he had formed far other plans. He loathed the idea that his daughter should be united to a Christian; but he feared the resentment of Felix if he should appear lukewarm; for he knew that he was still in the power of his deliverer, if he should choose to betray him to the Italian state which they inhabited. He revolved a thousand plans by which he should be enabled to prolong the deceit until it might be no longer necessary, and secretly to take his daughter with him when he departed. His plans were greatly facilitated by the news which arrived from Paris.

"The government of France were greatly enraged at the escape of their victim, and spared no pains to detect and punish his deliverer. The plot of Felix was quickly discovered, and De Lacey and Agatha were thrown into prison. The news reached Felix, and roused him from his dream of pleasure. His blind and aged father, and his gentle sister, lay in a noisome dungeon, while he enjoyed the free air, and the society of her whom he loved. This idea was torture to him. He quickly arranged with the Turk, that if the latter should find a favourable opportunity for escape before Felix could return to Italy, Safie should remain as a boarder at a convent at Leghorn; and then, quitting the lovely Arabian, he hastened to Paris, and delivered himself up to the vengeance of the law, hoping to free De Lacey and Agatha by this proceeding.

"He did not succeed. They remained confined for five months before the trial took place; the result of which deprived them of their fortune, and condemned them to a perpetual exile from their native country.

"They found a miserable asylum in the cottage in Germany, where I discovered them. Felix soon learned that the treacherous Turk, for whom he and his family endured such unheard-of oppression, on discovering that his deliverer was thus reduced to poverty and impotence, became a traitor to good feeling and honour, and had quitted Italy with his daughter, insultingly sending Felix a pittance of money to aid him, as he said, in some plan of future maintenance.

"Such were the events that preyed on the heart of Felix, and rendered him, when I first saw him, the most miserable of his family. He could have endured poverty, and when this distress had been the meed of his virtue, he would have gloried in it: but the ingratitude of the Turk, and the loss of his beloved Safie, were misfortunes more bitter and irreparable. The arrival of the Arabian now infused new life into his soul.

"When the news reached Leghorn, that Felix was deprived of his wealth and rank, the merchant commanded his daughter to think no more of her lover, but to prepare to return with him to her native country. The generous nature of Safie was outraged by this command; she attempted to expostulate with her father, but he left her angrily, reiterating his tyrannical mandate.

"A few days after, the Turk entered his daughter's apartment, and told her hastily, that he had reason to believe that his residence at Leghorn had been divulged, and that he should speedily be delivered up to the French government; he had, consequently, hired a vessel to convey him to Constantinople, for which city he should sail in a few hours. He intended to leave his daughter under the care of a confidential servant, to follow at her leisure with the greater part of his property, which had not yet arrived at Leghorn.

"When alone, Safie resolved in her own mind the plan of conduct that it would become her to pursue in this emergency. A residence in Turkey was abhorrent to her; her religion and feelings were alike adverse to it. By some papers of her father's, which fell into her hands, she heard of the exile of her lover, and learnt the name of the spot where he then resided. She hesitated some time, but at length she formed her determination. Taking with her some jewels that belonged to her, and a small sum of money, she quitted Italy, with an attendant, a native of Leghorn, but who understood the common language of Turkey, and departed for Germany.

"She arrived in safety at a town about twenty leagues from the cottage of De Lacey, when her attendant fell dangerously ill. Safie nursed her with the most devoted affection; but the poor girl died, and the Arabian was left alone, unacquainted with the language of the country, and utterly ignorant of the customs of the world. She fell, however, into good hands. The Italian had mentioned the name of the spot for which they were bound; and, after her death, the woman of the house in which they had lived took care that Safie should arrive in safety at the cottage of her lover.

CHAPTER VII

"Such was the history of my beloved cottagers. It impressed me deeply. I learned, from the views of social life which it developed, to admire their virtues, and to deprecate the vices of mankind.

"As yet I looked upon crime as a distant evil; benevolence and generosity were ever present before me, inciting within me a desire to become an actor in the busy scene where so many admirable qualities were called forth and displayed. But, in giving an account of the progress of my intellect, I must not omit a circumstance which occurred in the beginning of the month of August of the same year.

"One night, during my accustomed visit to the neighbouring wood, where I collected my own food, and brought home firing for my protectors, I found on the ground a leathern portmanteau, containing several articles of dress and some books. I eagerly seized the prize, and returned it to my hovel. Fortunately the books were written in the language the elements of which I had acquired at the cottage; they consisted of *Paradise Lost*, a volume of *Plutarch's Lives*, and the *Sorrows of Werter*. The possession of these treasures gave me extreme delight; I now continually studied and exercised my mind upon these histories, whilst my friends were employed in their ordinary occupations.

"I can hardly describe to you the effect of these books. They produced in me an infinity of new images and feelings, that sometimes raised me to ecstacy, but more frequently sunk me into the lowest dejection. In the *Sorrows of Werter*, besides the interest of its simple and affecting story, so many opinions are canvassed, and so many lights thrown upon what had hitherto been to me obscure subjects, that I found in it a never-ending source of speculation and astonishment. The gentle and domestic manners it described, combined with lofty sentiments and feelings, which had for their object something out of self, accorded well with my experience among my protectors, and with the wants which were for ever alive in my own bosom. But I thought Werter himself a more divine being than I had ever beheld or imagined; his character contained no pretension, but it sunk deep. The disquisitions upon death and suicide were calculated to fill me with wonder. I did not pretend to enter into the merits of the case, yet I inclined towards the opinions of the hero, whose extinction I wept, without precisely understanding it.

"As I read, however, I applied much personally to my own feelings and condition. I found myself similar, yet at the same time strangely unlike the beings concerning whom I read, and to whose conversation I was a listener. I sympathized with, and partly understood them, but I was unformed in mind; I was dependent on none, and related to none. 'The path of my departure was free;' and there was none to lament my annihilation. My person was hideous, and my stature gigantic: what did this mean? Who was I? What was I? Whence did I come? What was my destination? These questions continually recurred, but I was unable to solve them.

"The volume of *Plutarch's Lives* which I possessed, contained the histories of the first founders of the ancient republics. This book had a far different effect upon me from the *Sorrows of Werter.* I learned from Werter's imaginations despondency and gloom: but Plutarch taught me high thoughts; he elevated me above the wretched sphere of my own reflections, to admire and love the heroes of past ages. Many things I read surpassed my understanding and experience. I had a very confused knowledge of kingdoms, wide extents of country, mighty rivers, and boundless seas. But I was perfectly unacquainted with towns, and large assemblages of men. The cottage of my protectors had been the only school in which I had studied human nature; but this book developed new and mightier scenes of action. I read of men concerned in public affairs governing or massacring their species. I felt the greatest ardour for virtue rise within me, and abhorrence for vice, as far as I understood the signification of those terms, relative as they were, as I applied them, to pleasure and pain alone. Induced by these feelings, I was of course led to admire peaceable law-givers, Numa, Solon, and Lycurgus, in preference to Romulus and Theseus. The patriarchal lives of my protectors caused these impressions to take a firm hold on my mind; perhaps, if my first introduction to humanity had been made by a young soldier, burning for glory and slaughter, I should have been imbued with different sensations.

"But *Paradise Lost* excited different and far deeper emotions. I read it, as I had read the other volumes which had fallen into my hands, as a true history. It moved every feeling of wonder and awe, that the picture of an omnipotent God warring with his creatures was capable of exciting. I often referred the several situations, as their similarity struck me, to my own. Like Adam, I was created apparently united by no link to any other being in existence; but his state was far different from mine in every other respect. He had come forth from the hands of God a perfect creature, happy and prosperous, guarded by the especial care of his Creator; he was allowed to converse with, and acquire knowledge from beings of a superior nature: but I was wretched, helpless, and alone. Many times I considered Satan as the fitter emblem of my condition; for often, like him, when I viewed the bliss of my protectors, the bitter gall of envy rose within me.

"Another circumstance strengthened and confirmed these feelings. Soon after my arrival in the hovel, I discovered some papers in the pocket of the dress which I had taken from your laboratory. At first I had neglected them; but now that I was able to decypher the characters in which they were written, I began to study them with diligence. It was your journal of the four months that preceded my creation. You minutely described in these papers every step you took in the progress of your work; this history was mingled with accounts of domestic occurrences. You, doubtless, recollect these papers. Here they are. Every thing is related in them which bears reference to my accursed origin; the whole detail of that series of disgusting circumstances which produced it is set in view; the minutest description of my odious and loathsome person is given, in language which painted your own horrors, and rendered mine ineffaceable. I sickened as I read. 'Hateful day when I received life!' I exclaimed in agony. 'Cursed creator! Why did you form a monster so hideous that even you turned from me in disgust? God in pity made man beautiful and alluring, after his own image; but my form is a filthy type of your's, more horrid from its very resemblance. Satan had his companions, fellow-devils, to admire and encourage him; but I am solitary and detested.'

"These were the reflections of my hours of despondency and solitude; but when I contemplated the virtues of the cottagers, their amiable and benevolent dispositions, I persuaded myself that when they should become acquainted with my admiration of their virtues, they would compassionate me, and overlook my personal deformity. Could they turn from their door one, however monstrous, who solicited their compassion and friendship? I resolved, at least, not to despair, but in every way to fit myself for an interview with them which would decide my fate. I postponed this attempt for some months longer; for the importance attached to its success inspired me with a dread lest I should fail. Besides, I found that my understanding improved so much with every day's experience, that I was unwilling to commence this undertaking until a few more months should have added to my wisdom.

"Several changes, in the mean time, took place in the cottage. The presence of Safie diffused happiness among its inhabitants; and I also found that a greater degree of plenty reigned there. Felix and Agatha spent more time in amusement and conversation, and were assisted in their labours by servants. They did not appear rich, but they were contented and happy; their feelings were serene and peaceful, while mine became every day more tumultuous. Increase of knowledge only discovered to me more clearly what a wretched outcast I was. I cherished hope, it is true; but it vanished, when I beheld my person reflected in water, or my shadow in the moon-shine, even as that frail image and that inconstant shade.

"I endeavoured to crush these fears, and to fortify myself for the trial which in a few months I resolved to undergo; and sometimes I allowed my thoughts, unchecked by reason, to ramble in the fields of Paradise, and dared to fancy amiable and lovely creatures sympathizing with my feelings and cheering my gloom; their angelic countenances breathed smiles of consolation. But it was all a dream: no Eve soothed my sorrows, or shared my thoughts; I was alone. I remembered Adam's supplication to his Creator; but where was mine? he had abandoned me, and, in the bitterness of my heart, I cursed him.

"Autumn passed thus. I saw, with surprise and grief, the leaves decay and fall, and nature again assume the barren and bleak appearance it had worn when I first beheld the woods and the lovely moon. Yet I did not heed the bleakness of the weather; I was better fitted by my conformation for the endurance of cold than heat. But my chief delights were the sight of the flowers, the birds, and all the gay apparel of summer; when those deserted me, I turned with more attention towards the cottagers. Their happiness was not decreased by the absence of summer. They loved, and sympathized with one another; and their joys, depending on each other, were not interrupted by the casualties that took place around them. The more I saw of them, the greater became my desire to claim their protection and kindness; my heart yearned to be known and loved by these amiable creatures; to see their sweet looks turned towards me with affection, was the utmost limit of my ambition. I dared not think that they would turn them from me with disdain and horror. The poor that stopped at their door were never driven away. I asked, it is true, for greater treasures than a little food or rest; I required kindness and sympathy; but I did not believe myself utterly unworthy of it.

"The winter advanced, and an entire revolution of the seasons had taken place since I awoke into life. My attention, at this time, was solely directed towards my plan of introducing myself into the cottage of my protectors. I revolved many projects; but that on which I finally fixed was, to enter the dwelling when the blind old man should be alone. I had sagacity enough to discover, that the unnatural hideousness of my person was the chief object of horror with those who had formerly beheld me. My voice, although harsh, had nothing terrible in it; I thought, therefore, that if, in the absence of his children, I could gain the good-will and mediation of the old De Lacey, I might, by his means, be tolerated by my younger protectors.

"One day, when the sun shone on the red leaves that strewed the ground, and diffused cheerfulness, although it denied warmth, Safie, Agatha, and Felix, departed on a long country walk, and the old man, at his own desire, was left alone in the cottage. When his children had departed, he took up his guitar, and played several mournful, but sweet airs, more sweet and mournful than I had ever heard him play before. At first his countenance was illuminated with pleasure, but, as he continued, thoughtfulness and sadness succeeded; at length, laying aside the instrument, he sat absorbed in reflection.

"My heart beat quick; this was the hour and moment of trial, which would decide my hopes, or realize my fears. The servants were gone to a neighbouring fair. All was silent in and around the cottage: it was an excellent opportunity; yet, when I proceeded to execute my plan, my limbs failed me, and I sunk to the ground. Again I rose; and, exerting all the firmness of which I was master, removed the planks which I had placed before my hovel to conceal my retreat. The fresh air revived me, and, with renewed determination, I approached the door of their cottage.

"I knocked. 'Who is there?' said the old man—'Come in.'

"I entered; 'Pardon this intrusion,' said I, 'I am a traveller in want of a little rest; you would greatly oblige me, if you would allow me to remain a few minutes before the fire.'

" 'Enter,' said De Lacey; 'and I will try in what manner I can relieve your wants; but, unfortunately, my children are from home, and, as I am blind, I am afraid I shall find it difficult to procure food for you.'

" 'Do not trouble yourself, my kind host, I have food; it is warmth and rest only that I need.'

"I sat down, and a silence ensued. I knew that every minute was precious to me, yet I remained irresolute in what manner to commence the interview; when the old man addressed me—

" 'By your language, stranger, I suppose you are my countryman;—are you French?'

" 'No; but I was educated by a French family, and

understand that language only. I am now going to claim the protection of some friends, whom I sincerely love, and of whose favour I have some hopes.'

"'Are these Germans?'

"'No, they are French. But let us change the subject. I am an unfortunate and deserted creature; I look around, and I have no relation or friend upon earth. These amiable people to whom I go have never seen me, and know little of me. I am full of fears; for if I fail there, I am an outcast in the world for ever.'

"'Do not despair. To be friendless is indeed to be unfortunate; but the hearts of men, when unprejudiced by any obvious self-interest, are full of brotherly love and charity. Rely, therefore, on your hopes; and if these friends are good and amiable, do not despair.'

"'They are kind—they are the most excellent creatures in the world; but, unfortunately, they are prejudiced against me. I have good dispositions; my life has been hitherto harmless, and, in some degree, beneficial; but a fatal prejudice clouds their eyes, and where they ought to see a feeling and kind friend, they behold only a detestable monster.'

"'That is indeed unfortunate; but if you are really blameless, cannot you undeceive them?'

"'I am about to undertake that task; and it is on that account that I feel so many overwhelming terrors. I tenderly love these friends; I have, unknown to them, been for many months in the habits of daily kindness towards them; but they believe that I wish to injure them, and it is that prejudice which I wish to overcome.'

"'Where do these friends reside?'

"'Near this spot.'

"The old man paused, and then continued, 'If you will unreservedly confide to me the particulars of your tale, I perhaps may be of use in undeceiving them. I am blind, and cannot judge of your countenance, but there is something in your words which persuades me that you are sincere. I am poor, and an exile; but it will afford me true pleasure to be in any way serviceable to a human creature.'

"'Excellent man! I thank you, and accept your generous offer. You raise me from the dust by this kindness; and I trust that, by your aid, I shall not be driven from the society and sympathy of your fellow-creatures.'

"'Heaven forbid! even if you were really criminal; for that can only drive you to desperation, and not instigate you to virtue. I also am unfortunate; I and my family have been condemned, although innocent: judge, therefore, if I do not feel for your misfortunes.'

"'How can I thank you, my best and only benefactor? from your lips first have I heard the voice of kindness directed towards me; I shall be for ever grateful; and your present humanity assures me of success with those friends whom I am on the point of meeting.'

"'May I know the names and residence of those friends?'

"I paused. This, I thought, was the moment of decision, which was to rob me of, or bestow happiness on me for ever. I struggled vainly for firmness sufficient to answer him, but the effort destroyed all my remaining strength; I sank on the chair, and sobbed aloud. At that moment I heard the steps of my younger protectors. I had not a moment to lose; but, seizing the hand of the old man, I cried, 'Now is the time!—save and protect me! You and your family are the friends whom I seek. Do not you desert me in the hour of trial!'

"'Great God!' exclaimed the old man, 'who are you?'

"At that instant the cottage door was opened, and Felix, Safie, and Agatha entered. Who can describe their horror and consternation on beholding me? Agatha fainted; and Safie, unable to attend to her friend, rushed out of the cottage. Felix darted forward, and with supernatural force tore me from his father, to whose knees I clung: in a transport of fury, he dashed me to the ground, and struck me violently with a stick. I could have torn him limb from limb, as the lion rends the antelope. But my heart sunk within me as with bitter sickness, and I refrained. I saw him on the point of repeating his blow, when, overcome by pain and anguish, I quitted the cottage, and in the general tumult escaped unperceived to my hovel.

CHAPTER VIII

"Cursed, cursed creator! Why did I live? Why, in that instant, did I not extinguish the spark of existence which you had so wantonly bestowed? I know not; despair had not yet taken possession of me; my feelings were those of rage and revenge. I could with pleasure have destroyed the cottage and its inhabitants, and have glutted myself with their shrieks and misery.

"When night came, I quitted my retreat, and wandered in the wood; and now, no longer restrained by the fear of discovery, I gave vent to my anguish in fearful howlings. I was like a wild beast that had broken the toils; destroying the objects that obstructed me, and ranging through the wood with a stag-like swiftness. Oh! what a miserable night I passed! the cold stars shone in mockery, and the bare trees waved their branches above me: now and then the sweet voice of a bird burst forth amidst the universal stillness. All, save I, were at rest or in enjoyment: I, like the arch fiend, bore a hell within me; and, finding myself unsympathized with, wished to tear up the trees, spread havoc and destruction around me, and then to have sat down and enjoyed the ruin.

"But this was a luxury of sensation that could not endure; I became fatigued with excess of bodily exertion, and sank on the damp grass in the sick impotence of despair. There was none among the myriads of men that existed who would pity or assist me; and should I feel kindness towards my enemies? No: from that moment I declared everlasting war against the species, and, more than all, against him who had formed me, and sent me forth to this insupportable misery.

"The sun rose; I heard the voices of men, and knew that it was impossible to return to my retreat during that day. Accordingly I hid myself in some thick underwood, determining to devote the ensuing hours to reflection on my situation.

"The pleasant sunshine, and the pure air of day, restored me to some degree of tranquillity; and when I considered what had passed at the cottage, I could not help believing that I had been too hasty in my conclusions. I had certainly acted imprudently. It was apparent that my conversation had interested the father in my behalf, and I was a fool in having exposed my person to the horror of his children. I ought to have familiarized the old De Lacey to me, and by degrees have discovered myself to the rest of his family, when they should have been prepared for my approach. But I did not believe my errors to be irretrievable; and, after much consideration, I resolved to return to the cottage, seek the old man, and by my representations win him to my party.

"These thoughts calmed me, and in the afternoon I sank into a profound sleep; but the fever of my blood did not allow me to be visited by peaceful dreams. The horrible scene of the preceding day was for ever acting before my eyes; the females were flying, and the enraged Felix tearing me from his father's feet. I awoke exhausted; and, finding that it was already night, I crept forth from my hiding-place, and went in search of food.

"When my hunger was appeased, I directed my steps towards the well-known path that conducted to the cottage. All there was at peace. I crept into my hovel, and remained in silent expectation of the accustomed hour when the family arose. That hour past, the sun mounted high in the heavens, but the cottagers did not appear. I trembled violently, apprehending some dreadful misfortune. The inside of the cottage was dark, and I heard no motion; I cannot describe the agony of this suspence.

"Presently two countrymen passed by; but, pausing near the cottage, they entered into conversation, using violent gesticulations; but I did not understand what they said, as they spoke the language of the country, which differed from that of my protectors. Soon after, however, Felix approached with another man: I was surprised, as I knew that he had not quitted the cottage that morning, and waited anxiously to discover, from his discourse, the meaning of these unusual appearances.

"'Do you consider,' said his companion to him, 'that you will be obliged to pay three months' rent, and to lose the produce of your garden? I do not wish to take any unfair advantage, and I beg therefore that you will take some days to consider of your determination.'

"'It is utterly useless,' replied Felix, 'we can never again inhabit your cottage. The life of my father is in the greatest danger, owing to the dreadful circumstance that I have related. My wife and my sister will never recover [from] their horror. I entreat you not to reason with me any more. Take possession of your tenement, and let me fly from this place.'

"Felix trembled violently as he said this. He and his companion entered the cottage, in which they remained for a few minutes, and then departed. I never saw any of the family of De Lacey more.

"I continued for the remainder of the day in my hovel in a state of utter and stupid despair. My protectors had departed, and had broken the only link that held me to the world. For the first time the feelings of revenge and hatred filled my bosom, and I did not strive to controul them; but, allowing myself to be borne away by the stream, I bent my mind towards injury and death. When I thought of my friends, of the mild voice of De Lacey, the gentle eyes of Agatha, and the exquisite beauty of the Arabian, these thoughts vanished, and a gush of tears somewhat soothed me. But again, when I reflected that they had spurned and deserted me, anger returned, a rage of anger; and, unable to injure any thing human, I turned my fury towards inanimate objects. As night advanced, I placed a variety of combustibles around the cottage; and, after having destroyed every vestige of cultivation in the garden, I waited with forced impatience until the moon had sunk to commence my operations.

"As the night advanced, a fierce wind arose from the woods, and quickly dispersed the clouds that had loitered in the heavens: the blast tore along like a mighty avalanche, and produced a kind of insanity in my spirits, that burst all bounds of reason and reflection. I lighted the dry branch of a tree, and danced with fury around the devoted cottage, my eyes still fixed on the western horizon, the edge of which the moon nearly touched. A part of its orb was at length hid, and I waved my brand; it sunk, and, with a loud scream, I fired the straw, and heath, and bushes, which I had collected. The wind fanned the fire, and the cottage was quickly enveloped by the flames, which clung to it, and licked it with their forked and destroying tongues.

"As soon as I was convinced that no assistance could save any part of the habitation, I quitted the scene, and sought for refuge in the woods.

"And now, with the world before me, whither should I bend my steps? I resolved to fly far from the scene of my misfortunes; but to me, hated and despised, every country must be equally horrible. At length the thought of you crossed my mind. I learned from your papers that you were my father, my creator; and to whom could I apply with more fitness than to him who had given me life? Among the lessons that Felix had bestowed upon Safie geography had not been omitted: I had learned from these the relative situations of the different countries of the earth. You had mentioned Geneva as the name of your native town; and towards this place I resolved to proceed.

"But how was I to direct myself? I knew that I must travel in a southwesterly direction to reach my destination; but the sun was my only guide. I did not know the names of the towns that I was to pass through, nor could I ask information from a single human being; but I did not despair. From you only could I hope for succour, although towards you I felt no sentiment but that of hatred. Unfeeling, heartless creator! you had endowed me with perceptions and passions, and then cast me abroad an object for the scorn and horror of mankind. But on you only had I any claim for pity and redress, and from you I determined to seek that justice which I vainly attempted to gain from any other being that wore the human form.

"My travels were long, and the sufferings I endured intense. It was late in autumn when I quitted the district where I had so long resided. I travelled only at night, fearful of encountering the visage of a human being. Nature decayed around me, and the sun became heatless; rain and snow poured around me; mighty rivers were frozen; the surface of the earth was hard, and chill, and bare, and I found no shelter. Oh, earth! how often did I imprecate curses on the cause of my being! The mildness of my nature had fled, and all within me was turned to gall and bitterness. The nearer I approached to your habitation, the more deeply did I feel the spirit of revenge enkindled in my heart. Snow fell, and the waters were hardened, but I rested not. A few incidents now and then directed me, and I possessed a map of the country; but I often wandered wide from my path. The agony of my feelings allowed me no respite: no incident occurred from which my rage and misery could not extract its food; but a circumstance that happened when I arrived on the confines of Switzerland, when the sun had recovered its warmth, and the earth again began to look green, confirmed in an especial manner the bitterness and horror of my feelings.

"I generally rested during the day, and travelled only when I was secured by night from the view of man. One morning, however, finding that my path lay through a deep wood, I ventured to continue my journey after the sun had risen; the day, which was one of the first of spring, cheered even me by the loveliness of its sunshine and the balminess of the air. I felt emotions of gentleness and pleasure, that had long appeared dead, revive within me. Half surprised by the novelty of these sensations, I allowed myself to be borne away by them; and, forgetting my solitude and deformity, dared to be happy. Soft tears again bedewed my cheeks, and I even raised my humid eyes with thankfulness towards the blessed sun which bestowed such joy upon me.

"I continued to wind among the paths of the wood, until I came to its boundary, which was skirted by a deep and rapid river, into which many of the trees bent their branches, now budding with the fresh spring. Here I paused, not exactly knowing what path to pursue, when I heard the sound of voices, that induced me to conceal myself under the shade of a cypress. I was scarcely hid, when a young girl came running towards the spot where I was concealed, laughing as if she ran from some one in sport. She continued her course along the precipitous sides of the river, when suddenly her foot slipt, and she fell into the rapid stream. I rushed from my hiding place, and, with extreme labour from the force of the current, saved her, and dragged her to shore. She was senseless; and I endeavoured, by every means in my power, to restore animation, when I was suddenly interrupted by the approach of a rustic, who was probably the person from whom she had playfully fled. On seeing me, he darted towards me, and, tearing the girl from my arms, hastened towards the deeper parts of the wood. I followed speedily, I hardly knew why; but when the man saw me draw near, he aimed a gun, which he carried, at my body, and fired. I sunk to the ground, and my injurer, with increased swiftness, escaped into the wood.

"This was then the reward of my benevolence! I had saved a human being from destruction, and, as a recompence, I now writhed under the miserable pain of a wound, which shattered the flesh and bone. The feelings of kindness and gentleness, which I had entertained but a few moments before, gave place to hellish rage and gnashing of teeth. Inflamed by pain, I vowed eternal hatred and vengeance to all mankind. But the agony of my wound overcame me; my pulses paused, and I fainted.

"For some weeks I led a miserable life in the woods, endeavouring to cure the wound which I had received. The ball had entered my shoulder, and I knew not whether it had remained there or passed through; at any rate I had no means of extracting it. My sufferings were augmented also by the oppressive sense of the injustice and ingratitude of their infliction. My daily vows rose for revenge—a deep and deadly revenge, such as would alone compensate for the outrages and anguish I had endured.

"After some weeks my wound healed, and I continued my journey. The labours I endured were no longer to be alleviated by the bright sun or gentle breezes of spring; all joy was but a mockery, which insulted my desolate state, and made me feel more painfully that I was not made for the enjoyment of pleasure.

"But my toils now drew near a close; and, two months from this time, I reached the environs of Geneva.

"It was evening when I arrived, and I retired to a hiding-place among the fields that surround it, to meditate in what manner I should apply to you. I was oppressed by fatigue and hunger, and far too unhappy to enjoy the gentle breezes of evening, or the prospect of the sun setting behind the stupendous mountains of Jura.

"At this time a slight sleep relieved me from the pain of reflection, which was disturbed by the approach of a beautiful child, who came running into the recess I had chosen with all the sportiveness of infancy. Suddenly, as I gazed on him, an idea seized me, that this little creature was unprejudiced, and had lived too short a time to have imbibed a horror of deformity. If, therefore, I could seize him, and educate him as my companion and friend, I should not be so desolate in this peopled earth.

"Urged by this impulse, I seized on the boy as he passed, and drew him towards me. As soon as he beheld my form, he placed his hands before his eyes, and uttered a shrill scream: I drew his hand forcibly from his face, and said, 'Child, what is the meaning of this? I do not intend to hurt you; listen to me.'

"He struggled violently; 'Let me go,' he cried; 'monster! ugly wretch! you wish to eat me, and tear me to pieces—You are an ogre—Let me go, or I will tell my papa.'

" 'Boy, you will never see your father again; you must come with me.'

" 'Hideous monster! let me go; My papa is a Syndic—he is M. Frankenstein—he would punish you. You dare not keep me.'

" 'Frankenstein! you belong then to my enemy—to him towards whom I have sworn eternal revenge; you shall be my first victim.'

"The child still struggled, and loaded me with epithets which carried despair to my heart: I grasped his throat to silence him, and in a moment he lay dead at my feet.

"I gazed on my victim, and my heart swelled with exultation and hellish triumph: clapping my hands, I exclaimed, 'I, too, can create desolation; my enemy is not impregnable; this death will carry despair to him, and a thousand other miseries shall torment and destroy him.'

"As I fixed my eyes on the child, I saw something glittering on his breast. I took it; it was a portrait of a most lovely woman. In spite of my malignity, it softened and attracted me. For a few moments I gazed with delight on her dark eyes, fringed by deep lashes, and her lovely lips; but presently my rage returned: I remembered that I was for ever deprived of the delights that such beautiful creatures could bestow; and that she whose resemblance I contemplated would, in regarding me, have changed that air of divine benignity to one expressive of disgust and affright.

"Can you wonder that such thoughts transported me with rage? I only wonder that at that moment, instead of venting my sensations in exclamations and agony, I did not rush among mankind, and perish in the attempt to destroy them.

"While I was overcome by these feelings, I left the spot where I had committed the murder, and was seeking a more secluded hiding-place, when I perceived a woman passing near me. She was young, not indeed so beautiful as her whose portrait I held, but of an agreeable aspect, and blooming in the loveliness of youth and health. Here, I thought, is one of those whose smiles are bestowed on all but me; she shall not escape: thanks to the lessons of Felix, and the sanguinary laws of man, I have learned how to work mischief. I approached her unperceived, and placed the portrait securely in one of the folds of her dress.

"For some days I haunted the spot where these scenes had taken place; sometimes wishing to see you, sometimes resolved to quit the world and its miseries for ever. At length I wandered towards these mountains, and have ranged through their immense recesses, consumed by a burning passion which you alone can gratify. We may not part until you have promised to comply with my requisition. I am alone, and miserable; man will not associate with me; but one as deformed and horrible as myself would not deny herself to me. My companion must be of the same species, and have the same defects. This being you must create."

CHAPTER IX

The being finished speaking, and fixed his looks upon me in expectation of a reply. But I was bewildered, perplexed, and unable to arrange my ideas sufficiently to understand the full extent of his proposition. He continued—

"You must create a female for me, with whom I can live in the interchange of those sympathies necessary for my being. This you alone can do; and I demand it of you as a right which you must not refuse."

The latter part of his tale had kindled anew in me the anger that had died away while he narrated his peaceful life among the cottagers, and, as he said this, I could no longer suppress the rage that burned within me.

"I do refuse it," I replied; "and no torture shall ever extort a consent from me. You may render me the most miserable of men, but you shall never make me base in my own eyes. Shall I create another like yourself, whose joint wickedness might desolate the world. Begone! I have answered you; you may torture me, but I will never consent."

"You are in the wrong," replied the fiend; "and, instead of threatening, I am content to reason with you. I am malicious because I am miserable; am I not shunned and hated by all mankind? You, my creator, would tear me to pieces, and triumph; remember that, and tell me why I should pity man more than he pities me? You would not call it murder, if you could precipitate me into one of those ice-rifts, and destroy my frame, the work of your own hands. Shall I respect man, when he contemns me? Let him live with me in the interchange of kindness, and, instead of injury, I would bestow every benefit upon him with tears of gratitude at his acceptance. But that cannot be; the human senses are insurmountable barriers to our union. Yet mine shall not be the submission of abject slavery. I will revenge my injuries: if I cannot inspire love, I will cause fear; and chiefly towards you my arch-enemy, because my creator, do I swear inextinguishable hatred. Have a care: I will work at your destruction, nor finish until I desolate your heart, so that you curse the hour of your birth."

A fiendish rage animated him as he said this; his face was wrinkled into contortions too horrible for human eyes to behold; but presently he calmed himself, and proceeded—

"I intended to reason. This passion is detrimental to me; for you do not reflect that you are the cause of its excess. If any being felt emotions of benevolence towards me, I should return them an hundred and an hundred fold; for that one creature's sake, I would make peace with the whole kind! But I now indulge in dreams of bliss that cannot be realized. What I ask of you is reasonable and moderate; I demand a creature of another sex, but as hideous as myself: the gratification is small, but it is all that I can receive, and it shall content me. It is true, we shall be monsters, cut off from all the world; but on that account we shall be more attached to one another. Our lives will not be happy, but they will be harmless, and free from the misery I now feel. Oh! my creator, make me happy; let me feel gratitude towards you for one benefit! Let me see that I excite the sympathy of some existing thing; do not deny me my request!"

I was moved. I shuddered when I thought of the possible consequences of my consent; but I felt that there was some justice in his argument. His tale, and the feelings he now expressed, proved him to be a creature of fine sensations; and did I not, as his maker, owe him all the portion of happiness that it was in my power to bestow? He saw my change of feeling, and continued—

"If you consent, neither you nor any other human being shall ever see us again: I will go to the vast wilds of South America. My food is not that of man; I do not destroy the lamb and the kid, to glut my appetite; acorns and berries afford me sufficient nourishment. My companion will be of the same nature as myself, and will be content with the same fare. We shall make our bed of dried leaves; the sun will shine on us as on man, and will ripen our food. The picture I present to you is peaceful and human, and you must feel that you could deny it only in the wantonness of power and cruelty. Pitiless as you have been towards me, I now see compassion in your eyes; let me seize the favourable moment, and persuade you to promise what I so ardently desire."

"You propose," replied I, "to fly from the habitations of man, to dwell in those wilds where the beasts of the field will be your only companions. How can you, who long for the love and sympathy of man, persevere in this exile? You will return, and again seek their kindness, and you will meet with their detestation; your evil passions will be renewed, and you will then have a companion to aid you in the task of destruction. This may not be; cease to argue the point, for I cannot consent."

"How inconstant are your feelings! but a moment ago you were moved by my representations, and why do you again harden yourself to my complaints? I swear to you, by the earth which I inhabit, and by you that made me, that, with the companion you bestow, I will quit the neighbourhood of man, and dwell, as it may chance, in the most savage of places. My evil passions will have fled, for I shall meet with sympathy; my life will flow quietly away, and, in my dying moments, I shall not curse my maker."

His words had a strange effect upon me. I compassionated him, and sometimes felt a wish to console him; but when I looked upon him, when I saw the filthy mass that moved and talked, my heart sickened, and my feelings were altered to those of horror and hatred. I tried to stifle these sensations; I thought, that as I could not sympathize with him, I had no right to withhold from him the small portion of happiness which was yet in my power to bestow.

"You swear," I said, "to be harmless; but have you not already shewn a degree of malice that should reasonably make me distrust you? May not even this be a feint that will increase your triumph by affording a wider scope for your revenge?"

"How is this? I thought I had moved your compassion, and yet you still refuse to bestow on me the only benefit that can soften my heart, and render me harmless. If I have no ties and no affections, hatred and vice must be my portion; the love of another will destroy the cause of my crimes, and I shall become a thing, of whose existence every one will be ignorant. My vices are the children of a forced solitude that I abhor; and my virtues will necessarily arise when I live in communion with an equal. I shall feel the affections of a sensitive being, and become linked to the chain of existence and events, from which I am now excluded."

I paused some time to reflect on all he had related, and the various arguments which he had employed. I thought of the promise of virtues which he had displayed on the opening of his existence, and the subsequent blight of all kindly feeling by the loathing and scorn which his protectors had manifested towards him. His power and threats were not omitted in my calculations: a creature who could exist in the ice caves of the glaciers, and hide himself from pursuit among the ridges of inaccessible precipices, was a being possessing faculties it would be vain to cope with. After a long pause of reflection, I concluded, that the justice due both to him and my fellow-creatures demanded of me that I should comply with his request. Turning to him, therefore, I said—

"I consent to your demand, on your solemn oath to quit Europe for ever, and every other place in the neighbourhood of man, as soon as I shall deliver into your hands a female who will accompany you in your exile."

"I swear," he cried, "by the sun, and by the blue sky of heaven, that if you grant my prayer, while they exist you shall never behold me again. Depart to your home, and commence your labours: I shall watch their progress with unutterable anxiety; and fear not but that when you are ready I shall appear."

Saying this, he suddenly quitted me, fearful, perhaps, of any change in my sentiments. I saw him descend the mountain with greater speed than the flight of an eagle, and quickly lost him among the undulations of the sea of ice.

His tale had occupied the whole day; and the sun was upon the verge of the horizon when he departed. I knew that I ought to hasten my descent towards the valley, as I should soon be encompassed in darkness; but my heart was heavy, and my steps slow. The labour of winding among the little paths of the mountains, and fixing my feet firmly as I advanced, perplexed me, occupied as I was by the emotions which the occurrences of the day had produced. Night was far advanced, when I came to the half-way resting-place, and seated myself beside the fountain. The stars shone at intervals, as the clouds passed from over them; the dark pines rose before me, and every here and there a broken tree lay on the ground: it was a scene of wonderful solemnity, and stirred strange thoughts within me. I wept bitterly; and, clasping my hands in agony, I exclaimed, "Oh! stars, and clouds, and winds, ye are all about to mock me: if ye really pity me, crush sensation and memory; let me become as nought; but if not, depart, depart and leave me in darkness."

These were wild and miserable thoughts; but I cannot describe to you how the eternal twinkling of the stars weighed upon me, and how I listened to every blast of wind, as if it were a dull ugly siroc on its way to consume me.

Morning dawned before I arrived at the village of Chamounix; but my presence, so haggard and strange, hardly calmed the fears of my family, who had waited the whole night in anxious expectation of my return.

The following day we returned to Geneva. The intention of my father in coming had been to divert my mind, and to restore me to my lost tranquillity; but the medicine had been fatal. And, unable to account for the excess of misery I appeared to suffer, he hastened to return home, hoping the quiet and monotony of a domestic life would by degrees alleviate my sufferings from whatsoever cause they might spring.

For myself, I was passive in all their arrangements; and the gentle affection of my beloved Elizabeth was inadequate to draw me from the depth of my despair. The promise I had made to the dæmon weighed upon my mind, like Dante's iron cowl on the heads of the hellish hypocrites. All pleasures of earth and sky passed before me like a dream, and that thought only had to me the reality of life. Can you wonder, that sometimes a kind of insanity possessed me, or that I saw continually about me a multitude of filthy animals inflicting on me incessant torture, that often extorted screams and bitter groans?

By degrees, however, these feelings became calmed. I entered again into the every-day scene of life, if not with interest, at least with some degree of tranquillity.

END OF VOL. II.

Volume III

CHAPTER I

Day after day, week after week, passed away on my return to Geneva; and I could not collect the courage to recommence my work. I feared the vengeance of the disappointed fiend, yet I was unable to overcome my repugnance to the task which was enjoined me. I found that I could not compose a female without again devoting several months to profound study and laborious disquisition. I had heard of some discoveries having been made by an English philosopher, the knowledge of which was material to my success, and I sometimes thought of obtaining my father's consent to visit England for this purpose; but I clung to every pretence of delay, and could not resolve to interrupt my returning tranquillity. My health, which had hitherto declined, was now much restored; and my spirits, when unchecked by the memory of my unhappy promise, rose proportionably. My father saw this change with pleasure, and he turned his thoughts towards the best method of eradicating the remains of my melancholy, which every now and then would return by fits, and with a devouring blackness overcast the approaching sunshine. At these moments I took refuge in the most perfect solitude. I passed whole days on the lake alone in a little boat, watching the clouds, and listening to the rippling of the waves, silent and listless. But the fresh air and bright sun seldom failed to restore me to some degree of composure; and, on my return, I met the salutations of my friends with a readier smile and a more cheerful heart.

It was after my return from one of these rambles that my father, calling me aside, thus addressed me:—

"I am happy to remark, my dear son, that you have resumed your former pleasures, and seem to be returning to yourself. And yet you are still unhappy, and still avoid our society. For some time I was lost in conjecture as to the cause of this; but yesterday an idea struck me, and if it is well founded, I conjure you to avow it. Reserve on such a point would be not only useless, but draw down treble misery on us all."

I trembled violently at this exordium, and my father continued—

"I confess, my son, that I have always looked forward to your marriage with your cousin as the tie of our domestic comfort, and the stay of my declining years. You were attached to each other from your earliest infancy; you studied together, and appeared, in dispositions and tastes, entirely suited to one another. But so blind is the experience of man, that what I conceived to be the best assistants to my plan may have entirely destroyed it. You, perhaps, regard her as your sister, without any wish that she might become your wife. Nay, you may have met with another whom you may love; and, considering yourself as bound in honour to your cousin, this struggle may occasion the poignant misery which you appear to feel."

"My dear father, re-assure yourself. I love my cousin tenderly and sincerely. I never saw any woman who excited, as Elizabeth does, my warmest admiration and affection. My future hopes and prospects are entirely bound up in the expectation of our union."

"The expression of your sentiments on this subject, my dear Victor, gives me more pleasure than I have for some time experienced. If you feel thus, we shall assuredly be happy, however present events may cast a gloom over us. But it is this gloom, which appears to have taken so strong a hold of your mind, that I wish to dissipate. Tell me, therefore, whether you object to an immediate solemnization of the marriage. We have been unfortunate, and recent events have drawn us from that every-day tranquillity befitting my years and infirmities. You are younger; yet I do not suppose, possessed as you are of a competent fortune, that an early marriage would at all interfere with any future plans of honour and utility that you may have formed. Do not suppose, however, that I wish to dictate happiness to you, or that a delay on your part would cause me any serious uneasiness. Interpret my words with candour, and answer me, I conjure you, with confidence and sincerity."

I listened to my father in silence, and remained for some time incapable of offering any reply. I revolved rapidly in my mind a multitude of thoughts, and endeavoured to arrive at some conclusion. Alas! to me the idea of an immediate union with my cousin was one of horror and dismay. I was bound by a solemn promise, which I had not yet fulfilled, and dared not break; or, if I did, what manifold miseries might not impend over me and my devoted family! Could I enter into a festival with this deadly weight yet hanging round my neck, and bowing me to the ground. I must perform my engagement, and let the monster depart with his mate, before I allowed myself to enjoy the delight of an union from which I expected peace.

I remembered also the necessity imposed upon me of either journeying to England, or entering into a long correspondence with those philosophers of that country, whose knowledge and discoveries were of indispensable use to me in my present undertaking.

The latter method of obtaining the desired intelligence was dilatory and unsatisfactory: besides, any variation was agreeable to me, and I was delighted with the idea of spending a year or two in change of scene and variety of occupation, in absence from my family; during which period some event might happen which would restore me to them in peace and happiness: my promise might be fulfilled, and the monster have departed; or some accident might occur to destroy him, and put an end to my slavery for ever.

These feelings dictated my answer to my father. I expressed a wish to visit England; but, concealing the true reasons of this request, I clothed my desires under the guise of wishing to travel and see the world before I sat down for life within the walls of my native town.

I urged my entreaty with earnestness, and my father was easily induced to comply; for a more indulgent and less dictatorial parent did not exist upon earth. Our plan was soon arranged. I should travel to Strasburgh, where Clerval would join me. Some short time would be spent in the towns of Holland, and our principal stay would be in England. We should return by France; and it was agreed that the tour should occupy the space of two years.

My father pleased himself with the reflection, that my union with Elizabeth should take place immediately on my return to Geneva. "These two years," said he, "will pass swiftly, and it will be the last delay that will oppose itself to your happiness. And, indeed, I earnestly desire that period to arrive, when we shall all be united, and neither hopes or fears arise to disturb our domestic calm."

"I am content," I replied, "with your arrangement. By that time we shall both have become wiser, and I hope happier, than we at present are." I sighed; but my father kindly forbore to question me further concerning the cause of my dejection. He hoped that new scenes, and the amusement of travelling, would restore my tranquillity.

I now made arrangements for my journey; but one feeling haunted me, which filled me with fear and agitation. During my absence I should leave my friends unconscious of the existence of their enemy, and unprotected from his attacks, exasperated as he might be by my departure. But he had promised to follow me wherever I might go; and would he not accompany me to England? This imagination was dreadful in itself, but soothing, inasmuch as it supposed the safety of my friends. I was agonized with the idea of the possibility that the reverse of this might happen. But through the whole period during which I was the slave of my creature, I allowed myself to be governed by the impulses of the moment; and my present sensations strongly intimated that the fiend would follow me, and exempt my family from the danger of his machinations.

It was in the latter end of August that I departed, to pass two years of exile. Elizabeth approved of the reasons of my departure, and only regretted that she had not the same opportunities of enlarging her experience, and cultivating her understanding. She wept, however, as she bade me farewell, and entreated me to return happy and tranquil. "We all," said she, "depend upon you; and if you are miserable, what must be our feelings?"

I threw myself into the carriage that was to convey me away, hardly knowing whither I was going, and careless of what was passing around. I remembered only, and it was with a bitter anguish that I reflected on it, to order that my chemical instruments should be packed to go with me: for I resolved to fulfil my promise while abroad, and return, if possible, a free man. Filled with dreary imaginations, I passed through many beautiful and majestic scenes; but my eyes were fixed and unobserving. I could only think of the bourne of my travels, and the work which was to occupy me whilst they endured.

After some days spent in listless indolence, during which I traversed many leagues, I arrived at Strasburgh, where I waited two days for Clerval. He came. Alas, how great was the contrast between us! He was alive to every new scene; joyful when he saw the beauties of the setting sun, and more happy when he beheld it rise, and recommence a new day. He pointed out to me the shifting colours of the landscape, and the appearances of the sky. "This is what it is to live;" he cried, "now I enjoy existence! But you, my dear Frankenstein, wherefore are you desponding and sorrowful?" In truth, I was occupied by gloomy thoughts, and neither saw the descent of the evening star, nor the golden sun-rise reflected in the Rhine.—And you, my friend, would be far more amused with the journal of Clerval, who observed the scenery with an eye of feeling and delight, than to listen to my reflections. I, a miserable wretch, haunted by a curse that shut up every avenue to enjoyment.

We had agreed to descend the Rhine in a boat from Strasburgh to Rotterdam, whence we might take shipping for London. During this voyage, we passed by many willowy islands, and saw several beautiful towns. We staid a day at Manheim, and, on the fifth from our departure from Strasburgh, arrived at Mayence. The course of the Rhine below Mayence becomes much more picturesque. The river descends rapidly, and winds between hills, not high, but steep, and of beautiful forms. We saw many ruined castles standing on the edges of precipices, surrounded by black woods, high and inaccesible. This part of the Rhine, indeed, presents a singularly variegated landscape. In one spot you view rugged hills, ruined castles overlooking tremendous precipices, with the dark Rhine rushing beneath; and, on the sudden turn of a promontory, flourishing vineyards, with green sloping banks, and a meandering river, and populous towns, occupy the scene.

We travelled at the time of the vintage, and heard the song of the labourers, as we glided down the stream. Even I, depressed in mind, and my spirits continually agitated by gloomy feelings, even I was pleased. I lay at the bottom of the boat, and, as I gazed on the cloudless blue sky, I seemed to drink in a tranquillity to which I had long been a stranger. And if these were my sensations, who can describe those of Henry? He felt as if he had been transported to Fairy-land, and enjoyed a happiness seldom tasted by man. "I have seen," he said, "the most beautiful scenes of my own country; I have visited the lakes of Lucerne and Uri, where the snowy mountains descend almost perpendicularly to the water, casting black and impenetrable shades, which would cause a gloomy and mournful appearance, were it not for the most verdant islands that relieve the eye by their gay appearance; I have seen this lake agitated by a tempest, when the wind tore up whirlwinds of water, and gave you an idea of what the water-spout must be on the great ocean, and the waves dash with fury the base of the mountain, where the priest and his mistress were overwhelmed by an avalanche, and where their dying voices are still said to be heard amid the pauses of the nightly wind; I have seen the mountains of La Valais, and the Pays de Vaud: but this country, Victor, pleases me more than all those wonders. The mountains of Switzerland are more majestic and strange; but there is a charm in the banks of this divine river, that I never before saw equalled. Look at that castle which overhangs yon precipice; and that also on the island, almost concealed amongst the foliage of those lovely trees; and now that group of labourers coming from among their vines; and that village half-hid in the recess of the mountain. Oh, surely, the spirit that inhabits and guards this place has a soul more in harmony with man, than those who pile the glacier, or retire to the inaccessible peaks of the mountains of our own country."

Clerval! beloved friend! even now it delights me to record your words, and to dwell on the praise of which you are so eminently deserving. He was a being formed in the "very poetry of nature." His wild and enthusiastic imagination was chastened by the sensibility of his heart. His soul overflowed with ardent affections, and his friendship was of that devoted and wondrous nature that the worldly-minded teach us to look for only in the imagination. But even human sympathies were not sufficient to satisfy his eager mind. The scenery of external nature, which others regard only with admiration, he loved with ardour:

——— The sounding cataract
Haunted *him* like a passion: the tall rock,
The mountain, and the deep and gloomy wood,
Their colours and their forms, were then to him
An appetite; a feeling, and a love,
That had no need of a remoter charm,
By thought supplied, or any interest
Unborrowed from the eye.

And where does he now exist? Is this gentle and lovely being lost for ever? Has this mind so replete with ideas, imaginations fanciful and magnificent, which formed a world, whose existence depended on the life of its creator; has this mind perished? Does it now only exist in my memory? No, it is not thus; your form so divinely wrought, and beaming with beauty, has decayed, but your spirit still visits and consoles your unhappy friend.

Pardon this gush of sorrow; these ineffectual words are but a slight tribute to the unexampled worth of Henry, but they soothe my heart, overflowing with the anguish which his remembrance creates. I will proceed with my tale.

Beyond Cologne we descended to the plains of Holland; and we resolved to post the remainder of our way; for the wind was contrary, and the stream of the river was too gentle to aid us.

Our journey here lost the interest arising from beautiful scenery; but we arrived in a few days at Rotterdam, whence we proceeded by sea to England. It was on a clear morning, in the latter days of December, that I first saw the white cliffs of Britain. The banks of the Thames presented a new scene; they were flat, but fertile, and almost every town was marked by the remembrance of some story. We saw Tilbury Fort, and remembered the Spanish armada; Gravesend, Woolwich, and Greenwich, places which I had heard of even in my country.

At length we saw the numerous steeples of London, St. Paul's towering above all, and the Tower famed in English history.

CHAPTER II

London was our present point of rest; we determined to remain several months in this wonderful and celebrated city. Clerval desired the intercourse of the men of genius and talent who flourished at this time;

but this was with me a secondary object; I was principally occupied with the means of obtaining the information necessary for the completion of my promise, and quickly availed myself of the letters of introduction that I had brought with me, addressed to the most distinguished natural philosophers.

If this journey had taken place during my days of study and happiness, it would have afforded me inexpressible pleasure. But a blight had come over my existence, and I only visited these people for the sake of the information they might give me on the subject in which my interest was so terribly profound. Company was irksome to me; when alone, I could fill my mind with the sights of heaven and earth; the voice of Henry soothed me, and I could thus cheat myself into a transitory peace. But busy uninteresting joyous faces brought back despair to my heart. I saw an insurmountable barrier placed between me and my fellow-men; this barrier was sealed with the blood of William and Justine; and to reflect on the events connected with those names filled my soul with anguish.

But in Clerval I saw the image of my former self; he was inquisitive, and anxious to gain experience and instruction. The difference of manners which he observed was to him an inexhaustible source of instruction and amusement. He was for ever busy; and the only check to his enjoyments was my sorrowful and dejected mien. I tried to conceal this as much as possible, that I might not debar him from the pleasures natural to one who was entering on a new scene of life, undisturbed by any care or bitter recollection. I often refused to accompany him, alleging another engagement, that I might remain alone. I now also began to collect the materials necessary for my new creation, and this was to me like the torture of single drops of water continually falling on the head. Every thought that was devoted to it was an extreme anguish, and every word that I spoke in allusion to it caused my lips to quiver, and my heart to palpitate.

After passing some months in London, we received a letter from a person in Scotland, who had formerly been our visitor at Geneva. He mentioned the beauties of his native country, and asked us if those were not sufficient allurements to induce us to prolong our journey as far north as Perth, where he resided. Clerval eagerly desired to accept this invitation; and I, although I abhorred society, wished to view again mountains and streams, and all the wondrous works with which Nature adorns her chosen dwelling-places.

We had arrived in England at the beginning of October, and it was now February. We accordingly determined to commence our journey towards the north at the expiration of another month. In this expedition we did not intend to follow the great road to Edinburgh, but to visit Windsor, Oxford, Matlock, and the Cumberland lakes, resolving to arrive at the completion of this tour about the end of July. I packed my chemical instruments, and the materials I had collected, resolving to finish my labours in some obscure nook in the northern highlands of Scotland.

We quitted London on the 27th of March, and remained a few days at Windsor, rambling in its beautiful forest. This was a new scene to us mountaineers; the majestic oaks, the quantity of game, and the herds of stately deer, were all novelties to us.

From thence we proceeded to Oxford. As we entered this city, our minds were filled with the remembrance of the events that had been transacted there more than a century and a half before. It was here that Charles I. had collected his forces. This city had remained faithful to him, after the whole nation had forsaken his cause to join the standard of parliament and liberty. The memory of that unfortunate king, and his companions, the amiable Falkland, the insolent Goring, his queen, and son, gave a peculiar interest to every part of the city, which they might be supposed to have inhabited. The spirit of elder days found a dwelling here, and we delighted to trace its footsteps. If these feelings had not found an imaginary gratification, the appearance of the city had yet in itself sufficient beauty to obtain our admiration. The colleges are ancient and picturesque; the streets are almost magnificent; and the lovely Isis, which flows beside it through meadows of exquisite verdure, is spread forth into a placid expanse of waters, which reflects its majestic assemblage of towers, and spires, and domes, embosomed among aged trees.

I enjoyed this scene; and yet my enjoyment was embittered both by the memory of the past, and the anticipation of the future. I was formed for peaceful happiness. During my youthful days discontent never visited my mind; and if I was ever overcome by *ennui*, the sight of what is beautiful in nature, or the study of what is excellent and sublime in the productions of man, could always interest my heart, and communicate elasticity to my spirits. But I am a blasted tree; the bolt has entered my soul; and I felt then that I should survive to exhibit, what I shall soon cease to be—a miserable spectacle of wrecked humanity, pitiable to others, and abhorrent to myself.

We passed a considerable period at Oxford, rambling among its environs, and endeavouring to identify every spot which might relate to the most animating epoch of English history. Our little voyages of discovery were often prolonged by the successive objects that presented themselves. We visited the tomb of the illustrious Hampden, and the field on which that patriot fell. For a moment my soul was elevated from its debasing and miserable fears to contemplate the divine ideas of liberty and self-sacrifice, of which these sights were the monuments and the remembrancers. For an instant I dared to shake off my chains, and look around me with a free and lofty spirit; but the iron had eaten into my flesh, and I sank again, trembling and hopeless, into my miserable self.

We left Oxford with regret, and proceeded to Matlock, which was our next place of rest. The country in the neighbourhood of this village resembled, to a greater degree, the scenery of Switzerland; but every thing is on a lower scale, and the green hills want the crown of distant white Alps, which always attend on the piny mountains of my native country. We visited the wondrous cave, and the little cabinets of natural history, where the curiosities are disposed in the same manner as in the collections at Servox and Chamounix. The latter name made me tremble, when pronounced by Henry; and I hastened to quit Matlock, with which that terrible scene was thus associated.

From Derby still journeying northward, we passed two months in Cumberland and Westmoreland. I could now almost fancy myself among the Swiss mountains. The little patches of snow which yet lingered on the northern sides of the mountains, the lakes, and the dashing of the rocky streams, were all familiar and dear sights to me. Here also we made some acquaintances, who almost contrived to cheat me into happiness. The delight of Clerval was proportionably greater than mine; his mind expanded in the company of men of talent, and he found in his own nature greater capacities and resources than he could have imagined himself to have possessed while he associated with his inferiors. "I could pass my life here," said he to me; "and among these mountains I should scarcely regret Switzerland and the Rhine."

But he found that a traveller's life is one that

includes much pain amidst its enjoyments. His feelings are for ever on the stretch; and when he begins to sink into repose, he finds himself obliged to quit that on which he rests in pleasure for something new, which again engages his attention, and which also he forsakes for other novelties.

We had scarcely visited the various lakes of Cumberland and Westmoreland, and conceived an affection for some of the inhabitants, when the period of our appointment with our Scotch friend approached, and we left them to travel on. For my own part I was not sorry. I had now neglected my promise for some time, and I feared the effects of the dæmon's disappointment. He might remain in Switzerland, and wreak his vengeance on my relatives. This idea pursued me, and tormented me at every moment from which I might otherwise have snatched repose and peace. I waited for my letters with feverish impatience: if they were delayed, I was miserable, and overcome by a thousand fears; and when they arrived, and I saw the superscription of Elizabeth or my father, I hardly dared to read and ascertain my fate. Sometimes I thought that the fiend followed me, and might expedite my remissness by murdering my companion. When these thoughts possessed me, I would not quit Henry for a moment, but followed him as his shadow, to protect him from the fancied rage of his destroyer. I felt as if I had committed some great crime, the consciousness of which haunted me. I was guiltless, but I had indeed drawn down a horrible curse upon my head, as mortal as that of crime.

I visited Edinburgh with languid eyes and mind; and yet that city might have interested the most unfortunate being. Clerval did not like it so well as Oxford; for the antiquity of the latter city was more pleasing to him. But the beauty and regularity of the new town of Edinburgh, its romantic castle, and its environs, the most delightful in the world, Arthur's Seat, St. Bernard's Well, and the Pentland Hills, compensated him for the change, and filled him with cheerfulness and admiration. But I was impatient to arrive at the termination of my journey.

We left Edinburgh in a week, passing through Coupar, St. Andrews, and along the banks of the Tay, to Perth, where our friend expected us. But I was in no mood to laugh and talk with strangers, or enter into their feelings or plans with the good humour expected from a guest; and accordingly I told Clerval that I wished to make the tour of Scotland alone. "Do you," said I, "enjoy yourself, and let this be our rendezvous. I may be absent a month or two; but do not interfere with my motions, I entreat you: leave me to peace and solitude for a short time; and when I return, I hope it will be with a lighter heart, more congenial to your own temper."

Henry wished to dissuade me; but, seeing me bent on this plan, ceased to remonstrate. He entreated me to write often. "I had rather be with you," he said, "in your solitary rambles, than with these Scotch people, whom I do not know: hasten then, my dear friend, to return, that I may again feel myself somewhat at home, which I cannot do in your absence."

Having parted from my friend, I determined to visit some remote spot of Scotland, and finish my work in solitude. I did not doubt but that the monster followed me, and would discover himself to me when I should have finished, that he might receive his companion.

With this resolution I traversed the northern highlands, and fixed on one of the remotest of the Orkneys as the scene [of my] labours. It was a place fitted for such a work, being hardly more than a rock, whose high sides were continually beaten upon by the waves. The soil was barren, scarcely affording pasture for a few miserable cows, and oatmeal for its inhabitants, which consisted of five persons, whose gaunt and scraggy limbs gave tokens of their miserable fare. Vegetables and bread, when they indulged in such luxuries, and even fresh water, was to be procured from the main land, which was about five miles distant.

On the whole island there were but three miserable huts, and one of these was vacant when I arrived. This I hired. It contained but two rooms, and these exhibited all the squalidness of the most miserable penury. The thatch had fallen in, the walls were unplastered, and the door was off its hinges. I ordered it to be repaired, bought some furniture, and took possession; an incident which would, doubtless, have occasioned some surprise, had not all the senses of the cottagers been benumbed by want and squalid poverty. As it was, I lived ungazed at and unmolested, hardly thanked for the pittance of food and clothes which I gave; so much does suffering blunt even the coarsest sensations of men.

In this retreat I devoted the morning to labour; but in the evening, when the weather permitted, I walked on the stony beach of the sea, to listen to the waves as they roared, and dashed at my feet. It was a monotonous, yet ever-changing scene. I thought of Switzerland; it was far different from this desolate and appalling landscape. Its hills are covered with vines, and its cottages are scattered thickly in the plains. Its fair lakes reflect a blue and gentle sky; and, when troubled by the winds, their tumult is but as the play of a lively infant, when compared to the roarings of the giant ocean.

In this manner I distributed my occupations when I first arrived; but, as I proceeded in my labour, it became every day more horrible and irksome to me. Sometimes I could not prevail on myself to enter my laboratory for several days; and at other times I toiled day and night in order to complete my work. It was indeed a filthy process in which I was engaged. During my first experiment, a kind of enthusiastic frenzy had blinded me to the horror of my employment; my mind was intently fixed on the sequel of my labour, and my eyes were shut to the horror of my proceedings. But now I went to it in cold blood, and my heart often sickened at the work of my hands.

Thus situated, employed in the most detestable occupation, immersed in a solitude where nothing could for an instant call my attention from the actual scene in which I was engaged, my spirits became unequal; I grew restless and nervous. Every moment I feared to meet my persecutor. Sometimes I sat with my eyes fixed on the ground, fearing to raise them lest they should encounter the object which I so much dreaded to behold. I feared to wander from the sight of my fellow-creatures, lest when alone he should come to claim his companion.

In the mean time I worked on, and my labour was already considerably advanced. I looked towards its completion with a tremulous and eager hope, which I dared not trust myself to question, but which was intermixed with obscure forebodings of evil, that made my heart sicken in my bosom.

CHAPTER III

I sat one evening in my laboratory; the sun had set, and the moon was just rising from the sea; I had not sufficient light for my employment, and I remained idle, in a pause of consideration of whether I should leave my labour for the night, or hasten its conclusion by an unremitting attention to it. As I sat, a train of reflection occurred to me, which led me to consider the effects of what I was now doing. Three years before I was engaged in the same manner, and had created a fiend whose unparalleled barbarity had desolated my heart, and filled it for ever with the bitterest remorse. I was now about to form another being, of whose dispositions I was alike ignorant; she might become ten thousand times more malignant than her mate, and delight, for its own sake, in murder and wretchedness. He had sworn to quit the neighbourhood of man, and hide himself in deserts; but she had not; and she, who in all probability was to become a thinking and reasoning animal, might refuse to comply with a compact made before her creation. They might even hate each other; the creature who already lived loathed his own deformity, and might he not conceive a greater abhorrence for it when it came before his eyes in the female form? She also might turn with disgust from him to the superior beauty of man; she might quit him, and he be again alone, exasperated by the fresh provocation of being deserted by one of his own species.

Even if they were to leave Europe, and inhabit the deserts of the new world, yet one of the first results of those sympathies for which the dæmon thirsted would be children, and a race of devils would be propagated upon the earth, who might make the very existence of the species of man a condition precarious and full of terror. Had I a right, for my own benefit, to inflict this curse upon everlasting generations? I had before been moved by the sophisms of the being I had created; I had been struck senseless by his fiendish threats: but now, for the first time, the wickedness of my promise burst upon me; I shuddered to think that future ages might curse me as their pest, whose selfishness had not hesitated to buy its own peace at the price perhaps of the existence of the whole human race.

I trembled, and my heart failed within me; when, on looking up, I saw, by the light of the moon, the dæmon at the casement. A ghastly grin wrinkled his lips as he gazed on me, where I sat fulfilling the task which he had allotted to me. Yes, he had followed me in my travels; he had loitered in forests, hid himself in caves, or taken refuge in wide and desert heaths; and he now came to mark my progress, and claim the fulfilment of my promise.

As I looked on him, his countenance expressed the utmost extent of malice and treachery. I thought with a sensation of madness on my promise of creating another like to him, and, trembling with passion, tore to pieces the thing on which I was engaged. The wretch saw me destroy the creature on whose future existence he depended for happiness, and, with a howl of devilish despair and revenge, withdrew.

I left the room, and, locking the door, made a solemn vow in my own heart never to resume my labours; and then, with trembling steps, I sought my own apartment. I was alone; none were near me to dissipate the gloom, and relieve me from the sickening oppression of the most terrible reveries.

Several hours past, and I remained near my window gazing on the sea; it was almost motionless, for the winds were hushed, and all nature reposed under the eye of the quiet moon. A few fishing vessels alone specked the water, and now and then the gentle breeze wafted the sound of voices, as the fishermen called to one another. I felt the silence, although I was hardly conscious of its extreme profundity until my ear was suddenly arrested by the paddling of oars near the shore, and a person landed close to my house.

In a few minutes after, I heard the creaking of my

door, as if some one endeavoured to open it softly. I trembled from head to foot; I felt a presentiment of who it was, and wished to rouse one of the peasants who dwelt in a cottage not far from mine; but I was overcome by the sensation of helplessness, so often felt in frightful dreams, when you in vain endeavour to fly from an impending danger, and was rooted to the spot.

Presently I heard the sound of footsteps along the passage; the door opened, and the wretch whom I dreaded appeared. Shutting the door, he approached me, and said, in a smothered voice—

"You have destroyed the work which you began; what is it that you intend? Do you dare to break your promise? I have endured toil and misery: I left Switzerland with you; I crept along the shores of the Rhine, among its willow islands, and over the summits of its hills. I have dwelt many months in the heaths of England, and among the deserts of Scotland. I have endured incalculable fatigue, and cold, and hunger; do you dare destroy my hopes?"

"Begone! I do break my promise; never will I create another like yourself, equal in deformity and wickedness."

"Slave, I before reasoned with you, but you have proved yourself unworthy of my condescension. Remember that I have power; you believe yourself miserable, but I can make you so wretched that the light of day will be hateful to you. You are my creator, but I am your master;—obey!"

"The hour of my weakness is past, and the period of your power is arrived. Your threats cannot move me to do an act of wickedness; but they confirm me in a resolution of not creating you a companion in vice. Shall I, in cool blood, set loose upon the earth a dæmon, whose delight is in death and wretchedness.

Begone! I am firm, and your words will only exasperate my rage."

The monster saw my determination in my face, and gnashed his teeth in the impotence of anger. "Shall each man," cried he, "find a wife for his bosom, and each beast have his mate, and I be alone? I had feelings of affection, and they were requited by detestation and scorn. Man, you may hate; but beware! Your hours will pass in dread and misery, and soon the bolt will fall which must ravish from you your happiness for ever. Are you to be happy, while I grovel in the intensity of my wretchedness? You can blast my other passions; but revenge remains—revenge, henceforth dearer than light or food! I may die; but first you, my tyrant and tormentor, shall curse the sun that gazes on your misery. Beware; for I am fearless, and therefore powerful. I will watch with the wiliness of a snake, that I may sting with its venom. Man, you shall repent of the injuries you inflict."

"Devil, cease; and do not poison the air with these sounds of malice. I have declared my resolution to you, and I am no coward to bend beneath words. Leave me; I am inexorable."

"It is well. I go; but remember, I shall be with you on your wedding-night."

I started forward, and exclaimed, "Villain! before you sign my death-warrant, be sure that you are yourself safe."

I would have seized him; but he eluded me, and quitted the house with precipitation: in a few moments I saw him in his boat, which shot across the waters with an arrowy swiftness, and was soon lost amidst the waves.

All was again silent; but his words rung in my ears. I burned with rage to pursue the murderer of my peace, and precipitate him into the ocean. I walked up and down my room hastily and perturbed, while my imagination conjured up a thousand images to torment and sting me. Why had I not followed him, and closed with him in mortal strife? But I had suffered him to depart, and he had directed his course towards the main land. I shuddered to think who might be the next victim sacrificed to his insatiate revenge. And then I thought again of his words—*"I will be with you on your wedding-night."* That then was the period fixed for the fulfilment of my destiny. In that hour I should die, and at once satisfy and extinguish his malice. The prospect did not move me to fear; yet when I thought of my beloved Elizabeth,—of her tears and endless sorrow, when she should find her lover so barbarously snatched from her,—tears, the first I had shed for many months, streamed from my eyes, and I resolved not to fall before my enemy without a bitter struggle.

The night passed away, and the sun rose from the ocean; my feelings became calmer, if it may be called calmness, when the violence of rage sinks into the depths of despair. I left the house, the horrid scene of the last night's contention, and walked on the beach of the sea, which I almost regarded as an insuperable barrier between me and my fellow-creatures; nay, a wish that such should prove the fact stole across me. I desired that I might pass my life on that barren rock, wearily it is true, but uninterrupted by any sudden shock of misery. If I returned, it was to be sacrificed, or to see those whom I most loved die under the grasp of a dæmon whom I had myself created.

I walked about the isle like a restless spectre, separated from all it loved, and miserable in the separation. When it became noon, and the sun rose higher, I lay down on the grass, and was overpowered by a deep sleep. I had been awake the whole of the preceding night, my nerves were agitated, and my eyes inflamed by watching and misery. The sleep into which I now sunk refreshed me; and when I awoke, I again felt as if I belonged to a race of human beings like myself, and I began to reflect upon what had passed with greater composure; yet still the words of the fiend rung in my ears like a death-knell, they appeared like a dream, yet distinct and oppressive as a reality.

The sun had far descended, and I still sat on the shore, satisfying my appetite, which had become ravenous, with an oaten cake, when I saw a fishing-boat land close to me, and one of the men brought me a packet; it contained letters from Geneva, and one from Clerval, entreating me to join him. He said that nearly a year had elapsed since we had quitted Switzerland, and France was yet unvisited. He entreated me, therefore, to leave my solitary isle, and meet him at Perth, in a week from that time, when we might arrange the plan of our future proceedings. This letter in a degree recalled me to life, and I determined to quit my island at the expiration of two days.

Yet, before I departed, there was a task to perform, on which I shuddered to reflect: I must pack my chemical instruments; and for that purpose I must enter the room which had been the scene of my odious work, and I must handle those utensils, the sight of which was sickening to me. The next morning, at day-break, I summoned sufficient courage, and unlocked the door of my laboratory. The remains of the half-finished creature, whom I had destroyed, lay scattered on the floor, and I almost felt as if I had mangled the living flesh of a human being. I paused to collect myself, and then entered the chamber. With trembling hand I conveyed the instruments out of the room; but I reflected that I ought not to leave the relics of my work to excite the horror and suspicion of the peasants, and I accordingly put them into a basket, with a great quantity of stones, and laying them up, determined to throw them into the sea that very night; and in the mean time I sat upon the beach, employed in cleaning and arranging my chemical apparatus.

Nothing could be more complete than the alteration that had taken place in my feelings since the night of the appearance of the dæmon. I had before regarded my promise with a gloomy despair, as a thing that, with whatever consequences, must be fulfilled; but I now felt as if a film had been taken from before my eyes, and that I, for the first time, saw clearly. The idea of renewing my labours did not for one instant occur to me; the threat I had heard weighed on my thoughts, but I did not reflect that a voluntary act of mine could avert it. I had resolved in my own mind, that to create another like the fiend I had first made would be an act of the basest and most atrocious selfishness; and I banished from my mind every thought that could lead to a different conclusion.

Between two and three in the morning the moon rose; and I then, putting my basket aboard a little skiff, sailed out about four miles from the shore. The scene was perfectly solitary: a few boats were returning towards land, but I sailed away from them. I felt as if I was about the commission of a dreadful crime, and avoided with shuddering anxiety any encounter with my fellow-creatures. At one time the moon, which had before been clear, was suddenly overspread by a thick cloud, and I took advantage of the moment of darkness, and cast my basket into the sea; I listened to the gurgling sound as it sunk, and then sailed away from the spot. The sky became clouded; but the air was pure, although chilled by the north-east breeze that was then rising. But it refreshed me, and filled me with such agreeable sensations, that I resolved to prolong my stay on the water, and fixing the rudder in a direct position, stretched myself at the bottom of the boat. Clouds hid the moon, every thing was obscure, and I heard only the sound of the boat, as its keel cut through the waves; the murmur lulled me, and in a short time I slept soundly.

I do not know how long I remained in this situation, but when I awoke I found that the sun had already mounted considerably. The wind was high, and the waves continually threatened the safety of my little skiff. I found that the wind was north-east, and must have driven me far from the coast from which I had embarked. I endeavoured to change my course, but quickly found that if I again made the attempt the boat would be instantly filled with water. Thus situated, my only resource was to drive before the wind. I confess that I felt a few sensations of terror. I had no compass with me, and was so little acquainted with the geography of this part of the world that the sun was of little benefit to me. I might be driven into the wide Atlantic, and feel all the tortures of starvation, or be swallowed up in the immeasurable waters that roared and buffeted around me. I had already been out many hours, and felt the torment of a burning thirst, a prelude to my other sufferings. I looked on the heavens, which were covered by clouds that flew before the wind only to be replaced by others: I looked upon the sea, it was to be my grave. "Fiend," I exclaimed, "your task is already fulfilled!" I thought of Elizabeth, of my father, and of Clerval; and sunk into a reverie, so despairing and frightful, that even now, when the scene is on the point of closing before me for ever, I shudder to reflect on it.

Some hours passed thus; but by degrees, as the sun declined towards the horizon, the wind died away into a gentle breeze, and the sea became free from breakers. But these gave place to a heavy swell; I felt sick, and hardly able to hold the rudder, when suddenly I saw a line of high land towards the south.

Almost spent, as I was, by fatigue, and the dreadful suspense I endured for several hours, this sudden certainty of life rushed like a flood of warm joy to my heart, and tears gushed from my eyes.

How mutable are our feelings, and how strange is that clinging love we have of life even in the excess of misery! I constructed another sail with a part of my dress, and eagerly steered my course towards the land. It had a wild and rocky appearance; but as I approached nearer, I easily perceived the traces of cultivation. I saw vessels near the shore, and found myself suddenly transported back to the neighbourhood of civilized man. I eagerly traced the windings of the land, and hailed a steeple which I at length saw issuing from behind a small promontory. As I was in a state of extreme debility, I resolved to sail directly towards the town as a place where I could most easily procure nourishment. Fortunately I had money with me. As I turned the promontory, I perceived a small neat town and a good harbour, which I entered, my heart bounding with joy at my unexpected escape.

As I was occupied in fixing the boat and arranging the sails, several people crowded towards the spot. They seemed very much surprised at my appearance; but, instead of offering me any assistance, whispered together with gestures that at any other time might have produced in me a slight sensation of alarm. As it was, I merely remarked that they spoke English; and I therefore addressed them in that language: "My good friends," said I, "will you be so kind as to tell me the name of this town, and inform me where I am?"

"You will know that soon enough," replied a man

with a gruff voice. "May be you are come to a place that will not prove much to your taste; but you will not be consulted as to your quarters, I promise you."

I was exceedingly surprised on receiving so rude an answer from a stranger; and I was also disconcerted on perceiving the frowning and angry countenances of his companions. "Why do you answer me so roughly?" I replied: "surely it is not the custom of Englishmen to receive strangers so inhospitably."

"I do not know," said the man, "what the custom of the English may be; but it is the custom of the Irish to hate villains."

While this strange dialogue continued, I perceived the crowd rapidly increase. Their faces expressed a mixture of curiosity and anger, which annoyed, and in some degree alarmed me. I inquired the way to the inn; but no one replied. I then moved forward, and a murmuring sound arose from the crowd as they followed and surrounded me; when an ill-looking man approaching, tapped me on the shoulder, and said, "Come, Sir, you must follow me to Mr. Kirwin's, to give an account of yourself."

"Who is Mr. Kirwin? Why am I to give an account of myself? Is not this a free country?"

"Aye, Sir, free enough for honest folks. Mr. Kirwin is a magistrate; and you are to give an account of the death of a gentleman who was found murdered here last night."

This answer startled me; but I presently recovered myself. I was innocent; that could easily be proved: accordingly I followed my conductor in silence, and was led to one of the best houses in the town. I was ready to sink from fatigue and hunger; but, being surrounded by a crowd, I thought it politic to rouse all my strength, that no physical debility might be construed into apprehension or conscious guilt. Little did

I then expect the calamity that was in a few moments to overwhelm me, and extinguish in horror and despair all fear of ignominy or death.

I must pause here; for it requires all my fortitude to recall the memory of the frightful events which I am about to relate, in proper detail, to my recollection.

CHAPTER IV

I was soon introduced into the presence of the magistrate, an old benevolent man, with calm and mild manners. He looked upon me, however, with some degree of severity; and then, turning towards my conductors, he asked who appeared as witnesses on this occasion.

About half a dozen men came forward; and one being selected by the magistrate, he deposed, that he had been out fishing the night before with his son and brother-in-law, Daniel Nugent, when, about ten o'clock, they observed a strong northerly blast rising, and they accordingly put in for port. It was a very dark night, as the moon had not yet risen; they did not land at the harbour, but, as they had been accustomed, at a creek about two miles below. He walked on first, carrying a part of the fishing tackle, and his companions followed him at some distance. As he was proceeding along the sands, he struck his foot against something, and fell all his length on the ground. His companions came up to assist him; and, by the light of their lantern, they found that he had fallen on the body of a man, who was to all appearance dead. Their first supposition was, that it was the corpse of some person who had been drowned, and was thrown on shore by the waves; but, upon examination, they found that the clothes were not wet, and even that the body was not then cold. They instantly carried it to the cottage of an old woman near the spot, and endeavoured, but in vain, to restore it to life. He appeared to be a handsome young man, about five and twenty years of age. He had apparently been strangled; for there was no sign of any violence, except the black mark of fingers on his neck.

The first part of this deposition did not in the least interest me; but when the mark of the fingers was mentioned, I remembered the murder of my brother, and felt myself extremely agitated; my limbs trembled, and a mist came over my eyes, which obliged me to lean on a chair for support. The magistrate observed me with a keen eye, and of course drew an unfavourable augury from my manner.

The son confirmed his father's account: but when Daniel Nugent was called, he swore positively that, just before the fall of his companion, he saw a boat, with a single man in it, at a short distance from the shore; and, as far as he could judge by the light of a few stars, it was the same boat in which I had just landed.

A woman deposed, that she lived near the beach, and was standing at the door of her cottage, waiting for the return of the fishermen, about an hour before she heard of the discovery of the body, when she saw a boat, with only one man in it, push off from that part of the shore where the corpse was afterwards found.

Another woman confirmed the account of the fishermen having brought the body into her house; it was not cold. They put it into a bed, and rubbed it; and Daniel went to the town for an apothecary, but life was quite gone.

Several other men were examined concerning my

landing; and they agreed, that, with the strong north wind that had arisen during the night, it was very probable that I had beaten about for many hours, and had been obliged to return nearly to the same spot from which I had departed. Besides, they observed that it appeared that I had brought the body from another place, and it was likely, that as I did not appear to know the shore, I might have put into the harbour ignorant of the distance of the town of —— from the place where I had deposited the corpse.

Mr. Kirwin, on hearing this evidence, desired that I should be taken into the room where the body lay for interment that it might be observed what effect the sight of it would produce upon me. This idea was probably suggested by the extreme agitation I had exhibited when the mode of the murder had been described. I was accordingly conducted, by the magistrate and several other persons, to the inn. I could not help being struck by the strange coincidences that had taken place during this eventful night; but, knowing that I had been conversing with several persons in the island I had inhabited about the time that the body had been found, I was perfectly tranquil as to the consequences of the affair.

I entered the room where the corpse lay, and was led up to the coffin. How can I describe my sensations on beholding it? I feel yet parched with horror, nor can I reflect on that terrible moment without shuddering and agony, that faintly reminds me of the anguish of the recognition. The trial, the presence of the magistrate and witnesses, passed like a dream from my memory, when I saw the lifeless form of Henry Clerval stretched before me. I gasped for breath; and, throwing myself on the body, I exclaimed, "Have my murderous machinations deprived you also, my dearest Henry, of life? Two I have already destroyed; other victims await their destiny: but you, Clerval, my friend, my benefactor"——

The human frame could no longer support the agonizing suffering that I endured, and I was carried out of the room in strong convulsions.

A fever succeeded to this. I lay for two months on the point of death: my ravings, as I afterwards heard, were frightful; I called myself the murderer of William, of Justine, and of Clerval. Sometimes I entreated my attendants to assist me in the destruction of the fiend by whom I was tormented; and, at others, I felt the fingers of the monster already grasping my neck, and screamed aloud with agony and terror. Fortunately, as I spoke my native language, Mr. Kirwin alone understood me; but my gestures and bitter cries were sufficient to affright the other witnesses.

Why did I not die? More miserable than man ever was before, why did I not sink into forgetfulness and rest? Death snatches away many blooming children, the only hopes of their doating parents: how many brides and youthful lovers have been one day in the bloom of health and hope, and the next a prey for worms and the decay of the tomb! Of what materials was I made, that I could thus resist so many shocks, which, like the turning of the wheel, continually renewed the torture.

But I was doomed to live; and, in two months, found myself as awaking from a dream, in a prison, stretched on a wretched bed, surrounded by gaolers, turnkeys, bolts, and all the miserable apparatus of a dungeon. It was morning, I remember, when I thus awoke to understanding: I had forgotten the particulars of what had happened, and only felt as if some great misfortune had suddenly overwhelmed me; but when I looked around, and saw the barred windows, and the squalidness of the room in which I was, all flashed across my memory, and I groaned bitterly.

This sound disturbed an old woman who was sleeping in a chair beside me. She was a hired nurse, the wife of one of the turnkeys, and her countenance expressed all those bad qualities which often characterize that class. The lines of her face were hard and rude, like that of persons accustomed to see without sympathizing in sights of misery. Her tone expressed her entire indifference; she addressed me in English, and the voice struck me as one that I had heard during my sufferings:

"Are you better now, Sir?" said she.

I replied in the same language, with a feeble voice, "I believe I am; but if it be all true, if indeed I did not dream, I am sorry that I am still alive to feel this misery and horror."

"For that matter," replied the old woman, "if you mean about the gentleman you murdered, I believe that it were better for you if you were dead, for I fancy it will go hard with you; but you will be hung when the next sessions come on. However, that's none of my business, I am sent to nurse you, and get you well; I do my duty with a safe conscience, it were well if every body did the same."

I turned with loathing from the woman who could utter so unfeeling a speech to a person just saved, on the very edge of death; but I felt languid, and unable to reflect on all that had passed. The whole series of my life appeared to me as a dream; I sometimes doubted if indeed it were all true, for it never presented itself to my mind with the force of reality.

As the images that floated before me became more distinct, I grew feverish; a darkness pressed around me; no one was near me who soothed me with the gentle voice of love; no dear hand supported me. The physician came and prescribed medicines, and the old woman prepared them for me; but utter carelessness was visible in the first, and the expression of brutality was strongly marked in the visage of the second. Who could be interested in the fate of a murderer, but the hangman who would gain his fee?

These were my first reflections; but I soon learned that Mr. Kirwin had shewn me extreme kindness. He had caused the best room in the prison to be prepared for me (wretched indeed was the best); and it was he who had provided a physician and a nurse. It is true, he seldom came to see me; for, although he ardently desired to relieve the sufferings of every human creature, he did not wish to be present at the agonies and miserable ravings of a murderer. He came, therefore, sometimes to see that I was not neglected; but his visits were short, and at long intervals.

One day, when I was gradually recovering, I was seated in a chair, my eyes half open, and my cheeks livid like those in death, I was overcome by gloom and misery, and often reflected I had better seek death than remain miserably pent up only to be let loose in a world replete with wretchedness. At one time I considered whether I should not declare myself guilty, and suffer the penalty of the law, less innocent than poor Justine had been. Such were my thoughts, when the door of my apartment was opened, and Mr. Kirwin entered. His countenance expressed sympathy and compassion; he drew a chair close to mine, and addressed me in French—

"I fear that this place is very shocking to you; can I do any thing to make you more comfortable?"

"I thank you; but all that you mention is nothing to me: on the whole earth there is no comfort which I am capable of receiving."

"I know that the sympathy of a stranger can be but of little relief to one borne down as you are by so strange a misfortune. But you will, I hope, soon quit this melancholy abode; for, doubtless, evidence can easily be brought to free you from the criminal charge."

"That is my least concern: I am, by a course of strange events, become the most miserable of mortals. Persecuted and tortured as I am and have been, can death be any evil to me?"

"Nothing indeed could be more unfortunate and agonizing than the strange chances that have lately occurred. You were thrown, by some surprising accident, on this shore, renowned for its hospitality: seized immediately, and charged with murder. The first sight that was presented to your eyes was the body of your friend, murdered in so unaccountable a manner, and placed, as it were, by some fiend across your path."

As Mr. Kirwin said this, notwithstanding the agitation I endured on this retrospect of my sufferings, I also felt considerable surprise at the knowledge he seemed to possess concerning me. I suppose some astonishment was exhibited in my countenance; for Mr. Kirwin hastened to say—

"It was not until a day or two after your illness that I thought of examining your dress, that I might discover some trace by which I could send to your relations an account of your misfortune and illness. I found several letters, and, among others, one which I discovered from its commencement to be from your father. I instantly wrote to Geneva: nearly two months have elapsed since the departure of my letter.—But you are ill; even now you tremble: you are unfit for agitation of any kind."

"This suspense is a thousand times worse than the most horrible event: tell me what new scene of death has been acted, and whose murder I am now to lament."

"Your family is perfectly well," said Mr. Kirwin, with gentleness; "and some one, a friend, is come to visit you."

I know not by what chain of thought the idea presented itself, but it instantly darted into my mind that the murderer had come to mock at my misery, and taunt me with the death of Clerval, as a new incitement for me to comply with his hellish desires. I put by hand before my eyes, and cried out in agony—

"Oh! take him away! I cannot see him; for God's sake, do not let him enter!"

Mr. Kirwin regarded me with a troubled countenance. He could not help regarding my exclamation as a presumption of my guilt, and said, in rather a severe tone—

"I should have thought, young man, that the presence of your father would have been welcome, instead of inspiring such violent repugnance."

"My father!" cried I, while every feature and every muscle was relaxed from anguish to pleasure. "Is my father, indeed, come? How kind, how very kind. But where is he, why does he not hasten to me?"

My change of manner surprised and pleased the magistrate; perhaps he thought that my former exclamation was a momentary return of delirium, and now he instantly resumed his former benevolence. He rose, and quitted the room with my nurse, and in a moment my father entered it.

Nothing, at this moment, could have given me greater pleasure than the arrival of my father. I stretched out my hand to him, and cried—

"Are you then safe—and Elizabeth—and Ernest?"

My father calmed me with assurances of their welfare, and endeavoured, by dwelling on these subjects so interesting to my heart, to raise my desponding spirits; but he soon felt that a prison cannot be the abode of cheerfulness. "What a place is this that you inhabit, my son!" said he, looking mournfully at the barred windows, and wretched appearance of the room. "You travelled to seek happiness, but a fatality seems to pursue you. And poor Clerval—"

The name of my unfortunate and murdered friend was an agitation too great to be endured in my weak state; I shed tears.

"Alas! yes, my father," replied I; "some destiny of the most horrible kind hangs over me, and I must live to fulfil it, or surely I should have died on the coffin of Henry."

We were not allowed to converse for any length of time, for the precarious state of my health rendered every precaution necessary that could insure tranquillity. Mr. Kirwin came in, and insisted that my strength should not be exhausted by too much exertion. But the appearance of my father was to me like that of my good angel, and I gradually recovered my health.

As my sickness quitted me, I was absorbed by a gloomy and black melancholy, that nothing could dissipate. The image of Clerval was for ever before me, ghastly and murdered. More than once the agitation into which these reflections threw me made my friends dread a dangerous relapse. Alas! why did they preserve so miserable and detested a life? It was surely that I might fulfil my destiny, which is now drawing to a close. Soon, oh, very soon, will death extinguish these throbbings, and relieve me from the mighty weight of anguish that bears me to the dust; and, in executing the award of justice, I shall also sink to rest. Then the appearance of death was distant, although the wish was ever present to my thoughts; and I often sat for hours motionless and speechless, wishing for some mighty revolution that might bury me and my destroyer in its ruins.

The season of the assizes approached. I had already

been three months in prison; and although I was still weak, and in continual danger of a relapse, I was obliged to travel nearly a hundred miles to the county-town, where the court was held. Mr. Kirwin charged himself with every care of collecting witnesses, and arranging my defence. I was spared the disgrace of appearing publicly as a criminal, as the case was not brought before the court that decides on life and death. The grand jury rejected the bill, on its being proved that I was on the Orkney Islands at the hour the body of my friend was found, and a fortnight after my removal I was liberated from prison.

My father was enraptured on finding me freed from the vexations of a criminal charge, that I was again allowed to breathe the fresh atmosphere, and allowed to return to my native country. I did not participate in these feelings; for to me the walls of a dungeon or a palace were alike hateful. The cup of life was poisoned for ever; and although the sun shone upon me, as upon the happy and gay of heart, I saw around me nothing but a dense and frightful darkness, penetrated by no light but the glimmer of two eyes that glared upon me. Sometimes they were the expressive eyes of Henry, languishing in death, the dark orbs nearly covered by the lids, and the long black lashes that fringed them; sometimes it was the watery clouded eyes of the monster, as I first saw them in my chamber at Ingolstadt.

My father tried to awaken in me the feelings of affection. He talked of Geneva, which I should soon visit—of Elizabeth, and Ernest; but these words only drew deep groans from me. Sometimes, indeed, I felt a wish for happiness; and thought, with melancholy delight, of my beloved cousin; or longed, with a devouring *maladie du pays,* to see once more the blue lake and rapid Rhone, that had been so dear to me in early childhood: but my general state of feeling was a torpor, in which a prison was as welcome a residence as the divinest scene in nature; and these fits were seldom interrupted, but by paroxysms of anguish and despair. At these moments I often endeavoured to put an end to the existence I loathed; and it required unceasing attendance and vigilance to restrain me from committing some dreadful act of violence.

I remember, as I quitted the prison, I heard one of the men say, "He may be innocent of the murder, but he has certainly a bad conscience." These words struck me. A bad conscience! yes, surely I had one. William, Justine, and Clerval, had died through my infernal machinations; "And whose death," cried I, "is to finish the tragedy? Ah! my father, do not remain in this wretched country; take me where I may forget myself, my existence, and all the world."

My father easily acceded to my desire; and, after having taken leave of Mr. Kirwin, we hastened to Dublin. I felt as if I was relieved from a heavy weight, when the packet sailed with a fair wind from Ireland, and I had quitted for ever the country which had been to me the scene of so much misery.

It was midnight. My father slept in the cabin; and I lay on the deck, looking at the stars, and listening to the dashing of the waves. I hailed the darkness that shut Ireland from my sight, and my pulse beat with a feverish joy, when I reflected that I should soon see Geneva. The past appeared to me in the light of a frightful dream; yet the vessel in which I was, the wind that blew me from the detested shore of Ireland, and the sea which surrounded me, told me too forcibly that I was deceived by no vision, and that Clerval, my friend and dearest companion, had fallen a victim to me and the monster of my creation. I repassed, in my memory, my whole life; my quiet happiness while residing with my family in Geneva, the death of my mother, and my departure for

Ingolstadt. I remembered shuddering at the mad enthusiasm that hurried me on to the creation of my hideous enemy, and I called to mind the night during which he first lived. I was unable to pursue the train of thought; a thousand feelings pressed upon me, and I wept bitterly.

Ever since my recovery from the fever I had been in the custom of taking every night a small quantity of laudanum; for it was by means of this drug only that I was enabled to gain the rest necessary for the preservation of life. Oppressed by the recollection of my various misfortunes, I now took a double dose, and soon slept profoundly. But sleep did not afford me respite from thought and misery; my dreams presented a thousand objects that scared me. Towards morning I was possessed by a kind of night-mare; I felt the fiend's grasp in my neck, and could not free myself from it; groans and cries rung in my ears. My father, who was watching over me, perceiving my restlessness, awoke me, and pointed to the port of Holyhead, which we were now entering.

CHAPTER V

We had resolved not to go to London, but to cross the country to Portsmouth, and thence to embark for Havre. I preferred this plan principally because I dreaded to see again those places in which I had enjoyed a few moments of tranquillity with my beloved Clerval. I thought with horror of seeing again those persons whom we had been accustomed to visit together, and who might make inquiries concerning an event, the very remembrance of which made me again feel the pang I endured when I gazed on his lifeless form in the inn at ——.

As for my father, his desires and exertions were bounded to the again seeing me restored to health and peace of mind. His tenderness and attentions were unremitting; my grief and gloom was obstinate, but he would not despair. Sometimes he thought that I felt deeply the degradation of being obliged to answer a charge of murder, and he endeavoured to prove to me the futility of pride.

"Alas! my father," said I, "how little do you know me. Human beings, their feelings and passions, would indeed be degraded, if such a wretch as I felt pride. Justine, poor unhappy Justine, was as innocent as I, and she suffered the same charge; she died for it; and I am the cause of this—I murdered her. William, Justine, and Henry—they all died by my hands."

My father had often, during my imprisonment, heard me make the same assertion; when I thus accused myself, he sometimes seemed to desire an explanation, and at others he appeared to consider it as caused by delirium, and that, during my illness, some idea of this kind had presented itself to my imagination, the remembrance of which I preserved in my convalescence. I avoided explanation, and maintained a continual silence concerning the wretch I had created. I had a feeling that I should be supposed mad, and this for ever chained my tongue, when I would have given the whole world to have confided the fatal secret.

Upon this occasion my father said, with an expression of unbounded wonder, "What do you mean, Victor? are you mad? My dear son, I entreat you never to make such an assertion again."

"I am not mad," I cried energetically; "the sun and

the heavens, who have viewed my operations, can bear witness of my truth. I am the assassin of those most innocent victims; they died by my machinations. A thousand times would I have shed my own blood, drop by drop, to have saved their lives; but I could not, my father, indeed I could not sacrifice the whole human race."

The conclusion of this speech convinced my father that my ideas were deranged, and he instantly changed the subject of our conversation, and endeavoured to alter the course of my thoughts. He wished as much as possible to obliterate the memory of the scenes that had taken place in Ireland, and never alluded to them, or suffered me to speak of my misfortunes.

As time passed away I became more calm: misery had her dwelling in my heart, but I no longer talked in the same incoherent manner of my own crimes; sufficient for me was the consciousness of them. By the utmost self-violence, I curbed the imperious voice of wretchedness, which sometimes desired to declare itself to the whole world; and my manners were calmer and more composed than they had ever been since my journey to the sea of ice.

We arrived at Havre on the 8th of May, and instantly proceeded to Paris, where my father had some business which detained us a few weeks. In this city, I received the following letter from Elizabeth:—

"To Victor Frankenstein.

"My dearest Friend,

"It gave me the greatest pleasure to receive a letter from my uncle dated at Paris; you are no longer at a formidable distance, and I may hope to see you in less than a fortnight. My poor cousin, how much you must have suffered! I expect to see you looking even more ill than when you quitted Geneva. This winter has been passed most miserably, tortured as I have been by anxious suspense; yet I hope to see peace in your countenance, and to find that your heart is not totally devoid of comfort and tranquillity.

"Yet I fear that the same feelings now exist that made you so miserable a year ago, even perhaps augmented by time. I would not disturb you at this period, when so many misfortunes weigh upon you; but a conversation that I had with my uncle previous to his departure renders some explanation necessary before we meet.

"Explanation! you may possibly say; what can Elizabeth have to explain? If you really say this, my questions are answered, and I have no more to do than to sign myself your affectionate cousin. But you are distant from me, and it is possible that you may dread, and yet be pleased with this explanation; and, in a probability of this being the case, I dare not any longer postpone writing what, during your absence, I have often wished to express to you, but have never had the courage to begin.

"You well know, Victor, that our union had been the favourite plan of your parents ever since our infancy. We were told this when young, and taught to look forward to it as an event that would certainly take place. We were affectionate playfellows during childhood, and, I believe, dear and valued friends to one another as we grew older. But as brother and sister often entertain a lively affection towards each other, without desiring a more intimate union, may not such also be our case? Tell me, dearest Victor. Answer me, I conjure you, by our mutual happiness, with simple truth—Do you not love another?

"You have travelled; you have spent several years of your life at Ingolstadt; and I confess to you, my friend, that when I saw you last autumn so unhappy, flying to solitude, from the society of every creature, I could not help supposing that you might regret our connexion, and believe yourself bound in honour to fulfil the wishes of your parents, although they opposed themselves to your inclinations. But this is false reasoning. I confess to you, my cousin, that I love you, and that in my airy dreams of futurity you have been my constant friend and companion. But it is your happiness I desire as well as my own, when I declare to you, that our marriage would render me eternally miserable, unless it were the dictate of your own free choice. Even now I weep to think, that, borne down as you are by the cruelest misfortunes, you may stifle, by the word *honour,* all hope of that love and happiness which would alone restore you to yourself. I, who have so interested an affection for you, may increase your miseries ten-fold, by being an obstacle to your wishes. Ah, Victor, be assured that your cousin and playmate has too sincere a love for you not to be made miserable by this supposition. Be happy, my friend; and if you obey me in this one request, remain satisfied that nothing on earth will have the power to interrupt my tranquillity.

"Do not let this letter disturb you; do not answer it to-morrow, or the next day, or even until you come, if it will give you pain. My uncle will send me news of your health; and if I see but one smile on your lips when we meet, occasioned by this or any other exertion of mine, I shall need no other happiness.

"Elizabeth Lavenza.

"Geneva, May 18th, 17—."

This letter revived in my memory what I had before forgotten, the threat of the fiend—*"I will be with you on your wedding-night!"* Such was my sentence, and on that night would the dæmon employ every art to destroy me, and tear me from the glimpse of happiness which promised partly to console my sufferings. On that night he had determined to consummate his crimes by my death. Well, be it so; a deadly struggle would then assuredly take place, in which if he was victorious, I should be at peace, and his power over me be at an end. If he were vanquished, I should be a free man. Alas! what freedom? such as the peasant enjoys when his family have been massacred before his eyes, his cottage burnt, his lands laid waste, and he is turned adrift, homeless, pennyless, and alone, but free. Such would be my liberty, except that in my Elizabeth I possessed a treasure; alas! balanced by those horrors of remorse and guilt, which would pursue me until death.

Sweet and beloved Elizabeth! I read and re-read her letter, and some softened feelings stole into my heart, and dared to whisper paradisaical dreams of love and joy; but the apple was already eaten, and the angel's arm bared to drive me from all hope. Yet I would die to make her happy. If the monster executed his threat, death was inevitable; yet, again, I considered whether my marriage would hasten my fate. My destruction might indeed arrive a few months sooner; but if my torturer should suspect that I postponed it, influenced by his menaces, he would surely find other, and perhaps more dreadful means of revenge. He had vowed *to be with me on my wedding-night,* yet he did not consider that threat as binding him to peace in the mean time; for, as if to shew me that he was not yet satiated with blood, he had murdered Clerval immediately after the enunciation of his threats. I resolved, therefore, that if my immediate union with my cousin would conduce either to her's or my father's happiness, my adversary's designs against my life should not retard it a single hour.

In this state of mind I wrote to Elizabeth. My letter

was calm and affectionate. "I fear, my beloved girl," I said, "little happiness remains for us on earth; yet all that I may one day enjoy is concentered in you. Chase away your idle fears; to you alone do I consecrate my life, and my endeavours for contentment. I have one secret, Elizabeth, a dreadful one; when revealed to you, it will chill your frame with horror, and then, far from being surprised at my misery, you will only wonder that I survive what I have endured. I will confide this tale of misery and terror to you the day after our marriage shall take place; for, my sweet cousin, there must be perfect confidence between us. But until then, I conjure you, do not mention or allude to it. This I most earnestly entreat, and I know you will comply."

In about a week after the arrival of Elizabeth's letter, we returned to Geneva. My cousin welcomed me with warm affection; yet tears were in her eyes, as she beheld my emaciated frame and feverish cheeks. I saw a change in her also. She was thinner, and had lost much of that heavenly vivacity that had before charmed me; but her gentleness, and soft looks of compassion, made her a more fit companion for one blasted and miserable as I was.

The tranquillity which I now enjoyed did not endure. Memory brought madness with it; and when I thought on what had passed, a real insanity possessed me; sometimes I was furious, and burnt with rage, sometimes low and despondent. I neither spoke nor looked, but sat motionless, bewildered by the multitude of miseries that overcame me.

Elizabeth alone had the power to draw me from these fits; her gentle voice would soothe me when transported by passion, and inspire me with human feelings when sunk in torpor. She wept with me, and for me. When reason returned, she would remonstrate, and endeavour to inspire me with resignation. Ah! it is well for the unfortunate to be resigned, but for the guilty there is no peace. The agonies of remorse poison the luxury there is otherwise sometimes found in indulging the excess of grief.

Soon after my arrival my father spoke of my immediate marriage with my cousin. I remained silent.

"Have you, then, some other attachment?"

"None on earth. I love Elizabeth, and look forward to our union with delight. Let the day therefore be fixed; and on it I will consecrate myself, in life or death, to the happiness of my cousin."

"My dear Victor, do not speak thus. Heavy misfortunes have befallen us; but let us only cling closer to what remains, and transfer our love for those whom we have lost to those who yet live. Our circle will be small, but bound close by the ties of affection and mutual misfortune. And when time shall have softened your despair, new and dear objects of care will be born to replace those of whom we have been so cruelly deprived."

Such were the lessons of my father. But to me the remembrance of the threat returned: nor can you wonder, that, omnipotent as the fiend had yet been in his deeds of blood, I should almost regard him as invincible; and that when he had pronounced the words, *"I shall be with you on your wedding-night,"* I should regard the threatened fate as unavoidable. But death was no evil to me, if the loss of Elizabeth were balanced with it; and I therefore, with a contented and even cheerful countenance, agreed with my father, that if my cousin would consent, the ceremony should take place in ten days, and thus put, as I imagined, the seal to my fate.

Great God! if for one instant I had thought what might be the hellish intention of my fiendish adversary, I would rather have banished myself for ever from my native country, and wandered a friendless outcast over the earth, than have consented to this miserable marriage. But, as if possessed of magic powers, the monster had blinded me to his real intentions; and when I thought that I prepared only my own death, I hastened that of a far dearer victim.

As the period fixed for our marriage drew nearer, whether from cowardice or a prophetic feeling, I felt my heart sink within me. But I concealed my feelings by an appearance of hilarity, that brought smiles and joy to the countenance of my father, but hardly deceived the ever-watchful and nicer eye of Elizabeth. She looked forward to our union with placid contentment, not unmingled with a little fear, which past misfortunes had impressed, that what now appeared certain and tangible happiness, might soon dissipate into an airy dream, and leave no trace but deep and everlasting regret.

Preparations were made for the event; congratulatory visits were received; and all wore a smiling appearance. I shut up, as well as I could, in my own heart the anxiety that preyed there, and entered with seeming earnestness into the plans of my father, although they might only serve as the decorations of my tragedy. A house was purchased for us near Cologny, by which we should enjoy the pleasures of the country, and yet be so near Geneva as to see my father every day; who would still reside within the walls, for the benefit of Ernest, that he might follow his studies at the schools.

In the mean time I took every precaution to defend my person, in case the fiend should openly attack me. I carried pistols and a dagger constantly about me, and was ever on the watch to prevent artifice; and by these means gained a greater degree of tranquillity.

Indeed, as the period approached, the threat appeared more as a delusion, not to be regarded as worthy to disturb my peace, while the happiness I hoped for in my marriage wore a greater appearance of certainty, as the day fixed for its solemnization drew nearer, and I heard it continually spoken of as an occurrence which no accident could possibly prevent.

Elizabeth seemed happy; my tranquil demeanour contributed greatly to calm her mind. But on the day that was to fulfil my wishes and my destiny, she was melancholy, and a presentiment of evil pervaded her; and perhaps also she thought of the dreadful secret, which I had promised to reveal to her the following day. My father was in the mean time overjoyed, and, in the bustle of preparation, only observed in the melancholy of his niece the diffidence of a bride.

After the ceremony was performed, a large party assembled at my father's; but it was agreed that Elizabeth and I should pass the afternoon and night at Evian, and return to Cologny the next morning. As the day was fair, and the wind favourable, we resolved to go by water.

Those were the last moments of my life during which I enjoyed the feeling of happiness. We passed rapidly along: the sun was hot, but we were sheltered from its rays by a kind of canopy, while we enjoyed the beauty of the scene, sometimes on one side of the lake, where we saw Mont Salêve, the pleasant banks of Montalêgre, and at a distance, surmounting all, the beautiful Mont Blanc, and the assemblage of snowy mountains that in vain endeavour to emulate her; sometimes coasting the opposite banks, we saw the mighty Jura opposing its dark side to the ambition that would quit its native country, and an almost insurmountable barrier to the invader who should wish to enslave it.

I took the hand of Elizabeth: "You are sorrowful, my love. Ah! if you knew what I have suffered, and what I may yet endure, you would endeavour to let me taste the quiet, and freedom from despair, that this one day at least permits me to enjoy."

"Be happy, my dear Victor," replied Elizabeth; "there is, I hope, nothing to distress you; and be assured that if a lively joy is not painted in my face, my heart is contented. Something whispers to me not to depend too much on the prospect that is opened before us; but I will not listen to such a sinister voice. Observe how fast we move along, and how the clouds which sometimes obscure, and sometimes rise above the dome of Mont Blanc, render this scene of beauty still more interesting. Look also at the innumerable fish that are swimming in the clear waters, where we can distinguish every pebble that lies at the bottom. What a divine day! how happy and serene all nature appears!"

Thus Elizabeth endeavoured to divert her thoughts and mine from all reflection upon melancholy subjects. But her temper was fluctuating; joy for a few instants shone in her eyes, but it continually gave place to distraction and reverie.

The sun sunk lower in the heavens; we passed the river Drance, and observed its path through the chasms of the higher, and the glens of the lower hills. The Alps here come closer to the lake, and we approached the amphitheatre of mountains which forms its eastern boundary. The spire of Evian shone under the woods that surrounded it, and the range of mountain above mountain by which it was overhung.

The wind, which had hitherto carried us along with amazing rapidity, sunk at sunset to a light breeze; the soft air just ruffled the water, and caused a pleasant motion among the trees as we approached the shore, from which it wafted the most delightful scent of flowers and hay. The sun sunk beneath the horizon as we landed; and as I touched the shore, I felt those cares and fears revive, which soon were to clasp me, and cling to me for ever.

CHAPTER VI

It was eight o'clock when we landed; we walked for a short time on the shore, enjoying the transitory light, and then retired to the inn, and contemplated the lovely scene of waters, woods, and mountains, obscured in darkness, yet still displaying their black outlines.

The wind, which had fallen in the south, now rose with great violence in the west. The moon had reached her summit in the heavens, and was beginning to descend; the clouds swept across it swifter than the flight of the vulture, and dimmed her rays, while the lake reflected the scene of the busy heavens, rendered still busier by the restless waves that were beginning to rise. Suddenly a heavy storm of rain descended.

I had been calm during the day; but so soon as night obscured the shapes of objects, a thousand fears arose in my mind. I was anxious and watchful, while my right hand grasped a pistol which was hidden in my bosom; every sound terrified me; but I resolved that I would sell my life dearly, and not relax the impending conflict until my own life, or that of my adversary, were extinguished.

Elizabeth observed my agitation for some time in

timid and fearful silence; at length she said, "What is it that agitates you, my dear Victor? What is it you fear?"

"Oh! peace, peace, my love," replied I, "this night, and all will be safe: but this night is dreadful, very dreadful."

I passed an hour in this state of mind, when suddenly I reflected how dreadful the combat which I momentarily expected would be to my wife, and I earnestly entreated her to retire, resolving not to join her until I had obtained some knowledge as to the situation of my enemy.

She left me, and I continued some time walking up and down the passages of the house, and inspecting every corner that might afford a retreat to my adversary. But I discovered no trace of him, and was beginning to conjecture that some fortunate chance had intervened to prevent the execution of his menaces; when suddenly I heard a shrill and dreadful scream. It came from the room into which Elizabeth had retired. As I heard it, the whole truth rushed into my mind, my arms dropped, the motion of every muscle and fibre was suspended; I could feel the blood trickling in my veins, and tingling in the extremities of my limbs. This state lasted but for an instant; the scream was repeated, and I rushed into the room.

Great God! why did I not then expire! Why am I here to relate the destruction of the best hope, and the purest creature of earth? She was there, lifeless and inanimate, thrown across the bed, her head hanging down, and her pale and distorted features half covered by her hair. Every where I turn I see the same figure—her bloodless arms and relaxed form flung by the murderer on its bridal bier. Could I behold this, and live? Alas! life is obstinate, and clings closest where it is most hated. For a moment only did I lose recollection; I fainted.

When I recovered, I found myself surrounded by the people of the inn; their countenances expressed a breathless terror: but the horror of others appeared only as a mockery, a shadow of the feelings that oppressed me. I escaped from them to the room where lay the body of Elizabeth, my love, my wife, so lately living, so dear, so worthy. She had been moved from the posture in which I had first beheld her; and now, as she lay, her head upon her arm, and a handkerchief thrown across her face and neck, I might have supposed her asleep. I rushed towards her, and embraced her with ardour; but the deathly languor and coldness of the limbs told me, that what I now held in my arms had ceased to be the Elizabeth whom I had loved and cherished. The murderous mark of the fiend's grasp was on her neck, and the breath had ceased to issue from her lips.

While I still hung over her in the agony of despair, I happened to look up. The windows of the room had before been darkened; and I felt a kind of panic on seeing the pale yellow light of the moon illuminate the chamber. The shutters had been thrown back; and, with a sensation of horror not to be described, I saw at the open window a figure the most hideous and abhorred. A grin was on the face of the monster; he seemed to jeer, as with his fiendish finger he pointed towards the corpse of my wife. I rushed towards the window, and drawing a pistol from my bosom, shot; but he eluded me, leaped from his station, and, running with the swiftness of lightning, plunged into the lake.

The report of the pistol brought a crowd into the room. I pointed to the spot where he had disappeared, and we followed the track with boats; nets were cast, but in vain. After passing several hours, we returned hopeless, most of my companions believing it to have been a form conjured by my fancy. After having landed, they proceeded to search the country, parties going in different directions among the woods and vines.

I did not accompany them; I was exhausted: a film covered my eyes, and my skin was parched with the heat of fever. In this state I lay on a bed, hardly conscious of what had happened; my eyes wandered round the room, as if to seek something that I had lost.

At length I remembered that my father would anxiously expect the return of Elizabeth and myself, and that I must return alone. This reflection brought tears into my eyes, and I wept for a long time; but my thoughts rambled to various subjects, reflecting on my misfortunes, and their cause. I was bewildered in a cloud of wonder and horror. The death of William, the execution of Justine, the murder of Clerval, and lastly of my wife; even at that moment I knew not that my only remaining friends were safe from the malignity of the fiend; my father even now might be writhing under his grasp, and Ernest might be dead at his feet. This idea made me shudder, and recalled me to action. I started up, and resolved to return to Geneva with all possible speed.

There were no horses to be procured, and I must return by the lake; but the wind was unfavourable, and the rain fell in torrents. However, it was hardly morning, and I might reasonably hope to arrive by night. I hired men to row, and took an oar myself, for I had always experienced relief from mental torment in bodily exercise. But the overflowing misery I now felt, and the excess of agitation that I endured, rendered me incapable of any exertion. I threw down the oar; and, leaning my head upon my hands, gave way to every gloomy idea that arose. If I looked up, I saw the scenes which were familiar to me in my happier time, and which I had contemplated but the day before in the company of her who was now but a shadow and a recollection. Tears streamed from my eyes. The rain had ceased for a moment, and I saw the fish play in the waters as they had done a few hours before; they had then been observed by Elizabeth. Nothing is so painful to the human mind as a great and sudden change. The sun might shine, or the clouds might lour; but nothing could appear to me as it had done the day before. A fiend had snatched from me every hope of future happiness: no creature had ever been so miserable as I was; so frightful an event is single in the history of man.

But why should I dwell upon the incidents that followed this last overwhelming event. Mine has been a tale of horrors; I have reached their *acme,* and what I must now relate can but be tedious to you. Know that, one by one, my friends were snatched away: I was left desolate. My own strength is exhausted; and I must tell, in a few words, what remains of my hideous narration.

I arrived at Geneva. My father and Ernest yet lived; but the former sunk under the tidings that I bore. I see him now, excellent and venerable old man! his eyes wandered in vacancy, for they had lost their charm and their delight—his niece, his more than daughter, whom he doated on with all that affection which a man feels, who, in the decline of life, having few affections, clings more earnestly to those that remain. Cursed, cursed be the fiend that brought misery on his grey hairs, and doomed him to waste in wretchedness! He could not live under the horrors that were accumulated around him; an apoplectic fit was brought on, and in a few days he died in my arms.

What then became of me? I know not; I lost sensation, and chains and darkness were the only objects that pressed upon me. Sometimes, indeed, I dreamt that I wandered in flowery meadows and pleasant vales with the friends of my youth; but awoke, and found myself in a dungeon. Melancholy followed, but by degrees I gained a clear conception of my miseries and situation, and was then released from my prison. For they had called me mad; and during many months, as I understood, a solitary cell had been my habitation.

But liberty had been a useless gift to me had I not, as I awakened to reason, at the same time awakened to revenge. As the memory of past misfortunes pressed upon me, I began to reflect on their cause—the monster whom I had created, the miserable dæmon whom I had sent abroad into the world for my destruction. I was possessed by a maddening rage when I thought of him, and desired and ardently prayed that I might have him within my grasp to wreak a great and signal revenge on his cursed head.

Nor did my hate long confine itself to useless wishes; I began to reflect on the best means of securing him; and for this purpose, about a month after my release, I repaired to a criminal judge in the town, and told him that I had an accusation to make; that I knew the destroyer of my family; and that I required him to exert his whole authority for the apprehension of the murderer.

The magistrate listened to me with attention and kindness: "Be assured, sir," said he, "no pains or exertions on my part shall be spared to discover the villain."

"I thank you," replied I; "listen, therefore, to the deposition that I have to make. It is indeed a tale so strange, that I should fear you would not credit it, were there not something in truth which, however wonderful, forces conviction. The story is too connected to be mistaken for a dream, and I have no motive for falsehood." My manner, as I thus addressed him, was impressive, but calm; I had formed in my own heart a resolution to pursue my destroyer to death; and this purpose quieted my agony, and provisionally reconciled me to life. I now related my history briefly, but with firmness and precision, marking the dates with accuracy, and never deviating into invective or exclamation.

The magistrate appeared at first perfectly incredulous, but as I continued he became more attentive and interested; I saw him sometimes shudder with horror, at others a lively surprise, unmingled with disbelief, was painted on his countenance.

When I had concluded my narration, I said, "This is the being whom I accuse, and for whose detection and punishment I call upon you to exert your whole power. It is your duty as a magistrate, and I believe and hope that your feelings as a man will not revolt from the execution of those functions on this occasion."

This address caused a considerable change in the physiognomy of my auditor. He had heard my story with that half kind of belief that is given to a tale of spirits and supernatural events; but when he was called upon to act officially in consequence, the whole tide of his incredulity returned. He, however, answered mildly, "I would willingly afford you every aid in your pursuit; but the creature of whom you speak appears to have powers which would put all my exertions to defiance. Who can follow an animal which can traverse the sea of ice, and inhabit caves and dens, where no man would venture to intrude? Besides, some months have elapsed since the commission of his crimes, and no one can conjecture to what place he has wandered, or what region he may now inhabit."

"I do not doubt that he hovers near the spot which I inhabit; and if he has indeed taken refuge in the Alps, ne may be hunted like the chamois, and destroyed as a beast of prey. But I perceive your thoughts: you do not credit my narrative, and do not intend to pursue my enemy with the punishment which is his desert."

As I spoke, rage sparkled in my eyes; the magistrate was intimidated; "You are mistaken," said he, "I will exert myself; and if it is in my power to seize the monster, be assured that he shall suffer punishment proportionate to his crimes. But I fear, from what you have yourself described to be his properties, that this will prove impracticable, and that, while every proper measure is pursued, you should endeavour to make up your mind to disappointment."

"That cannot be; but all that I can say will be of little avail. My revenge is of no moment to you; yet, while I allow it to be a vice, I confess that it is the devouring and only passion of my soul. My rage is unspeakable, when I reflect that the murderer, whom I have turned loose upon society, still exists. You refuse my just demand: I have but one resource; and I devote myself, either in my life or death, to his destruction."

I trembled with excess of agitation as I said this; there was a phrenzy in my manner, and something, I doubt not, of that haughty fierceness, which the martyrs of old are said to have possessed. But to a Genevan magistrate, whose mind was occupied by far other ideas than those of devotion and heroism, this elevation of mind had much the appearance of madness. He endeavoured to soothe me as a nurse does a child, and reverted to my tale as the effects of delirium.

"Man," I cried, "how ignorant art thou in thy pride of wisdom! Cease; you know not what it is you say."

I broke from the house angry and disturbed, and retired to meditate on some other mode of action.

CHAPTER VII

My present situation was one in which all voluntary thought was swallowed up and lost. I was hurried away by fury; revenge alone endowed me with strength and composure; it modelled my feelings, and allowed me to be calculating and calm, at periods when otherwise delirium or death would have been my portion.

My first resolution was to quit Geneva for ever; my country, which, when I was happy and beloved, was dear to me, now, in my adversity, became hateful. I provided myself with a sum of money, together with a few jewels which had belonged to my mother, and departed.

And now my wanderings began, which are to cease but with life. I have traversed a vast portion of the earth, and have endured all the hardships which travellers, in deserts and barbarous countries, are wont to meet. How I have lived I hardly know; many times have I stretched my failing limbs upon the sandy plain, and prayed for death. But revenge kept me alive; I dared not die, and leave my adversary in being.

When I quitted Geneva, my first labour was to gain some clue by which I might trace the steps of my fiendish enemy. But my plan was unsettled; and I wandered many hours around the confines of the town, uncertain what path I should pursue. As night approached, I found myself at the entrance of the cemetery where William, Elizabeth, and my father, reposed. I entered it, and approached the tomb which marked their graves. Every thing was silent, except the leaves of the trees, which were gently agitated by the wind; the night was nearly dark; and the scene would have been solemn and affecting even to an uninterested observer. The spirits of the departed seemed to flit around, and to cast a shadow, which was felt but seen not, around the head of the mourner.

The deep grief which this scene had at first excited quickly gave way to rage and despair. They were dead, and I lived; their murderer also lived, and to destroy him I must drag out my weary existence. I knelt on the grass, and kissed the earth, and with quivering lips exclaimed, "By the sacred earth on which I kneel, by the shades that wander near me, by the deep and eternal grief that I feel, I swear; and by thee, O Night, and by the spirits that preside over thee, I swear to pursue the dæmon, who caused this misery, until he or I shall perish in mortal conflict. For this purpose I will preserve my life: to execute this dear revenge, will I again behold the sun, and tread the green herbage of earth, which otherwise should vanish from my eyes for ever. And I call on you, spirits of the dead; and on you, wandering ministers of vengeance, to aid and conduct me in my work. Let the cursed and hellish monster drink deep of agony; let him feel the despair that now torments me."

I had begun my adjuration with solemnity, and an awe which almost assured me that the shades of my murdered friends heard and approved my devotion; but the furies possessed me as I concluded, and rage choaked my utterance.

I was answered through the stillness of night by a loud and fiendish laugh. It rung on my ears long and heavily; the mountains re-echoed it, and I felt as if all hell surrounded me with mockery and laughter. Surely in that moment I should have been possessed by phrenzy, and have destroyed my miserable existence, but that my vow was heard, and that I was reserved for vengeance. The laughter died away: when a well-known and abhorred voice, apparently close to my ear, addressed me in an audible whisper—"I am satisfied: miserable wretch! you have determined to live, and I am satisfied."

I darted towards the spot from which the sound proceeded; but the devil eluded my grasp. Suddenly the broad disk of the moon arose, and shone full upon his ghastly and distorted shape, as he fled with more than mortal speed.

I pursued him; and for many months this has been my task. Guided by a slight clue, I followed the windings of the Rhone, but vainly. The blue Mediterranean appeared; and, by a strange chance, I saw the fiend enter by night, and hide himself in a vessel bound for the Black Sea. I took my passage in the same ship; but he escaped, I know not how.

Amidst the wilds of Tartary and Russia, although he still evaded me, I have ever followed in his track. Sometimes the peasants, scared by this horrid apparition, informed me of his path; sometimes he himself, who feared that if I lost all trace I should despair and die, often left some mark to guide me. The snows descended on my head, and I saw the print of his huge step on the white plain. To you first entering on life, to whom care is new, and agony unknown, how can you understand what I have felt, and still feel? Cold, want, and fatigue, were the least pains which I was destined to endure; I was cursed by some devil, and carried about with me my eternal hell; yet still a spirit of good followed and directed my steps, and, when I most murmured, would suddenly extricate me from seemingly insurmountable difficulties. Sometimes, when nature, overcome by hunger, sunk under the exhaustion, a repast was prepared for me in the desert, that restored and inspirited me. The fare was indeed coarse, such as the peasants of the country ate; but I may not doubt that it was set there by the spirits that I had invoked to aid me. Often, when all was dry, the heavens cloudless, and I was parched by thirst, a slight cloud would bedim the sky, shed the few drops that revived me, and vanish.

I followed, when I could, the courses of the rivers; but the dæmon generally avoided these, as it was here that the population of the country chiefly collected. In other places human beings were seldom seen; and I generally subsisted on the wild animals that crossed my path. I had money with me, and gained the friendship of the villagers by distributing it, or bringing with me some food that I had killed, which, after taking a small part, I always presented to those who had provided me with fire and utensils for cooking.

My life, as it passed thus, was indeed hateful to me, and it was during sleep alone that I could taste joy. O blessed sleep! often, when most miserable, I sank to repose, and my dreams lulled me even to rapture. The spirits that guarded me had provided these moments, or rather hours, of happiness, that I might retain strength to fulfil my pilgrimage. Deprived of this respite, I should have sunk under my hardships. During the day I was sustained and inspirited by the hope of night: for in sleep I saw my friends, my wife, and my beloved country; again I saw the benevolent countenance of my father, heard the silver tones of my Elizabeth's voice, and beheld Clerval enjoying health and youth. Often, when wearied by a toilsome march, I persuaded myself that I was dreaming until night should come, and that I should then enjoy reality in the arms of my dearest friends. What agonizing fondness did I feel for them! how did I cling to their dear forms, as sometimes they haunted even my waking hours, and persuade myself that they still lived! At such moments vengeance, that burned within me, died in my heart, and I pursued my path towards the destruction of the dæmon, more as a task enjoined by heaven, as the mechanical impulse of some power of which I was unconscious, than as the ardent desire of my soul.

What his feelings were whom I pursued, I cannot know. Sometimes, indeed, he left marks in writing on the barks of the trees, or cut in stone, that guided me, and instigated my fury. "My reign is not yet over," (these words were legible in one of these inscriptions); "you live, and my power is complete. Follow me; I seek the everlasting ices of the north, where you will feel the misery of cold and frost, to which I am impassive. You will find near this place, if you follow not too tardily, a dead hare; eat, and be refreshed. Come on, my enemy; we have yet to wrestle for our lives; but many hard and miserable hours must you endure, until that period shall arrive."

Scoffing devil! Again do I vow vengeance; again do I devote thee, miserable fiend, to torture and death. Never will I omit my search, until he or I perish; and then with what ecstacy shall I join my Elizabeth, and those who even now prepare for me the reward of my tedious toil and horrible pilgrimage.

As I still pursued my journey to the northward, the snows thickened, and the cold increased in a degree almost too severe to support. The peasants were shut up in their hovels, and only a few of the most hardy ventured forth to seize the animals whom starvation had forced from their hiding-places to seek for prey. The rivers were covered with ice, and no fish could be procured; and thus I was cut off from my chief article of maintenance.

The triumph of my enemy increased with the difficulty of my labours. One inscription that he left was in these words: "Prepare! your toils only begin:

wrap yourself in furs, and provide food, for we shall soon enter upon a journey where your sufferings will satisfy my everlasting hatred."

My courage and perseverance were invigorated by these scoffing words; I resolved not to fail in my purpose; and, calling on heaven to support me, I continued with unabated fervour to traverse immense deserts, until the ocean appeared at a distance, and formed the utmost boundary of the horizon. Oh! how unlike it was to the blue seas of the south! Covered with ice, it was only to be distinguished from land by its superior wildness and ruggedness. The Greeks wept for joy when they beheld the Mediterranean from the hills of Asia, and hailed with rapture the boundary of their toils. I did not weep; but I knelt down, and, with a full heart, thanked my guiding spirit for conducting me in safety to the place where I hoped, notwithstanding my adversary's gibe, to meet and grapple with him.

Some weeks before this period I had procured a sledge and dogs, and thus traversed the snows with inconceivable speed. I know not whether the fiend possessed the same advantages; but I found that, as before I had daily lost ground in the pursuit, I now gained on him; so much so, that when I first saw the ocean, he was but one day's journey in advance, and I hoped to intercept him before he should reach the beach. With new courage, therefore, I pressed on, and in two days arrived at a wretched hamlet on the sea-shore. I inquired of the inhabitants concerning the fiend, and gained accurate information. A gigantic monster, they said, had arrived the night before, armed with a gun and many pistols; putting to flight the inhabitants of a solitary cottage, through fear of his terrific appearance. He had carried off their store of winter food, and, placing it in a sledge, to draw which he had seized on a numerous drove of trained dogs, he had harnessed them, and the same night, to the joy of the horror-struck villagers, had pursued his journey across the sea in a direction that led to no land; and they conjectured that he must speedily be destroyed by the breaking of the ice, or frozen by the eternal frosts.

On hearing this information, I suffered a temporary access of despair. He had escaped me; and I must commence a destructive and almost endless journey across the mountainous ices of the ocean,—amidst cold that few of the inhabitants could long endure, and which I, the native of a genial and sunny climate, could not hope to survive. Yet at the idea that the fiend should live and be triumphant, my rage and vengeance returned, and, like a mighty tide, overwhelmed every other feeling. After a slight repose, during which the spirits of the dead hovered round, and instigated me to toil and revenge, I prepared for my journey.

I exchanged my land sledge for one fashioned for the inequalities of the frozen ocean; and, purchasing a plentiful stock of provisions, I departed from land.

I cannot guess how many days have passed since then; but I have endured misery, which nothing but the eternal sentiment of a just retribution burning within my heart could have enabled me to support. Immense and rugged mountains of ice often barred up my passage, and I often heard the thunder of the ground sea, which threatened my destruction. But again the frost came, and made the paths of the sea secure.

By the quantity of provision which I had consumed I should guess that I had passed three weeks in this journey; and the continual protraction of hope, returning back upon the heart, often wrung bitter drops of despondency and grief from my eyes. Despair had indeed almost secured her prey, and I should soon have sunk beneath this misery; when once, after the poor animals that carried me had with incredible toil gained the summit of a sloping ice mountain, and one sinking under his fatigue died, I viewed the expanse before me with anguish, when suddenly my eye caught a dark speck upon the dusky plain. I strained my sight to discover what it could be, and uttered a wild cry of ecstacy when I distinguished a sledge, and the distorted proportions of a well-known form within. Oh! with what a burning gush did hope revisit my heart! warm tears filled my eyes, which I hastily wiped away, that they might not intercept the view I had of the dæmon; but still my sight was dimmed by the burning drops, until, giving way to the emotions that oppressed me, I wept aloud.

But this was not the time for delay; I disencumbered the dogs of their dead companion, gave them a plentiful portion of food; and, after an hour's rest, which was absolutely necessary, and yet which was bitterly irksome to me, I continued my route. The sledge was still visible; nor did I again lose sight of it, except at the moments when for a short time some ice rock concealed it with its intervening crags. I indeed perceptibly gained on it; and when, after nearly two days' journey, I beheld my enemy at no more than a mile distant, my heart bounded within me.

But now, when I appeared almost within grasp of my enemy, my hopes were suddenly extinguished, and I lost all trace of him more utterly than I had ever done before. A ground sea was heard; the thunder of its progress, as the waters rolled and swelled beneath me, became every moment more ominous and terrific. I pressed on, but in vain. The wind arose; the sea roared; and, as with the mighty shock of an earthquake, it split, and cracked with a tremendous and overwhelming sound. The work was soon finished: in a few minutes a tumultuous sea rolled between me and my enemy, and I was left drifting on a scattered piece of ice, that was continually lessening, and thus preparing for me a hideous death.

In this manner many appalling hours passed; several of my dogs died; and I myself was about to sink under the accumulation of distress, when I saw your vessel riding at anchor, and holding forth to me hopes of succour and life. I had no conception that vessels ever came so far north, and was astounded at the sight. I quickly destroyed part of my sledge to construct oars; and by these means was enabled, with infinite fatigue, to move my ice-raft in the direction of your ship. I had determined, if you were going southward, still to trust myself to the mercy of the seas, rather than abandon my purpose. I hoped to induce you to grant me a boat with which I could still pursue my enemy. But your direction was northward. You took me on board when my vigour was exhausted, and I should soon have sunk under my multiplied hardships into a death, which I still dread,—for my task is unfulfilled.

Oh! when will my guiding spirit, in conducting me to the dæmon, allow me the rest I so much desire; or must I die, and he yet live? If I do, swear to me, Walton, that he shall not escape; that you will seek him, and satisfy my vengeance in his death. Yet, do I dare ask you to undertake my pilgrimage, to endure the hardships that I have undergone? No; I am not so selfish. Yet, when I am dead, if he should appear; if the ministers of vengeance should conduct him to you, swear that he shall not live—swear that he shall not triumph over my accumulated woes, and live to make another such a wretch as I am. He is eloquent and persuasive; and once his words had even power over my heart: but trust him not. His soul is as hellish as his form, full of treachery and fiend-like malice.

Hear him not; call on the manes of William, Justine, Clerval, Elizabeth, my father, and of the wretched Victor, and thrust your sword into his heart. I will hover near, and direct the steel aright.

Walton, in continuation.

August 26th, 17—.

You have read this strange and terrific story, Margaret; and do you not feel your blood congealed with horror, like that which even now curdles mine? Sometimes, seized with sudden agony, he could not continue his tale; at others, his voice broken, yet piercing, uttered with difficulty the words so replete with agony. His fine and lovely eyes were now lighted up with indignation, now subdued to downcast sorrow, and quenched in infinite wretchedness. Sometimes he commanded his countenance and tones, and related the most horrible incidents with a tranquil voice, suppressing every mark of agitation; then, like a volcano bursting forth, his face would suddenly change to an expression of the wildest rage, as he shrieked out imprecations on his persecutor.

His tale is connected, and told with an appearance of the simplest truth; yet I own to you that the letters of Felix and Safie, which he shewed me, and the apparition of the monster, seen from our ship, brought to me a greater conviction of the truth of his narrative than his asseverations, however earnest and connected. Such a monster has then really existence; I cannot doubt it; yet I am lost in surprise and admiration. Sometimes I endeavoured to gain from Frankenstein the particulars of his creature's formation; but on this point he was impenetrable.

"Are you mad, my friend?" said he, "or whither does your senseless curiosity lead you? Would you also create for yourself and the world a demoniacal enemy? Or to what do your questions tend? Peace, peace! learn my miseries, and do not seek to increase your own."

Frankenstein discovered that I made notes concerning his history: he asked to see them, and then himself corrected and augmented them in many places; but principally in giving the life and spirit to the conversations he held with his enemy. "Since you have preserved my narration," said he, "I would not that a mutilated one should go down to posterity."

Thus has a week passed away, while I have listened to the strangest tale that ever imagination formed. My thoughts, and every feeling of my soul, have been drunk up by the interest for my guest, which this tale, and his own elevated and gentle manners have created. I wish to soothe him; yet can I counsel one so infinitely miserable, so destitute of every hope of consolation, to live? Oh, no! the only joy that he can now know will be when he composes his shattered feelings to peace and death. Yet he enjoys one comfort, the offspring of solitude and delirium: he believes, that, when in dreams he holds converse with his friends, and derives from that communion consolation for his miseries, or excitements to his vengeance, that they are not the creations of his fancy, but the real beings who visit him from the regions of a remote world. This faith gives a solemnity to his reveries that render them to me almost as imposing and interesting as truth.

Our conversations are not always confined to his own history and misfortunes. On every point of general literature he displays unbounded knowledge, and a quick and piercing apprehension. His eloquence is forcible and touching; nor can I hear him, when he relates a pathetic incident, or endeavours to move the passions of pity or love, without tears. What a glorious creature must he have been in the days of his prosperity, when he is thus noble and godlike in ruin. He seems to feel his own worth, and the greatness of his fall.

"When younger," said he, "I felt as if I were destined for some great enterprise. My feelings are profound; but I possessed a coolness of judgment that fitted me for illustrious achievements. This sentiment of the worth of my nature supported me, when others would have been oppressed; for I deemed it criminal to throw away in useless grief those talents that might be useful to my fellow-creatures. When I reflected on the work I had completed, no less a one than the creation of a sensitive and rational animal, I could not rank myself with the herd of common projectors. But this feeling, which supported me in the commencement of my career, now serves only to plunge me lower in the dust. All my speculations and hopes are as nothing; and, like the archangel who aspired to omnipotence, I am chained in an eternal hell. My imagination was vivid, yet my powers of analysis and application were intense; by the union of these qualities I conceived the idea, and executed the creation of a man. Even now I cannot recollect, without passion, my reveries while the work was incomplete. I trod heaven in my thoughts, now exulting in my powers, now burning with the idea of their effects. From my infancy I was imbued with high hopes and a lofty ambition; but how am I sunk! Oh! my friend, if you had known me as I once was, you would not recognize me in this state of degradation. Despondency rarely visited my heart; a high destiny seemed to bear me on, until I fell, never, never again to rise."

Must I then lose this admirable being? I have longed for a friend; I have sought one who would sympathize with and love me. Behold, on these desert seas I have found such a one; but, I fear, I have gained him only to know his value, and lose him. I would reconcile him to life, but he repulses the idea.

"I thank you, Walton," he said, "for your kind intentions towards so miserable a wretch; but when you speak of new ties, and fresh affections, think you that any can replace those who are gone? Can any man be to me as Clerval was; or any woman another Elizabeth? Even where the affections are not strongly moved by any superior excellence, the companions of our childhood always possess a certain power over our minds, which hardly any later friend can obtain. They know our infantine dispositions, which, however they may be afterwards modified, are never eradicated; and they can judge of our actions with more certain conclusions as to the integrity of our motives. A sister or a brother can never, unless indeed such symptoms have been shewn early, suspect the other of fraud or false dealing, when another friend, however strongly he may be attached, may, in spite of himself, be invaded with suspicion. But I enjoyed friends, dear not only through habit and association, but from their own merits; and, wherever I am, the soothing voice of my Elizabeth, and the conversation of Clerval, will be ever whispered in my ear. They are dead; and but one feeling in such a solitude can persuade me to preserve my life. If I were engaged in any high undertaking or design, fraught with extensive utility to my fellow-creatures, then could I live to fulfil it. But such is not my destiny; I must pursue and destroy the being to whom I gave existence; then my lot on earth will be fulfilled, and I may die."

September 2d.

My beloved Sister,

I write to you, encompassed by peril, and ignorant whether I am ever doomed to see again dear England, and the dearer friends that inhabit it. I am surrounded by mountains of ice, which admit of no escape, and threaten every moment to crush my vessel. The brave fellows, whom I have persuaded to be my companions, look towards me for aid; but I have none to bestow. There is something terribly appalling in our situation, yet my courage and hopes do not desert me. We may survive; and if we do not, I will repeat the lessons of my Seneca, and die with a good heart.

Yet what, Margaret, will be the state of your mind? You will not hear of my destruction, and you will anxiously await my return. Years will pass, and you will have visitings of despair, and yet be tortured by hope. Oh! my beloved sister, the sickening failings of your heart-felt expectations are, in prospect, more terrible to me than my own death. But you have a husband, and lovely children; you may be happy: heaven bless you, and make you so!

My unfortunate guest regards me with the tenderest compassion. He endeavours to fill me with hope; and talks as if life were a possession which he valued. He reminds me how often the same accidents have happened to other navigators, who have attempted this sea, and, in spite of myself, he fills me with cheerful auguries. Even the sailors feel the power of his eloquence: when he speaks, they no longer despair; he rouses their energies, and, while they hear his voice, they believe these vast mountains of ice are mole-hills, which will vanish before the resolutions of man. These feelings are transitory; each day's expectation delayed fills them with fear, and I almost dread a mutiny caused by this despair.

September 5th.

A scene has just passed of such uncommon interest, that although it is highly probable that these papers may never reach you, yet I cannot forbear recording it.

We are still surrounded by mountains of ice, still in imminent danger of being crushed in their conflict. The cold is excessive, and many of my unfortunate comrades have already found a grave amidst this scene of desolation. Frankenstein has daily declined in health: a feverish fire still glimmers in his eyes; but he is exhausted, and, when suddenly roused to any exertion, he speedily sinks again into apparent lifelessness.

I mentioned in my last letter the fears I entertained of a mutiny. This morning, as I sat watching the wan countenance of my friend—his eyes half closed, and his limbs hanging listlessly,—I was roused by half a dozen of the sailors, who desired admission into the cabin. They entered; and their leader addressed me. He told me that he and his companions had been chosen by the other sailors to come in deputation to me, to make me a demand, which, in justice, I could not refuse. We were immured in ice, and should probably never escape; but they feared that if, as was possible, the ice should dissipate, and a free passage be opened, I should be rash enough to continue my voyage, and lead them into fresh dangers, after they might happily have surmounted this. They desired, therefore, that I should engage with a solemn promise, that if the vessel should be freed, I would instantly direct my course southward.

This speech troubled me. I had not despaired; nor had I yet conceived the idea of returning, if set free. Yet could I, in justice, or even in possibility, refuse this demand? I hesitated before I answered; when Frankenstein, who had at first been silent, and, indeed, appeared hardly to have force enough to attend, now roused himself; his eyes sparkled, and his cheeks flushed with momentary vigour. Turning towards the men, he said—

"What do you mean? What do you demand of your captain? Are you then so easily turned from your design? Did you not call this a glorious expedition? and wherefore was it glorious? Not because the way was smooth and placid as a southern sea, but because it was full of dangers and terror; because, at every new incident, your fortitude was to be called forth, and your courage exhibited; because danger and death surrounded, and these dangers you were to brave and overcome. For this was it a glorious, for this was it an honourable undertaking. You were hereafter to be hailed as the benefactors of your species; your name adored, as belonging to brave men who encountered death for honour and the benefit of mankind. And now, behold, with the first imagination of danger, or, if you will, the first mighty and terrific trial of your courage, you shrink away, and are content to be handed down as men who had not strength enough to endure cold and peril; and so, poor souls, they were chilly, and returned to their warm fire-sides. Why, that requires not this preparation; ye need not have come thus far, and dragged your captain to the shame of a defeat, merely to prove yourselves cowards. Oh! be men, or be more than men. Be steady to your purposes, and firm as a rock. This ice is not made of such stuff as your hearts might be; it is mutable, cannot withstand you, if you say that it shall not. Do not return to your families with the stigma of disgrace marked on your brows. Return as heroes who have fought and conquered, and who know not what it is to turn their backs on the foe."

He spoke this with a voice so modulated to the different feelings expressed in his speech, with an eye so full of lofty design and heroism, that can you wonder that these men were moved. They looked at one another, and were unable to reply. I spoke; I told them to retire, and consider of what had been said: that I would not lead them further north, if they strenuously desired the contrary; but that I hoped that, with reflection, their courage would return.

They retired, and I turned towards my friend; but he was sunk in languor, and almost deprived of life.

How all this will terminate, I know not; but I had rather die, than return shamefully,—my purpose unfulfilled. Yet I fear such will be my fate; the men, unsupported by ideas of glory and honour, can never willingly continue to endure their present hardships.

September 7th.

The die is cast; I have consented to return, if we are not destroyed. Thus are my hopes blasted by cowardice and indecision; I come back ignorant and disappointed. It requires more philosophy than I possess, to bear this injustice with patience.

September 12th.

It is past; I am returning to England. I have lost my hopes of utility and glory;—I have lost my friend. But I will endeavour to detail these bitter circumstances to you, my dear sister; and, while I am wafted towards England, and towards you, I will not despond.

September 9th, the ice began to move, and roarings like thunder were heard at a distance, as the islands split and cracked in every direction. We were in the most imminent peril; but, as we could only remain passive, my chief attention was occupied by my unfortunate guest, whose illness increased in such a degree, that he was entirely confined to his bed. The ice cracked behind us, and was driven with force towards the north; a breeze sprung from the west, and on the 11th the passage towards the south became perfectly free. When the sailors saw this, and that their return to their native country was apparently assured, a shout of tumultuous joy broke from them, loud and long-continued. Frankenstein, who was dozing, awoke, and asked the cause of the tumult. "They shout," I said, "because they will soon return to England."

"Do you then really return?"

"Alas! yes; I cannot withstand their demands. I cannot lead them unwillingly to danger, and I must return."

"Do so, if you will; but I will not. You may give up your purpose; but mine is assigned to me by heaven, and I dare not. I am weak; but surely the spirits who assist my vengeance will endow me with sufficient strength." Saying this, he endeavoured to spring from the bed, but the exertion was too great for him; he fell back, and fainted.

It was long before he was restored; and I often thought that life was entirely extinct. At length he opened his eyes, but he breathed with difficulty, and was unable to speak. The surgeon gave him a composing draught, and ordered us to leave him undisturbed. In the mean time he told me, that my friend had certainly not many hours to live.

His sentence was pronounced; and I could only grieve, and be patient. I sat by his bed watching him; his eyes were closed, and I thought he slept; but presently he called to me in a feeble voice, and, bidding me come near, said—"Alas! the strength I relied on is gone; I feel that I shall soon die, and he, my enemy and persecutor, may still be in being. Think not, Walton, that in the last moments of my existence I feel that burning hatred, and ardent desire of revenge, I once expressed, but I feel myself justified in desiring the death of my adversary. During these last days I have been occupied in examining my past conduct; nor do I find it blameable. In a fit of enthusiastic madness I created a rational creature, and was bound towards him, to assure, as far as was in my power, his happiness and well-being. This was my duty; but there was another still paramount to that. My duties towards my fellow-creatures had greater claims to my attention, because they included a greater proportion of happiness or misery. Urged by this view, I refused, and I did right in refusing, to create a companion for the first creature. He shewed unparalleled malignity and selfishness, in evil: he destroyed my friends; he devoted to destruction beings who possessed exquisite sensations, happiness, and wisdom; nor do I know where this thirst for vengeance may end. Miserable himself, that he may render no other wretched, he ought to die. The task of his destruction was mine, but I have failed. When actuated by selfish and vicious motives, I asked you to undertake my unfinished work; and I renew this request now, when I am only induced by reason and virtue.

"Yet I cannot ask you to renounce your country and friends, to fulfil this task; and now, that you are returning to England, you will have little chance of meeting with him. But the consideration of these points, and the well-balancing of what you may esteem your duties, I leave to you; my judgment and ideas are already disturbed by the near approach of death. I dare not ask you to do what I think right, for I may still be misled by passion.

"That he should live to be an instrument of mischief disturbs me; in other respects this hour, when I momentarily expect my release, is the only happy one which I have enjoyed for several years. The forms of the beloved dead flit before me, and I hasten to their arms. Farewell, Walton! Seek happiness in tranquillity, and avoid ambition, even if it be only the apparently innocent one of distinguishing yourself in science and discoveries. Yet why do I say this? I have myself been blasted in these hopes, yet another may succeed."

His voice became fainter as he spoke; and at length, exhausted by his effort, he sunk into silence. About half an hour afterwards he attempted again to speak, but was unable; he pressed my hand feebly, and his eyes closed for ever, while the irradiation of a gentle smile passed away from his lips.

Margaret, what comment can I make on the untimely extinction of this glorious spirit? What can I say, that will enable you to understand the depth of my sorrow? All that I should express would be inadequate and feeble. My tears flow; my mind is overshadowed by a cloud of disappointment. But I journey towards England, and I may there find consolation.

I am interrupted. What do these sounds portend? It is midnight; the breeze blows fairly, and the watch on deck scarcely stir. Again; there is a sound as of a human voice, but hoarser; it comes from the cabin where the remains of Frankenstein still lie. I must arise, and examine. Good night, my sister.

Great God! what a scene has just taken place! I am yet dizzy with the remembrance of it. I hardly know whether I shall have the power to detail it; yet the tale which I have recorded would be incomplete without this final and wonderful catastrophe.

I entered the cabin, where lay the remains of my ill-fated and admirable friend. Over him hung a form which I cannot find words to describe; gigantic in stature, yet uncouth and distorted in its proportions. As he hung over the coffin, his face was concealed by long locks of ragged hair; but one vast hand was extended, in colour and apparent texture like that of a mummy. When he heard the sound of my approach, he ceased to utter exclamations of grief and horror, and sprung towards the window. Never did I behold a vision so horrible as his face, of such loathsome, yet appalling hideousness. I shut my eyes involuntarily, and endeavoured to recollect what were my duties with regard to this destroyer. I called on him to stay.

He paused, looking on me with wonder; and, again turning towards the lifeless form of his creator, he seemed to forget my presence, and every feature and gesture seemed instigated by the wildest rage of some uncontrollable passion.

"That is also my victim!" he exclaimed; "in his murder my crimes are consummated; the miserable series of my being is wound to its close! Oh, Frankenstein! generous and self-devoted being! what does it avail that I now ask thee to pardon me? I, who irretrievably destroyed thee by destroying all thou lovedst. Alas! he is cold; he may not answer me."

His voice seemed suffocated; and my first impulses, which had suggested to me the duty of obeying the dying request of my friend, in destroying his enemy, were now suspended by a mixture of curiosity and compassion. I approached this tremendous being; I dared not again raise my looks upon his face, there was something so scaring and unearthly in his ugliness. I attempted to speak, but the words died away on my lips. The monster continued to utter wild and incoherent self-reproaches. At length I gathered resolution to address him, in a pause of the tempest of his passion: "Your repentance," I said, "is now superfluous. If you had listened to the voice of conscience, and heeded the stings of remorse, before you had urged your diabolical vengeance to this extremity, Frankenstein would yet have lived."

"And do you dream?" said the dæmon; "do you think that I was then dead to agony and remorse?—He," he continued, pointing to the corpse, "he suffered not more in the consummation of the deed;—oh! not the ten-thousandth portion of the anguish that was mine during the lingering detail of its execution. A frightful selfishness hurried me on, while my heart was poisoned with remorse. Think ye that the groans of Clerval were music to my ears? My heart was fashioned to be susceptible of love and sympathy; and, when wrenched by misery to vice and hatred, it did not endure the violence of the change without torture, such as you cannot even imagine.

"After the murder of Clerval, I returned to Switzerland, heart-broken and overcome. I pitied Frankenstein; my pity amounted to horror: I abhorred myself. But when I discovered that he, the author at once of my existence and of its unspeakable torments, dared to hope for happiness; that while he accumulated wretchedness and despair upon me, he sought his own enjoyment in feelings and passions from the indulgence of which I was for ever barred, then impotent envy and bitter indignation filled me with an insatiable thirst for vengeance. I recollected my threat, and resolved that it should be accomplished. I knew that I was preparing for myself a deadly torture; but I was the slave, not the master of an impulse, which I detested, yet could not disobey. Yet when she died!—nay, then I was not miserable. I had cast off all feeling, subdued all anguish to riot in the excess of my despair. Evil thenceforth became my good. Urged thus far, I had no choice but to adapt my nature to an element which I had willingly chosen. The completion of my demoniacal design became an insatiable passion. And now it is ended; there is my last victim!"

I was at first touched by the expressions of his misery; yet when I called to mind what Frankenstein had said of his powers of eloquence and persuasion, and when I again cast my eyes on the lifeless form of my friend, indignation was re-kindled within me.

"Wretch!" I said, "it is well that you come here to whine over the desolation that you have made. You throw a torch into a pile of buildings, and when they are consumed you sit among the ruins, and lament the fall. Hypocritical fiend! if he whom you mourn still lived, still would he be the object, again would he become the prey of your accursed vengeance. It is not pity that you feel; you lament only because the victim of your malignity is withdrawn from your power."

"Oh, it is not thus—not thus," interrupted the being; "yet such must be the impression conveyed to you by what appears to be the purport of my actions. Yet I seek not a fellow-feeling in my misery. No sympathy may I ever find. When I first sought it, it was the love of virtue, the feelings of happiness and affection with which my whole being overflowed, that I wished to be participated. But now, that virtue has become to me a shadow, and that happiness and affection are turned into bitter and loathing despair, in what should I seek for sympathy? I am content to suffer alone, while my sufferings shall endure: when I die, I am well satisfied that abhorrence and opprobrium should load my memory. Once my fancy was soothed with dreams of virtue, of fame, and of enjoyment. Once I falsely hoped to meet with beings, who, pardoning my outward form, would love me for the excellent qualities which I was capable of bringing forth. I was nourished with high thoughts of honour and devotion. But now vice has degraded me beneath the meanest animal. No crime, no mischief, no malignity, no misery, can be found comparable to mine. When I call over the frightful catalogue of my deeds, I cannot believe that I am he whose thoughts were once filled with sublime and transcendant visions of the beauty and the majesty of goodness. But it is even so; the fallen angel becomes a malignant devil. Yet even that enemy of God and man had friends and associates in his desolation; I am quite alone.

"You, who call Frankenstein your friend, seem to have a knowledge of my crimes and his misfortunes. But, in the detail which he gave you of them, he could not sum up the hours and months of misery which I endured, wasting in impotent passions. For whilst I destroyed his hopes, I did not satisfy my own desires. They were for ever ardent and craving; still I desired love and fellowship, and I was still spurned. Was there no injustice in this? Am I to be thought the only criminal, when all human kind sinned against me? Why do you not hate Felix, who drove his friend from his door with contumely? Why do you not execrate the rustic who sought to destroy the saviour of his child? Nay, these are virtuous and immaculate beings! I, the miserable and the abandoned, am an abortion, to be spurned at, and kicked, and trampled on. Even now my blood boils at the recollection of this injustice.

"But it is true that I am a wretch. I have murdered the lovely and the helpless; I have strangled the innocent as they slept, and grasped to death his throat who never injured me or any other living thing. I have devoted my creator, the select specimen of all that is worthy of love and admiration among men, to misery; I have pursued him even to that irremediable ruin. There he lies, white and cold in death. You hate me; but your abhorrence cannot equal that with which I regard myself. I look on the hands which executed the deed; I think on the heart in which the imagination of it was conceived, and long for the moment when they will meet my eyes, when it will haunt my thoughts, no more.

"Fear not that I shall be the instrument of future mischief. My work is nearly complete. Neither your's nor any man's death is needed to consummate the series of my being, and accomplish that which must be done; but it requires my own. Do not think that I shall be slow to perform this sacrifice. I shall quit your vessel on the ice-raft which brought me hither, and shall seek the most northern extremity of the globe; I shall collect my funeral pile, and consume to ashes this miserable frame, that its remains may afford no light to any curious and unhallowed wretch, who would create such another as I have been. I shall die. I shall no longer feel the agonies which now consume me, or be the prey of feelings unsatisfied, yet unquenched. He is dead who called me into being; and when I shall be no more, the very remembrance of us both will speedily vanish. I shall no longer see the sun or stars, or feel the winds play on my cheeks. Light, feeling, and sense, will pass away; and in this condition must I find my happiness. Some years ago, when the images which this world affords first opened upon me, when I felt the cheering warmth of summer, and heard the rustling of the leaves and the chirping of the birds, and these were all to me, I should have wept to die; now it is my only consolation. Polluted by crimes, and torn by the bitterest remorse, where can I find rest but in death?

"Farewell! I leave you, and in you the last of human kind whom these eyes will ever behold. Farewell, Frankenstein! If thou wert yet alive, and yet cherished a desire of revenge against me, it would be better satiated in my life than in my destruction. But it was not so; thou didst seek my extinction, that I might not cause greater wretchedness; and if yet, in some mode unknown to me, thou hast not yet ceased to think and feel, thou desirest not my life for my own misery. Blasted as thou wert, my agony was still superior to thine; for the bitter sting of remorse may not cease to rankle in my wounds until death shall close them for ever.

"But soon," he cried, with sad and solemn enthusiasm, "I shall die, and what I now feel be no longer felt. Soon these burning miseries will be extinct. I shall ascend my funeral pile triumphantly, and exult in the agony of the torturing flames. The light of that conflagration will fade away; my ashes will be swept into the sea by the winds. My spirit will sleep in peace; or if it thinks, it will not surely think thus. Farewell."

He sprung from the cabin-window, as he said this, upon the ice-raft which lay close to the vessel. He was soon borne away by the waves, and lost in darkness and distance.

THE END.

Mary Shelley on *Frankenstein*

The following is Mary Shelley's Introduction to the 1831 edition of *Frankenstein.*

The Publishers of the Standard Novels, in selecting "Frankenstein" for one of their series, expressed a wish that I should furnish them with some account of the origin of the story. I am the more willing to comply, because I shall thus give a general answer to the question, so very frequently asked me—"How I, then a young girl, came to think of, and to dilate upon, so very hideous an idea?" It is true that I am very averse to bringing myself forward in print; but as my account will only appear as an appendage to a former production, and as it will be confined to such topics as have connection with my authorship alone, I can scarcely accuse myself of a personal intrusion.

It is not singular that, as the daughter of two persons of distinguished literary celebrity, I should very early in life have thought of writing. As a child I scribbled; and my favourite pastime, during the hours given me for recreation, was to "write stories." Still I had a dearer pleasure than this, which was the formation of castles in the air—the indulging in waking dreams—the following up trains of thought, which had for their subject the formation of a succession of imaginary incidents. My dreams were at once more fantastic and agreeable than my writings. In the latter I was a close imitator—rather doing as others had done, than putting down the suggestions of my own mind. What I wrote was intended at least for one other eye—my childhood's companion and friend; but my dreams were all my own; I accounted for them to nobody; they were my refuge when annoyed—my dearest pleasure when free.

I lived principally in the country as a girl, and passed a considerable time in Scotland. I made occasional visits to the more picturesque parts; but my habitual residence was on the blank and dreary northern shores of the Tay, near Dundee. Blank and dreary on retrospection I call them; they were not so to me then. They were the eyry of freedom, and the pleasant region where unheeded I could commune with the creatures of my fancy. I wrote then—but in a most common-place style. It was beneath the trees of the grounds belonging to our house, or on the bleak sides of the woodless mountains near, that my true compositions, the airy flights of my imagination, were born and fostered. I did not make myself the heroine of my tales. Life appeared to me too common-place an affair as regarded myself. I could not figure to myself that romantic woes or wonderful events would ever be my lot; but I was not confined to my own identity, and I could people the hours with creations far more interesting to me at that age, than my own sensations.

After this my life became busier, and reality stood in place of fiction. My husband, however, was from the first, very anxious that I should prove myself worthy of my parentage, and enrol myself on the page of fame. He was for ever inciting me to obtain literary reputation, which even on my own part I cared for then, though since I have become infinitely indifferent to it. At this time he desired that I should write, not so much with the idea that I could produce any thing worthy of notice, but that he might himself judge how far I possessed the promise of better things hereafter. Still I did nothing. Travelling, and the cares of a family, occupied my time; and study, in the way of reading, or improving my ideas in communication with his far more cultivated mind, was all of literary employment that engaged my attention.

In the summer of 1816, we visited Switzerland, and became the neighbours of Lord Byron. At first we spent our pleasant hours on the lake, or wandering on its shores; and Lord Byron, who was writing the third canto of Childe Harold, was the only one among us who put his thoughts upon paper. These, as he brought them successively to us, clothed in all the light and harmony of poetry, seemed to stamp as divine the glories of heaven and earth, whose influences we partook with him.

But it proved a wet, ungenial summer, and incessant rain often confined us for days to the house. Some volumes of ghost stories, translated from the German into French, fell into our hands. There was the History of the Inconstant Lover, who, when he thought to clasp the bride to whom he had pledged his vows, found himself in the arms of the pale ghost of her whom he had deserted. There was the tale of the sinful founder of his race, whose miserable doom it was to bestow the kiss of death on all the younger sons of his fated house, just when they reached the age of promise. His gigantic, shadowy form, clothed like the ghost in Hamlet, in complete armour, but with the beaver up, was seen at midnight, by the moon's fitful beams, to advance slowly along the gloomy avenue. The shape was lost beneath the shadow of the castle walls; but soon a gate swung back, a step was heard, the door of the chamber opened, and he advanced to the couch of the blooming youths, cradled in healthy sleep. Eternal sorrow sat upon his face as he bent down and kissed the forehead of the boys, who from that hour withered like flowers snapt upon the stalk. I have not seen these stories since then; but their incidents are as fresh in my mind as if I had read them yesterday.

"We will each write a ghost story," said Lord Byron; and his proposition was acceded to. There were four of us. The noble author began a tale, a fragment of which he printed at the end of his poem of Mazeppa. Shelley, more apt to embody ideas and sentiments in the radiance of brilliant imagery, and in the music of the most melodious verse that adorns our language, than to invent the machinery of a story, commenced one founded on the experiences of his early life. Poor Polidori had some terrible idea about a skull-headed lady, who was so punished for peeping through a key-hole—what to see I forget—something very shocking and wrong of course; but when she was reduced to a worse condition than the renowned Tom of Coventry, he did not know what to do with her, and was obliged to despatch her to the tomb of the Capulets, the only place for which she was fitted. The illustrious poets also, annoyed by the platitude of prose, speedily relinquished their uncongenial task.

I busied myself *to think of a story,*—a story to rival those which had excited us to this task. One which would speak to the mysterious fears of our nature, and awaken thrilling horror—one to make the reader dread to look round, to curdle the blood, and quicken the beatings of the heart. If I did not accomplish these things, my ghost story would be unworthy of its name. I thought and pondered—vainly. I felt that blank incapability of invention which is the greatest misery of authorship, when dull Nothing replies to our anxious invocations. *Have you thought of a story?* I was asked each morning, and each morning I was forced to reply with a mortifying negative.

Every thing must have a beginning, to speak in Sanchean phrase; and that beginning must be linked to something that went before. The Hindoos give the world an elephant to support it, but they make the elephant stand upon a tortoise. Invention, it must be humbly admitted, does not consist in creating out of void, but out of chaos; the materials must, in the first place, be afforded: it can give form to dark, shapeless substances, but cannot bring into being the substance itself. In all matters of discovery and invention, even of those that appertain to the imagination, we are continually reminded of the story of Columbus and his egg. Invention consists in the capacity of seizing on the capabilities of a subject, and in the power of moulding and fashioning ideas suggested to it.

Many and long were the conversations between Lord Byron and Shelley, to which I was a devout but nearly silent listener. During one of these, various philosophical doctrines were discussed, and among others the nature of the principle of life, and whether there was any probability of its ever being discovered and communicated. They talked of the experiments of Dr. Darwin, (I speak not of what the Doctor really did, or said that he did, but, as more to my purpose, of what was then spoken of as having been done by him,) who preserved a piece of vermicelli in a glass case, till by some extraordinary means it began to move with voluntary motion. Not thus, after all, would life be given. Perhaps a corpse would be re-animated; galvanism had given token of such things: perhaps the component parts of a creature might be manufactured, brought together, and endued with vital warmth.

Night waned upon this talk, and even the witching hour had gone by, before we retired to rest. When I placed my head on my pillow, I did not sleep, nor could I be said to think. My imagination, unbidden, possessed and guided me, gifting the successive images that arose in my mind with a vividness far beyond the usual bounds of reverie. I saw—with shut eyes, but acute mental vision,—I saw the pale student of unhallowed arts kneeling beside the thing he had put together. I saw the hideous phantasm of a man stretched out, and then, on the working of some powerful engine, show signs of life, and stir with an uneasy, half vital motion. Frightful must it be; for supremely frightful would be the effect of any human endeavour to mock the stupendous mechanism of the Creator of the world. His success would terrify the artist; he would rush away from his odious handywork, horror-stricken. He would hope that, left to itself, the slight spark of life which he had communicated would fade; that this thing, which had received such imperfect animation, would subside into dead matter; and he might sleep in the belief that the silence of the grave would quench for ever the transient existence of the hideous corpse which he had looked upon as the cradle of life. He sleeps; but he is awakened; he opens his eyes; behold the horrid thing stands at his bedside, opening his curtains, and looking on him with yellow, watery, but speculative eyes.

I opened mine in terror. The idea so possessed my mind, that a thrill of fear ran through me, and I wished to exchange the ghastly image of my fancy for the realities around. I see them still; the very room, the dark *parquet,* the closed shutters, with the moonlight struggling through, and the sense I had that the glassy lake and white high Alps were beyond. I could not so easily get rid of my hideous phantom; still it haunted me. I must try to think of something else. I recurred to my ghost story,—my tiresome unlucky ghost story! O! if I could only contrive one which would frighten my reader as I myself had been frightened that night!

Swift as light and as cheering was the idea that broke in upon me. "I have found it! What terrified me will terrify others; and I need only describe the spectre which had haunted my midnight pillow." On the morrow I announced that I had *thought of a story.* I began that day with the words, *It was on a dreary night of November,* making only a transcript of the grim terrors of my waking dream.

At first I thought but of a few pages—of a short tale; but Shelley urged me to develope the idea at greater length. I certainly did not owe the suggestion of one incident, nor scarcely of one train of feeling, to my husband, and yet but for his incitement, it would never have taken the form in which it was presented to the world. From this declaration I must except the preface. As far as I can recollect, it was entirely written by him.

And now, once again, I bid my hideous progeny go forth and prosper. I have an affection for it, for it was the offspring of happy days, when death and grief were but words, which found no true echo in my heart. Its several pages speak of many a walk, many a drive, and many a conversation, when I was not alone; and my companion was one who, in this world, I shall never see more. But this is for myself; my readers have nothing to do with these associations.

I will add but one word as to the alterations I have made. They are principally those of style. I have changed no portion of the story, nor introduced any new ideas or circumstances. I have mended the language where it was so bald as to interfere with the interest of the narrative; and these changes occur almost exclusively in the beginning of the first volume. Throughout they are entirely confined to such parts as are mere adjuncts to the story, leaving the core and substance of it untouched.

London, October 15. 1831.

Critical Excerpts

1. [T]he author seems to us to disclose uncommon powers of poetic imagination. The feeling with which we perused the unexpected and fearful, yet, allowing the possibility of the event, very natural conclusion of Frankenstein's experiment, shook a little even our firm nerves. . . . It is no slight merit in our eyes, that the tale, though wild in incident, is written in plain and forcible English, without exhibiting that mixture of hyperbolical Germanisms with which tales of wonder are usually told, as if it were necessary that the language should be as extravagant as the fiction. The ideas of the author are always clearly as well as forcibly expressed; and his[1] descriptions of landscape have in them the choice requisites of truth, freshness, precision, and beauty. . . . Upon the whole, the work impresses us with a high idea of the author's original genius and happy power of expression. . . . If Gray's definition of Paradise, to lie on a couch, namely, and read new novels, come any thing near truth, no small praise is due to him, who, like the author of *Frankenstein,* has enlarged the sphere of that fascinating enjoyment.

Sir Walter Scott,
"Remarks on *Frankenstein;*
or, The Modern Prometheus: A Novel,"
in *Blackwood's Edinburgh Magazine,* 1818

---

[1] *Frankenstein* was first published anonymously in 1818.

2. This novel rests its claim on being a source of powerful and profound emotion. . . . The sentiments are so affectionate and so innocent—the characters of the subordinate agents in this strange drama are clothed in the light of such a mild and gentle mind—the pictures of domestic manners are of the most simple and attaching character: the father's is irresistible and deep. Nor are the crimes and malevolence of the single Being, though indeed withering and tremendous, the offspring of any unaccountable propensity to evil, but flow irresistibly from certain causes fully adequate to their production. They are the children, as it were, of Necessity and Human Nature. In this the direct moral of the book consists; and it is perhaps the most important, and of the most universal application, of any moral that can be enforced by example. Treat a person ill, and he will become wicked. Requite affection with scorn;—let one being be selected, for whatever cause, as the refuse of his kind—divide him, a social being, from society, and you impose upon him the irresistible obligations—malevolence and selfishness. It is thus that, too often in society, those who are best qualified to be its benefactors and its ornaments, are branded by some accident with scorn, and changed, by neglect and solitude of heart, into a scourge and a curse.

Percy Bysshe Shelley,
"On *Frankenstein,*"
in *The Athenaeum,* 1832

3. The Monster in *Frankenstein,* sublime in his ugliness, his simplicity, his passions, his wrongs, and his strength, physical and mental, embodies in the wild narrative more than one distinct and important moral theory or proposition. In himself he is the type of a class deeply and cruelly aggrieved by nature—the Deformed or hideous in figure or countenance, whose

sympathies and passions are as strong as their bodily deformity renders them repulsive. An amount of human woe, great beyond reckoning, have such experience. When the Monster pleads his cause against cruel man, and when he finally disappears on his raft on the icy sea to build his own funeral pile, he pleads the cause of all that class who have so strong a claim on the help and sympathy of the world, yet find little else but disgust or, at best, neglect.

The Monster created by Frankenstein is also an illustration of the embodied consequences of our actions. As he, when formed and endowed with life, became to his imaginary creator an everlasting, ever-present curse, so may one single action, nay a word, or it may be a thought, thrown upon the tide of time, become to its originator a curse, never to be recovered, never to be shaken off.

Richard Hengist Horne,
"Mrs. Shelley," *A New Spirit of the Age,*
ed. Richard Hengist Horne (1844),
in *The World's Classics,*
Oxford University Press, 1907

4. Even the protracted descriptions of domestic life assume a new and deeper meaning, for the shadow of the monster broods over them. One by one those whom Frankenstein loves fall victims to the malice of the being he has endowed with life. Unceasingly and unrelentingly the loathsome creature dogs our imagination, more awful when he lurks unseen than when he stands actually before us. With hideous malignity he slays Frankenstein's young brother, and by a fiendish device causes Justine, an innocent girl, to be executed for the crime. Yet ere long our sympathy, which has hitherto been entirely with Frankenstein, is unexpectedly diverted to the monster who, it would

seem, is wicked only because he is eternally divorced from human society.

Edith Birkhead,
The Tale of Terror: A Study of the Gothic Romance (1921),
Russell & Russell, 1963

5. If we stand back from Mary Shelley's novel in order better to view its archetypal shape, we see it as the quest of a solitary and ravaged consciousness first for consolation, then for revenge, and finally for a self-destruction that will be apocalyptic, that will bring down the creator with his creature. . . . The profound dejection endemic in Mary Shelley's novel is fundamental to the Romantic mythology of the self, for all Romantic horrors are diseases of excessive consciousness, of the self unable to bear the self. . . .

A Romantic poet fought against self-consciousness through the strength of what he called imagination, a more than rational energy by which thought could seek to heal itself. But Frankenstein's daemon . . . can win no release from his own story by telling it. . . .

. . . Frankenstein's creature can help neither himself nor others, for he has no natural ground to which he can return. . . . Mary Shelley, with marvelous appropriateness, brings her Romantic novel to a demonic conclusion in a world of ice. . . . There is a heroism fully earned in the being who cries farewell in a claim of sad triumph: "I shall ascend my funeral pile triumphantly and exult in the agony of the torturing flames." . . .

The fire of increased consciousness stolen from heaven ends as an isolated volcano cut off from other selves by an estranging sea. "The light of that conflagration will fade away; my ashes will be swept into the sea by the winds" is the exultant cry of Frankenstein's creature.

Harold Bloom,
from the Afterword to *Frankenstein*,
Signet-NAL, 1965

6. *Frankenstein* is constructed of three concentric layers, one within the other. In the outermost layer, Robert Walton . . . describes his voyage towards the North Pole and his encounter with Victor Frankenstein. In the main, middle layers, Frankenstein tells Walton how he created the monster and abandoned it in disgust, how it revenged itself by murdering all those he loved and how he finally turned and pursued it. In the very centre, the monster himself describes the development of his mind after the flight from the laboratory and his bitterness when men reject him. . . .

. . . At the centre of the triple structure is the story of the education of a natural man and of his dealings with his creator. . . . [H]ere . . . Mary Shelley is constructing something with the schematic character of a philosophic romance. The story of the monster's beginnings is the story of a child, and at the same time he recapitulates the development of aboriginal man. He awakens to the world of the senses, discovers fire and searches for food. When men reject him, he discovers society by watching the De Laceys in their cottage. Having thus acquired language, from Felix's reading of Volney he learns of human history; having learned to read, he discovers private sentiment in *Werther* and public virtue in Plutarch.

Most of all, it is through *Paradise Lost* that he comes to understand himself and his situation. . . . At the same time, through the copy of Frankenstein's journal . . . he learns that his situation is yet more desparate than theirs since he has been rejected without guilt and is utterly companionless.

M. K. Joseph,
from the Introduction to *Frankenstein,*
Oxford University Press, 1969

7. [Mary Shelley] hurtled into teen-age motherhood without any of the financial or social or familial supports that made bearing and rearing children a relaxed experience for the normal middle-class woman of her day. . . . She was an unwed mother, responsible for breaking up a marriage of a young woman just as much a mother as she. The father whom she adored broke furiously with her when she eloped; and Mary Wollstonecraft, the mother whose memory she revered, and whose books she was rereading throughout her teen-age years, had died in childbirth—died giving birth to Mary herself.

Surely no outside influence need be sought to explain Mary Shelley's fantasy of the newborn as at once monstrous agent of destruction and piteous victim of parental abandonment. "I, the miserable and the abandoned," cries the monster at the end of *Frankenstein,* "I am an abortion to be spurned at, and kicked, and trampled on. . . . I have murdered the lovely and the helpless. . . . I have devoted my creator to misery; I have pursued him even to that irremediable ruin."

. . . Mary Shelley comes honestly to grips with the dilemma of a newly created human being, a giant adult male in shape, who must swiftly recapitulate, and without the assistance of his terrified parent, the infantile and adolescent stages of human development.

. . . The material in *Frankenstein* about the abnormal, or monstrous, manifestations of the child-parent tie justifies, as much as does its famous monster,

Mary Shelley's reference to the novel as "my hideous progeny."

What Mary Shelley actually did in *Frankenstein* was to transform the standard Romantic matter of incest, infanticide, and patricide into a phantasmagoria of the nursery. . . .

Ellen Moers,
Literary Women,
Doubleday and Company, 1976

8. Shelley seems to suggest that, if the family is to be a viable institution for the transmission of domestic affection from one generation to the next, it must redefine that precious commodity in such a way that it can extend to the "outsiders" and become hardy enough to survive in the world outside the home. . . .

The one character who clearly exemplifies such a redefined notion of domestic affection is Safie, the daughter of a Christian Arab woman who, "born in freedom, spurned the bondage to which she was now reduced" upon her marriage to the Turk. Safie's father had rescued his wife from slavery, just as Victor's father had rescued Caroline Beaufort from poverty. But instead of translating her gratitude into lifelong subservience and sporadic charity, this woman taught her daughter "to aspire to higher powers of intellect, and an independence of spirit forbidden to the female followers of Mahomet" . . .

Although Safie is, like Mary Shelley, motherless when she must put her early training to the test, she applies her mother's teachings in a way that is intended to contrast, I believe, with the behavior of the passive Elizabeth, equally influenced by her adopted mother's teachings and example. Safie discovers that her mind is "sickened at the prospect of again returning to Asia, and being immured within the walls of a harem, allowed only to occupy herself with infantile amusements, ill suited to the temper of her soul, now accustomed to grand ideas and the noble emulation of virtue." In consequence, she not only refuses to wait for the possibility that her lover will miraculously find her, but actively seeks Felix out, traveling through Europe with only an attendant for protection. Had Elizabeth been encouraged "to aspire to higher powers of intellect, and an independence of spirit," she might have followed Victor to Ingolstadt and perhaps even insisted that he provide the Monster a companion for his wanderings. As it is, Victor cannot conceive of involving Elizabeth in his work on any level; both are petrified in fatally polarized worlds.

Kate Ellis,
"Monsters in the Garden: Mary Shelley and the Bourgeois Family,"
in *The Endurance of* Frankenstein: *Essays on Mary Shelley's Novel,*
ed. George Levine and U.C. Knoepflmacher, University of California Press, 1979

9. In the Romantic universe extremes meet, contraries are reconciled and even fused. *Frankenstein* begins with Walton's dream of a tropical paradise at the North Pole, and his Romantic vision in turn introduces Frankenstein's dream of the vital fire or "spark" interpenetrating and animating matter otherwise cold and dead. Both visions recall Coleridge's enthusiasm for the reconciliation of elements opposed or different *in kind,* whether in nature or in art. . . .

. . . The Monster's narrative reveals a conservative distrust of Romantic extremes, a Victorian longing for security, society, and self-command, symbolized (as in *Jane Eyre*) by the domestic hearth. Only when he loses all hope of companionship does he run, as it were, to extremes: first to fire; next, in bitterness of heart, to cold and ice; finally, in a condition of almost philosophical despair, to a "Romantic" synthesis of both in his dramatic suicide-by-fire at the North Pole.

Andrew Griffin,
"Fire and Ice in *Frankenstein*,"
in *The Endurance of* Frankenstein:
Essays on Mary Shelley's Novel,
University of California Press, 1979

10. [The] equation of femininity with a passivity that borders on the ultimate passivity of death is, in *Frankenstein* and in Mary Shelley's own life, associated with a dead mother. Caroline Beaufort Frankenstein, who nurses her dying father "with the greatest tenderness" and is the perfect daughter-wife to Alphonse Frankenstein, is a model accepted by Justine and by Elizabeth yet rejected (or forgotten) by the Monster and by Victor. Caroline is found by the elder Frankenstein near her father's coffin; on her own deathbed, she enjoins the "yielding" Elizabeth to take her place as mother and "supply my place to your younger cousins." It is significant that both she and Elizabeth are invoked in Victor's dream just after he has seen "the dull yellow eyes of the creature" to which he has given life. Presumably one of Victor's objects in finding "a passage to life" is to restore his mother and "renew life where death had apparently devoted the body to corruption"; but his dream only underscores his rejection of the maternal or female model.

U. C. Knoepflmacher,
"Thoughts on the Aggression of Daughters,"
in *The Endurance of* Frankenstein:
Essays on Mary Shelley's Novel,
University of California Press, 1979

11. Mary Shelley's entire literary career is characterized by . . . two competing impulses. . . . On the

one hand, she repeatedly bowed to the conventional prejudice against aggressive women by apologizing for or punishing her self-assertion: she claimed that her writing was always undertaken to please or profit someone else, she dreaded exposing her name or personal feelings to public scrutiny, and she subjected her ambitious characters to pain and loneliness. On the other hand, both in her numerous comments about her profession and by her ongoing literary activity, Mary Shelley demonstrated that imaginative self-expression was for her an important vehicle for proving her worth and, in that sense, for defining herself.

Shelley's characteristic ambivalence with regard to female self-assertion was largely a response to her very particular position within the competing value systems of the turbulent first decades of the nineteenth century. Mary Wollstonecraft Godwin Shelley internalized two conflicting models of behavior that became sharply delineated in the wake of the French Revolution As the daughter of William Godwin and Mary Wollstonecraft and the lover, then the wife, of Percy Shelley, Mary was always encouraged to live up to the Romantic ideal of the creative artist, to prove herself by means of her pen and her imagination. . . . [The] pressure to be "original" and "great" was, however, exerted by a relatively small number of artists and radicals; far more pervasive was what we have already seen to be the increasingly rigid social expectation that a woman should conform to the conventional model of feminine propriety.

Mary Poovey,
The Proper Lady and the Woman Writer: Ideology as Style in the Works of Mary Wollstonecraft, Mary Shelley, and Jane Austen,
University of Chicago Press, 1984

12. [E]x-nuclear physicist and science historian Brian Easlea detects in *Frankenstein* "Mary Shelley's indictment of masculine ambition" and an exposure of "the compulsive character of masculine science."[2] . . . Easlea focuses much of his attention upon the sexual and parenting metaphors used by "probing" scientists from the natural philosophers of the sixteenth century to the nuclear scientists of the present. He notes that Francis Bacon, the "Patriarck of Experimental Philosophy", called on his fellow men to inaugurate with him "the truly masculine birth of time", so as to achieve "the domination of man over the universe."[3] Easlea's point that such a universe was and overwhelmingly still is seen as a "resisting female" who must be "aggressively penetrated" and conquered can hardly be denied. He quotes science historian Carolyn Merchant's description of how, from Bacon's time onward, "official" attitudes toward Nature altered: "The constraints against penetration associated with the earth-mother image were transformed into sanctions for denudation. After the Scientific Revolution *Natura* no longer complains that her garments of modesty are being torn by the wrongful thrusts of man."[4]

Maurice Hindle,
from the Introduction to *Frankenstein*,
Penguin Books, 1985

13. By far the most important literary source for *Frankenstein* . . . is Milton's *Paradise Lost*, as repeated allusions in the novel remind us, beginning

---

[2]Brian Easlea, *Fathering the Unthinkable: Masculinity, Scientists, and the Nuclear Arms Race* (Pluto Press, London, 1983), pp. 28, 35.
[3]Quoted in ibid., p. 19.
[4]ibid., p. 22

with the title-page itself and culminating in the monster's own avid reading of the epic poem, which he takes to be true history. As the monster reflects upon his reading, he first compares his condition with Adam's, but then feels a frustration akin to Satan's, if not worse. Victor, who ought to correspond to God in this new creation, comes also to feel like Satan; he too bears a hell within him. The monster's earliest memories resemble those of Adam in *Paradise Lost* Book VIII, while his first sight of his own reflection in water is a travesty of Eve's similar revelation in Book IV. Likewise, the monster's vengeful declaration of war against human kind arises from a bitter feeling of exclusion from human joys, a hopeless envy described in terms similar to Satan's (*Paradise Lost,* iv. 505 ff.; ix. 114 ff.).

Frankenstein's relationship to Milton's epic is, however, more than a matter of incidental borrowings. . . . [I]t elaborates upon the connections between *two* kinds of myth: a myth of creation and a myth of transgression. *Frankenstein* does this too, but its sinister travesty collapses the two kinds of myth together so that now creation and transgression appear to be the same thing. . . . The accusations of impiety which greeted the publication of *Frankenstein* may surprise us today, but it seemed to some of Mary Shelley's first readers that the novel was calling into question the most sacred of stories, equating the Supreme Being with a blundering chemistry student.

Chris Baldick,
In Frankenstein's Shadow: Myth, Monstrosity, and Nineteenth-century Writing,
Oxford University Press-Clarendon, 1987

14. Victor Frankenstein embodies certain elements of Percy Shelley's temperament and character that had begun to trouble Mary Shelley. She perceived in

Percy an intellectual hubris or belief in the supreme importance of mental abstractions that led him to be insensitive to the feelings of those who did not share his ideas and enthusiasms. The Percy Shelley that Mary knew and loved lived in a world of abstract ideas; his actions were primarily motivated by theoretical principles, the quest for perfect beauty, love, freedom, goodness. While Mary Shelley endorsed and shared these goals, she had come to suspect that in Percy's case they sometimes masked an emotional narcissism, an unwillingness to confront the origins of his own desires or the impact of his demands on those most dependent upon him. . . .

Clerval embodies Mary Shelley's heroic ideal, the imaginative man who is capable of deep and abiding love and who takes responsibility for those dependent upon him. Clerval both embarks on "a voyage of discovery to the land of knowledge" and also immediately delays that voyage to nurse his sick friend back to health. He thus combines intellectual curiosity with a capacity for nurturing others. . . . Clerval and Victor Frankenstein together comprise the Percy Shelley with whom Mary Godwin had fallen in love. But the murder of Clerval annihilates the most positive dimensions of Percy Shelley in the novel, leaving Frankenstein as the image of all that Mary Shelley most feared in both her husband and in the Romantic project he served.

Anne K. Mellor,
Mary Shelley: Her Life, Her Fiction, Her Monsters,
Routledge, 1989

15. Both Walton and Frankenstein devote their emotional energy not to empathic feelings or domestic affections but to egoistic dreams of conquering the boundaries of nature or of death. Not only have they diverted their libidinal desires away from normal

erotic objects, but in the process they have engaged in a particular mode of thinking which we might call "scientific." Frankenstein and Walton are both the products of the scientific revolution of the seventeenth century. They have been taught to see nature "objectively," as something separate from themselves, as passive and even dead matter—as the "object of my affection"—that can and should be penetrated, analyzed and controlled. They thus accord nature no living soul or "personhood" requiring recognition or respect.

Wordsworth had articulated the danger inherent in thinking of nature as something distinct from human consciousness. A reader of Wordsworth, Mary Shelley understood nature in his terms, as a sacred all-creating mother, a living organism or ecological community with which human beings interact in mutual dependence. To defy this bond, as both Frankenstein and Walton do, is to break one's ties with the source of life and health. Hence Frankenstein literally becomes sick in the process of carrying out his experiment: "every night I was oppressed by a slow fever, and I became nervous to a most painful degree"; and at its completion, he collapses in "a nervous fever" that confines him to his sickbed for several months.

Anne K. Mellor,
Mary Shelley: Her Life, Her Fiction, Her Monsters,
Routledge, 1989

16. . . . Taken as a whole, the novel can be understood to show the relation between creature and creator as a reflection of the relation between workers and those who control the forces of production. The paradoxes in *Frankenstein*—that the Creature is much larger and apparently more powerful than Victor yet is incapable of producing anything without him and that Victor is inextricably bound to it and it

to him—accurately represent the bond between worker and capitalist as both become involved in the process of production.

. . . Victor's story . . . lays out, in narrative form, the series of stages that Marx's writings describe workers going through as they become alienated from the objects they produce. . . .

. . . The literal details Shelley uses to convey Victor's state of mind while he is making the Creature—his isolated apartment, his inability to contact his family or even notice the changing of the seasons—can be read to represent what Marx describes as the two most immediate consequences of the worker's alienation for the product of his . . . labor: alienation from nature and from other men. . . . In Marx's terms, the Creature represents the externalization of Victor's alienation. The Creature, once produced, works to break any attachment Victor might form to the outside world. . . .

. . . [T]he materials Victor uses to make the Creature, parts of dismembered corpses, are emblematic of the way production breaks down what Marx calls the "body" of the natural world into a series of "dead" component parts to be used in manufacturing. . . . While Victor consciously insists he was intent only on creating ideal beauty and was horrified at the results when the Creature was completed, [his] journal entry reveals his awareness of what was happening during the process of production. Shelley's novel thus suggests that the ultimate nineteenth-century self-alienation arises not from production itself but from the denial of the materiality of that process.

Elsie B. Michie,
"Frankenstein and Marx's Theories of Alienated Labor,"
in *Approaches to Teaching Shelley's* Frankenstein,
ed. Stephen C. Behrendt,
The Modern Language Association of America, 1990

17. Through her family relations, ambitions, values, intelligence, and imagination, Mary Shelley mirrored the major questions of her era—and ours. She lived at the very beginning of an era of rapid social and technological change in which fixed values were largely replaced by relative ones and a stable order replaced by one in constant flux. Her Creature can be seen as a metaphor for the unprotected being who seeks its rights in a new, potentially hostile world. While she welcomed change, she was convinced of the need for a sound philosophy to deal with that change. For Mary Shelley, a world with no absolutes requires individuals and governments to make decisions on the basis of love and responsibility for the general good. In *Frankenstein,* she gives us her vision of the outcome should we fail. We are increasingly drawn to *Frankenstein* as we recognize in our society the shadow of Frankenstein and his Creature.

Betty T. Bennett,
"*Frankenstein* and the Uses of Biography,"
in *Approaches to Teaching Shelley's* Frankenstein,
The Modern Language Association of America, 1990

18. Some [readers] may want to suggest that . . . the domestic sphere defined by the women in *Frankenstein* bears Shelley's moral approval: it keeps men human, fosters their capacity for tenderness and affection, and restrains the excesses of their ambition—specifically, given Shelley's subtitle, their tendency to self-mythologizing Promethean transgression and isolation. Most [readers] will sense that, despite Victor's alternately self-lacerating and self-aggrandizing rhetoric, the novel does not indict him so much for violating the boundaries of life and death as for abdicating parental responsibility for the life he

has created. One may extend this view by considering all the caregivers in the novel and their recipients: [readers] will observe that while some characters are both, Victor is always a recipient and never a giver, and the Creature (before he is embittered) is always a giver and never a recipient (even in their final chase, the Creature leaves food for his pursuer). Equally notable are the instances of men who feed, warm, protect, rescue, nurse, or nurture those needing their care and remain generously devoted to the welfare of others: Walton, his shipmaster, Alphonse, Clerval, Felix, Kerwin, the Creature.

Susan J. Wolfson,
"Feminist Inquiry and *Frankenstein,*"
in *Approaches to Teaching Shelley's* Frankenstein,
The Modern Language Association of America, 1990

19. . . . [The Creature's] entire existence is a pitiful record of the breakdown of communication, despite his poignant efforts to express himself. . . .

. . . [O]nly the Creature seems to appreciate the liberating and humanizing potential of language. . . . In observing the "godlike science" of speech practiced among the family of cottagers, for instance, he remarks that "every conversation . . . now opened new wonders" to him. . . . In his earliest stages of consciousness the Creature seeks interaction with others; by contrast Victor increasingly withdraws to the secrecy of his laboratory. The Creature wishes to bring pleasure to others, while Victor wishes to bring fame and adulation to himself. One is generous, the other selfish. . . .

To clarify these essential differences in language use, I cite . . . Victor's fondness for passive-voice constructions, as opposed to the Creature's preference for the active voice. . . . Victor repeatedly invokes the responsibility-shifting power of the passive voice to exonerate himself rhetorically from the catastrophic chain of events for which he is directly . . . responsible. The Creature's final speech, in which the active voice predominates, is startling by comparison: "I have murdered the lovely and the helpless; I have strangled the innocent. . . . I have devoted my creator . . . to misery; I have pursued him even to that irremediable ruin. . . . I shall quit your vessel . . . I shall collect my funeral pile and consume to ashes this miserable frame.

. . . Elsewhere, [Victor] relegates to dependent clauses his acts and activities whose consequences are the greatest and most terrible. . . . In tracing them, students come to appreciate how much this man of words isolates . . . himself in a fabric of deception whose raw material is language itself.

Stephen C. Behrendt,
"Language and Style in *Frankenstein,*"
in *Approaches to Teaching Shelley's* Frankenstein,
The Modern Language Association of America, 1990

20. Between 1818 and 1831, Mary Shelley's philosophical views changed radically, [convincing her] that human events are decided not by personal choice or free will but by an indifferent destiny or fate. The values implicitly espoused in the first edition of *Frankenstein*—that nature is a nurturing and benevolent life force that punishes only those who transgress against its sacred rights, that Victor is morally responsible for his acts, that the Creature is potentially good but driven to evil by social and parental neglect, that a family like the De Laceys that loves all its children equally offers the best hope for human happiness, and that human egotism causes the greatest suffering in the world—are all rejected in the 1831 revisions.

In the 1818 version, Victor Frankenstein possessed free will: he could have abandoned his quest for the "principle of life," he could have cared for his Creature, he could have protected Elizabeth. But in the 1831 edition, he is the pawn of forces beyond his knowledge or control. As he comments, "Destiny was too potent, and her immutable laws had decreed my utter and terrible destruction" (Rieger, app. 239). . . .

In the 1831 edition, . . . Victor's downfall is caused not so much by his egotistical "presumption and rash ignorance" as by bad influences, whether his father's ignorance or Professor Waldman's . . . manipulations. Victor's only sin is not his failure to love and care for his Creature but his original decision to construct a human being. . . .

Not only is Frankenstein portrayed in 1831 as a victim rather than an originator of evil, but Clerval—who had functioned in the first edition as the touchstone of moral virtue against which Victor's fall was measured—is now portrayed as equally ambitious of fame and power. . . . Furthermore, the ideology of the egalitarian and loving bourgeois family that Mary Shelley inherited from her mother's writings and that sustained the first edition of *Frankenstein* is now undercut. Maternal love is identified with self-destruction when Caroline Beaufort deliberately sacrifices her life to nurse Elizabeth. And Elizabeth Lavenza has become a passive "angel in the house," no longer able to speak out in the law courts against Justine's execution.

Anne K. Mellor,
"Choosing a Text of *Frankenstein* to Teach,"
in *Approaches to Teaching Shelley's* Frankenstein,
The Modern Language Association of America, 1990

22. Mary Wollstonecraft Shelley's *Frankenstein* (1818), her first and most celebrated novel, contrasts a scientist of a good family and seemingly lofty aspirations with his own malformed creature. The

creature is a noble savage, loving and humanistic until driven to murder by human cruelty. The scientist, representing the values of his culture, emerges as egocentric and irresponsible—a failed "New Prometheus." His obsessive quest for power leads to his own and his creature's moral and physical destruction, symbolizing a central dilemma of the early nineteenth century: how will the dawning age establish moral values that keep pace with rapidly changing technological advances and political idealogies? In Mary Shelley's era, the question applied equally to formative research in air-flight and electricity as it did to government based on an increasingly expanded and enlightened electorate deciding the fate of the nation. Substitute nuclear energy and gene research, and we recognize the questions as the same we continue to struggle with today.

Betty T. Bennett and Charles E. Robinson, eds., from the Introduction to *The Mary Shelley Reader,* Oxford University Press, 1990

23. We know Frankenstein's creature as if we had always known him: Boris Karloff, tall, lurching, mute, shabbily clad, a humanlike thing with a square head and electronic pegs sticking out of his neck and a look of baffled innocence on his face. We remember him best in the great scene in which, still giddy, still scarred by his newly acquired life, he stands, with his arms raised. His hands tremble as he tries to seize what some dim instinct tells him is important: light. An effulgence, a mystery. When he fails to seize it, he whimpers gently, and the rest of the film unreels its tale of incoherence, misplaced wisdom, cruel pride, and misunderstood love.

Since the James Whale–Boris Karloff production of *Frankenstein* (1931) there have been scores of sequels, film adaptations, cartoons, parodies, and travesties of the Frankenstein story. The range of film interpretations need not surprise us. The emblematic tale that Mary Shelley invented in 1816 had an equally varied stage life for nearly a century before film was invented. By now, the name Frankenstein represents, in the popular imagination, an instantly recognizable myth. That the myth was created by Mary Shelley in a novel she wrote when she was eighteen years old is not quite so well known.

Leonard Wolf,
The Essential Frankenstein:
The Definitive, Annotated Edition,
NAL-Dutton, 1993

Suggestions for Further Reading

Aldiss, Brian W. *Billion Year Spree—The History of Science Fiction.* London: Weidenfeld and Nicolson, 1973.

Baldick, Chris. *In Frankenstein's Shadow: Myth, Monstrosity, and Nineteenth-Century Writing.* Oxford: Oxford University Press-Clarendon, 1987.

Behrendt, Stephen C., ed. *Approaches to Teaching Shelley's* Frankenstein. New York: The Modern Language Association of America, 1990.

Cantor, Paul A. *Creature and Creator: Myth-Making and English Romanticism.* New York: Cambridge University Press, 1984.

Easlea, Brian. *Science and Sexual Oppression—Patriarchy's Confrontation with Woman and Nature.* London: Weidenfeld and Nicolson, 1981.

Forry, Steven Earl. *Hideous Progenies: Dramatizations of* Frankenstein *from Mary Shelley to the Present.* Philadelphia: University of Pennsylvania Press, 1990.

Gilbert, Sandra and Susan Gubar. *The Madwoman in the Attic.* New Haven: Yale University Press, 1979.

Homans, Margaret. *Bearing the Word: Language and Female Experience in Nineteenth-Century Women's Writing.* Chicago: University of Chicago Press, 1986.

Levine, George, and U.C. Knoepflmacher, eds. *The Endurance of Frankenstein.* Berkeley and Los

Angeles, and London: University of California Press, 1979.

Mellor, Anne K. *Mary Shelley: Her Life, Her Fiction, Her Monsters.* New York: Routledge, 1989.

Moers, Ellen. *Literary Women.* Garden City, New Jersey: Doubleday, 1976.

Poovey, Mary. *The Proper Lady and the Woman Writer: Ideology as Style in the Works of Mary Wollstonecraft, Mary Shelley and Jane Austen.* Chicago and London: University of Chicago Press, 1984.

Small, Christopher. *Ariel Like a Harpy: Shelley, Mary, and Frankenstein.* London: Gollancz, 1972.

Sunstein, Emily W. *Mary Shelley: Romance and Reality.* Boston: Little Brown, 1989.

Veeder, William. *Mary Shelley & Frankenstein—The Fate of Androgyny.* Chicago: University of Chicago Press, 1986.

Notes

Volume I

page 5: **Dr. Darwin.** Erasmus Darwin, an eighteenth-century physician and the grandfather of the famous evolutionist Charles Darwin.

page 14: **post-road.** A road used for transporting mail.

page 16: **keeping.** A term used by painters that denotes the ability to render things in proper proportion.

page 17: **shroud.** A nautical term for describing the ropes that connect a ship's masthead to its sides.

page 18: **but I shall kill no albatross.** A reference to Coleridge's poem, *The Rime of the Ancient Mariner.*

page 20: **the sea room.** Enough space for a ship to safely maneuver amid the ice floes.

page 20: **sledge.** A sled, in this case drawn by dogs.

page 20: **the ground sea.** A heavy sea in which large waves rise and dash upon the coast without apparent cause.

page 24: **pedantry.** An overly learned presentation or application of knowledge.

page 32: **Natural philosophy.** The field we now refer to as the physical sciences.

page 34: **the philosopher's stone.** Alchemists had believed such a stone had the power to transform base metals into gold.

page 42: **chimera.** A monster originating in Greek mythology, composed of incongruous parts of a lion, a goat, and having the tail of a serpent.

page 53: **lassitude.** A weakened or fatigued condition.

page 56: **watching.** Staying awake.

page 65: **encomiums.** Glowing expressions of praise.

page 67: **perambulations.** Strolls.

page 72: **prognosticate.** Foretell; predict.

Volume II

page 96: ***aiguilles.*** French for "needles"; used here to describe pointed mountain peaks.

page 105: **impervious.** Impenetrable; unable to be damaged or hurt.

page 107: **offals.** Leftovers.

page 133: **portmanteau.** A large travelling bag.

page 150: **Syndic.** A municipal magistrate.

page 157: **siroc.** A hot, dry wind that travels across Italy, Spain and France from Africa.

Volume III

page 162: **exordium.** A beginning or introduction.

page 172: **Isis.** Refers to the Thames river, which is located north of the Oxford river.

page 172: ***ennui.*** A state of weariness, dissatisfaction, and boredom.

page 174: **remissness.** Negligence or lack of attention to work or a duty.

page 184: **skiff.** A small, light sailing ship or rowboat.

page 189: **augury.** Interpretation or conclusion based on physical appearance or chance events; an omen or portent.

page 191: **gaolers.** Jailers.

page 191: **turnkeys.** Prison guards.

page 214: ***acme.*** The highest point or summit; the climax.

page 214: **apoplectic fit.** Another term for a cerebral hemorrhage or stroke.

page 220: **repast.** A meal.

page 227: **imprecations.** Curses.

page 227: **asseverations.** Expressions of affirmation.

page 234: **despond.** Become discouraged or disheartened.

page 241: **contumely.** Rude language and treatment arising from contempt.